I0819685

# EULOGY FOR THE DAWN

Also by Jeramy Goble

Fantasy:

*Coven Queen*
*Briz and Bayla: The Bronze Age Bounty Hunters*

Science-fiction/space opera:

The Akallian Tales Trilogy:
*Souls of Astraeus*
*Games of Astraeus*
*Fates of Astraeus*

# EULOGY FOR THE DAWN

North Carolina

JERAMY GOBLE

Noachian Books
North Carolina
Noachian-books.com



Printed in the United States of America

jeramygoble.com
facebook.com/JeramyGoble
twitter.com/JeramyGoble
Cover art by Felix Ortiz
Jacket design by STK Kreations

Publisher's Cataloging-in-Publication Data

Names: Goble, Jeramy, author.
Title: Eulogy for the dawn : the epic legend of gods, dragons, demons, beasts, & men / Jeramy Goble.
Description: Maggie Valley, NC : Noachian Books, 2021. | Series: Wrathlore, bk. 1. | Also available in audiobook format.
Identifiers: LCCN 2021905942 (print) | ISBN 978-0-9990435-6-1 (hardcover) | ISBN 978-0-9990435-7-8 (paperback) | ISBN 978-0-9990435-5-4 (ebook)
Subjects: LCSH: Mythology, Norse--Fiction. | Gods--Fiction. | Elves--Fiction. | Dragons--Fiction. | Magic--Fiction. | Fantasy fiction. | BISAC: FICTION / Fantasy / Epic. | FICTION / Fantasy / Dragons & Mythical Creatures. | GSAFD: Fantasy fiction.
Classification: LCC PS3607.O26 E95 2021 (print) | LCC PS3607.O26 (ebook) | DDC 813/.6--dc23.

First Edition

10 9 8 7 6 5 4 3 2 1

For Emma, our own Wiggly.

Field of Frigid Fire
Kathon
Wyrminster
Cenzia
Kimozoa
Ashka
Kimoba
Onadion
Wattre
Komara
Azizam
Zirakzar
Nuledzad
Hornercruck
Baicmauh
Bundinul
The Vulgar Gap
Vordzinad
Forgiving Sea
Neceith

N
Deshemn
Glacier
Andein
Nekhsemn
Beybluff
Naucha
Moseyr
Tricca
Greyley
Sea of
Jorcheg
Grat
Lugadlurtz
Opham Falls
Akänse Ocean
Stä Bläsjä

# Prologue

*In the time of the 72nd ring*
*562 ABV (After the Birth of the Virtues)*

Domaren raced onto the bridge and blinked up through the rain in time to see Isnyra fold her wings back and land solidly next to him. Her massive dragon frame shot a wooden thud booming out in all directions. After swinging off his horse and tossing a torch to the nearby guard, he wiped his face and waited for Isnyra.

After a rapid flash that basked the dark and wet bridge in light, she shifted to her human form and joined him in a jog towards Prumo Hald's main doors.

"What do you think they will say?" She asked.

A younger red dragon, and recently knighted, Isnyra was full of questions.

"I am confident they will be quite furious," Domaren said. He sighed with dread as he spoke and glanced at Isnyra, who seemed locked in a forward stare before focusing back on the entrance. After the pair hopped to a stop in front of the doors, Domaren swung his arm back and pounded on them. Only the rain replied.

Isnyra added a kick.

"The guards saw us coming," she said, as she leaned back and looked up the walls.

Domaren added his complaint.

"What is the delay? Open the doors!" He yelled. After one last bang, he tilted his head back towards Isnyra.

"But yes, I cannot imagine what they will say when they hear the news that we are about to deliver," he added. "I only know that it will be at a level of rage you have never witnessed before." His comments of uncertainty landed solidly with a measured concern.

The two godknights listened as the massive beams behind the doors slid out from their typical positions of prone reinforcement.

"Just as I was beginning to enjoy the rain," Isnyra said.

After dense rattles and bangs, the doors shook and cracked open, squeaking and groaning on their ancient hinges. The sound of the rain echoed back at them from the front hall. Domaren and Isnyra marched through the moment there was room, just as they and the other knights had countless times before. They then set off at a brisk pace while a guard shuffled along in a clumsy stumble, attempting to keep up.

"Lord Domaren, Lady Isnyra," the Prumo Hald guard said. "Please, this is highly irregular," the guard said, each subsequent syllable escalating with agitation. He motioned for other guards farther back in the corridor to join him. As they stepped out from the shadow, their movements sent the dust and bits in the air whooshing and scattering about. After rushing over, the additional contingent of six guards stepped in front of the godknights and blocked their path.

"I must insist you wait here while we confirm your visitation with the Kihdai," the original guard said firmly. His hand rested on his sword's pommel, but he had not yet drawn it. Domaren looked down and smiled as the guard repositioned his hand. But like a parent tiring quickly of their cute but frustrating child after a vexing day, Domaren's smile fell.

"You can insist all you like," Domaren said. His voice dripped with annoyed emphasis. "But the Kihdai instructed me and Isnyra to report back to them at the earliest viable opportunity as to the status of the errand they charged us with. Do you understand?"

The guard's hand slowly slipped down off the pommel towards the handle while Domaren tracked his movements. He then turned his head enough only to lock eyes quickly with Isnyra.

"I absolutely understand your statement, Lord Domaren, but we receive our directives from the Kihdai, just as you do. Now, if you can respect the instructions they have given us, we will simply confer with our mutual... superiors... and arrange to escort you as soon as they have given us permission to do so."

Domaren had a reply, but inspected the entire group of guards for their hand placements instead. Each now had their hands on their weapons. Their tense bodies stood rigid and ready. Feigning a sigh in order to look down and towards Isnyra, a sharp light growing brighter by the moment caught Domaren's eye.

"Now Isnyra!"

Before the knight's name finished leaving Domaren's lips, Isnyra's firestone unleashed a torrent of blinding light from her chest, across the entire expanse of Prumo Hald's main hall. Almost as quickly as the light shot out, it subsided. Standing before the guards now were Domaren, Godknight of the Humans with Verikta, his ancient longsword in his hand, and Isnyra, Godknight of the Dragons, in her natural, red dragon form.

"Now, you must truly let us pass," Isnyra said. Her vocal cords had morphed and swelled with her transformation from human to dragon. As she spoke, her normal volume smacked against the walls and rattled iron fixtures. She also sent paintings sliding on their hooks, leaving them unleveled and teetering.

Domaren slid his feet from his preparatory stance into an offensive one.

"Your delay is costing lives," Domaren said. "Stand aside!"

Before the provocations escalated to violence, however, a voice bellowed from the opposite end of the hall.

"Isnyra?"

Domaren held Verikta over his head, but let his sight fall to the side to peer between the guards. A large silhouette, a bit less than twice as tall as Domaren, loomed imposingly in the threshold of the distant room's firelight.

"Where are the others?" The distant figure asked. "Please, come speak with us. Tell us what you have learned. Guards, thank you. You may let them pass."

Domaren let his hand-and-a-half grip break apart as he slowly lowered Verikta. But as his arms fell, the corners of his mouth raised. Without saying a word, Domaren reiterated his authority with the guards and slid Verikta into her scabbard.

"Come now," the figure said. "We must have the latest news." As he pivoted to return to the room he entered from, he heaved into another set of interior doors to open them far wider than needed only for himself. "Man and dragon, come along," he announced playfully.

Isnyra walked around the group of guards while Domaren walked straight forward and split them down the middle. The guards said nothing as the knight forced them to step back or bump into their fellow guards. Domaren held the eyes of the only guard that had spoken with them and continued silently reminding them of their place. After a few seconds, and once Domaren felt he had made his point, he turned and jogged to catch up with Isnyra. Isnyra turned her massive head and neck toward him just as he caught up with her.

"Maybe we can discuss the topic of Prumo Hald guards needlessly delaying godknights from seeing to their business," she whispered. But even in a whisper, Isnyra's dragon voice carried.

"What? Yes, perhaps," the waiting figure replied. "But that isn't quite as pressing as other news I believe you have for us."

"Yes, of course," Isnyra said in her dragon form's rumbling, alto voice.

The two knights arrived at the threshold of the next room and finally confirmed the identity of the figure whose voice they were confident they had recognized. The human Kihdai had been the one to welcome them. His chosen form at the birth of the virtues was that of a human, though noticeably larger and taller than a natural human.

"Kihdai," Domaren said after stopping to bow.

Isnyra followed suit with a head bow of her own. "Kihdai."

"Hello friends, yes, come, come," he said. "Come in. Where are the others?"

"The answer to that forms the bulk of our news,"

Isnyra said.

"I see," answered the Kihdai. "Follow me. Let us share your news with the others as well."

The Kihdai turned and marched towards the center of the sprawling and sparse room. As Domaren and Isnyra followed, they noticed the other Kihdai sitting in their massive but plain thrones, as they usually do when discussing matters of their creation. But the two knights could not determine the sensitivity or significance of any prior chatter as they approached the center of the room, for none of the Kihdai spoke. They merely turned their heads and watched their knights step closer.

The responsibility of filling the silence fell to the popping and crackling of a substantial fire arrangement in front of the thrones. Running in a circular ditch a few meters in front of the Kihdai, the fire basked the gods in a gently wavering wealth of light. A bulky chandelier made of iron, matched in circumference to the fiery ring below, dangled freely from an anchor high above. The large iron ring accommodated some hundreds of candles. Layers of overlapping and dried wax drippings caked the sides and obscured large portions of the fixture's metal.

"Please, knights," the god suggested, "enter the circle and tell us what you have learned."

The duo obliged as they were told and proceeded towards the fire circle as the creator returned to his throne. Domaren easily hopped over the fire, with Isnyra following quickly after. The cavernous chamber and distance between thrones accommodated dragons easily. With another two dozen human-sized paces, the two knights reached the center of the circle.

"Thank you for coming to us with whatever news you may have," said the human Kihdai. "Please, begin when you are ready."

"Why have only two of you come?" Another Kihdai asked. Her assumed form was that of a dragon. The dancing fire reflected off her scales and gave the impression that her body changed colors with the flames.

"That is our news, dragon Kihdai," Domaren replied. His words came slowly, and with a weight that frequently pulled his head down as he spoke. After looking to Isnyra as if still in disbelief, he continued. "It seems that the source of the uprisings across Stä Bläsjä are our some of our very own knights."

The dwarf Kihdai roared as he shoved himself up out of his throne. "What? What evidence do you have of this?"

"A large, combined force confronted us when we arrived in the city of Mashka, dwarf Kihdai. Tens of thousands from most races as far as we could tell." Isnyra paused to let the initial wave of unfortunate news settle before continuing.

Her next words carried with them a melancholy lilt as if still in disbelief, herself.

"Domaren and I had spoken with the other knights just days before and agreed to meet them in Mashka before traveling farther east to investigate various revolts, but... that meeting never happened. At least not as we had discussed previously."

Another godknight, a female orc who had vacated her throne as well, paced in slow circles around it. Holding her hands behind her, she stared down, deep in thought, but stopped for another question. She hinted at having hope that the allegations were false, but wavered towards certainty.

"And how did you confirm the other knights were part of this opposing force?"

"We saw them, orc Kihdai," Domaren replied. As with his previous comments, Domaren struggled to speak what, until that time, had been unthinkable. "We spoke with them. And after, we had to fight them."

Many of the Kihdai stopped pacing or peeled themselves away from their distractions of thought. Each creator then snapped their eyes into sharp focus on the pair of knights at the center of the circle.

"We all planned to meet at an abandoned farm on the outside of town," Isnyra said, before Domaren continued.

"And when I arrived on the morning we had agreed to, I only found Isnyra, waiting. There was also a child who had apparently been compensated to stand and wait for our arrival to deliver us a message."

"The message conveyed something that we would soon learn was in actuality, a ruse," Isnyra continued. "It said that an ambush had delayed the others and to come quickly to assist. Naturally, we raced off to the defense of our fellow knights. But when we arrived at the new location, we found a large army, formed and ready."

Domaren took a turn in continuing the account.

"Many races were on the field, but we could not confirm which, definitively. I don't recall seeing any dragons," he said, nodding thankfully at Isnyra.

"After we relayed this news to you," Isnyra said, "we were planning to confirm who isn't part of this treachery and organize a proper response."

"Thank you. We do appreciate your inclination," said the dwarf Kihdai, "but you still haven't mentioned specifics regarding the other knights."

"Yes, I apologize," Domaren said. "Upon seeing the army, Isnyra and I approached."

"Just the two of you?" the human Kihdai asked.

"Yes. We wanted to learn more about what was transpiring, and felt comfortable we could repulse them, or flee if necessary."

"Unfortunately," Isnyra continued, "we ended up having to flee."

Domaren nodded at his fellow godknight, and then at the Kihdai before resuming.

"After crossing the field and closing the distance between the gathered army and ourselves, the other knights stepped out from behind the front ranks."

Incredulous at what she must have felt were impending revelations of treachery, the dragon Kihdai folded her wings behind her and stomped towards Domaren and Isnyra. As she stepped wide over the recessed band of fire, she flipped her large tail up to protect it. Once in the circle's interior, she relaxed her wings and let her tail slam to the floor with a meaty smack. She marched over to the two knights and slowed only when she was within half a wingspan of them. While looming over the knights, she spit her next words out sharply and slowly as her face twitched to contain her anger.

"What... did... they... say?" She asked.

Domaren took a careful moment to gather his thoughts and consider how he would present them. Not out of intimidation or worry about how the Kihdai would treat him or Isnyra—knowing the dragon Kihdai reserved her anger for the others—but again, because he still had trouble believing what he was about to say.

"The other knights spoke of dissatisfaction, Kihdai," Domaren said, respectfully. "They cited a growing concern for the welfare of their people, mismanagement of creation, and regarding the proxies, what they felt was an exploitation of their rank."

The human god spun towards Domaren and glared down at him with a newly manifested stare of hate. The truant knights were not there to receive his admonishment, but as the Kihdai blasted out in a primordial rage, Domaren and Isnyra would temporarily have to do.

"Mismanagement?" He shouted. He turned towards the other Kihdai as he flailed and continued his roaring tirade. As he boomed and yelled louder and moved about with added animation, he squeezed a fist and fanned the ring of flame so that it grew three times in height.

"How dare those to whom we have given everything, aspire to such egregious levels of idiocy that they think they can take issue with us, over anything?"

The god's thundering question tore through the halls of Prumo Hald's corridors, his disgusted and furious volume eclipsing Isnyra's earlier rattles and vibrations. Sounds of falling frames and decorations rang out from various locations in Prumo Hald. Immediately following the human creator's rhetorical question, yet another Kihdai, the elf creator, wasted no time in planning a response. The human Kihdai released his fist and allowed the flames to return to normal.

"Where are these fools at currently?" The elf god asked.

In an effort to reset his thoughts, Domaren blinked for the first time in what felt like decades. Glancing at Isnyra, he then swallowed only to wet his throat.

"We weren't able to glean very many specifics—" Domaren attempted, before the dwarf Kihdai interrupted.

"Wait," the dwarf Kihdai blurted. "What happened after they voiced their concerns? Was anything else said?"

Isnyra stammered slightly as she recalled the rest of the encounter.

"Oh, only that they had these concerns and that they wanted our help," she said.

"Help with what?" The elf god asked. Her brewing assumptions caused her question to snip sharply.

"Help with fighting you," Domaren said after hesitating. "Fighting the proxies. An absolute rebellion."

"And how did you respond?" asked the human Kihdai, with an unsettling softness.

"We absolutely rejected the notion," Domaren said as he motioned at Isnyra. "We challenged them on their motives, their thinking, and not only told them we disagreed with their justification, but told them why they would fail."

For the first time since the conversation began, the Kihdai had no immediate reply. Isnyra concluded the story.

"We argued back and forth for a time," she said, "but soon after that is when they gave their armies the order to charge. We fought for hours. At one point Domaren and I had become separated, but once we finally regrouped, we decided to break off and report what had transpired."

Again, the room fell silent as the Kihdai processed the news, and undoubtedly considered their response. Breaking the silence, Isnyra spoke up once again.

"Kihdai, Domaren and I are loyal. We have confidence in you and are grateful for this existence. There are countless untold throughout the world who feel the same way, and I know your proxies are of the same mind. Whatever action you wish taken, we will see to it."

Domaren nodded at Isnyra's prudence and her sentiment. "I agree with every word, absolutely."

The elf Kihdai turned and added her dark encouragement.

"Good," the elf Kihdai said, lingering on the word.

"Good. And I'm sure we will want to discuss specific tactics, but I believe I speak for all Kihdai when I say we encourage you to conscript, recruit, or otherwise press anyone necessary into our cause. We will not tolerate rebellion from our own knights."

"Agreed," boomed the dwarf god.

"Understood," Domaren said. He was then prepared to let the conversation continue, but the notion of recruitment reminded him of an opportunity.

"I wonder, Kihdai," he said. "There have been rumors for some time now, that there are some... demons that wish to abandon their ways. To escape eternal purgatory..."

The orc god bounced with a hearty a laugh.

"You can't possibly be suggesting that we have anything to do with any of *them,"* she said.

Before she could continue, the dragon Kihdai responded.

"Their power... their decay magic... could potentially serve us as a significant benefit in this," the Kihdai said. "Does anyone disagree?"

The human god looked up from his thoughts, but returned to them just as quickly. There were no objections.

The two knights stood patiently and dutifully, waiting for their next command from the Kihdai. The Kihdai that had originally remained seated were all standing now. Some stared into the fire, pensive with thought, while others continued pacing. Finally, the human Kihdai came to a halt, his ceased movement and loud, hearty stop catching the attention of the others. He looked around at the faces of his fellow creators to measure their disposition, as if silently asking for their agreement on what he was about to say. He then turned slowly to face the two knights and stepped towards them.

"Listen to each word that I am about to say and keep them close," he began. In contrast to his hints of rage, his tone had returned to its earlier warmth and kindness. "Both of you should leave here knowing that we empower you and sanction you to acquire anything or enlist anyone," he said as he motioned to the elf god in acknowledgment of her suggestion, "and execute any task that you deem necessary to accomplish your charge to peacefully or violently dismantle any such attempt at a rebellion. It will fail. You will see to it. Negotiate agreements. Have treaties signed between nations. Get the proxies together. All of it. Assemble a response that has no equal, and that none can counter or overcome. Do not rest until you eliminate this threat. Educate them on the repercussions of their misplaced ambitions and ignorant grievances. Deliver pain. Be the very definition of consequence and our unrelenting instruments of wrath."

# Part I

*"We never considered a rebellion, or until then, the notion of a rebellion, as improbable. What we did admittedly underestimate, however, was who might perpetrate one."*
*- Kihdai Reflections on Wrathlore, 564 ABV*

# One

*In the time of the 72nd ring*
*1217 ABV*

"There are moments when I find your stubbornness amusing, Munch, but now is not one of them," Domaren said. "You have done this a thousand times. We have to go. Come on."

The loyal but obstinate horse lifted its head from the grass and looked back at Domaren.

"Hello," Domaren said. He accompanied his simple greeting with a sarcastic wave. "Back here. Yes, please. At your service. Whenever you're ready."

As the horse swung its head back towards the ground, Domaren sighed and looked down at his newest dog, Wiggly.

"You have been riding with us for only, what, six weeks?"

Wiggly exhibited her namesake activity and wiggled her rear with wild enthusiasm. Her mouth then popped open into a smiling pant.

"And when I give the command, you mount up every time, without hesitation."

Wiggly ran up to Domaren and jumped on his leg before bouncing off and running back to her previous spot.

"I have had countless dogs through the ages, and you are absolutely one of the quickest learners," Domaren said. He continued, accentuating his embellished pride by occasionally jutting his jaw out in Munch's direction. "Thousands upon thousands of dogs, yet you are one of the finest of all the fine boys and girls of the canine persuasion with which I have ever had the pleasure to travel."

Domaren exaggerated his inflection and pitch every handful of syllables and playfully continued to shun Munch.

"In fact, I cannot easily think of a quicker learner," he said. "Well, there was, of course Bellow, that lanky hound King Raefan gifted me, I think it was. I don't quite remember."

As if comprehending, though seemingly uninterested, Munch snorted.

"King Raefan," Domaren repeated, as he thrust his fingers into his beard to grab his chin. "Raefan. Raefan. King of..."

Domaren looked back to Wiggly as he tried to remember.

"Ederiand! I had almost forgotten. Yes, Ederiand. Used to be on the south side of the Lugadlurtz Delta. The Ederians were wiped out ages ago. Great painters. Regardless, yes, Bellow was not necessarily the quickest study, but once he learned something, he could always repeat the task. While you are a quick learner, Wiggly Butt, we shall see if your ability to retain commands rivals old Bellow."

Wiggly dropped down and stretched her front legs as

Domaren continued speaking to her.

"And then Munch over here," Domaren said, while waving his hand at the horse, "has been with me for some twelve years. The most loyal horse in at *least* my last two dozen. I trained him to stick out his leg for dogs to mount up almost that long ago. And you, Wiggly, you have caught on well, when Munch complies of course..."

Domaren lifted his head and craned his neck in the direction of Munch's ears.

"Yet, each and every time he does *not* do it, I know he is choosing to ignore me."

Domaren looked back to Wiggly.

"He knows we need to go, but alas, he does not care."

Wiggly tilted her head mid-sentence, as Domaren spoke.

"Did you not like something I said? Or maybe you *liked* one of those words, hmm? Go? Is that it? Shall we go?"

Wiggly barked, lunging and lifting up a few inches off her front paws. As Wiggly bounded about and shouted at the air, Munch finally extended his right rear leg. With no hesitation, Wiggly ran up onto Munch's back before bouncing into her makeshift saddle, which was attached to Domaren's.

"Well, isn't that something," Domaren said. With a feigned pride, he quickly clapped three times at Munch. "You will take orders from the dog before you will me!"

As the green pommel stone on Domaren's sword flashed, Munch whipped his head up. Domaren interpreted it as a horse's version of an eye-roll.

Domaren stepped into the stirrups and swung his leg over before plopping into his saddle.

"I hope you are quite pleased with yourself," Domaren said. He then offered Munch a quick and playful pat on the neck. The horse gently flicked his head again and flipped the reins into a more comfortable position. Domaren tapped the grove calling stone on his armor.

"Hello, yes, we're finally ready now," Domaren said.

A male's calm voice replied, emanating softly into the open air from the general area surrounding the grove calling stone.

"Is it not about time you get a bird, now, Domaren?"

"Extremely humorous. I'm ready now," he replied.

"Or, perhaps a cat!"

"Whenever you are finished..." Domaren said.

The voice at the other end of the communication chuckled heartily.

"All right, all right," the voice said. "Off you go. Talk with you soon."

With a smile, Domaren shook his head and reached over to pet Wiggly in her saddle.

He grabbed Munch's reins and pulled them just shy of taut. As he did, a thick stream of rocky debris washed over Domaren's vision. Only at the end of the experience did the stream of debris morph into a series of white limbs. Beginning at the ends of the bone-colored branches, Domaren's visual experience raced along the limbs, getting thicker and thicker until his sight pierced the trunk of the Limb of Life with its seventy-two growth rings. Down towards the base, his vision plummeted until finally it penetrated the ground and traced the magnificent web of supernatural roots.

When the tree's branches receded back to the Grove and his sight cleared, Domaren swung out of his saddle and landed solidly in the new location that the groveknights had sent him. He shifted his feet in the patch of gritty soil as a female's loud tirade in the distance abruptly stopped.

A flood of Varoahn defenders from outside Cenzia caught Domaren's attention.

As they emerged from the tree-line, their light footsteps and shuffling of clothes, leathers, and spears were all but indistinguishable from the violent, northern winds harassing the canopy of the nearby pine forest. While the tail of Varoahn emerged from the trees, the men whooped, hollered and chanted melodies of war, assembling haphazardly as if gathering in the town square for an ale, or five, and a minstrel's song, rather than to prepare for battle. Four men walked out from the primary force, escorting a hooded woman dressed in leather and linen. With her hands tied behind her, she thrashed about wildly.

"You two," Domaren said, pointing to Munch and Wiggly. "Stay here." Wiggly spun in her saddle and sat before watching Domaren walk away.

Glancing to the opposite side of the field, Domaren compared the imposing armies of Onadion. Their orderly ranks stood still and quiet, conveying their own brand of intimidation through discipline. Their force was sturdy and motionless. They sang no songs. And while both forces contained hearty and rugged men of varying sizes and fighting disciplines, the Onadion army also included a cavalry, mounted entirely by generations of expert female riders.

As Domaren approached, he caught sight of the woman whose admonition he assumed he had interrupted. As she looked down to the base of the gentle hill at him, the sun bounced harshly off his suit of armor. She held up a hand and squinted.

"Am I really seeing this?" The woman said. "A godknight? How is our business here of any consequence to you, much less the fate of the world?"

Domaren ascended the moderate hill and offered quick but courteous nods. "War Maiden Silaya," He greeted flatly. "Lord Bin." A hand rested casually on the pommel of his sheathed sword.

"Oh, pleasantries," Silaya said, rolling her eyes. "Lords and maidens and knights and m'ladies and all that."

Domaren stood rigid, his face reflecting patience and experience.

"Yes, Maiden Silaya," he continued calmly. "Despite what you may think, I do indeed respect the position you have attained and earned in accordance with the ways of your people."

"I'm sure," Silaya replied, extending the final syllable with a thick sarcasm.

"You're addressing a godknight!" Lord Bin yelled. Incredulous, he flailed about as he spoke. "Perhaps you should show some respect!"

"You dare scold me, Bin, with my captive sister mere yards from me?" Silaya bit back. "I see you're still using your gall to compensate for your... endowment. The knight's presence here can only be a good thing for you, and don't you deny it!"

Bin looked at Domaren and back to Silaya. His chest rose and fell rapidly as he strained to bite his tongue.

Before addressing the entire gathering, Domaren sighed sharply and mentally sorted through unending variations of word combinations he felt he had already spoken countless times to other warring factions over the centuries.

"MenofCenzia.WarriorsofOnadion!"Heannounced. His eyes shifted between groups. "If your ignorance is somehow more keen than the judgment that brings you here, and you do not know who I am, I am Domaren—

godknight for the Kihdai. I am responsible for carrying out their wishes and directives across the whole continent, but specifically, throughout each country of the realms of men. The Kihdai have summoned me here today to..."

Domaren paused while gently amusing himself.

"...*urge* you to seek a peaceful resolution to your disagreement and avoid coming to any form of violent conflict."

He listened for a reply while only faint movements at each group's front lines nipped at Domaren's attention. A voice bellowed something at the rear of Varoahn's forces which caused a ripple of hearty laughter, but it was too faint for Domaren to understand. Soon after, a new taunt rang out from the Onadion line that Domaren could hear.

"And what if we idiots insist, lord master professor godknight?"

Domaren grinned first and then spun his sight back to Maiden Silaya who half-heartedly waved off the question.

"You say you are here to urge us?" Silaya continued proudly. "That would imply that is the extent of your intentions. If that is the case, though I have no desire to speak for Bin or the men across the field, then I would thank you and the Kihdai for your concern and request that you leave us and let us solve our quarrel on our own time, and by a manner in which we deem best. Nothing will prevent me from returning home with my sister."

The striking woman walked her horse out a few feet from their front lines as she spoke. Silaya's long and thick hair, braided and decorated with rings of carved wood and twine, appeared greater in volume than that of the horse's mane and tail combined. Her back was firm and proud, and the armor she wore gradually transitioned from mostly steel on her legs to overlapping panels of leather on her torso and shoulders. She clutched her helmet and held the horse's reins with one arm. With the other, she held her longsword off to the horse's side. Strapped on her back was another blade—a second sword, and a buckler.

Domaren maintained an intrigued glare at the Onadion war maiden. As the sun slipped behind the rounded mountains, Domaren relaxed his eyes and gave his full attention to the woman's deliberate approach. Her agitated words were like those from previous generations, and Domaren let the shuffling of restless infantry or booing from the Varoahn distract him from her grievance. Only her movements and gestures towards either army concerned him.

"For years, in the name of peace," the maiden shouted, "the Onadion people have overlooked Varoahn encroachments on our shared border—a border created in good faith by our collective ancestors as a result of gifted land for saving you from the dragons who are mere miles to the north! And do not forget that you needed saving, because your ancestors foolishly took it upon themselves to invade dragon lands!"

Bin, the solid and rectangular leader finely chiseled with muscle, looked back at his men to wave and acknowledge the booing that had already swelled in volume.

"That is an outright lie, Silaya. Not only a lie, but an insult. Our people have never invaded any dragon territory. We have only ever fought for the preservation or protection of our people, to defend what is ours, or to reclaim that which was taken unlawfully! That's exactly why we're here today! And we only have your sister as a means of securing your abandonment of these lands so we can be done with you for good!"

Silaya looked over her shoulder and rolled her eyes

while Bin continued.

"My forefathers had no desire to confront the dragons at will. They had no desire for a conflict. They had to put up with centuries of starvation and famine because those malicious and selfish monsters disrespected our borders. Disrespected our treaties. Took advantage of us and treated us with contempt. They raided and torched our villages for centuries, killing and eating our horses and cattle, and destroyed crops out of spite. My people had no other choice than to fight!"

"As noble and heartbreaking as your... story is," Silaya said, "you and your people are the only ones who consider it true."

The Varoahn men bristled in waves of contemptuous mannerisms. Their arms, hands, and fingers gesticulated in a wild variety of derogatory gestures and symbols. And what began as spotty booing of annoyance had grown to the point of almost drowning out the maiden's retort. Domaren rubbed his face and laughed to himself.

"There are many documented accounts from proxies and godknights alike," she replied. "Probably including a few from Domaren here," she added, flinging her hand in Domaren's direction. "Accounts from humans, seavers, orcs, bears, dwarves, elves, and probably even demons alike, that speak to having to deal with the fallout from your peoples' antagonizing of the dragons!"

The war maiden's golden hair, plaited tightly behind her, swung wildly as her animated complaint washed over the field outside Cenzia. Both the Onadion and Varoahn were her captive audience. As she spoke, she addressed her own people with outstretched and relaxed arms. She met the Varoahn, however, with pointed fingers and jagged slices with the side of one hand into the palm of the other.

"Back to your earlier point, Silaya, yes, I hope that my presence here is good for everyone," Domaren said. He broke in softly hoping to calm the situation.

"What are you talking about?" She challenged. "You're only here to keep the peace. You have no interest in justice. And as you can see, my sister is right over there, being held prisoner!"

"I will work to have your sister returned safely," Domaren said. "And while we are absolutely concerned with justice, yes, you're right. We are also concerned with peace. And sometimes, peace outweighs justice."

"Of course that's what someone who has never been wronged by another would say," Silaya said. She dismounted and walked closer. "Bin's people have been encroaching on our lands acre by acre for generations, and we've ignored it long enough."

Bin dismounted as he shouted back in kind. "You lie! My ancestors settled these lands, including the Korolo Prairie, long before the Onadion wandered into this region!"

Silaya lunged at Bin with a pointed finger in his face. Both Bin's and Silaya's guards jumped closer to their respective leaders.

"You are completely ignoring the Korolo Trade Pact of 124 ABV!" She growled. "In exchange for food that saved your people from famine, you ceded the prairie to us! It has been legally bound to us for thousands of years!"

"This is ridiculous," Bin huffed. With an outstretched arm, he then turned to Domaren. "My lord, godknight, please. Is there anything at all you can lend to help resolve this misunderstanding?"

"Misunderstanding? I understand perfectly..." Silaya said.

"Yes, I believe I can be of assistance," Domaren found space to reply. He exchanged glances with Bin and Silaya. The maiden's eyes appeared as though they could not be wider.

"I was there," Domaren continued. "I was a godknight then, just as I am now. And though it has been quite a long time since the negotiating of that trade pact, I still recall much of the original terms of the agreement."

Silaya and Bin stared at Domaren with impatient anticipation.

"The pact's language was indeed as Silaya describes," the godknight said.

"I told you! I am no liar!" Silaya shouted triumphantly. "Now, return my sister!" She drew her sword and pointed it at Bin as she stepped back from him. After turning to her forces gathered behind her and sprawling down a side of the hill, she thrust her sword up once more for their benefit. Her bloodthirsty forces erupted in approving cheers.

"Forgive me," Bin said, his volume harsher than his words. "While I appreciate your insight, Lord Godknight Domaren, perhaps we should review the actual document to confirm."

Silaya's arm dropped slowly as she approached Bin once again.

"What? You were just deferring to Domaren seconds ago, and now you doubt him?"

"Well, neither of us should trust the resolution of this matter to the words of one man."

"Look at you trying to weasel out of this," Silaya said. "That is a godknight," she added, pointing her sword at Domaren. "Not just a man. And he was there! I trust everyone here today will take note of your attempted deceit."

Bin's men flailed angrily behind him. Hateful jeers,

boos, and shouts of 'Prove it!' mixed with the cheering from Silaya's people muddled the air. Bin spun around slowly, silently goading on the ire of his men. The guards at the front struggled to restrain Silaya's sister as she kicked and jerked her arms. At last, Bin held up his arms to quiet them.

"Surely, you would not deny us a simple review of the document, lord godknight, to confirm the language for the benefit of all?"

Silaya watched the exchange unfold silently. Her own people's ruckus quieted down.

"Though I was present and helped contribute to the language used in it, I think it is more than fair to show a contract to a party who challenges it—despite, or perhaps especially because of, their level of ignorance. Wouldn't you agree, Silaya?" Domaren asked.

Bin cut his eyes at Domaren, and his insult, while Silaya dipped her chin and then scooped it back up.

"If that will settle this once and for all and result in my sister being returned to me, then so be it," she said. "But if there is any further delay to a resolution after this... concession, then I will not be so accommodating."

Her people began jeering while Bin's forces started cheering.

"Well, it's settled," Domaren said to Bin. "A peaceful resolution. Shall we make arrangements to journey back to Onadion? I believe they have a copy in their archives there."

"A copy?" Bin barked. He turned his head towards his men and repeated himself.

"A copy?"

"What legitimacy does a copy have?" Bin asked. "Any decent calligrapher can reproduce any writing, and with the right sponsor, can reproduce it with appropriate ink on proper paper! No," he said. "No. No lasting agreement on this matter can be sustained on some copy, a likely forgery. If there is to be a peaceful concession, then I'm afraid I must demand to see the original!"

Domaren turned to Silaya. After taking in a chest and diaphragm full of air, he huffed it out in bitter frustration.

"War maiden," he said, extending his hand. "Is letting Bin review the original document acceptable to you?"

Silaya stood firm, only moving her eyes between Domaren and Bin. The jeering from one side and cheering on the other swelled as she finally settled back on Domaren.

"The original agreement, along with many of our other original, historical documents, were lost during the great fire of 388."

"Lost?" Bin yipped with delight.

He spun around towards his men once again.

"Lost? Well, I'm afraid I must decline your suggestion, lord godknight," he said. "I can not possibly expect my people to respect dubious claims when there are no original documents to prove them!"

Portions of Silaya's fighters stopped jeering, and instead shouted, "What?" Or, "What did he say?"

"It was not a suggestion," Domaren said, lifting his chin up slightly as he exaggerated his annunciation.

Bin's smirk, rooted in confidence, fell to a harsh squint.

"You have the word of a godknight!" Silaya yelled. "And I'm sure, many identical copies of the trade agreement at your disposal!"

"Regardless, you know the entire understanding is a half truth at best, our Onadion cousin!" Bin said. The men surrounding him grumbled in agreement. "There has been no clear border between our lands since just after the time of Wrathlore. It is widely known and widely accepted, war maiden, that the land which was originally ours, has since been returned to us by your ancestors, long ago! The land is ours, not yours, and even if it was still yours, there isn't even any agreement amongst our people, or the Onadion, on what that original border looked like!"

The Varoahn man swung an open hand in Domaren's direction, silently asking for the godknight's input.

"Words of any man not of my people, and duplicates of documents written long after the fact, are things to which no people should be bound. Here," Bin continued with exaggerated animation. "Let me go draft something up where your father agreed to relinquish the wealth of Onadion to us. What? See? Absurd you say?"

"If that's the extreme you want to jump to, Lord Bin," Silaya replied, "then we're back where we started and that's fine with me! These aren't your lands. They never were your lands, and we will expel you from them by force!"

As Silaya finished speaking, she held up her sword and made a great display of slowly inspecting the blade. As she did, Bin erupted with in a frenzied laugh and drew his own weapon. Domaren stepped closer to the pair as they inched closer to each other.

"It would be a shame if your sister paid for your hastiness," Bin said. His thinly veiled threat accompanied his raised arm as a signal to the guards holding Silaya's sister.

"Bin, Silaya," Domaren snapped. "You were seconds from an agreement. Don't do this. Don't do this to your people. There are very few things worth the death of one, not to mention thousands."

"No, no, no," the maiden said. She lashed back in anger as though she hadn't even heard Domaren.

"Do not attempt to sell me or anyone behind me, or the godknight for that matter, on any of your poorly conceived machinations. We have documents that show when the land was originally granted to us. There are chronicles of the wars our people have fought over the Varoahns' subsequent claims to take it back—none of which have ever been won by the Varoahn. We even have records of fabricated claims, some of which I believe you're attempting to invoke now. You will not advance this futile endeavor. Do not try to deny that my people have been settling villages, without challenge, on what is legitimate Onadion land even as recently as when I was a child. I will not allow it!"

"The fabricated claim you reference was an isolated incident!" The Varoahn leader gnashed back in response. "We all know that! My grandfather often spoke of how much he regretted what transpired. How dare you use that as a justification for war! It is not that fabrication that I am citing. I am in fact referring to the legitimate claims that resulted from the treaty our fathers entered into. And to think you would so conveniently—"

"Remind me, Bin," Domaren interrupted. "What was your father's name?"

Bin turned towards Domaren, mouth frozen mid-sentence. After a moment, he dashed his tongue across his drying lips. He then squinted and grimaced with impatience as he continued.

"With all due respect, godknight, I have to agree with my cousin here. Let us be and let us settle our issues amongst ourselves."

"No, please," Domaren insisted as he held his arms behind him. "You both have looked to me for input. Humor me. What was your father's name?"

Bin looked at Silaya, puzzled, before settling back upon Domaren.

"Galand," Bin snapped proudly.

Domaren nodded and turned to Silaya.

"And *your* father's name?"

"My *mother's* name is Vilivia, and my father's name is Holthan," Silaya answered without hesitation. Domaren smiled wider.

"Wonderful. And what is your grandfather's name, Bin?"

Bin tilted his head and let out something between a sigh and a growl.

"Please, just bear with me a moment," Domaren pleaded. He twirled his hand gently as he spoke.

"Brandon," Bin huffed.

"Yes," Domaren acknowledged. "Silaya, what about your... great grandmother's name?"

Silaya looked down, but almost immediately looked back up.

"Ursula," she answered.

"Thank you both! Grandfather Brandon and Great Grandmother Ursula!"

Domaren released his arms and began tapping his chin as he approached the two leaders. But before he could continue his lesson, a shuffle in the grass caught his ear. In a single, smooth flash, he instinctively drew his sword and spun towards the sound. But rather than encountering a master assassin lashing out with lethal prowess, it was Wiggly. She had leapt from her saddle and met Domaren with another broad smile, happily panting. Her rear and tail wagged heartily.

"I told you to stay," he reprimanded gently. After sheathing his sword, he grinned and shook his head. When he looked up, Munch had also disobeyed their master. The horse shook his head as well in apparent disapproval.

"What is this about?" Silaya asked. One side of her mouth drew up in irritation and disbelief.

"You need to stay up there in your saddle, girl," he said, ignoring Silaya. As he escorted Wiggly back towards Munch, he shook a finger at them and scolded them. "Hop back up and stay put," he added. "And Munch, you get back down to the base of the hill. This shouldn't take too long."

Munch stood in place and blinked.

Domaren snapped at Munch.

"Okay. We *just* went over this. I am through arguing with you."

Munch's legs remained motionless as a crow cawed, drawing attention to the horse's stubbornness.

"Sure, fine. There is no need to rush. Nowhere to go and nothing to do," Domaren said to Munch. He stepped closer and reached into a pouch strapped to his saddle.

"We will just help ourselves to some food while we wait."

Domaren pulled his hand from the pouch and came out with a palm full of meat. He pinched at it with his other hand, but immediately paused.

"Ah yes, this is pork. Have you had pork before?" Domaren asked Wiggly. "I do not believe you have had this yet. Well, not from me anyway." He clicked his tongue. "Come on over here."

Domaren grabbed a slice of pork and knelt down.

"Come on, girl. Try this out."

Before he could finish speaking, Wiggly shot over. The cattle dog's black and white patches tightened with definition as she launched towards him.

"Ah! It seems the pork is a success." Domaren said. As Wiggly ravished the remaining pork in his hand, Domaren addressed his horse.

"I have some snacks for you, but not until you stick that leg out!"

Silaya's agitated voice boomed and startled Wiggly.

"I'm sorry, my good lord sir magistrate godknight, but could I trouble you to finish your involvement with our previous discussion? We have a few more pressing things to settle here than that of the appetite of a dog! Surely you must understand the severity—"

Before she could finish, Domaren shot up to his feet and tossed the other piece of pork to Wiggly. He stormed across the hill and replied as he stomped.

"What I understand, Silaya, is the futility of this discussion, and the inevitable battle. What I understand is that no matter the agreement, or concession, one of you here will find your way into a fight. I hope your sister survives it. What I also understand, is that regardless of the outcome, and any eventual, but tenuous peace, you all will find a way to fight about something else and waste more of my time. A century and an agreement will come, and the next century and a war will go. Over and over and over again. Land that has changed shape and hands more than your minds can comprehend will continue shifting shape and owners at the expense of your peoples' peace and your brief flickers of life."

Silaya and Bin stood silently next to their horses. They stopped blinking for a moment and leaned forward with furled brows.

As Domaren continued, he raised his voice for more to hear.

"This example of humanity's continued pride and eternal, cyclic stupidity that I dare interrupt, is precisely why I care a great deal more about this dog, than I do about the outcome of this inconsequential argument."

The godknight stepped closer to the arguing leaders once more and spoke more intimately.

"You see... The dog concerns itself only with food, water, and warmth, her contentment and peace defined only by the things necessary for survival. Her motivations are pure. Sure, there may be an element of loyalty in a dog's mind, but even that is entirely objective. A dog will be loyal up until it is given a very legitimate reason to become disloyal."

Bin's jaw dropped open as he prepared to reply, but Domaren anticipated what he felt would be a meaningless retort.

"But, no, please," he roared, returning his focus to the gathered armies. "Grandfather Brandon and Great Grandmother Ursula. Let us continue the history lesson! Who might know the name of the shared great uncle between Brandon and Ursula?"

Domaren stopped and looked up. Bin and Silaya exchanged uneasy glances between themselves.

"Second uncle to Brandon and Ursula? Anyone?" Domaren asked again, yelling into the opposing armies.

Finally, someone deep within the Onadion ranks bellowed back.

"Gaithor!"

Domaren spun and pointed in the reply's general direction.

"Ah! Yes! Gaithor!" He said. "A mere six generations before those that stand here today."

As Domaren continued, he increasingly addressed the entirety of the gathered warriors. He moved about quickly, looking into the eyes of more and more soldiers.

"And this will be easy," he suggested. "Who was Gaithor's great-grandfather? Only a few more generations back—the last king of your unified kin?"

In a roar of sound, almost each man and woman shouted out.

"Tradavin!"

Domaren raised his fist in the air, mockingly celebrating the two groups' revelation.

"Tradavin! Yes! A great king during a great time for your two great peoples."

Domaren dropped his fist as he let a silence fall once more throughout the fields. His smile slid down as well, before turning back to Silaya and Bin.

"And who was Tradavin's father?" Domaren asked the pair of leaders. His arms and eyebrows rose as he waited for a response. "Hmm? No?"

He spun in a circle and yelled at the armies.

"Tradavin's father? Who was he?"

Bin mumbled, summoning Domaren's attention once more.

"Enough of these ridiculous—" Bin started.

Domaren's arms dropped in disappointment.

"Sundarre," Domaren interrupted.

The godknight stepped closer to Bin with each subsequent response and rhetorical question.

"And Sundarre's grandfather? Fortus. Fortus' grandfather? Mallach. His grandfather? Sceptin. Sceptin's grandfather? Gimgast. And let's get really adventurous. How about Gimgast's seventh great-grandfather?"

Less than an arm's length from Bin, Domaren repeated his latest question to all those in the area.

"Gimgast's seventh great-grandfather? Anyone?"

Domaren bore into Bin's eyes with his own, with the gaping silence being interrupted only once by a pair of mocking crows. As Domaren allowed the silence to creep into and fester in the minds of Bin, Silaya, the Onadion and Varoahn alike, Domaren stepped away from Bin and walked in a circle to once again look as many men and women in the eye as possible.

"Xoradin," Domaren finally said. "Xoradin," he said again, almost whispering.

"I think I speak for everyone, Domaren," Silaya said, "when I say that we know what you're trying to do."

Domaren turned and walked towards Silaya with no discernible expression or disposition.

"We understand that our grievances and quarrels are minor in the overall unfolding of time," she continued. "We understand that we do not view things on the same scale as you do. But we live in such a way that makes sense for us. We hold things dear to us in a way that can not make sense to you, in a way that must not make sense to you. You must have enough wisdom in your many eons of life to have the capacity to appreciate that, no?"

Domaren took a step back, but continued looking at Silaya. He crossed his arms, but quickly dropped them before pointing out to the horizon.

"What do your people call the tallest mountain peak in the ridge at the end of the valley there?"

Silaya sighed and looked.

"Mount Awinda."

"Yes," Domaren confirmed. "And why is that mountain significant to your people?"

Silaya leaned forward and pointed at Domaren with her sword.

"I'm tired of your questions, godknight, and I'm tired of your condescension! Go lecture someone else."

Domaren stood where he was, but said nothing, and only held up his hands. His eyes snapped towards the mountain and then back to Silaya.

She sighed again and allowed the flat of her blade to drop and smack into the side of her leg.

"The base of Awinda," she offered. "It's where our first ancestors are said to have settled after the Birth of the Virtues."

"Ah!" Domaren said, resuming an animated circle around the officers of the two gathered armies.

"The birth of the virtues! Ages ago! And do you know what Awinda looked like at that time?"

Domaren examined the faces of the silent warriors as he passed them. Occasionally, he would look to Silaya or Bin.

"Does no one know?" He prodded.

"What nonsense are you speaking, Domaren?" Silaya finally challenged. "Awinda has always—"

"*Always?*" Domaren interrupted. "How do you presume to have any idea what *always* means? To what can you possibly relate it? To centuries ago? Eons ago? To the beginning? You do not know of what you speak! Because none of you were there. None of you! I was!"

"Speaking of forever, Domaren... You may, but my people don't have forever," Silaya shot back. "When might we be able to expect you to arrive at your point?"

Domaren stopped pacing in his frustrated circle and looked to Wiggly before setting his focus on Mount Awinda.

"The area was originally nothing more than a common pond," Domaren said. His voice floated gently and melodically, as if singing a long-forgotten lullaby to a youthful world. "The amount of water was just enough as to not evaporate between seasons of rain but quenched the thirst of countless species of fledgling creatures."

Domaren's vision blurred slightly as he allowed his

eyes to rest and his memory to stretch its legs.

"But no one remembers those creatures," he added with a noticeable dip towards the somber. "No one remembers that pond."

Domaren cleared his throat and shuffled his feet and looked down. As he brought his head back up, he focused his vision once again on Bin.

"And no one will remember you," he concluded.

The initial silence following his comments allowed Domaren to slip away and slide into the past more than he already had, into a plethora of random memories and ages that Domaren hadn't remembered in some time. But the silence was not to last.

Bin erupted in laughter and shook Domaren out of his thoughts. The godknight looked at him in annoyed confusion.

"What could you possibly find humorous? How can you be laughing?" Domaren asked. "The lands of the world will rise and fall. Time will beat and weather the mountains into submission. Creatures, cultures, and species will come into and fall out of existence. Generations will come and go, and your actions from birth to death will amount to nothing. No one will remember you!"

Bin's stoic posture had given way to lung-emptying laughter as he collapsed clumsily onto one of his officer's shoulders. After a break and a few deep breaths, Bin finally found air to reply.

"You will!" He blurted out after a snort.

In another unexpected response, Silaya and her fellow Onadion also burst into laughter. Domaren's head turned back and forth in bewilderment at the two groups' shortsightedness, but his bewilderment quickly shifted into disgust.

"But I can *choose* whether or not to speak of you. I can *choose* whether you are remembered. Is that what you wish? For the persistence of your memory to depend on one person's whim?"

The accumulating contempt between Domaren and the others grew more and more tangible with each syllable.

"The pitiful disagreements between your two clans will not end with one battle today," Domaren yelled, shouting the laughter down. "You must already know that. There is always an argument, always a battle, always a conflict. It will only be a catalyst—a catalyst for more blood. A catalyst for a civil war that will claim the lives of countless innocents."

He turned his head to the armies of Onadion, and then to the Varoahn defenders of Cenzia. A voice erupted out from the Onadion side. Domaren flung his head around.

"Our people are willing to pay that price, godknight!" The voice screamed, boldly. The rest of the Onadion erupted into boisterous chants of support. Domaren squinted to focus in. As the chanting died down, a response came from the Varoahn.

"As are we! And once we route these invaders, perhaps we should march to Onadion!"

The Varoahn defenders whooped and mocked. Their sounds echoed and ricocheted off the city walls. As the Varoahn army quieted down, Domaren addressed both groups once more.

"Yes, yes, of course. The honor of battle," Domaren mocked. "Glorifying your ancestors' past conflicts by spilling new blood. Sacrificing yourselves in the name of arbitrary stubbornness and meaningless contempt. You think you are accomplishing something and standing up for something worth the sacrifice. And like millions of others that came before you, you bleat and posture over the glory of battle and welcome death. But it is only when the darkness creeps in during those last breaths, and your lie's facade weakens under the weight of mortality, that you finally understand. When you realize that death is mere moments away, you will grasp desperately at the truth and beg for it to spare you. You will give anything for one more night with your wife, or dinner with your children, instead of dying for a cause that, in the end, is of no consequence."

"Enough, Domaren," Silaya replied. "That's quite enough. That's what you don't understand. We know death is on our horizon. Whether it's just over the next hill or far beyond in the mountains, valleys, and plateaus... we see it. It will *always* be on the horizon. We don't let that decide what is worth a fight. Now, it's time to be on your way with your lessons and scolding, or you can prepare to join us as we settle this matter."

"Yes, that's all easy for a godknight to say," Bin hollered in agreement. "Living and persisting through all the ages, never needing to care about death. Never experiencing it. Never living a second in fear of it!"

"It's true. You could never value a life like we do," Silaya said, surprising Domaren with the continued shared viewpoints. "You can never care about something so much that you would risk your life for it. You won't support us fighting to take our land back even though you know we're in the right!"

"Silaya, I'm not here to support you or Bin. I'm not here to help either of you win a fight. I'm here to keep thousands of people on both sides from dying."

"That is the crux of the matter, Domaren! We want to be here! We want to fight! We want our land back! The honor of our people and the honor of our ancestors' agreements, and the commitment of their neighbors is worth dying for!"

Bin brandished his sword and smiled widely, waiting for Silaya to finish.

"And keeping what we have taken and settled families on already, is worth us dying for," Bin said. "I can't think of a death more honorable."

"Death is as foreign a concept to you as time is," Domaren growled. "You both are speaking on matters which you don't properly understand."

Both Bin and Silaya opened their mouths, ready to cut him off, but Domaren spit as he continued.

"Yes, yes," he said. "I know. You've seen loss. You've lost family and friends. Loved ones have been cut down in war. You live to die, for the glory. But again, you yourself have never experienced death. Don't talk to me about death. I've watched the young snipped down before their parents, villages and cities burned, civilizations crumble, and complete histories of people evaporate into time. I've seen the true nature of death, and it is the only truth. You only know to rail against death. But you don't even know what it really is you're thrashing futilely to avoid. There is nothing beautiful about death. Death is not glorious. There are only eternal questions with no answers. Lives come and go. Memories and stories of people fade to dust shortly after their bodies. You both think your ancestors settled that land first? Such is the conceit of mortals. There were three other civilizations on this spot before yours, and they're barely known to current historians. And Silaya, even if you got that area back today, the current generations would settle on it and develop it, sure, but so too would your civilization crumble into the limited memory of the entirety of time. And that's what you don't understand. That will happen *no matter* your actions here today. If any of you or your people had any sense, you'd leave this field and go home to a lover's bed and a barrel of wine and try to forget that, eventually, it will be as if none of you ever walked this land."

Silaya and Bin stood silent and wide-eyed, fixed on Domaren. He couldn't tell if they were enraged or mortified. After a moment, Silaya turned and spoke to her captains. Bin appeared to do something similar, though Domaren could not hear either of them.

"You only continue to prove our points," Silaya said. "More now than ever, my will to fight is strong. You would have us retreat and live in submissive silence. You would have us turn a blind eye to those that wrong us. Day in and day out, the same, with no struggle, no challenges, and no growth. Our dreams, homes, and children would shrivel up, learning to live for nothing and just wait to die."

Domaren stood patiently, letting Silaya have her say. But before he could reply, Bin had to add another unsolicited comment.

"For the first time today, the war maiden has said something with which I can completely agree!" Bin bellowed. "The very fact that we will die, lord godknight, is why we fight, to try and ensure that our children won't have to."

Some of Silaya's captains turned their horses and rode to the side of their forces. Silaya sheathed her sword and stepped back to size Bin up one last time.

"Good," Bin said gently, nodding. "It is almost time, at last."

"This will not end how either of you wish it to," Domaren warned.

Bin chuckled as he held his sword up and spoke, almost as if he was addressing the blade.

"But you can not deny us our attempt," Bin said slyly.

The Onadion army bristled and jeered at Domaren. The Varoahn defenders seemed to agree with their would-be aggressors. Along with the Onadion, the Varoahn also shouted disapprovingly at Domaren.

"Yes. Leave us to our business, godknight," Bin added. "We have given you time to speak and we have listened to you. We don't expect you to understand or relate to our positions. You live apart. You exist apart. And I believe it is at least on that, that we and our Onadion cousins agree."

"Now," Bin continued, "I must ensure our argument begins as originally planned." With a rapid spin, Bin turned and waved his arm at the guards at the front of his army. A guard then drew a sword and shoved it through the back of Silaya's sister.

Silaya crumpled at the knees slightly and shrieked out in hateful horror.

"Vonna!" She screamed.

Silaya drew her sword and spun feverishly, looking for her horse.

Bin raced away, having sprinted for his own horse the moment he gave the command to have Silaya's sister run through.

DOMAREN

# Two

Silaya screamed every obscenity she knew until she ran out of air. After taking another quick but deep breath, she repeated herself and held out her sword in a signal to her waiting forces to prepare a charge. Spit flew from her lips and tears ran down her cheeks.

After looking back at Domaren with a scowl of disdain and contempt, she sarcastically bowed her head before slipping on her helmet. The Onadion horns in the front sounded her instruction. Additional horns farther back in the Onadion ranks answered in acknowledgment. While the brassy rattle of the Onadion battle call reverberated across the foothills, Bin and his Varoahn officers reached their forces and blended back in with the front lines.

Domaren watched as the two clans shifted ranks and settled into their initial starting positions. As units moved around and the shape of the armies rippled about in the distance, Domaren addressed his horse and dog.

"The two of you," he started. "Get out of here and go wait for me at the city outskirts." As he gave them instructions, he pointed towards Cenzia before slapping Munch on the backside. Wiggly's panting face looked back at Domaren as Munch road away. The knight then turned and stepped farther out into the field.

"Well done, yes, Silaya," Domaren said. He sighed and continued with patronizing excitement. "Prepare your horses for a wedge. Bin will never see that coming."

Domaren took one last glance to make sure Munch was heading in the right direction, but then focused across the field on the Varoahn.

"Oh, what's this, Bin? Are you bringing the bowmen and pikemen forward to counter? What a brilliant and original strategy!"

After reaching the center of the battlefield, Domaren reached for his sword.

"Glory to the dead," he huffed to himself. "Hmm, actually—" he continued, grinning.

Domaren heard the Varoahn war chant start up.

"Live for the north! Fight for the north!" A lone voice began.

He looked up and confirmed Bin was waving his sword and working his men up. They answered him back as one.

"Live for the north! Fight for the north!"

"Oh, right," Domaren said under his breath. "Live for this. Fight for that."

Domaren pumped a mocking fist into the air.

The Onadion horns stole Domaren's attention.

*Barrroooooooo!* Domaren sang in silly imitation.

"Here we go, Silaya! Time to make those ancestors proud!"

Once the next blast of the Onadion horns spilled out into the distant trees, the Varoahn shot out towards their adversary. In return, Silaya waved her sword over her head and reared her steed. With a war cry of her own, in the Onadion's dialect of the same root language shared with their related Varoahn cousins, Silaya launched her people into battle.

"What was that again?" Domaren said to himself. His disinterested eyes looked to the ground as he tried to remember. "Doesn't matter. They're all the same."

While calmly standing between the two forces, Domaren looked up and huffed a breath of fresh disappointment before slapping and rubbing his hands together, absentmindedly enjoying the friction. With a reach under his arm, he grabbed his gauntlets and quickly fastened them. He then slid his hand along the top half of his scabbard towards his sword's hilt while the two armies raced towards each other. As his hand moved, his palm throbbed with an ancient kinship that bonded him to his sword. He focused on its power before settling his hand on the handle.

Domaren's fingers quickly fell into their normal and comfortable place. He then pressed one of the sword's many handlestones to make use of his weapon's magic. Having activated the yellow gem, Domaren could deal devastating blows, but none would be fatal. Finally, Domaren drew his ancient, dawn-forged weapon, Verikta. The blade pulsed with yellow energy before quickly subsiding.

Domaren held his sword up for the charging armies to see. He whipped his free hand up and slapped the flat of the blade, blasting a wave of percussive sound throughout the area. As he struck the blade, a torrent of fire and lightning engulfed the sword.

As the sword put on its display, Domaren looked back and forth between the armies. They were not slowing down.

"Have it your way," Domaren grumbled.

He dropped Verikta to his side, then brandished the sword to secure his grip for it before the fight began. He took off in a sprint. As he did, the latest wave of energy evaporated away—just in time for the first encounter.

Domaren slashed across at the Onadion forces. A wave of energy rippled out from the tip of Domaren's sword and sent Silaya and the front point of her cavalry's wedge tumbling through the air. As he followed through, he spun to meet the first of the Varoahn.

"You could save yourself a lot of time, my friends," he admonished.

The Varoahn approached in a more sporadic manner, requiring Domaren to engage in rapid successions of clashes with individuals. In each encounter, Domaren landed killing blows. With expert precision, as if he had invented the art of the blade himself, Domaren sliced and hacked into the stubborn armies. But when he landed decapitating slices, lethal stabs to the heart, or deep lacerations to bellies and chests, each attacker registered the force and pain, though no physical damage took hold. Man after man, woman after woman, horse after horse, all fell to the ground at Domaren's feet, writhing in excruciating and temporarily incapacitating pain.

But they would live.

In the initial hours of the sprawling battle, Domaren kept the two armies focused on him, just far enough away from the shared border with the dragons for Domaren to feel confident that they would not disturb their mighty northern neighbors. Fighting primarily centered on Domaren in increasingly larger concentric circles of people waiting their turn to give the godknight their best effort. And though most of the fighting focused on Domaren, there were also small, isolated encounters between the two mortal clans in and around the primary sparring with Domaren.

As the fighting progressed, Domaren realized he was looking up less and less, seeing fewer horses, and the sounds of horse neighing had all but disappeared. No longer was the ground slammed and pounded by rearing and landing horses. He no longer heard the sounds of scared or angry beasts. The cavalry had noticeably disengaged and Domaren attempted to scan slivers of the horizon for horses between swipes of his blade, parrying pikes, and dodging shield swipes.

Finally, he spied them. At the northern end of the conflict, a quickly moving contingent of Varoahn infantry split off from the primary conflict and appeared to be attempting to flank the rear of the Onadion cavalry. To fight on two fronts against Domaren and their quarreling cousins, the Onadion horses disengaged and maneuvered to counter their sneaky foe.

Domaren's blood pulsed with dread, and his mind throbbed with annoyance.

*You frustrating fools,* he thought.

He immediately pivoted and shifted his weight in order to face north and slog his way through the meatiest center of the fight. For the moment, Domaren no longer attempted to land what would normally be killing blows to neutralize attackers, but deflected and avoided them instead. On his way to the truant group, Domaren passed Vonna's unconscious body. As he raced by, he jabbed her in the leg.

At every opportunity, Domaren blocked and slid blades away. He ducked and jumped. He sprinted when he could or stopped mid-stride, and let rushing attackers run past due to their armored momentum.

When Domaren reached the outer bands of the primary confrontation, the delays and attacks grew less frequent. He took advantage of greater expanses of open ground and sprinted towards the flanking Varoahn and countering Onadion cavalry. He ran with increasing speed, beginning with that of the fastest human, to the unparalleled speed of a godknight. Domaren finally broke away entirely from the major battle and made straight for the others. He hoped to reach them before crossing into dragon territory, but as he ran, he saw something in the blur of his speed that sent his nerves stinging in a fresh blister of frustration—the blackened ground of the dragons' scorched border passed under his feet. The dragons did not require walls, towers, turrets, or artificial defenses of any means, at their borders at least. The known repercussions for trespassing were defense enough.

The sight of the border sent Domaren's senses into a heightened state, with his hearing and vision more attuned to the surrounding environment. His intentions shifted from tending to the overall battle to getting the humans out of dragon territory as quickly as possible. He had no concern for his health, safety, or survival, but the lasting implications of a renewed animosity between the dragons and any clan of humans were a burdening weight for which only Domaren had an appropriate appreciation.

Domaren sheathed his sword and raced deeper into the increasingly rocky hills, feverishly looking to the horizon, nearby peaks, and skies overhead for any hints of dragon scouts. With no signs that any dragons had noticed the incursion yet, Domaren pressed on.

Domaren tore across the hills and sped along the ground, the grainy dirt feeling like a stream under his supernatural feet. And just before catching up to them,

Domaren watched as the Varoahn entered a moderately cut canyon, disappearing from sight. On the other end, the Onadion cavalry sprinted down to meet the Varoahn. Domaren split the difference and ran to meet them in the middle from the top of the canyon edge.

Domaren spotted the edge of the approaching cliff and drew his sword. He dug his heels in, sliding in the gravel to a scratching and skittering stop, and prepared to jump down into the canyon between the two approaching adversaries.

But, just before launching down into the canyon, two masses of movement at the top of his periphery broke his attention. He raised his head slowly under the gravity of his exponentially increasing dread.

A sharp breeze slapped at his face, and then another. As Domaren's eye level rose to meet the sight of two approaching dragons, the hulking creatures erupted in clashing tears of dense screams. After landing at the opposite cliff edge in a crunching and violent slam, the two dragons folded their wings flat behind them and leaned over to unleash two horrific streams of flame.

The bolts of fire shot across the canyon and framed Domaren on each side. Domaren and the entire path of the canyon below were lit up as if it were noon on the clearest of days. The dragons had arrived to investigate the trespassing upon their land and brought the men and women in the canyon to a standstill. Domaren could only faintly hear the sounds of the primary conflict behind him.

Domaren stood calmly, using every moment to measure possible actions and to consider what to say, if there was anything to be said.

*The Onadion and Varoahn below. Stopped. Not fighting. Good,* he thought.

The dragons ended their streams of fire. Domaren looked over his shoulder at the primary battle before spinning back in panic.

*Are they going to attack? Can't give them time to consider it.*

"I apologize, immediately, on behalf of the fools below us, respected friends," Domaren said. "I am Domaren, friend to all dragons and Godkn—"

"We know who you are," the matte red dragon to the left interrupted. As she spoke, she casually stretched, her wingspan easily matching half the length of the canyon. "And we see how terribly hard it appears to be for you, to simply keep your species from crossing our borders."

The second dragon, a lighter but richer red, spoke up.

"Do you need our help in removing these humans from our lands?" He asked. "We are, of course, perfectly justified in assisting, regardless of your response. Or perhaps we should have our own godknight join us?"

"No, no," Domaren quickly but calmly replied. "I assure you it is my intention to end this ridiculous skirmish and get this segment here back across the border as quickly as possible."

"How many times must we say it?" A Varoahn officer shouted from the belly of the canyon. "We have our own affairs and our own disagreements. Quit bothering and interfering with us! Leave us be! We have no need for godknights or monsters from the north here!"

"Monsters?" The brighter dragon echoed back. "I guess everything is a monster to you, hmm? You're nothing but simple, trivial ants crawling through a ditch, who don't know how to respect something as simple as a border!"

The leading segment of Onadion in the canyon grew uneasy and slowly backed their horses out while the

Varoahn provoked the dragons. However, the pass through which they had entered the canyon was quite narrow and prevented them from withdrawing quickly. As the dragon admonished the Varoahn, its throat glowed with mustering fire. Domaren let his head fall in fatigue from the altercation's predictability and swung it around in a preemptive stretch.

The dragon closest to the Onadion unleashed its spray of fiery punishment as it jumped into the canyon, spooking the horses into a flurry of neighing and chaotic rearing. Domaren followed suit and jumped down before plunging Verikta into the ground. With a rumble of seismic disorientation, he sent the Varoahn stumbling and rolling backwards, and out of the path of the dragon's torrent of fire. He then spun around and addressed the nearest dragon calmly.

"I'm telling you, I will remove these fools from your lands," Domaren said.

"From where I stand, you're just another one of the fools," the dragon said.

The dragon whipped a wing around, swiping at the human knight, but Domaren rolled out of the way into a kneeling crouch to center his gravity as the wing's wind blew over him. As if he could see the energy pass over, Domaren immediately brought his sword around and pointed its energy at the side of the canyon. With a slap to the flat of his blade, he shot out a concussive wave and dislodged dozens of boulders. The boulders, each one at least the size of a dragon, shook loose and rumbled down a destructive path, breaking the dragon's wings and bones before finally pinning it into what would typically be a permanent grave. As the boulders and dirt settled, they blocked Domaren's sight of the other dragon harassing the Onadion.

But Domaren needed to manage the troublesome Varoahn first. Those left standing advanced. He dispatched the initial challengers with multiple twirling, x-shaped slashes from left to right before a thrust to someone else's belly. Domaren dealt with the next few with violent slashes that, instead of making contact with the Varoahn attackers, sent them flying into the nearby canyon walls. Once he handled those that hadn't already turned to flee or rejoin the primary battle, he turned back to see what had become of the Onadion and the other dragon at the opposite end of the canyon.

Domaren turned and sprinted for the tower of boulders and resting place of the first dragon. He raced up, leaping up in wide strides, climbing higher and higher. Just as he hit the summit, the heat of a stream of fire bit at his skin. He threw himself down onto the boulders, narrowly missing an attack from the other dragon. The pinned Onadion, which had attempted to escape to the other side of the canyon, were not so lucky. Domaren watched as the flames consumed the Onadion. While most perished, Domaren watched a few escape the canyon from where they entered.

*Well, if the dragons didn't get you, I would have,* Domaren thought.

He stood up and leapt down the other side of the boulder tower, flicking his eyes up and down between determining the dragon's disposition and confirming his footing—one hectic hop at a time. After landing securely back at the floor of the canyon, Domaren found himself eye to eye with the remaining dragon.

"Your kin will live, dragon. Just let me pass and I'll finish driving the remaining humans back to their side of the border."

"You can proceed all you wish, Domaren, but let us have a contest to see who can clear the rest out the fastest, hmm?"

As the dragon finished challenging the human godknight, the enormous creature grinned, revealing its rows of threatening teeth. Before Domaren could reply, however, the dragon jumped and launched itself out of the canyon. With a subsequent beating of its wings, the dragon turned and faced the fleeing Onadion.

"There isn't time for this," Domaren said.

Before the dragon could bring its wings down a second time, Domaren reached up to the sky and clawed at the air with one hand as if searching for something in an upside down pouch. After rummaging around in apparent nothingness, his hand froze and locked into place. Having found what he was looking for, he crushed his fingers into a tense fist and jerked his arm down. As Domaren's fingers grappled down onto his palm and his muscles tensed against what seemed to be an invisible rope held by the stars themselves, a bolt of lightning ripped out from the bruised clouds and struck down straight through the dragon's skull. Its body went limp and crashed straight down to the ground from where it took flight.

"I'm sorry, friend," Domaren said.

The dragon's right wing was the last extremity to land. Domaren watched as it rolled flat onto the ground.

"See you soon."

With the canyon subdued and empty, Domaren shot out through the pass in pursuit of the fleeing Onadion.

*They're headed back south,* he thought. *Good.*

He dug his heels in once again and jumped into another sprint. He shook his head and sighed in relief as the burned border of the northern dragon territories passed back under his feet. And just as the Onadion caught back up with the primary battle, so too did Domaren. When the Onadion and Varoahn realized that Domaren had returned to the battle's primary focus, word spread and an eerie calmness brought the fighting to a halt.

Domaren watched with intrigue as the violent scene stopped so suddenly. He could hear the two adversaries mumble gently as they pointed and nodded sharply in Domaren's direction.

"I'll say it again. Your countrymen would be far better served by expending all this time and energy on negotiating a peace instead of entertaining me," Domaren scolded.

Reunited, for the moment, in their desire to expel the godknight from their quarrel, the armies sounded their war cries once again and rushed at Domaren. Some landed blows against the godknight, but his armor absorbed everything without so much as a scrape, blemish, or dulling of its shine. The occasionally coordinated volleys of arrows bounced off him with the harmlessness of raindrops. Domaren fought cleanly and easily. Though there was no legitimate challenge from the armies or threat to his safety, he fought with a calculated consideration and wise regard, taking nothing for granted.

"You are fighting fairly well," Domaren said. He smiled as he amused himself when he found time to yell to any who could hear. "But I'm afraid there are other things to which I will eventually need to attend."

Having recently regenerated his supernatural energy from his last grove stone, he could fight the quaint mortal armies continuously for months upon months. He merely needed to wait them out.

The two disagreeing populations continued finding common ground in their effort to expel the godknight.

Brothers, cousins, mothers, and sisters forgot their feuds. Opposing captains crossed the field to coordinate flanking maneuvers upon Domaren, which failed. Time after time, they tried new tactics, or charged with fresh fighters. Each failed. Domaren repulsed each wave. Each new effort. Every attempt to stop Domaren resulted in the same disappointment. No scrapes. No bangs, cuts, or bruises. He waded through every attack with ease, never breaking a sweat, and never doubting the inevitable outcome.

But he waited. He waited them out. It only took him nine additional hours to outlast two armies after the altercation in the canyon.

By the end of the fight, many that Domaren repulsed earlier crawled away to seek refuge in Cenzia. Exhausted and pained fighters, Varoahn and Onadion alike, collapsed at the gates and doors of the city and watched the rest of the struggle against Domaren unfold. With each passing minute, the futility of their effort became more apparent. Humility and exhaustion, it seemed, were good catalysts for helping reveal common ground.

The time between rushes and attacks against Domaren increased. As the hours progressed, he went from no breaks between fights, to seconds, to minutes. When there was a lull in hostilities, he even helped some exhausted mortals off the field just to walk back into the center of the battlefield to wait for a fresh attack. He planned to outlast them and waited for them to see reason. At last, the spent Varoahn and Onadion finally relented. Domaren breathed heavily for about twenty seconds, but that was all.

Domaren spun in place, slowly, many times, but no longer saw any threats nearby, nor on the horizon, or in any direction on the field. He sheathed Verikta and leaned over. He picked up a man and gently draped him over his shoulder.

"Come on, friend," Domaren said. "Up with you. Let's get to the city."

He crossed the field diagonally and met the short stretch of road leading to the gates of Cenzia. He leaned up under the arm of another exhausted man nearby and helped him shuffle back to the city walls as well.

As Domaren and the two men approached the city's front gates, many who hadn't already made their way also found energy to stumble or creep back.

Domaren helped the wounded men find a comfortable place on the nearby thick grass to sit. The sprawling gathering of men and women along the road, in the fields, and at the gates were mostly quiet, groaning occasionally from aches and pains, or panting heavily. Domaren stepped out into the middle of the road.

"I think it's quite obvious that the Kihdai will not allow this civil war to take place," Domaren boomed. He turned slowly as he addressed the two factions. "Maybe you'll recognize the futility. Not only in fighting me, but the pointlessness in fighting each other as well."

"Now, I can come back here to Cenzia, elsewhere in the area, or anywhere in Onadion to try again to encourage you to resolve your differences by other means. But, I believe every one of you, your families, and villages, would benefit more by agreeing to sit down with each other to seek a peaceful consensus to your disagreements."

Domaren continued to scan the sea of men and women as he spoke.

"Are there any thoughts or comments?" He asked.

Pained coughs, additional rapid breathing, and grunts of discomfort were the only response.

"All right," Domaren added. "I truly do wish each of

you health and peace."

As he completed one last circle of inspection, he nodded and reached for Verikta's handle. After wrapping his fingers around the sword, though still sheathed, his fingers once again found the yellow gem he pressed before the battle.

He tapped it.

A wave of energy rippled across the expanse of the battlefield. It raced along the road and on the outskirts of Cenzia, and rolled miles north across the border at the canyon. As the energy fell across the land, it healed any men, women, or dragons harmed by Domaren's direct or indirect attacks. It revived any who were dead. Exhaustion was the only remaining effect of the fighting.

"You smug bastard!" A voice shouted.

Domaren grinned and whistled for Munch. After approximately ten seconds, the horse weaved through the tired fighters and galloped over.

"Hey, you listened!" Domaren said. After a neck scratch for Munch and a ruffle of the ears for Wiggly, Domaren climbed up.

He then closed his eyes for the length of a long blink. When he opened them, another beam that resembled rocky sediment encompassed Domaren and his traveling companions. After another pinch of time, the Grove removed Domaren from the road outside Cenzia and placed him at his previous location on the outskirts of the village of Lilibrun.

* * *

Domaren sucked in a contented gulp of air and exhaled. His lungs hadn't yet emptied when the emerald on

Verikta's pommel flashed.

"They've got to be joking," he said to Wiggly. "I *just* got back."

Before he could tend to the attempted communication, a pitiful and distraught voice interrupted.

"Excuse me, young man? Could you please help me catch my chicken?"

*Young man,* Domaren thought. *Ha!*

Verikta's brilliant pommel stone flashed a second time.

"I'm afraid I don't have time to assist," Domaren offered. He tugged at his sword, still in its scabbard, and gestured at the shining stone with his other hand. The gem's light faded.

The weary farmer shuffled quickly towards Domaren and came to a stop. Wiggly sniffed the air and apparently felt no need to growl at the stranger. The man sighed as his head sagged. "Oh, I know a busy godknight got'sa go when called, but sure you've the time to help me catch this chicken first? I'm too long in the tooth, you know. She'd outrun me for days!"

Besides the stone on Domaren's sword, the matching emeralds on his gauntlets pulsed with new light.

"I apologize, my friend, but I must see to this," Domaren said. He leaned over in his saddle and placed his hand on the farmer's shoulder. "I will gladly help you when I get back if you haven't caught her by then."

The farmer sighed again but said nothing. Domaren looked up to the sky and then surveyed the road. He backed Munch away from the farmer's fence and pressed his calling stone.

After pressing the grove calling stone, another stream of sandy energy tore down from the sky. While the material pulsed down, Domaren removed his gauntlets, slipped them under his arm, and swung off his horse. The cylinder of sediment shot into the ground in front of him and left behind a grove stone—a circular bank of stone that came up to just above his waist. Initially shining yellow with an intense heat, the stone quickly cooled. Vibrant symbols carved themselves into the stone as the last bit of energy from the sky finished sinking into the ground.

With a space in the bank of round stone that allowed him to enter, Domaren walked into the center of the platform of rock and placed his hands inside indentations that perfectly accommodated the size and shape of his palms and fingers. The symbols around the stone and the spaces under his hands glowed. He had established a connection with the Grove.

A voice emanated from the altar of circular stone, having no discernible source.

"Domaren," an agitated voice began. "We're already hearing about the reckless way in which you handled the situation near Cenzia. Why did you feel it necessary to offend the dragons the way you did? We not only wanted you to keep the Onadion and Varoahn from bothering them, but we surely didn't want you disrupting them either!"

As the voice spoke, and with his hands still resting in the stone's indentations, Domaren's pommelstone, two different calling stones, as well as the emeralds on his gauntlets and pauldrons—glowed with sustained light. While the bitter voice continued ranting, the light from the stones glowed brighter as Domaren's celestial energy regenerated.

"Calba?" Domaren replied in mild disgust. "I haven't received a message from you in some time. How long has it been?"

Domaren's power finished regenerating. He removed his hands from the indentations as he turned to talk under his breath.

"Not long enough..." he added.

"Yes," Calba agreed. "Not long enough."

"Well, spit it out. Who's in an uproar and wh—" Domaren attempted.

"Don't pretend to be so dense," Calba interrupted in contempt. "I just told you, as if you didn't already know. Not only did you allow the Onadion and Varoahn to cross the border, you killed two dragon border guards! What is the matter with you?"

"I killed no one," Domaren replied dismissively. "If you were down here, rather than sitting under your tree sending messages, you would know that."

Domaren waited for a reply. There was none.

"And why don't you know that? Because you're not a Kihdai, a proxy, or a godknight. You sit up there removed from reality, removed from danger, removed from authority. You have no appreciation for the fact that you are, at the most, a mere messenger. Please remember that when relaying messag—"

Calba interrupted again.

"I know no one is dead *now,*" Calba finally responded. "But two things remain. You allowed the humans to cross the border, and you offended the dragons by killing their guards, even though you revived them."

Domaren smiled to himself as Calba continued his admonishment.

"You practically failed your last directive," he said.

"A pleasure to speak with you, Calba," Domaren said. As he replied, he placed his hands back in the stone indentations and made every effort to remove all sincerity from his voice.

"Fine. I was asked to pass along the displeasure of the Kihdai as requested, and I have done so. Prepare for—" Calba started. Domaren took the opportunity to interrupt this time.

"Yes, fantastic, I know. I'm ready."

The stone encircling Domaren surged red with natural heat, and with a pop of blinding light, the stone ring disintegrated out from around him. Domaren stood alone only with his thoughts and the sound of rustling leaves. And the sound of truant chickens.

*Chickens.*

Domaren huffed and attempted to clear his mind as he looked up to the horizon, settling his vision on the chimneys of homes and markets, and thatched barns of Lilibrun, a prominent town on the edges of Komara. Komara was the largest city occupied by humans and was the traditional home of the human godknight. Domaren rarely spent a night in his home, however, being constantly beckoned by the Kihdai. But he was home for now, and as he looked away from the city, he turned and caught the old farmer looking at him, smiling warmly. Rather than reciprocating a smile out of kindness, the old man's missing teeth made Domaren smile. He stepped over to the chicken farmer's fence and sought to make good on his promise.

"Looks like I won't be leaving just yet, my friend. Let's get those rascals back in their coop."

He spotted the original chicken, but now also a second one.

"I thought you only needed help with one," Domaren teased.

The old man chuckled and shrugged. Regardless, Domaren moved slowly towards the nearby gate and crept in. Wiggly jumped down from Munch and ran over.

"No, no," Domaren said. "You're made to herd, sure, but I don't need you getting all dirty. Go on, get back up."

Instead of obeying, Wiggly tilted her head and sat.

"Okay," Domaren said. "As long as you stay there."

He turned back towards the farm.

"Where do you silly little things think you're going?" Domaren posed softly to the chickens. "Time to go home."

Domaren stared down at the original, mischievous chicken and mentally mapped his plan of attack. While he knew he would successfully catch the chickens, he thought he'd have some fun with it.

"Okay, time to pounce! What's your name by the way?"

The old man hobbled over and leaned on a rotten post as he waited for the altercation between godknight and chicken.

"The name's Minchet!"

"Okay, Minchet. My plan is to lean over and spread my arms. Kind of like you do with pigs, right? Going to make myself look wider than I am and hopefully be a bit more nimble while I'm closer to the ground. You ready?"

Minchet replied in the affirmative with a wheezy chuckle.

Domaren spotted the chicken coop and heard the muffled squawks of other hens inside. With a glance at the second chicken, and then back to the original, Domaren darted off.

The second chicken stood between him and the original troublemaker. Being careful not to startle the second one, Domaren snatched it up by its legs. In a zig-zagging blur of movement, Domaren confused the first chicken and made his move. But as he reached down to scoop it up, despite his announced—and what he thought would be a fool-proof—plan, his momentum had other plans and shifted his center of gravity such that he lost his footing and slid onto his muddied and humbled side.

Still holding one chicken, Domaren rolled his head and watched as the other skipped off in a flapping and noisy racket.

"Well, that's one of two! A success so far, I'd say," Minchet said with approving laughter.

While wiping his nose and chuckling also, Domaren stood up and approached the coop to deposit the one he had caught.

"Out-maneuvered by dinner!" Domaren said, still laughing.

With a quick slap of his hand, he swiped some mud off his armor and eyed the second stubborn chicken once again. As he did, his sword's pommelstone flashed again.

Domaren scoffed and stepped slowly towards the second chicken.

The pommelstone flashed a second time, along with his gauntlets.

"They are especially needy today," he complained to himself.

He continued his approach towards the chicken, being sure to confirm the driest path this time.

"Without the help of mud, oh poultried-one, you won't escape me this time!"

His pommelstone, gauntlets, and pauldrons flashed for a total of three new attempts.

Domaren launched off in another sprint. He ran towards the chicken in a blur of godly zig-zags, and this time swooped down and successfully snatched up the chicken by its legs. As Domaren jumped up and came to a triumphant stop, he chuckled, but not before all of his stones, including his two calling stones, flashed a fourth time. After the fourth attempt at contact, Domaren felt a sharp pain stab at his entire existence.

"All right!" He shouted. After angrily stomping back to the coop, he opened the door and tossed the chicken in harmlessly. He skipped backwards to an adequate clearing in the middle of the old farmer's larger corral, looked up, and tapped his grove calling stone. Munch took some steps towards him, but Domaren waved him away for the moment.

A new grove stone and its accompanying torrent of pebbles and dirt shot down across from Domaren once again. The stream of material subsided, and the glowing stone cooled.

"I'm really not in the mood for—" Domaren started.

As the godknight addressed his summons, the old farmer whispered, "thank you," and slapped Domaren on his back before heading back to the coop with a basket, ready to fill it with eggs.

"Domaren!" The voice from the grove stone called.

He looked around aimlessly as he placed the voice. After quickly doing so, his mood lightened immediately.

"Bahvan," he replied in a relieved breath. Domaren jogged through the opening and placed his hands in the stone's indentations as he continued. "It's good to hear from you."

"Ha! Why is that?"

Domaren offered a laugh of his own while the fraction of his recently refilled energy regenerated.

"Oh," he said, dismissing his frustrations. "I don't know. I just enjoy hearing from some of you more than others on most days."

"Ah, I know what you're getting at," Bahvan said. "I don't always like being stuck here in the Grove with some of the same few you're probably referring to. The resentment some of us here have for some of you down there gets awfully tiresome. But, it's nothing that hasn't existed for eons I guess."

As Bahvan spoke to Domaren through the grove stone, Domaren nodded.

"True," he acknowledged. "It's just nice to get directives from those who... act like equals, rather than superiors. A little humility goes a long way. There's good and bad about both groups though, I guess. You all are stuck there. And we're stuck here."

The two friends who hadn't been in each other's physical presence in ages shared laughs through the grove stone connection.

"I'd probably find something to complain about there though," Bahvan offered.

"Heh, exactly," Domaren said. "Same for me, there, I'm sure."

"Well, maybe someday the Kihdai will let us visit, or let you all visit us."

"Mm," Domaren grunted. "I've never heard of that happening, but it would be nice. I've always wanted to see the new Grove. One can hope."

"And I've always wanted to see the lands of the mortals," Bahvan said. "The stories and legends have always fascinated me."

"It definitely is that," Domaren returned with a laugh. "It really is an intriguing place."

After a few more shared laughs, Domaren inquired about his next directive.

"All right, my friend. What do you have for me?"

"Yes, yes, right," Bahvan said. "I'm afraid it doesn't sound all that exciting."

"Well, I'm sure it's more exciting than chasing chickens," Domaren quipped.

"Hmm?" Bahvan asked in a puzzled lilt.

"Oh," Domaren said, laughing. "Never mind."

"Hmm, sure," Bahvan said with a giggle. "Anyway, Brikana's helping mediate a new trade agreement between two major dragon broods and one of them has some fairly significant dealings with a few human kingdoms. As the human godknight, the Kihdai would like you to visit and lend some advice on the language of the agreement and help inform the whole situation. They want you to act only in a consultative capacity."

Domaren leaned away from the grove stone.

"Domaren?" Bahvan asked.

"Yes, I'm here," he replied. "They want me to go, right now? After the um, situation I just dealt with?"

"I thought it might be a bit too soon as well, if that's what you're getting at," Bahvan teased.

"Does Brikana know I'm being asked to visit?"

"Not yet," Bahvan replied.

Domaren grinned.

"I didn't think so," he responded through a snicker. "Out of all of us, the last one I'd expect to reach out for anything is our beloved dragon godknight."

"Oh," Bahvan began. "She's just a little stubborn is all." He let a chuckle loose as he finished speaking.

"Stubborn?" Domaren scoffed. "Remember that time she challenged the dragon tribunal a while back? Refused to leave after they proposed a vote to have her replaced as their godknight?"

Before Domaren could finish, Bahvan was choking

with fresh laughter.

"She challenged each of them to a fight!" He said, barely finding breath to blurt.

"Right!" Domaren confirmed. "She was always bending the directives she got from the Kihdai... would get into arguments with the dragon tribunal, constantly."

"Well, she's not like that anymore, though, right?" Bahvan asked.

"Oh, ha! That's what she wants us all to believe," Domaren playfully admonished. "She's just learned how to obscure her opinions better!"

"Well, she always sees things done, though," Bahvan added.

"Yes, I know," Domaren admitted. "I know. She does, and if I could only have one other godknight to help me in a fight, it'd be her."

"Oh, don't ever let her hear you say that!" Bahvan said, bursting out again.

Domaren only replied with hearty laughter. When they caught their breath, Bahvan brought the conversation back to its focus.

"All right, all right. Please go ahead and visit, and lend whatever help you can to these negotiations."

Domaren sniffed through a few last laughs before responding.

"Of course. No problem," Domaren obliged. "A little diplomatic directive will be a pleasant change of pace. It's been awfully busy over the past few centuries."

"Mmm," Bahvan mumbled. "Peace takes work."

"Lately, all the work seems to be war."

Bahvan had no immediate reply, but finally responded.

"Well, sometimes the godknights have to wage what they wish to prevent."

Domaren took a second.

"Trust me. I know," he said.

"Anyway," Bahvan said, trying to press on. "As you said, a little diplomatic directive will be a pleasant change of pace, and hopefully will help lead to even more of these, more civil directives. The world seems to be in a fairly haggard state lately, with most of the races getting along together quite poorly. That's why directives like this are so important."

"I understand, my friend," Domaren said. "You will have no argument from me. I just hope that my next directive..."

Domaren trailed off as a noise in Bahvan's background distracted him.

"Bahvan?"

He didn't answer.

The noise increased. White noise of agitated voices and unintelligible commotion grew louder. Inside the grove stone, Domaren could only lean into the indentions, blur his vision, and listen.

"There's," Bahvan said. "There's something wrong."

"What is it, Bahvan?" Domaren said. He rushed his words with a hurried calm. "Tell me what you see."

"Everyone's pouring out from Vals Hald and scattering out into the fields... Headed this way, towards the forest."

A crunching explosion tore out over Domaren's connection with the grove stone. Crisp sounds of breaking trees stabbed at Domaren's ears.

"Bahvan! Get away from there! Get out!"

Another percussive punch of noise blasted out from the grove stone. Domaren instinctively flinched from the harsh blast.

"Domar..." Bahvan screamed. But the communication

bond was severed. Domaren stood still, shocked in confused fear.

With no initiation from Domaren this time, a new stroke of rocky energy lashed out from the sky. It rained down onto the grove stone and pummeled it to dust.

# Three

Domaren could do nothing but watch the grove stone crumble to the ground. Typically, they disintegrated when the Grove ended their communications, or when a knight ended the conversation by pressing their grove calling stone again. But never did they seemingly dismiss themselves.

Domaren immediately slapped his grove calling stone, hoping to open a new conversation.

Nothing happened.

He slapped it again and then tried another time.

"Bahvan," he said, barking in exasperation.

One more smash of the stone.

"Bahvan!"

He looked up, scouring the sky for any hints of a fresh stream of energy. Nothing.

Holding his gaze to sky, he spun and spun, squinting most of the time, waiting for some kind of interaction. Nothing.

Looking back down, he slowly raised his hand up to

his calling stone again and, after a moment's hesitation, pressed it. Nothing.

Domaren slowly lowered to his knees and placed his hands in the small piles of debris left over from the last grove stone. He closed his eyes to focus his thoughts.

*What was that explosion?*

*What happened?*

*Grove stones have accidentally been severed before, sure, but that explosion.*

*There were two!*

*I hope it was just an accident.*

He looked back up at the sky and blinked rapidly. Nothing.

He stood up and let his eyes dance around the ground aimlessly

He looked back down at the pile of pitiful gravel.

Back up to the sky.

*Nothing.*

*Do I still have my abilities? My strength?*

He dropped his hand down to Verikta's handle and felt a small zap to his palm as he ran his fingers over the handlestones.

With the realization that Verikta seemed normal, his nerves relaxed by a fraction. He used the reassurance as fuel to focus and calm himself.

He inspected Verikta's pommelstone and the stones on his gauntlets. They were dim.

*I need to check with the other godknights.*

He looked around the area again to help himself focus and calm down even more. But something tugged at his attention.

*The chickens.*

They were still in the coop, it seemed, and Domaren

could still hear the old farmer rummaging around inside.

Unable to make sense of what happened, Domaren dashed over to Munch and hopped on. He trotted past the farmer's corral and joined the main road leading back to his home. There, he didn't have a grove stone, but a common traveling stone. As he, Munch, and Wiggly returned to the village, he tapped a different calling stone. This onyx stone, attuned to Domaren and used to communicate between godknights rather than with the Grove, knew who he wished to speak with.

An incensed alto voice answered almost immediately. Her monotone reply bit each syllable with confident brevity.

"I'm extremely busy. What is it, Domaren?"

"Listen. Something's wrong at the Grove," he said, his voice weighted with urgency even while riding.

"What?"

"I was in the middle of speaking with the Grove when I heard panic and explosions. The communication was severed and the grove stone disintegrated."

"I really doubt there's anything to worry about. Did you even try to call a new stone?"

Domaren pulled back on Munch's reins.

"Yes, Brikana," he said. His words snapped in anger. "I'm telling you. Something's wrong."

"I've lost contact in the middle of a grove stone before," she replied. "I'm sure it's just a temporary issue."

"Did you hear what I said, Brikana? Explosions. Plural. Panic. And I couldn't re-establish contact."

Brikana had no retort. Domaren pressed on with his concern.

"When was the last time you heard from them?"

"Two days ago," she answered. "They've got me dealing with some silly negotiations."

Domaren huffed a sharp sigh as his patience dwindled.

"Can you just try to summon a grove stone?"

"No. I don't have time for that or you. I'm sure it will be—"

"It isn't fine, Brikana. Please try to summon the stone!"

Domaren spun awkwardly in his saddle as nearby field hands eyed him, a man that probably seemed to them to be shouting at himself.

"Just try. If you get through, I'll leave you be, all right?" Domaren implored.

Brikana breathed in slowly and then shot her breath out in frustration. The bond between the two godknights went silent.

"Are you there?" Domaren snipped. "Are you going to try?"

"Yes!" She shouted back. "I'm getting ready to!"

Domaren relented and rubbed his eyes.

"Anything?"

"Hold on."

Domaren waved at the onlooking field hands.

"What the..."

"See?" Domaren chided.

"Wait," Brikana said.

There was only silence as Domaren assumed Brikana was trying repeatedly to summon a grove stone.

"I told you, Brikana," he said sternly. "Something is *wrong.*"

"Stop for a second," she said. "Let me think. Why did you contact me first? What was your message from the Grove about?"

"It was about you and the dragons," he impatiently answered. "The Kihdai knew there was a new trade agreement being negotiated between some of the dragon broods, which have some fairly significant human influence and impact. They wanted me to visit and lend my advice."

"Lend your advice?" Brikana said. "I don't need your hel—"

Domaren lashed out.

"Can you put your pride away for a minute, Brikana? That was my directive, but I'm not concerned with that right now. Even though I have every right, as well as obligation, to oversee any language involving humanity, there is a bigger concern for us to consider. I need your help in figuring out what's happened. Now, since it pertains to my last directive, I am going to use my traveling stone and come to where you are. Once I'm there, I think we should speak with the other knights, see what they've experienced, fill them in on what I heard, and start looking into this. Do you disagree with that?"

"You can do whatever you want," Brikana replied coldly. "But I would suggest you remember when speaking to me that I don't get my directives from you."

With that, the connection between the two godknights ended.

Domaren, Munch, and Wiggly stood awkwardly in the narrow path of dirt, worn through the years by countless wagon wheels. Munch tapped gently at the ground. Domaren caught eyes with a curious field hand.

"And this is one of her better days," Domaren joked. He waved again and resumed his ride to the village.

* * *

The public knew of the godknights, their fabled immortality, and their duties. Through all the ages of life, each race has had its own godknight to enforce the will of the Kihdai. Throughout time, they protected the various cultures within their particular population, and intervened in wars or disputes. Godknights were generally liked and respected, and as Domaren rode through the streets of the human godknight's traditional home, he offered and returned many greetings, waves, and shouts of friendliness.

Domaren frequently stopped and spoke with people as he traversed the streets. They sprinted down alleys to catch up with him. They left customers standing at counters to rush out and thank him for some noble deed, or for staving off a violent conflict with a neighboring village. Others rushed out with pies baked especially for him, or insisted on buying him a pint.

Today, his face dragged with concern, and citizens' usual stops and calls went ignored or dismissed. After a ride distracted with worry and thought, he reached his humble home and raced up the rickety steps.

He crashed through the door and surveyed the first room as if he'd never seen it before. Maps and books cluttered the room in wobbly stacks, but at that moment, he couldn't remember which books he had reviewed recently, or for what purpose. He stomped through his home, mindlessly wandering around like a possessed beast whose only purpose in life was to eat or find a mate. After remembering the travel stone was outside and below his home in his small stable, he raced back out and grabbed Munch's reins.

"Apologies, you two," he said to his animal friends. "My mind is everywhere."

As he approached his private, one stall stable, he shoved open the gate and walked in. His eyes locked on the stone as he led Munch to it.

Unlike the grove stones that encircled him almost

entirely, with only one entry point, travel stones had many gaps through which the owner could enter. Domaren led Much in and, after letting go of the reins, placed his hands in the indentations—very similar to those in grove stones. But another difference between the travel and grove stones was that rather than providing and regenerating his energy, the indentations in the travel stone consumed his power. And instead of establishing a connection with the Grove, the travel stone simply streamed him to another location in the world, placing him at the desired location.

After confirming Munch and Wiggly were ready, a downpour of sandy energy enveloped them and whisked them off to the dragon city of Kimozoa.

Domaren's stream of shifting rock struck out from his home and rapidly blended into the sky. As it raced transparently between locations, it arced along the curve of the world's shape before slamming down into the center of a public receiving stone. Even though he landed in Kimozoa at the height of the mid-day sun, a gigantic shadow fellow over him.

Before moving any other muscles or shifting his gaze, Domaren brought his hands up slowly, touching the tips of his two index fingers together, forming two sides of a triangle. Only after he had showed a non-dragon's proper gesture of respect to the approaching creatures, did he turn his eyes up to them.

"Ah, Domaren," Kistora greeted. Kistora was a remarkable dragon and one of Kimozoa's most renowned public servants. He curled his gigantic tail slowly behind him before bringing it up against his side. Kistora's thick voice coated Domaren's chest with the reverberations of a rumbling bass. "Even Brikana doesn't always show us similar degrees of respect. It is good to see you."

"Likewise, Lord Kistora. Thank you." Domaren repeated the gesture of respect with his hands as he bowed. "Would you know happen to know where Brikana might be?"

"Mmm, yes. I'm fairly confident she is at the theatre," Kistora said. "I believe the negotiations are set to begin for the proposed Rijonian Accords, if they haven't already begun. Is there something the matter?"

Domaren shifted uneasily, but replied quickly.

"I do have an urgent matter I need to broach with her, but it's nothing I need trouble you with."

Kistora smiled warmly. The seam of his mouth parted, giving way to the sight of a seemingly endless bank of teeth, each one a quarter of Domaren's height.

"Well, I won't press you," Kistora added. "But should you need our assistance, know that you shall have it."

Domaren offered the gesture of respect a final time.

"Thank you, Kistora. I wish you well."

Domaren dropped his hands and clicked his tongue, prompting Munch to enter into a quick walk towards the theatre. Though preoccupied with concern and weighed down by constant extrapolations of what might have transpired, Domaren found focus enough to scan the massive crowd of dragons. He looked along and through the thick sea of dragons, gathered or traveling along the crowded thoroughfare, being careful where he strode. There was very little he could see through or above the throng of dragons. Most were some twenty feet tall at the chest, with some shorter and some larger. Luckily, the scale and size of Kimozoa's buildings were such that he could determine where he was by looking at the horizon. He steered Munch carefully and pressed on through the streets.

Upon arriving at the tribunal's semi-circular theatre,

Domaren smiled at having forgotten the scale of the steps for most of the city's buildings. He sniffed in a quick breath and dismounted. After tying Munch's reins through a decorative loop in a nearby column, he gave his friends some advice.

"Try not to get stomped, or... cooked," he said. He offered both of his friends a pat and smile before jogging towards the steps leading to the entrance.

The rise of the steps was quite tall for someone the size of a human, and they were rather deep. Luckily, the depth gave Domaren enough room to jog towards the next step, grab on to the edge, and vault himself up and onto each subsequent step. His efforts inspired him to wonder why some areas of the city seemed to accommodate species other than dragons more than others. Regardless, he made quick work of the stairs, and if anything, the difference in perspective amused Domaren.

As he finally topped the massive stairs, the shadows of two enormous dragons draped over him. Tending towards the taller amongst the dragon species, the two creatures stepped into his path. They weren't quite challenging his arrival, because they knew him and Domaren knew them. It was, however, understood that Domaren would present them with his cause for being there.

Domaren brought his hands up and touched the tips of his fingers once again.

"Hello, Lord Dragons," he began. "The Kihdai have directed me here to rendezvous with Brikana, and assist however I can with the Rijonian Accords. I would request your permission to be allowed to pass."

The two imposing creatures immediately parted and removed themselves from his path.

"Thank you, knight Domaren," the dragon to his

left responded. "You are welcome here and are permitted to pass."

Domaren bowed and offered the salute of respect a final time before continuing on.

He resumed his march of urgency and passed between the dragons into a towering portico. Its ceiling was an alternating checkered pattern of stone lattice and vibrant fabric of garnet and crimson. After passing through the portico, Domaren walked out into the open-air theatre and immediately slowed his pace to lessen the noise he made.

Far across at the other side of the theatre, five dragon tribunes elected to represent their respective dragon brood presided over the session. Each dragon sat atop its dedicated portion of the highest and outermost level of the theatre, with steps similar to those at the theatre's entrance leading down to the lowest level of the structure. It was here that a dragon would plead its case or concerns to the tribunal. As Domaren stepped closer and immediately started scouring the area for Brikana, a prospective member of the proposed Rijonian Accords addressed the assembled tribunal, which loomed high overhead.

Domaren stepped farther in, but didn't enter the speaker's area. Instead, he walked along the wall just outside the primary theatre structure, attempting to be inconspicuous in his hunt for Brikana. As he searched, he let the speaker's comments register.

"Lords tribunal," the dragon continued. "If I may be so bold... It would be nothing less than foolish to reject the terms outlined in these accords. The Frillincian and Morig broods would both benefit from this agreement, and would only strengthen the mutual protection agreements the Frillincians have with the humans on their borders. And I maintain that a strong relationship with any race on any of our borders can only be a good thing."

One of the five tribunes stirred, unfurling his wings and rippling them out to their maximum extent. He strained through a stretch as he spoke.

"I appreciate your enthusiasm, Lord Mediator," the tribune started. "But while there are mutually beneficial aspects of these proposed accords, can someone please remind me why this requires the attention of the tribunal?"

The mediator shuffled his four feet briefly before replying.

"Yes, the primary reason is because of the... shared border between the humans and the Frillincian brood I referenced previously."

"Right," the tribute responded. "And if this was a proposed agreement between broods that share no borders with outside races, there would be no need for it to be brought to the attention of the full tribunal, is that correct?"

The mediator looked to the side galleries before turning back to the tribunal.

"Yes, that is correct."

"Then I'm afraid the need to have this addressed by the tribunal is still lost on me. There have been agreements and treaties struck between broods and other races in the past, including humans. Can we please get to the heart of what this tribunal needs to be made aware of and pass judgment on?"

The mediator let his head and long neck droop as he shuffled his feet again. He stuttered a fumbled response, but movement from the gallery to the mediator's right drew everyone's attention.

"Lords tribunal," a female dragon began. "I would like to speak to this point if I may be permitted."

The mediator looked at her before turning back to

the tribunal.

"I will yield my current allotment to our Godknight, Lady Brikana."

Domaren dropped his head and rolled his eyes behind closed eyelids. He rubbed them gently while feeling silly for not immediately recognizing Brikana's voice.

The mediator stepped back and withdrew to the rear of the speaking level as Brikana took his place. Domaren's skin itched and his stomach groaned with anxiety. He wasn't sure what Brikana had to say, or how she intended to say it.

"Lords and Ladies of the Tribunal," Brikana began. "There is quite a complicated matter involved here. One that the mediator is understandably reluctant to state outright. And please, Lord Mediator, do not take my comments as a slight, but just a means of broaching the sensitivity of the issue."

Domaren's eyebrows rose slightly at Brikana's unexpected and gentle touch of diplomacy. The tribunal sat in silence as Brikana continued.

"You see. This is not as simple a situation as it may appear. The humans sharing a border with some of our own race, are not just any segment of humans—"

The most senior tribune, who had not yet spoken, launched up onto all fours and snapped his wings out in a crisp slap before bringing them back down. His dark blue scales were dull and irregularly worn. His face wore the worries of an entire culture, but the resolve of hundreds of years. Of all the characteristics of his features, weakness or ineptitude were not amongst them.

"Wait!" His seismic voice growled. "The Frillincian brood, you say?"

The entire theatre became restless as they started

focusing on the specifics surrounding the Frillincian brood. Some tribunes risked toppling off their columns to lean towards others and whisper. The galleries, filled with hundreds of dragons spanning the entire societal and political spectrum, rippled with activity. Silence became whispers. Whispers became exclamations. Exclamations grew into ancient roars of hate and culminated in the elder tribune's realization.

"The Frillincian brood shares a border with the Vriden!"

Brikana cut a glance at Domaren as the gallery screamed out in anger. The first tribune who had questioned the need for the tribunal's involvement erupted over the frenzied theatre.

"Which imbecile contemplated the notion that this tribunal would permit an agreement that could in any way benefit the Vriden? What involvement did you have, Brikana? I demand an answer! Choose your words carefully!"

"Lords Tribunal," Brikana rushed through confident strength, "the only motivation for even asking you to consider this arrangement is because of the significant benefit that we dragons would benefit from the nurtured relationship between our people—the Frillincians and the Morig. The existing agreements between the Frillincians and Vriden are a minor detail, but yes, one that exists, and one that we knew to reference because of the history we have with the Vriden."

"That history," screamed the original, incensed tribune, "includes the hunting of dragons! The Vriden hunted us! They tracked us down in mobs, chased us, drew us out, and terrorized us. They hacked our heads off and mounted them in their halls. Our wings were ripped off and used to protect their markets from the sun. They used the blood and bone of our kind as furniture and decoration! Yes, you would do well to remember exactly what that history entails!"

Brikana drooped her majestic head before looking back up to the tribunal. She slowly turned in a circle to connect with as many of the other dragons as she could. Having outlined the horror of the history with the Vriden, the tribune's comments drew the other outrage to a close. The theatre assumed a tenuous silence as Brikana moved.

"My fellow dragons," Brikana started solemnly. "Much to the chagrin of some, I have very frequently thought of myself as a dragon first, and as our race's godknight, second. There is nothing I hold closer to my heart than that of being a dragon. Dragons are an absolutely singular phenomenon of existence. When the Kihdai kissed that catalyst of life, I'm fairly confident they knew that dragons would have no equal."

Brikana paused, if only to gauge how much of an impact her initial reply was making.

"I want to make sure each and every dragon here knows, that I am immensely cognizant of our history with the Vriden. I am keenly aware that our laws dictate that all interactions that have any involvement with the Vriden be scrutinized. I understand that and support that. But I can only say again that the primary reason I have any amount of support for this proposed agreement is because of the benefit that our Frillincian and Morig broods would realize. And with that said, my Lords and Ladies tribunal, I would also like to assure you that the malice, violence, and savagery that those Vriden generations exhibited centuries ago have long-since been bred out of their blood."

The oldest tribune, and the one that reminded the theatre that the Vriden were the humans that shared the border with the Frillincians, responded next.

"Though the current generations of Vriden may not remember those times, lady godknight," he said. "There are most assuredly dragons still alive that remember that darkness. I am one of them. It is not always so easy to find peace in the simple passage of time."

Though unsure of how the tribunal would receive any input from him, Domaren stepped away from the wall, compelled to speak.

"If it might be permitted, may I address the tribunal?" Domaren asked. He spoke slowly, and with a respectful softness.

Brikana looked at him as he approached. Her gigantic eyes, full of pride and stress, squinted with an ire added for his benefit. But after a wink from Domaren, they reluctantly relaxed into a stare of reluctant patience. She then turned to the tribunal.

"I yield my remaining time to Godknight Domaren."

Domaren paused after his initial request, but after hearing no objection from the tribunal, walked farther into the heart of the theatre.

He strode slowly, and respectfully, looking to the galleries, nodding to each side as he did. After peering up at the tribunal, he closed his eyes and opened them. As some of the onlooking dragons froze and whispered, Domaren's body took on a new form. Quickly, but smoothly, Domaren's body grew. His overall size swelled. His neck lengthened. He pitched forward. His arms and hands bulged into immense trunks of flesh and bone, and feet with massive claws. Wings pierced through his armor and unfurled into massive curtains of webbing behind him. His brilliant armor of shiny steel, with accents of bronze and gold, grew in conjunction with his body and transformed into thousands of bright green scales.

Most in the vicinity who knew godknights could assume a form representative of any race watched silently as Domaren changed shape. Still, even some who knew, and especially those who didn't, gasped in reverent awe as the human godknight temporarily became one of them. As Domaren completed his transformation, his respectable form as a dragon flexed and stretched into a comfortable posture.

"Brikana, native dragons, and of course, the tribunal, please forgive me for this display. If I was to be honored with your time and attention, I wanted to address this tribunal, as a dragon. Though the power of each individual godknight is confined to their natural form, we have the ability to assume an individual likeness associated with each race. I thought it would be a sign of respect, and I intended it as such."

"Just because you look like us," roared the eldest dragon, "does not mean you are one of us. How dare you presume to..."

A female dragon, quiet until that point, interrupted with a refined grace.

"At the risk of perpetuating an endless loop of presumptions, my fellow tribune, I would think that the godknight knows what his native form is, and isn't. Let's accept his sign of respect and hear what he has to say."

The elder tribune held the gaze of the female tribune, but eventually relented and turned his head back to Domaren. As the sound in the theatre dwindled to its lowest volume since his arrival, he turned to Brikana. She jerked her head in the tribunal's direction, urging him to continue.

"Thank you, Lady Tribune, and thank you all for

your time. The truth is, I would like to agree with the elder tribune and I also wanted to echo some of the points he made. Time does indeed not wash away the sins of our past. They do not erase memories. In fact, my friends, I remember. I remember the fight waged against the Vriden of those past generations. The disease of ignorance, hate, and violence they attempted to spread throughout humanity—I remember that as well. I was there. Just as I was the human godknight then, I am their knight now. I was the human godknight that fought against those humans. I fought against segments of the race which I represent, because they were wrong. What they did was wrong. How they thought, felt, and acted was wrong. They united the rest of humanity against them. At that moment, the Vriden were a group apart. They were rightfully disowned, disavowed, and shunned by the rest of humanity."

Domaren continued speaking, though as he did, he allowed his form to shift back to his native, human semblance.

"That was not the first time, and will not be the last time, that a knight has taken their own species to task. It was not the first time that a godknight has waged war against those of his native form. It will not be the last. We will, as we have always, seek to destroy those who wish harm against any good in this world. We will seek out any who wish to do harm. To our own, or to others."

Domaren dropped his head and collected his thoughts.

"Just as I would vouch for today's living dragons in the face of those who would cite the Slaughter of Stenvurna as justification for hating you, I would stick up for the Vriden of today. Just as the ancestors of the Vriden hunted the dragons, your ancestors obliterated entire villages of unknowing orcs, suspected of encroaching upon dragon territory, only to discover later that they actually hadn't infringed on your lands."

As Domaren prepared his closing comments, he stepped even closer to the base of the massive columns supporting the dragons from where they perched. His neck bent back almost to its fullest extent.

"What I'm getting at, my friends, is that while we must hold each and everyone accountable for their despicable acts, we can not penalize the future for the deeds of the past. We must not project hate for an unreasonable amount of time or let a long-dead generation prevent the hope and promise for peace and growth. Please consider, if not approve these accords. A human-Vriden relationship with one of your broods, would in no way endanger the dragons. I assure you that these are good people and have been for some time. They cherish their dragon neighbors. The same dragon neighbors that would benefit mutually from this agreement."

The tribunal and the entire gallery fell completely silent. Each dragon seemed to reflect sincerely on Domaren's words. While he spoke, he could hear mumbles and moans of approval. Domaren felt good about what he had said. He felt good about it, because he felt it was true.

Finally, a member of the tribunal offered a response.

"You speak with eloquence and passion, my Lord Godknight, Domaren. I can appreciate what you mean to say, and what you mean to accomplish..."

The tribune's voice trailed off. Just before Domaren or any of the dragons in the gallery had time to feel uneasy at the silence, the tribune shot his wings out. He flapped them once in a violent slap of power, shot himself up into the air, off his column, and allowed himself to fall in a thunderous but controlled crash to the ground—immediately in front of Domaren.

"But I will allow no one, much less a godknight, to disguise their ulterior motives in flowery diplomacy. You will not toy with us like puppets, sitting from a suspended platform higher than our own perches!"

Dragons throughout the theatre shot out from their positions into the sky, or down onto the ground at speaking level. Shouting and arguments for or against the proposed accords slammed into one another. The sharp cacophony amplified the tension exponentially. Domaren threw his hands up as if pleading with an attacker to spare him. Though Domaren was unafraid, the rapid escalation concerned him.

"My lord, tribune, I meant no offense at all. I only wished to convey my experience with the..."

The remaining tribunes had jumped from their columns as well, with the rest of the tribunal split evenly in support of, or against, the topic at hand. Half loomed over Domaren, while the other half assumed a defensive posture at Domaren's side.

"I've already said that I know what you are doing, Domaren," the tribune lashed out in response. "I'm tired of the godknights seeking to manipulate this world to their will, based on what they claim is the will of the Kihdai!"

Another tribune stepped towards the enraged dragon, unintentionally forcing Domaren to step away from the confrontation. As he did, he felt the breeze from Brikana rushing forward smack him in the face.

"Brikana. Brikana! Don't!"

"How dare you think you can say such a stupid thing without being challenged," she began. "If you think the godknights have been manipulating the world, then what is it that you think I've been doing since I became your knight? How dare you!"

"This is ridiculous," argued one of the defensive tribunes. "Where is this coming from? Why such paranoia?"

"Brikana," a tribune standing to the side of the accusing tribune began. "You should be very careful with how you proceed right now. Yes, you are our godknight, and yes, I regard you as a dragon as much as my family or any other dragon in this gallery. But what you are not, is a member of our tribunal. I would ask that you show some restraint and not intervene in our actions."

Another tribune standing to Domaren's side laughed. "As a member of the tribunal, I say that you, Brikana, are welcome to stand by my side. The tribune looked back at his angry counterparts before continuing.

"You do not speak for the entire tribunal, my friend. That is why I stand across from you now. Your judgment of the Vriden is uncalled for, and your basis for objecting to the accords is out of line. Your logic is flawed."

The gallery fell quiet. The divided tribunal of dragons, along with Brikana, slowly spread out.

Domaren reached for Verikta's handle slowly and pressed the green handlestone, setting the blade's power to mirror. Instead of withstanding any impact, the sword would instantly absorb and return the energy it sustained. He had no intention of initiating a fight, but would defend his fellow knight and his sympathetic dragon allies. If there had been no support for his position from any of the tribunal, he would not even consider interfering.

He stepped backwards slowly, more than he already had. He knew he would need exptra space to analyze the situation if a fight began. If it came to that, the heart of the theatre and the space in it, as well as the sky above it, would become a thick jumble of massive dragons.

His eyes danced from one potential target to another, and then to his allies and back. He breathed deep and exhaled smoothly.

The eldest dragon, standing across from Brikana, grinned.

"Right or wrong, Brikana, you will not overpower those of us on this side."

She smiled back.

"Win or lose," she started. "We are *right.*"

The youngest dragon on the accusing side shot off the ground. Before launching into the air, the others, along with the eldest, darted forward and charged at Brikana. They struck and knocked her over as her allies darted out of the way and immediately turned to launch a stream of fire at their attackers. Before chasing after them into the sky, Brikana rolled out of the momentum from her charging attackers and considered the best plan of attack.

"Brikana?" Domaren shouted. She didn't answer. In the time it took for him to consider shifting into a dragon, and then discounting the thought as he would be far less powerful in his dragon form, he saw three dragons jump from their spot in the gallery and make their way towards them.

"I am an ally of the dragons," he said to them. "Your decisions are your own. The Kihdai asked that I simply share my thoughts."

He drew Verikta. The sword pulsed with a thick, green brightness, confined close to the blade before dissipating.

The dragons drew nearer. They slowed and lowered themselves closer to the ground. One dragon to the side reared back and launched a massive torrent of concentrated flame. Domaren flourished his blade and waved his free hand along the blade, causing the energy close to the blade to expand out to multiple feet in width. The dragon's flame struck it and immediately ricocheted back. Immune to its own fire, the dragon flinched and turned away as the wave of fire washed over it, temporarily confusing and blinding it. With another quick flick of his hand, Domaren shrunk his sword's surrounding energy to its resting location.

With his sword's standard reflectiveness restored, Domaren registered movement to his side. Just as he turned to block, he brought the sword up, and with the flat of his blade, blocked an incoming tail swipe just in time. The massive creature's tail struck the sword, and while in its mirror form, absorbed the force of the hit and flung the energy back at the dragon. The result left the dragon appearing to be kicked and spun around before toppling over and rolling into the outer walls of the gallery.

Only one dragon remained as an immediate threat, though Domaren wanted to see if Brikana was alright. He looked up and searched the sky.

He immediately had to squint. The piercing sun was directly overhead. But with a sea of dragons in the sky, weaving their broad shadows around and about to the ground, he finally located Brikana.

The nearest dragon rewarded Domaren's concern for Brikana with a gleaming sparkle off its teeth as it swung its neck down and snatched him up in a violent chomp. If the dragon had chewed on any other beast, being, or human, they wouldn't have survived. But Domaren's armor easily resisted the force of the dragon's bite and provided him with a much-needed moment to think.

While being pinned in the dragon's mouth, Verikta wouldn't have any impacts to absorb, so Domaren shifted his fingers on the handle and changed Verikta's power to a multiplicative magic by pressing the sword's purple gem.

Any hits from Verikta would now land with exponential force and with minimum effort from Domaren.

A translucent film of dark plum flashed onto the blade and then disappeared. After changing Verikta's magic, Domaren lifted the sword up and stabbed it through a gap in the dragon's teeth. After thrusting it down until the crossbar hit the dragon's harrowing fangs, he pulled it out a bit to make room to angle and leverage the blade before pulling down on the handle as aggressively as he could.

Domaren sliced the blade back, getting it stuck against the roof of the dragon's mouth. The handle lodged into the lower gums of the massive creature.

At first, there was no sign that Domaren and Verikta were having any effect on the dragon, but soon after, he saw the space between the dragon's top and bottom teeth separate. Ever so slightly, he felt himself slide down from the bonds of its mouth.

The dragon couldn't help but relent and let go of its weakening bite. Domaren fell to the ground and rolled onto his feet, sprinting away from the wave of flame released by his previous captor. He sheathed his sword and spun to face the largest jumble of fighting dragons.

"The godknights are not against you! I am not against you!"

His voice only barely crept through clashes and bashes of dragons and destruction. His plea had no effect. Just as Domaren shouted another plea for peace, a dragon surprised him by slamming him into the ground and pinned him under its foot. Domaren grunted at the concussive slam and strained to move under the massive beast's weight. Before he could free himself, another dragon plummeted from the sky and slammed into the nearest section of the theatre, collapsed it, and revealed the dragon city's skyline behind it. Surprised by the dragon's violent landing, Domaren focused in on the sound of the surrounding fights, which quickly gave way to a mumble of surprise and shame. The dragon queen had responded to the commotion. As she roared in anger, the fighting quickly came to a halt.

"What is the matter with you all? What fools have allowed this to take place? Do you see what you are doing to our city? Stop it! Quit now or you will answer to me!"

The largest dragon in the vicinity by far, second only to Brikana, the elected queen of the united dragon broods was selected by the subordinate tribunes and voted as a tie-breaker when needed. Her overall hue was bright green and rivaled the vivid purity of the most persistent and verdant forest grasses. The queen's body was narrow, though nevertheless substantial, and her lengthy and muscular legs made her stand taller than most dragons. Calloused, black skin lined the edges of her wings, and through their thin webbing, black bones outlined their skeletal structure. She marched deeper into the theatre as her striking appearance and demeanor commanded attention.

Rather than let someone else explain his presence, Domaren took the initiative to address it himself.

"Queen Kire," Domaren said. The queen spun around and snarled, only out of an instinctive response to seeing anything other than a dragon. But upon realizing it was Domaren, she relaxed her disappointment.

"I was unfortunately involved in this disturbance," he said. "And for that, I apologize—not only to you, but to all of you. If and when you may be interested in any of my insight as to what transpired, I will, of course, be at your disposal."

"Well, please, by all means," the queen said. Her voice maintained its flippant disapproval of the entire situation.

"Yes, let's start with you."

"Yes, of course," Domaren said. He sneaked a peek at Brikana and fought to contain a laugh. As she let her head droop to the side, she returned a stare of apathy while he attempted to work his charm he so frequently lauded. A charm that, as Brikana often argued in return, wasn't as potent as he believed. Domaren continued.

"Just earlier, I received a grove stone where the Kihdai directed me to visit Kimozoa and lend any insight I could regarding the debate of the proposed Rijonian Accords."

"The Kihdai ordered you here?" Kire said, sounding somewhat surprised.

"Correct, Queen Kire."

"Very well, continue."

"Yes, and so, I... traveled here from Lilibrun to follow through on that directive, and upon arriving here at the theatre, I found the tribunal already in session, discussing the proposition."

"I must say," Kire said, "I can't wait to find out when such a civil situation turned sour like it apparently did."

"It did go downhill quite rapidly from there," Domaren said. "Though, I can't exactly point to an individual or position that seemed to be at fault more than another."

"Is that so?" Kire asked.

Domaren nodded before wrapping up his summary.

"Yes, I believe so, Queen Kire. The debate centered on support and rejection of the proposed language of the Rijonian Accords. And though I found myself on one side of the debate, I personally found value in all voiced positions."

The queen stepped back and squinted. She then let a playful smirk slide across her long and majestic face. While the queen seemed to consider Domaren's viewpoint, he hid a glance at Brikana behind a feigned scratch to his chin. His dragon godknight counterpart shook her head.

Queen Kire stepped farther away from Domaren before swinging around to address the various smatterings of dragons in and around the theatre.

"Well, speak up members of the tribunal, and those in the gallery," the queen said. "Is it as the human knight portrays? Could you not reach a consensus or convene to vote peacefully on matters as this body has been charged to do?"

No objection or challenge came from anywhere in the theatre.

"I see," the queen said. She then turned abruptly back towards Domaren. Her voice was respectful and amiable towards Domaren, but quickly veered towards an aggravated impatience with, as Domaren hoped, the other dragons.

"Do you feel you have adequately provided any input you have on this matter, as directed by the Kihdai?"

Domaren stammered as he considered her question.

"Um, y... Yes, I... believe I have," Domaren said. He held his hands and looked around the theatre, somewhat confused by the unexpected request.

"Wonderful," the queen replied. With a nod to her nearby guards, she issued additional instructions. "Thank you for your assistance, Domaren. And with that, I would ask that you leave us to our continued deliberations."

Domaren froze, obliged to comply with the queen's rightful request, but he still wanted to discuss the severed grove stone with Brikana.

"Tribunal," Queen Kire bellowed, addressing all the gathered dragons once again. "Take a moment to gather yourselves and to do some initial cleanup. Afterward, I expect you to reconvene and follow this debate through to a professional and civilized conclusion. Yes?"

The theatre and gallery dragons signaled their compliance with silent bows of subservience.

Domaren took a few steps away to avoid the approaching guards for a moment longer.

"Brikana," Domaren said. He waved at her and shouted another whisper. "Brikana!"

She widened her eyes and scowled as she shook her head, just as the guards cut off his line of sight. Domaren sighed.

"Please, I just need to have a quick—"

After having his path to Brikana cut off, one of the dragon guards shifted to Domaren's side and started walking, encouraging Domaren to make his way towards the exit.

"I just wanted to tell her..." he said, before giving up. "Never mind. Fine. Let's go."

# Four

With a guard leading and one behind him, the dragons marched Domaren through the streets of the city. Domaren walked at a quick pace to accommodate the dragons' leisurely gait, but the one at the rear occasionally flipped a foot out and shoved him forward. Domaren stopped and turned slowly.

"You really don't need to keep doing that," he said.

The giant beast lowered its head down to Domaren's level. His nostrils flared slowly. The skin around his eyes tightened.

"Don't concern yourself with what *I* need to do," the dragon replied. Its voice dragged along with a hateful scratchiness. "You just need to leave the city. Now turn around."

The lead dragon stopped and approached the quarreling duo behind him.

"No, no," he said in a hurry. "We did all the fighting we're going to do back in the theatre. Come on, Domaren. We just need to let things cool down. Everyone knows the dragons are allies to the godknights. All of them. This will all blow over and everyone will eventually calm down. And you," the dragon said to his kin, "keep your hands off him. But Domaren, for now, please get your horse and—"

"Yes, okay, I understand," he replied.

The trio resumed their march—now with Domaren leading Munch and Wiggly—frequently passing through groups of onlooking dragons. Some scowled at their brethren while some blew smoke through their nose at the godknight, or both, and some were apathetic. But shortly after, without additional shoving or harassment, Domaren and his two escorts reached Kimozoa's mammoth southern gatehouse. With neither pomp nor humiliation, the two dragons flanked Domaren as he approached the heavily fortified gate. The huge inner doors, made of countless strips of intertwined iron, swung open. The dragons watched as Domaren passed through to the exterior gate.

Once outside, Domaren turned and watched the gates shut while dragons heaved on various lengths of rope and chain. Not only was the city closed off to him, but so too was his first chance at learning what Brikana or any other dragon might know about what happened at the Grove. As the decorative doors outside the gate slowly careened into one another, he couldn't help but smile at the absurdity of the day's events.

His sense of humor failed him quickly, however. He turned back to the road's sprawling distance and tapped his grove calling stone.

*There probably hasn't been any change, but can they hear me now?*

Nothing.

He tried again. Same result.

Domaren's pulse throbbed with anger. He hated

being lost for information.

With his left hand, he then reached over for his knight calling stone towards his right shoulder. But before he could make contact, the stone surged with light.

*Oh. Perfect timing. I guess word is spreading.*

Though he hesitated for a second at the thought of speaking with the Redeemed godknight, Domaren prioritized a need for information over his lack of enthusiasm for speaking with the stuffy and verbose demon. He dropped his arm and huffed, but quickly swung his hand back up and tapped the stone.

"Hello Crizichial," Domaren said.

"Domaren," Crizichial replied. "Do you know of anything odd going on?" The godknight of the Redeemed spoke with a reserved concern.

Domaren forced a sarcastic laugh.

"Um, yes," Domaren said. "There are quite a few things going on today."

Crizichial said nothing.

"I had a grove stone severed mid-conversation," Domaren continued. "And I haven't been able to re-establish contact. What about you?"

For a moment, Domaren thought he was going to be met with silence again, but finally, Crizichial responded.

"Your grove stone connection was severed? I do not believe that I have ever experienced that."

"Yeah, it happened to me," Domaren said. "When did you speak with them last?"

"My last stone yesterday," Crizichial answered.

"Can you try now?" Domaren asked.

"Um, yes, of course."

Domaren waited while listening to Crizichial shuffle and stir through their connection.

"It is not working," Crizichial said.

Domaren nodded to himself. "Mmm. Yes, I didn't think it would."

"Has that happened to any of us before?" Crizichial wondered.

"It happened to me a long time ago, but I don't remember if anyone else has experienced anything similar," Domaren said. "I'm still trying to find out if anyone else has had recent issues. I came to Kimozoa to try and confirm with Brikana, but, other than learning she couldn't initiate a connection with the Grove either, I wasn't able to speak with her much."

"She could not make any time to discuss a topic such as this with you?" Crizichial asked.

"No, not exactly," Domaren replied. "She seemed to be more concerned with other matters."

"Ah, Brikana," Crizichial sighed. "Why am I not surprised?"

Domaren huffed a disappointed laugh through his nose.

"Well, perhaps you can help me with something else until we figure it out," Crizichial suggested.

"What's that?"

"There is a large army marching towards the calling tower over here," Crizichial explained. "They are still a few days out, but I am not sure of their intentions and was curious if you could help me look into the matter."

"Wait," Domaren blurted. "There's an army marching on one of the calling towers, just after my last stone with the Grove was severed?"

Crizichial paused a moment. "And? What does one have to do with the other?"

"I don't know, Crizichial. I just think it's odd that

the two events happened so close together."

"Ah, yes, I see," Crizichial replied. In contrast to Domaren's tone, Crizichial was calm and patient. "I only meant that our calling towers have been attacked before, for various reasons, and they were always repaired or rebuilt."

Domaren shifted his weight.

"You're not at all concerned that there may be something larger going on?"

"I do not know enough to make that leap, yet, no."

Domaren rubbed his eyes and felt his frustrated huff of breath flow up along the inside of his hand.

"All right, well, I'll head your way and help regardless, but first I want to stop and speak with the dragon proxy. I'm sure these odd occurrences are something the proxies need to know about if they don't already."

"I understand. Thank you, Domaren. Travel well."

With the connection to Crizichial ended, Domaren turned his gaze back to the closed gates of Kimozoa before turning opposite to look down the road towards the outskirts of Kimoba in the distance.

Though the town of Kimoba wasn't as extravagant or fortified as Kimozoa, its scale and breadth still rivaled that of the largest cities of any other race. The stretch of road from Kimozoa's gates was wide and well kept, and paved with massive stones, which Domaren assumed would only seem like small cobblestones to a dragon. He often steered Munch off the road and into the grass to minimize the chance of injury.

As Domaren grew closer to the town, the blood red buildings which sprawled out to the horizon simultaneously comforted and intimidated him. Most building exteriors, like many in Kimozoa, were constructed of large, flat stones overlapping from top to bottom. Dragon masons welded them together by heating the top and bottom edges until they glowed yellow before slamming them together with their significant strength. Once cooled, the stones would then be painted a rich crimson. Most roofs were conical and pointed at the center, constructed of similar flat stones, though these were left with their natural color or sometimes painted black.

Rather than doors and gates, most buildings in Kimoba had large windows or openings leading to massive terraces dragons could fly out from or land on. There were similar openings in the ceilings of a building's top floor, which provided for a dragon's easy arrival or exit. And if there was a threat of significant weather, or during times of war, dragons pushed sizable slabs of stone into place to close off various entryways in walls indefinitely, or placed them on top of additional supports to secure the ceilings.

There were smaller doors and staircases for species other than dragons as well, but they were often hard to find. Newcomers to Kimoba frequently had to ask locals where they could find the 'small' door at a particular location.

After passing into the town outskirts, Domaren felt more relaxed than he did in Kimozoa. The town was host to a larger variety of species when compared with its larger sister city back up the road to the north, so his presence was less noticed. The busier traffic and increased bustle of a thriving trade center allowed for a bit more unintended anonymity. And lesser, too, was the concern for politics and world news in Kimoba. Moods towards outsiders and strangers were more relaxed. Life was more casual, and less distrusting. As being a human goes in dragon territory, Domaren felt less out of place in Kimoba than in Kimozoa.

The large streets teamed with outsiders, mostly human, with a smaller number of dwarves and seavers immediately noticeable. Most movements that caught Domaren's eyes, however, were the huge curtains of dragon wings shifting, flapping, or whipping about throughout the streets, similar to how humans move their arms around when avoiding others in crowds. Dense slaps of wings from dragons taking off were interspersed with the heavy thuds of those landing. Countless blotches of shadow peppered the streets from dragons flying overhead.

Domaren walked along the village's main road with a fair degree of anonymity. Most of those that noticed him at all showed no concern, or if anything, harmlessly poked at a companion to bring their attention to the godknight. His and Munch's uninterrupted walk allowed him to focus on his concerns and his worry while making his way towards Kimoba Cathedral.

Kimoba Cathedral was the largest structure in the town. And while there were overall, larger buildings in Kimozoa, nothing in Kimozoa, even on top of its hill, climbed higher into the sky than Kimoba Cathedral with its towering spire, perches, and landing balconies.

Domaren marveled at the structure as he neared it. Just as many races had their own representative godknight to enforce the gods' will, so too did many races have a center of faith where citizens can commune with the spiritual elements of the world. Kimoba Cathedral was arguably the grandest of all. There, and at the other places of worship, citizens can pray and receive guidance from their respective race's proxy, who serves in the role of a spiritual representative for the Kihdai.

The cathedral was constructed in a manner complimentary to the rest of surrounding Kimoba, with its similar red stone and black roof. And while the majority of Kimoba's buildings appeared dark and unpolished from the shadows cast by surrounding buildings, the largest portion of the cathedral and entirety of the spire soared above the rest of the village, catching the sunlight through most of any given day. The painted and polished stones reflected brilliantly, almost resembling the scales on the neck of a gargantuan dragon.

Expansive gardens encircled the entire cathedral, and though surprisingly subdued, they were verdant and refined. Where giant sunflowers, striking bushes, and manicured hedges didn't command an onlooker's attention, towering trees, unique to dragon territory, shadowed the ground beneath. Vines and weeping branches dangled freely from the trees, teasing the tops of the gardens below.

The rich emerald of the interspersed grasses gave the impression of an ancient sea that had washed the perfectly centered cathedral into the middle of the garden. Throughout the area, dragons rested and strolled about, some alone, others with companions.

The main entrance to the cathedral, like that of so many other structures in the region, was a vast mouth through which only dragons could reach and fly through. Domaren, however, as he had for centuries, knew where the small door was and veered off to the side towards it, just slightly around the corner from the immense facade of the cathedral. Seeing nothing obvious to tie Munch to, he posed a question to the horse.

"If I leave you here, will you stay here? Please?"

The horse didn't answer, of course, but Domaren then pleaded with Wiggly as he headed for the door.

"Come get me if he causes any trouble."

The small door and stairwell were plain and practical. During construction, dragons cared little for decorating these passages, as their kind would never use them. They were just slightly more than an afterthought, but were much appreciated by the smaller species of the world. And even though he ascended the stairs at a brisk pace, it took some time for Domaren to reach the first level of the cathedral.

After finally reaching the top of the stairs, even the godknight was short of breath, albeit slightly. He found humor in his harmless fatigue, more than any annoyance. And before he had enough time to contemplate any notion of any further thought on the matter, he was struck—as he had been so many times before—by the singular and stunning sight before him.

Having emerged just to the side of where dragons enter, Domaren's breath involuntarily paused at the sight of the sun shooting in through the spacious portico. Ornate frescos on the portico's floor flaunted their magnificence in the sun, almost moving and brought to life by the streaming beams of light. Before reaching the bulk of the cathedral's sanctuary, the portico's exquisite art captured primordial scenes of the dragon proxies through the ages, standing watch over Kimoba Cathedral. Domaren was extremely familiar with them, but to a new, non-dragon visitor, the frescos would be hard to discern from only five or six feet off the floor.

Just as Domaren turned to make his way into the sanctuary, a flash of shadow and snap of sound startled him. Turning back to the large opening, Domaren stepped back and watched as a dragon landed. The momentum of its landing forced its head down gently. A strong gust of wind rolled over Domaren as the magnificent creature folded its wings into a comfortable position along the length of its body. Unaware of the godknight, the dragon stepped through the portico and into the sanctuary. Domaren followed suit.

After passing through the portico, Domaren paused at the sanctuary threshold as if looking at the interior of the cathedral for the first time. While the dragon continued on deeper into the sanctuary, Domaren scanned the inspiring and cavernous room with a familiar awe.

The ceiling, high overhead even by dragon standards, resembled a sea of large hemispheres connected but rippling out at the edges as if someone had turned the head of a massive ale upside down. The rounded shapes were made of curved glass which magnified and provided a glossy appearance to the intricate scenes painted on the ceiling.

Closest to the entrance, the ceiling depicted Prumo Hald, the dwelling of the Kihdai as it was when time began. The gigantic tower of petrified wood housed the Limb of Life which was connected to the center of the world and shot out through its surface where it climbed up to tickle the underbelly of the heavens. While the Kihdai sat on their thrones in the earliest days of existence, the painting showed their chamber as dark and plain. The walls of their chamber were without decoration, ornament, or embellishment. The narrow halls which surrounded their throne room were also dank, uninspiring, and empty. Stretching to the horizon, a large expanse of evenly lit and grey grass surrounded the fortress and lay uninterrupted by not so much as a tree, mountain, or river.

The scene above the next section of glass spheres showed the same grey grass and lonely tower, but in this frame, some of the Kihdai had risen from their thrones. Unlike the first frame, there were now visible gaps between the Kihdai and their seats. Though each individual Kihdai had no discernible form, the scene portrayed each one as a loosely clumped mass of luminescent sediment. As if scooped up in the palm of a giant from the riverbed of existence and placed inside the tower, each entity now appeared to be moving. Restless.

In the following three illustrations, the Kihdai slowly glide away from their throne room, into the connecting corridors, and out into the grey prairie around the tower.

The next depiction in the series shows the Kihdai and their first encounter with the life of the world. Though the Kihdai had themselves caused life to come into being ages before, they had done so from within the chambers of Prumo Hald and had not yet interacted with their creation.

Traditionally, the stories told to Domaren and the rest of the world describe the Kihdais' first experience with their creation as a joyous one. In the next scene that seemed to reflect that, the Kihdai are surrounded by countless other entities who also resemble nebulous masses of sediment—though to a smaller degree when compared with the Kihdai. One of the small, mortal entities is shown approaching, before expressing its gratitude for life by a form of silent communication. It then offered its compliments and respect.

The powerful group of Kihdai listened as the humble creature communicated, before replying to it with a single question.

'Is there anything we might do to enhance your experience with our world?' They ask silently.

The small entity then retreated into the massive gathering of his identical siblings to confer. And though the story says that the world's life discussed it for eons, only one scene depicts the conversation. In the next, they present a decision to the Kihdai.

Despite the long stretch of time spent, the Kihdai waited quietly without interrupting the discussion. It is thought that patience, or impatience, was simply not a concept in those early ages of the world. But finally, the single representative of life spoke up.

'We have decided,' the little creature communicated.

'And do you want to live forever?' A Kihdai asked.

'No. We considered that, but we want others to have an opportunity to experience the world.'

'Are you wanting us to provide you with food?' Another Kihdai wondered.

'No,' the small offspring replied. 'There is nothing we require that we can not generate ourselves.'

A different Kihdai glided closer.

'Is it that you want to make worlds of your own?' It asked.

'No. We are thankful for and pleased with the world you have already provided.'

Still another Kihdai asked its own question.

'Then what is it that you would ask of us?'

The small mass of sediment and energy glided closer to the Kihdai.

'We all look the same and travel throughout perfectly uniform and sterile lands. Might you help us distinguish between ourselves as well as give dimension to the vast distances of this world?'

There was no immediate reply from the Kihdai, who turned and conferred between themselves this time. Again, ages passed with the tiny beings showing no sign of needing to rush the Kihdai towards an answer. It is sometimes thought that mortality was not conceived until after the birth of the virtues. Regardless, the Kihdai finally turned back towards their polite progeny and answered. The next batch of scenes on the ceiling depict the legendary solutions.

'We believe we have conceived of something you might find pleasing, our dear ones. Follow us through the world as we give further definition to it and we will find a way to do the same for you.'

The mass of identical beings agreed silently and followed their Kihdai as proposed.

While the majority of the world's inhabitants disagree over which feature of the world the Kihdai added first, most of the world's races like to claim it was something involving their specific race by citing additional stories and legends beyond the core story. Of course, in Kimoba Cathedral, the first illustration to show a feature being granted involves the dragon species.

'Cast your sight out upon the world,' one of the Kihdai said to the gathered creatures. 'The first act of change on our virgin world will be that of calling upon the energy and heat of the world in the form of fire. Deep from the unknowable recesses of the world, we will sculpt volcanoes and have them house portions of the fire. When the world stirs just right, these will spew fire out through the sky and surrounding land to remind those who witness it of its raw power. To commemorate this added feature of the world, we will transform one of you into the form of a dragon.'

The Kihdai then communicated directly to a single, different entity.

'You, here. You will be made our first godknight of the dragons and you will be named Ashrion. We charge you with protecting these volcanoes, these monuments of singular strength, and to represent us outside the walls of Prumo Hald. You and others who we also make dragons will bear the virtue of primal energy. As do the volcanoes, so too will you breathe fire and wear brilliant scales which resemble the hardened throat of volcanoes. And as this is my contribution to our suggested features, I will take on the semblance of a dragon as well.'

The Kihdai grew nearer still to the little creature and, after extending branches of its muddy sentiment, touched the small mass, and transformed it into a magnificent dragon. Ashrion swelled in size, quickly growing into its tail, legs, body, wings, neck, and head. Its scales were the color of neglected pewter, resembling an ancient but reliable set of plate armor. The dragon Kihdai, now also in the form of a dragon, had scales which spanned the colors of the spectrum of fire. At its tail, the dragon's scales were the shade of dried blood. As the Kihdai finalized its evolution, its coloring transitioned gradually up its body into lighter reds, then oranges, before shifting to yellows, and finally, white and then a blue face.

Ashrion stretched and flexed into his new form. He shifted in place to look at his legs and tail. And as he looked behind, he unfolded his wings. As one of the first volcanoes far in the distance erupted, his wings extended to their full width before rising up and slamming back down towards the ground, launching him into the air.

The others who had not yet been transformed remained in place, motionless, ignorant as to what fear was, and only felt the world's first inclinations of awe. Once Ashrion and the dragon Kihdai had completed their transformations, the Kihdai audibly spoke to Ashrion for the first time.

"If you would return to us, Godknight Ashrion," the Kihdai began, "we will transform some of the others into forms similar to yours, and then continue with the rest of the world."

While still flying, Ashrion dipped his head and long neck in respect, and stilled his wings before landing. The original grey mass that had provided the Kihdai with their requests felt within itself, the equivalent of a mental smile upon seeing the wondrous, new dragons.

Following the illustration depicting the elevation of Ashrion came smaller and less grand illustrations of the elevations of the other races, which were less revered by the dragons.

'Come, everyone,' a different and still shapeless Kihdai beckoned. 'Let us continue through the world and we will further define it, and you.'

Shown in the next scene were the Kihdai—one of which was now a dragon, Godknight Ashrion, the other dragons, and the remaining, formless population of the world. After traveling beyond the volcanoes, the Kihdai stopped the group.

'Here, our friends,' said one of the undefined Kihdai. 'In some parts of the world, there will be hills and mountains. Some of these mountains have risen to similar heights as volcanoes. But rather than being brought forth by fire, they will spring to life from the great disagreements of friction and time below ground. Hills are not yet mountains but aspire to be so.'

The Kihdai continued.

'The hills and mountains will represent the virtue of heartiness and will be embodied by their representative race, the dwarf. And just as we have left one of you unchanged after creating the dragons, we will leave another of you unchanged as we create the dwarves. In fact, we will leave one of you unchanged for each race we create, and each of you will be immortal so that this act of creation will be remembered throughout all generations. Those who are left unchanged shall be known as the Ständ. May each of you be forever revered and respected.'

As the Kihdai finished communicating the creation of the mountains, hills, and details of the Ständ, it stretched out and connected with another of the smaller, mortal masses. Karindi was shaped to life, first godknight of the dwarves. Karindi was a stout and stalwart dwarf. His head was wide but chiseled as it narrowed slightly down to his hearty chin. Wrapped around his face and extending down in thick ropes of braided hair was an ebony beard. His long and dense hair fell across his back and muscular shoulders. Every muscle in his arms and legs was clearly defined and noticeably large, perfectly complimenting his broad chest. The Kihdai of the mountains then transformed a large portion of the shapeless entities into dwarves and took on its own form of a dwarf. The dwarf Kihdai then pointed at one of the unchanged entities, identifying it as one of the Ställd. Its soul smiled.

The next scene had the Ställd, dragons, dwarves, along with their Kihdai and godknights, journeying over the mountains and down the hills with the remaining formless population and formless Kihdai. And though the elves would later lose their right to a godknight as a result of their involvement in the events of Wrathlore, the original knights are still those most revered and celebrated in art and texts.

'And now we will sow vegetation and generate fauna, which will further define the face of the world,' a formless Kihdai said silently. 'From the slopes of volcanoes and mountains, down the hills and to the flatlands, there will be a host of grasses, plants, trees, creatures, and insects that will assist each of you with the stewardship of the world. The virtue assigned to this segment of our creation will be purity and shall be represented by the elven race. Step closer, our child,' the Kihdai requested. 'You will be known as Jyraleth, the elven godknight. As you take your form, so shall I become an elf.'

Jyraleth's energy whipped into a frenzy as the others' had when touched by a Kihdai. It spun and twisted into a solid shape that gave way to feet, legs, arms, hands and fingers, a torso, neck, and head. Jyraleth's lengthy hair, darker than Karindi's but just lighter than black, rippled out and unfurled down her back. A gown the color of mint green enveloped Jyraleth, bound and stitched with thin vines and malleable branches. As Jyraleth's ears gently extended up to a subtle point, the elven Kihdai transformed yet another portion of the lifeless entities into elves as well. The formless mass selected to be a Stäld for the elves raced over to admire the new species.

The ceiling's next illustration, and portion of the godknight creation story often omitted by some in more recent times, conveyed the creation of the orc godknight. Also as a result of Wrathlore, the orcs were yet another group who unfortunately would later lose its privilege to godknight representation in the world.

The large gathering, now composed of more of those with form than without, was shown traversing through an almost completed transformation of the world. Another shapeless Kihdai motioned for the group to pause again.

'If I may, my friends,' the Kihdai started. 'I would like to bring water into the world. It will be a necessary luxury required by all that we have brought into being to survive. And with this world's water, I shall create darkness and light. The sun and the moon. With the cycle these celestial bodies will bring, there will come a time for activity and a time for rest. The possibilities of light and the wonders of the dark. The water, sun, and moon will be forever more so long as this world endures, and will demonstrate resiliency, and stamina. I will create and have the race of orcs be the steward of these virtues and I will also take this form.'

Once again, a shapeless Kihdai is shown stepping away from his group of fellow creators and reaching out to touch one of the mortal creatures. As the Kihdai named the orc godknight, another large grouping of the formless entities assumed semblances of various orcs.

"I name you, Godknight Gazduru, and charge you with the representation of the water, sun, and moon, and their stamina."

The mass flashed and sparked with activity, popping instantly into a similar overall form as Jyraleth's. But this was male, a good deal larger overall, and had a powerful, yet proportionate physique. Protruding out from just above his eyes were two horns that poked out and curved straight up for only the height of his forehead. His skin, mostly covered by the thick leathers that spun into existence around him, was a combination of a green similar to Jyraleth's gown. But his skin was darker with occasional streaks of color the shade of dry soil. Another Stäld could be seen hopping and bowing at the sight of the new species.

As Domaren walked deeper into the Kimoba Cathedral sanctuary, he came to the last illustration—the story of his own elevation.

The final depiction shows the entire population of the world and their Kihdai continuing on their path to explore and define the world when finally, they returned to the spot they originally left from. In addition to the Stäld, there was still one Kihdai, and a portion of the population without form. One of the small, formless masses floated out from the remaining entities and posed a question silently to the Kihdai.

'What becomes of us, those who still have no virtue or assigned form?' The small being asked. 'Is there nothing that we may represent? I saw nothing left requiring improvement.'

The final undefined Kihdai stepped forward without hesitance and slowly reached out to touch the timid jumble of energy.

'Here at the crossroads of the world,' the Kihdai said, 'you will discover that there is indeed a fate and form for you. You shall encompass all virtues, and none. You are the steward of the entire world, as it is your steward. As a godknight of the humans, you will be able to harness parts of all virtues we have previously bestowed on your brethren. You should feel at home in any part of the world, and you are to treat it as such. Your virtue is adaptability and your name will be Domaren.'

The Kihdai released its connection with the new human godknight and gave form to the remaining entities while also taking the shape of a male human for himself. The remaining entity was the last to be recognized as one of the Stäld.

As his formation completed, Domaren grew into his human form, toned and muscular like Gazduru, but smaller in stature. A set of armor sprung forth from the ground and snapped itself into place around Domaren in a series of metallic crashes. As the armor settled into place, the world's first storm brewed overhead and ejected a stream of lightning down at Domaren. After the sky's fury immediately receded into nothing, the sword of the human godknight, Verikta was left in Domaren's palm.

While Domaren stared at his sword and armor in awe, the Kihdai addressed the entire gathering of humans, elves, dwarves, orcs, dragons, as well as the Stäld.

"You have honored us all with your request, and with the resulting experience," said the elven Kihdai. "Your request, your ideas, and your inspiration have helped us create wonders throughout the world that we could never have conceived on our own. Please, go and enjoy this creation that you have helped wrought."

"These things you have done for us," Gazduru started. "They are magnificent. They are beautiful."

"This is beyond anything that I could have imagined," Ashrion added.

"How could we possibly be worthy of these gifts?" Jyraleth asked.

The dwarf Kihdai shook his head.

"Our children," he replied. "It is not a matter of worthiness. It is as it should have been from the beginning. We realize that now, thanks to you."

"How might we go about repaying you?" Karindi wondered.

The dragon Kihdai also shook his head.

"Relish it," he answered. "Relish it. Respect it. Share it. Help others prosper, and so also will you prosper. You are our children, and we want you to be happy."

"Can we at least thank you properly?" Domaren asked. "What are your names? What should we call you?"

"We do not have names, nor do we require them," the orc Kihdai answered. "You can simply call us Kihdai individually, Kihdai collectively, or Kihdai following the name of one of your races, virtues, or features of the world."

The humility of the Kihdai carries consistently from story to story, regardless of which race or individual tells it, or which region of the world it's told in. One of the defining characteristics of the relationship between the Kihdai and the beings of the world is the Kihdais' overall desire to make sure the world is an enjoyable experience for everyone. But as he approached the end of the series, Domaren resisted, but finally allowed himself to grin. It wasn't a grin rooted in sentimental regard, but rather a bittersweet regret at how the world's innocent enthusiasm has since been supplanted by apathy and mediocrity.

The last scene on the ceiling of Kimoba Cathedral shows the Kihdai returning to Prumo Hald, but upon their return, the structure is now bright and inspiring. Dragons, humans, orcs, elves, and dwarves are seen crowding the halls and corridors of the gigantic fortress. The creatures and people inside, as well as the fully formed Kihdai, are happy and feasting. The bland nature of existence was gone, or rather, it had been given meaning and definition. Artists sat off to the side and captured the early days of creation, later to have their works adorn Prumo Hald. Musicians entertained and ushered in adventure and possibility with fanfares and dance.

Domaren's eyes quickly retraced the progression of the ancient events many times up above him. If not for being a godknight, Domaren's neck would have long seized and begun hurting from glancing up for so long. Finally, after his third or fourth review of the series of illustrations, something stole his attention.

"Lord Godknight Domaren?" The dragon proxy asked in astonishment. "You do me great honor by being here! My, I almost can't believe it! It's such a rare treat that an outside godknight visits our humble sanctuary!"

Domaren turned and looked up to meet the eyes of the dragon proxy. Vinlaza was a significant dragon, one of the biggest Domaren had ever seen. His scales were a dark blue with white spines running along his back. His neck transitioned from a rich blue of the deep ocean to completely black at the head.

"Humble?" Domaren laughed. "No, no," he said, whispering, and looking back to the ceiling. "There is nothing here that is humble."

Vinlaza didn't reply, but tilted his head to the side.

"Oh, I only meant that it's nothing less than stunning," Domaren clarified. "I meant nothing negative at all."

The proxy grinned with understanding.

"I have always meant to ask, though," Domaren said, glancing back to Vinlaza. "Why is there no scene depicting the elevation of the Redeemed or seavers? I could have sworn there were mentions of them in some of the other holy places in the world."

The proxy recoiled gently, as if confused.

"The Redeemed and seavers?" asked Vinlaza, raising his nose and turning to the side. "They were not among the *original* forms granted the gift of a godknight. That is known."

"Yes," Domaren quickly obliged. "But they were granted a knight, eventually. And the Redeemed do represent the virtue of forgiveness and were, in fact, elevated. They have their own representative godknight. The same can be said of the seavers and their virtue of humility."

"Well, yes, of course," Vinlaza admitted, "but they were not present for the original elevations, or the creation of the world's physical features."

Domaren replied immediately.

"So, they have been judged unworthy of commemoration in these artworks, then?" He asked.

"My lord godknight," the proxy said confidently. "I'm afraid it is just a matter of these scenes being completed long before the Redeemed or seaver godknights were anointed."

"Ah, a simple matter of *timing*," Domaren said.

"Yes, yes, absolutely," the proxy rushed to agree.

"How unfortunate," Domaren said, in an exaggerated

breath.

Vinlaza frowned and dipped his chin. "Mmm, yes."

"Well, despite the missing representation of the Redeemed and seavers, it is still nothing less than an absolute masterwork of art and architecture," Domaren said. "But while I wish I had more time to discuss art with you, I need to report a most troubling occurrence, proxy."

The proxy's face compressed into squints and wrinkles of concern.

"Is everything all right?" Vinlaza inquired.

"I don't know, honestly," Domaren answered. "I was right in the middle of a discussion with the Grove, and receiving information on my next directive, when I heard terrible sounds of destruction and chaos. My connection was severed, and I could not establish a new connection. The directive involved checking on an agreement Brikana was working on. So, I came to Kimozoa and tried to speak with her. She was her usual self, so we didn't converse long. I then reached out to Crizichial, who also couldn't establish a connection with the Grove. While he is checking on a matter concerning an army marching towards a calling tower, I told him I would check with you and see if you had any relevant information to add."

While Domaren spoke, Vinlaza paced and stopped to glance up at the most concerning bits of the story. When Domaren finished, the proxy shuffled over and leaned down. He spoke in a low whisper. His eyes sprung wide and didn't blink.

"Domaren, I don't have to tell you how alarming this is."

"No, you don't," Domaren said.

Vinlaza turned and jumped into low flight towards the center of the sanctuary.

"We should contact the other proxies," he yelled, waving for Domaren to follow him towards the cathedral's altars to the virtues. "They may have news or know if anything untoward is happening."

Domaren hesitated, opening his mind to the chaotic web of possibility, but finally took off at a jog. He fell in behind the proxy, who was shouting in spurts over his shoulder and flapping of his wings.

"Should we just ask if they've heard of similar occurrences from other godknights or anything that may be related?"

Domaren opened his mouth to reply but marveled instead at the dragon that entered with him, sitting atop a large, massive column in the sanctuary.

"Well, wait a moment," Domaren finally replied, still jogging. He didn't immediately continue, however. Vinlaza had flown ahead and gained quite a lead. Domaren waited until he was closer to the altars, where the proxy landed.

"Wait," Domaren continued. "Untoward? What is it exactly that you think might be happening?" Domaren's mind raced as he extrapolated the possibilities, but didn't want to influence the proxy.

The proxy recoiled and looked around as if he had misplaced the obviousness of the moment.

"What might be happening?" Vinlaza said. "Why, a rebellion, of course. A new rebellion against the Kihdai!"

Domaren lowered his head and took in a massive breath, and used the moment to think.

"Dear, respected proxy," Domaren said. He held out his hands to frame the seriousness of his reply. "A rebellion? A new rebellion? Are you truly suggesting that is possible again?"

"Yes," Vinlaza replied sternly. "Wrathlore! You know

better than anyone! The godknights didn't succeed with it before, so maybe some of them are trying again now!"

"I don't understand how you're coming to this concern," Domaren said. "I haven't heard of any hint of anything like that being planned or suggested."

The proxy scoffed and flung a dismissive foot out. "You didn't the first time either, apparently."

Vinlaza looked up immediately and turned to Domaren.

"Forgive me, Domaren," he said. "I was not thinking. It just slipped—"

Domaren waved off the awkward disruption to their conversation.

"Think nothing of it," Domaren said. "You're right."

Vinlaza's eyes danced manically as he rushed to resume the conversation.

"So, you have not heard of anything? What about your viciously severed grove stone? Anything that might seem similar to the events of the first deception?"

Domaren paused and dropped his hands.

"Nothing. No one..." Domaren began before interrupting himself. He looked away, distracted, and continued as if speaking to himself.

"There's been no sign..."

Vinlaza huffed and rippled his wings in frustration.

"Well, how would you like to proceed?" The proxy asked. His voice had become short and impatient. "Do you still want to speak with the other proxies?"

Domaren sighed and let his shoulders fall.

"Yes," he said. "More information is most always better than less."

As they returned to constructive planning, Vinlaza nodded and smiled warmly. He then turned around and gestured at the altars, asking Domaren silently which of the other proxies he would like to speak with.

"Oh, anyone we can get a hold of," Domaren said. "I've only spoken with you so far."

"Right," the proxy said. "I'll... just... go to the nearest altar. The dwarves? Want to speak with Tobati?"

Vinlaza looked at Domaren to confirm, who received a quick nod followed by an extended hand. The dragon then walked over to the altar for the dwarven virtue and outstretched his wings before curling them inward in front of him to surround the altar.

"Wait," Domaren interrupted again.

Vinlaza turned around.

"It might be best that we not communicate in this method," Domaren said. His eyes flicked about, looking at nothing in particular. "Do you understand?" He asked the proxy. "If there is anything untoward going on, as you have considered, then, unless we're in contact with someone, in person, there is absolutely no guarantee who else may be listening... or who else may be in the company of those we wish to speak with."

Vinlaza relaxed his wings and let them fall to his side.

"I hadn't thought of that," the dragon said. "Perhaps you're right."

The proxy turned and approached Domaren once more.

"What should we do?"

"I'll have to try and make contact in person," Domaren said, still spinning plans to life in his mind.

"With who?" Asked the proxy. "Other knights? Proxies?"

"I don't know yet. I'd like to confirm the status of all the knights first," Domaren added.

The dragon looked out into the sanctuary and back to Domaren.

"What about me? Should I go? Can I help? I'd be happy to."

Domaren looked up at the dragon and focused for the first time in minutes.

"No, I don't think so. I think it may be worth staying to your normal routine here in case you hear anything from the dragon community. And maybe you can check in again with Brikana. Hopefully you'll be more successful than I was."

The massive dragon chuckled but stifled any further laughter. He then hummed deeply from within his scaled body.

"I doubt that," Vinlaza said. His voice shifting to a darker and softer tone. "Be careful, Domaren."

# Five

Domaren exited the sanctuary with a flurry of concerns rushing through his mind. After another quick glance up to the worshiping dragon in the sanctuary, Domaren shifted his sight a final time to the depictions on the ceiling, as if rewinding time as he neared the exit. Reversing the elevations. Reversing the world to lifelessness. Before the virtues. Before definition. Before conflict.

After leaving the cathedral and entering the sprawling garden once more, Domaren squinted towards Kimozoa on the northern horizon and wondered if he should try to contact Brikana again. But her initial disinterest and his temporary exile from the city made him think twice. Instead, Domaren reached for his knight's calling stone to tell Crizichial he was on his way. But his paranoia stopped him just short of initiating the connection.

His discussion with Vinlaza regarding the potential for unfriendly ears had taken root. Hoping to avoid drawing unwanted attention, Domaren instead simply decided to set out straight for the lands of the Redeemed far to the south. But after dismissing the notion of contacting the other knights, he did still want to try contacting the Grove again. Domaren reached up and tapped the corresponding stone.

Nothing.

Unable to use or being leery of most of the methods of communicating and easy travel he had used for ages—whether by choice or by the unknowns of what was wrong in the Grove—Domaren hopped up onto Munch and mentally prepared to set out. But before departing, he reviewed his equipment out loud with Wiggly.

"Looks like we might have a fair amount of old-fashioned travel ahead of us," Domaren said. "May need to upgrade this saddle and bags, hmm? What do you think?"

Wiggly responded by standing, circling, and scratching at her blanket before sitting back down.

"Okay, then. Let's go see what we can find."

With no objection from Wiggly, Domaren clicked his teeth and meandered Munch back into the throngs of Kimoba's streets. His goal was to seek out a saddler to find something to pack and store more than he could currently, and to minimize trips into a given town.

"Excuse me," Domaren said to a passing dwarf. "Would you happen to know where I can find a saddler? I seem to remember there being—"

"Do I look like a resident of this town?" The dwarf said, snapping at Domaren without stopping. "And I don't believe dragons use horses, for travel anyway!"

Domaren stopped to take in the dwarf's less-than-courteous response as he walked by, but rather than causing a scene, he only smiled and continued on. Domaren cut a playful glance at Wiggly.

"Well, I am obviously not a dragon," Domaren said.

Domaren steered Munch farther down the street, but registered a sudden pain in his stomach. He grimaced as he walked and considered what the source may be.

*Oh yes,* he said to himself. *I think I'm hungry.*

"I haven't felt that in ages," he said.

Domaren's communions with the Grove usually replenished his energy and nutrition when he connected with a grove stone, so his urge to eat or drink was rare. Only when he had exerted himself tremendously or had gone a time without a grove stone did he experience hunger pangs. With the ability to refresh his energy unavailable at the moment, Domaren veered for a food stall at the edge of Kimoba's market.

He jumped down and approached the stall and its high counter, but stood back from it so that the dragon operating it could see him.

"Hello there, friend," he shouted. "Could I trouble you for whatever you might have available?"

The dragon stepped back from his carving station and looked around before finally looking down.

"What, you want a whole horse?" The gruff butcher asked, poking fun at the man-sized godknight.

Domaren grimaced and looked over his shoulder at Munch. After turning back, he noticed the slaughtered whole and half horses hanging from hooks in a semi-circle curing towards the rear of the stall.

"Why is everyone being so discourteous today?" Domaren asked, feigning offense. "It's almost as though Kimoba hasn't been a crossroads for many of the races for centuries."

Domaren continued without letting the grouchy butcher reply.

"Can I just have a few slices of something other than horse?" He asked. "I'll pay what it's worth."

The dragon let his arms fall and sighed in exasperation.

"Fine, fine," he said, stepping back over to his carving station. "I'll get you set up with some rat sticks."

"Hmm, actually..."

"Oh, don't get in a fix," the dragon said. "I'm joking. I have some hog over here."

"Thank you," Domaren forced himself to say.

The butcher reached for a dragon-sized hatchet and swiped it superficially at the side of a long pine log leaning up against the side of the stall. Once the dragon had some slivers, he held the axe close to its head and sliced at one of them a few times more, making a skewer of sorts. After breaking the skewer in half, he threaded a long chunk of pork onto it. Finally, once he snatched up a large frond to place the skewer on, the butcher plopped the meat on it and handed it to Domaren. The portion went from a small bit in the dragon's grasp, to a forearm's length of meat in Domaren's.

"Wonderful," Domaren said. He spoke flatly, but sincerely. "How much?"

"Twenty," the dragon shouted.

"Twenty?" Domaren said, recoiling. "Twenty what? Twenty thank-yous?"

"Hey, what's worth five coins to a dragon is worth twenty to you, right? Do you want it or not?"

"Fine, fine," Domaren said. He dismissed the dragon quickly as he reached into the pouch on his belt. "Yes, here's your twenty coins. But you don't get a thank-you."

"Yeah, okay," the butcher said, taking the coins from Domaren. "I'm devastated."

Domaren shook his head but smiled at the dragon.

"Can you tell me where to find the saddler? There is one in Kimoba, right?" Domaren asked.

"Yeah, back the way you came," answered the butcher. "Towards the northern gate facing Kimozoa, one row back."

"Back the way—" Domaren started. "Wait. How do you know which direction I came from?"

The dragon dropped his carving knives to his side again and stared ahead at a tower of horse meat.

"What?" The dragon said. He turned to Domaren with a face annoyed with contempt. "Word spreads quickly when one of you knights is in town," he said.

Domaren instinctively took a few looks around before turning back.

"All right," he said to the butcher. "Fine." Domaren waved.

The butcher held up a knife in acknowledgment between slices and went back to his work.

Back atop Munch, Domaren sized up the huge stick of meat in his hands. He leaned down for a bite and ripped off a huge chunk before making his way back towards the gate, occasionally reaching down with one hand to steer Munch. As he approached the saddler's stall, he hopped off and took another bite. He tore a chunk off the piece hanging out of his mouth and dropped it into Wiggly's patient but drooling mouth.

"Ah, right, I knew Kimoba had a saddler!" Domaren said to his dog. An elf dropped his hammer on the horseshoe he was working and lowered the flame of his forge. After slapping his hands against his filthy apron, the elf walked over.

"Ah, a farrier, too? Hello, friend," Domaren greeted. He had to chew a bit more, but swallowed his huge bite of hog meat.

"I need some bigger bags, and perhaps a different saddle," he said to the elf.

The elf turned and looked back to another farrier who was distracted from brushing a horse. Both looked at Domaren's skewer of meat as he took another bite.

"Oh, no," Domaren said. "This is pork."

"You're Domaren," the elf said before looking back at his colleague. "You're a godknight. Why would you be in need of such... common items? Looks like you have all you need right there."

While the shop keeper pointed towards Munch, Domaren stopped chewing and lowered his skewer.

"Do you have anything available?" Domaren asked.

The man brushing the horse tossed his tool down and approached Domaren.

"I don't understand," Domaren said. "Do you ask all your customers why they want to give you their money?"

"No," the man said. "Just the ones who normally don't need to spend it."

Domaren looked between the elf and the man and sniffed out a laugh before slapping his mostly empty skewer down on the counter. He then turned and walked back towards Munch.

"All right, all right, never mind," said the elf. "Just curious is all. What are you looking for?"

"I need a saddle I can tie a bunch of things to, and bags made to hold a lot over long distances," he answered.

The elf turned and leaned back on the counter as he pointed.

"Well, we have these saddles made of leather from Opham Falls. Strong, and I'm pretty confident of the long distances part. We're asking, what, a hundred and eighty coins for those? But we also have some used but restored saddles from…"

The elf closed his eyes, apparently trying to remember. He opened them and snapped his fingers at the man.

"Balcmauh," the man said. The elf echoed him in acknowledgment.

"Balcmauh!"

"And how much are those?" Asked Domaren.

"A hundred coins."

"A hundred?" Domaren said, astounded. "That's absurd. For used saddles? New or used, how did such quality leather come to be available at Kimoba's corner stable, anyway?"

The man and elf looked at each other.

Domaren shifted his weight in annoyance.

"Come on, don't make me walk away again. Quit wasting my time and just tell me," he said.

"Eighty," the man said. Domaren laughed.

"Now I'm really intrigued!" He added, crossing his arms.

"If you will stop asking your questions," the man said, "we'll sell you one of them for seventy-five."

"Forty," Domaren replied.

"What?" The elf asked angrily. "That's insulting!"

The man slowly reached for the elf's arm. When the elf felt his touch, he whipped his eyes over before turning back to Domaren. He sighed and shook his head.

"Seventy," countered the elf.

Domaren smiled.

"Forty-five."

"Sixty-five."

Domaren pointed at the elf and man as he replied again.

"Fifty and that's it for me," he said.

The elf turned to the man and waited to gauge his reaction. After exchanging glances of disappointment, the elf conceded.

"Fine," the elf said. "Fifty coins."

Domaren smiled and bowed quickly, sincere but playful. As he bent back up, a sharp and snappy voice growled from behind him.

"Now that you have your wares, lord godknight, I believe it's time that you travel on."

Before turning around, Domaren watched the elf's and man's eyes float up, and then, still farther up.

When he turned, Domaren saw three dragons standing across from him. Each one looked as though they had been in as many fights as they had scales on their hides. And, while two were very small, approximately ten feet tall at the top of their head, the third was three times that.

"My, my," Domaren started. "I must say that I have never been met with such hostility before, in Kimoba, or Kimozoa for that matter."

"Well, isn't that a shame?" The largest dragon asked flippantly. "We definitely have a significant amount of hostility to offer you, especially since you apparently can not take a hint."

"What hint is that?" Domaren asked calmly.

"The fact that you are not wanted here," replied one of the smaller dragons.

"And who is it that doesn't want me here?" Domaren challenged. "I was just received quite hospitably in Kimozoa, and only moments ago had a most enjoyable conversation with your proxy."

The third dragon spoke up.

"Our godknight and proxy do not speak for all

of us," the dragon said with a sneer. "They live in their towers and cathedrals, blind to our needs and busy with the machinations of manipulating the rest of the world to their whims. They shove the will of the Kihdai down our throats without taking our say into account."

Domaren allowed the dragon to complete his complaint, but immediately replied with stern annoyance.

"I am not currently enforcing anything and am not shoving anything down anyone's throat. I am simply trying to buy a saddle."

The biggest dragon stepped forward.

"Well, I would ask that you quickly complete your transaction," it said, "and leave Kimoba."

"Ask?" Domaren sought to clarify.

"Strongly recommend," said the dragon.

Domaren looked back at the elf and man. With a quick twitch of his eyes, he motioned for them to get away.

"Do you know how many fights I have lost?" Domaren asked as he turned back, wrapping his fingers around Verikta. "Do you know how many fights any godknight has lost, for that matter?"

Domaren pulled on Verikta slightly, just enough for a click from the scabbard to be heard. The largest dragon's throat started to glow cherry red, the orange of a sunrise, and finally, the yellow of the sun.

The dragon shot its mouth open and launched a river of fire at Domaren. As it did, Domaren ripped Verikta from its scabbard and held it in front of him. As soon as Verikta's blade pointed up, a white hot shield of light blasted forth, forming a complete circle, easily deflecting the large dragon's attack. Domaren walked forward, forcing the dragon to back up from the heat of its own fire. The other pair leaped out of the way.

"Do you not think I've learned at some point over the countless ages how to fight dragons?"

Domaren shook Verikta quickly, dismissing the shield, but continued walking forward.

"I don't care if you don't want me here. I don't care if you don't want the godknights here," he added.

The gigantic dragon stood its ground while the smaller dragons continued spreading out to either side of Domaren.

"With each passing generation, I have to hear more of you whine. There is always more whining, more complaining. More complete obliviousness. More ignorance of the past, and less concern for the future."

The smaller pair of dragons had almost slipped out of each side of Domaren's periphery.

Domaren stopped.

"I'm growing tired of having to explain to this world that we do what we do to increasingly save you from yourselves."

The enormous dragon lowered its head and spread its wings.

"The irony," Domaren said, brandishing Verikta, "is palpable."

In a preemptive surprise, Domaren spun a particularly wild flourish up and over his head before bringing it down into a hateful slice into the ground, as if trying to sever the world in two. The strike landed with a catastrophic blast of sound, shooting a tearing rip through the ground, racing across the distance between Domaren and the largest dragon, and taking with it, a tall shop near the beast.

As the tear in the ground sped along, the two dragons on either side rushed at him. Domaren stepped back and lowered into a defensive posture. As the crevasse sped towards the gigantic dragon, it widened and deepened, and did its best to swallow the enormous creature.

With the biggest dragon preoccupied for the moment, Domaren remained in his defensive posture and stared ahead, timing his reaction to the two flanking dragons perfectly.

Just before the two rushing creatures closed within striking distance, Domaren pressed his blue handlestone and flung Verikta up into the air where it created a duplicate of itself. Domaren shot forward and jumped to grab them both and landed just in time to spin a defensive circle, deflecting the tail of one dragon and the open arms of the other. The sword strikes were mere defensive hits and caused no damage to the dragons, but sent them stumbling and rolling into various corners of the street.

"Well, here we are, my scaly and hot-tempered friends," Domaren said, his voice dripping with condescension. "What a challenging predicament I've found myself in."

As he spoke, Domaren tapped the flat of his two blades together, dismissing the duplicate. While the two smaller dragons recovered, the largest dragon scratched out from the crevasse.

"I'd rather face the threat of annihilation from my kin or foreigners if it meant we could be rid of your arrogance, godknight," the formidable dragon said, spitting with disgust.

"It's not arrogance," Domaren replied. "It's perspective. And while most of the world doesn't have any, it can be beaten into some."

The dragon let loose a punishing tear of sound and launched into the air, its shadow swallowing Domaren and the street in darkness. Domaren turned and looked for the other two dragons.

"Come on," he goaded them. "Hurry or you're going to miss the rest of the fight!"

Domaren held his sword up to his mouth and whispered something to the blade. And as the primary dragon plummeted from the sky, Domaren dug his feet into the gravel and held Verikta up over his shoulder.

"Oh, no!" Domaren shouted. "Will I ever survive the onslaught of the mighty dragon?"

The immense beast elongated its neck, spread its wings out wide, and stretched its back legs out behind it, picking up as much speed as possible.

Within a few hundred feet of the ground, the dragon flipped over and poised its punishing hind legs so that it could stomp and pound Domaren into the ground, but before the dragon could land its devastating attack, an even larger shadow swooped into view.

The extra shadow swallowed up the others and caused the two smaller dragons that had once again approached Domaren, to stumble back from the scene again. Domaren shuffled and lunged to catch sight of the recent addition to the fight.

It was Brikana.

The dragon godknight shot in and rammed the other dragon out of the air, sending it rolling through the sky before crashing into a nearby roof.

"Domaren!" Brikana shouted, her voice sounding more annoyed than anything.

"Ah," he said as he sheathed his sword. "Now can I have a moment of your time?"

Brikana spun down in a steep descent and landed in the street. Her gargantuan dragon frame marched ferociously towards her human godknight counterpart.

"Was this absolutely necessary?" Brikana asked with

a snarl. She stopped just in front of Domaren and looked down at him, burning a proverbial hole through him with her displeasure.

Domaren turned back and forth between her and the shop counter as he replied.

"I was just... trying... to buy a saddle," he said. "But your fellow countrymen here," he continued, gesturing at the scared lesser dragons, frozen nearby, "and their larger friend, over there somewhere, desired to quarrel with me."

"And, I'm sure you didn't exacerbate the matter in any way," Brikana said. Before Domaren could reply, she snarled at the two lesser dragons, sending them scampering away.

"As I said," Domaren stated stoically. "I was simply trying to buy some bags and a saddle and take my leave of Kimoba."

"Fine, fine," she said dismissively.

"What are you doing here?" Domaren asked. "How did you know where I'd be?"

"I didn't," she said. "I launched up out of Kimozoa to try to find you and saw that big guy flying around and decided to come and see what was happening. I should've known you'd be involved."

"I told you—" Domaren attempted.

"Yes, buying a saddle," she interrupted.

Domaren's eyes popped wide as he snapped his fingers. He turned around to the shop counter once again.

"Can I have that saddle now?" He asked. As he spoke, he scanned the stall and saw no one. But a head finally raised up from behind the most distant wall.

"There you are," Domaren said. "Everything's okay now. I'll take that saddle now, please."

He turned back to Brikana.

"See?"

Brikana snorted in contempt, sending a bit of smoke escaping through her intimidating nose.

"But I did want to catch up with you," she said. "I didn't have the time to talk when you first reached out and I want to find out what's going on with the Grove. Especially with what you did and said in the theatre earlier. Thank you for that."

Domaren grinned gently as he switched to a more serious and concerned tone.

"Well, I'm glad you came looking for me," he said. "We can't reach the Grove, and after speaking with your proxy, he's worried that history may be trying to repeat itself."

"What?" Brikana said. Her head jerked back in disbelief. "A new revolt?"

Domaren tilted his head to the side and shrugged, unsure of the possibilities.

"That's what I was saying to the proxy. I just don't see how that's possible. But his concern has somewhat exacerbated my own. He suggested we refrain from communicating using any other method but in person."

"We need to speak with the others as soon as possible," Brikana said. "If someone has engineered this, we need to uncover that as quickly as possible."

Domaren nodded.

"You and Criz are the only ones I have been able to contact before everything failed," he said. And before continuing, he stopped himself and let his focus drift.

"Brikana," he said, snapping his gaze back up to her massive eyes. "There isn't anything you're not telling me, is there?"

The dragon godknight stepped back, but lowered her

head closer to Domaren.

"What in your tiny human brain justifies your impulse to ask me that?"

Domaren closed the distance between them even more.

"I have to ask," he replied. "It's somewhat alarming that you wouldn't want to ask me the same question, or at least want to understand why the question needs to be asked."

Their eyes remain locked for a time as both knights stood in silence. After a deep breath, Brikana swung her long neck slowly to each side.

"No, there is nothing I'm not telling you," she said in an even softer and more secret tone.

Domaren nodded once and turned to his horse.

"At your own suggestion," Brikana started, "is there anything you might want to share with me?"

Domaren turned back slowly. A friendly grin crept up from one side of his lips.

"No," he answered, before turning back to fiddle with Munch's harness, girth, and saddle. He heard Brikana sigh behind him.

"Fine, good," she said. "How do we proceed? How do we check with the others?"

Domaren ran his hand through Munch's mane before resting his hands on the new saddle.

"I don't know if we should check with the others as much as we should check *on* the others."

Domaren turned to measure Brikana's reaction.

"How did Criz sound when you spoke with him?" She asked.

"He sounded as calm as he always is," Domaren said, shrugging his shoulders and hands as they rested on the saddle. "If he was aware of whatever might be happening, I couldn't tell."

A silence found its way between the two friends as Domaren, and seemingly Brikana, extrapolated from a host of unknowns. Brikana abruptly turned to look up the road before turning back. Domaren watched, curious about what startled Brikana.

"Could they really do it, Domaren?" She asked. "*Would* any of them?"

BRIKANA

The rapidly moving clouds above beckoned his eye and sent his gaze upwards. Their speed caught his mind, his thoughts, and his concentration. In a moment, Domaren's consideration raced from certainty to doubt. What he felt were truths and fact constructed by experience and relationships throughout centuries, suddenly flattened into thin, slippery condensates of foreign unfamiliarity. The sky above him, perpetually unique and forever new, seemed to reflect a blanket of familiar textures and ominous hues. But even as paranoia tapped its fingertips on the windowpanes of Domaren's conviction, he found a mental curtain he could draw to disavow his worry.

"I don't believe they would," he replied in a quick monotone.

Brikana's face remained devoid of expression while, Domaren imagined, she waited for him to elaborate.

"The first time, there were signs," he added. "They came to me. They hinted at their concerns. Their frustrations. They all did, but they grew quiet the closer it came to the actual rebellion."

"Interesting that you refer to it as the first time," Brikana said.

The two friends caught each other's eye quickly.

"No, you're right." Domaren said. "There were signs. There were signs of Wrathlore. I don't know what's happening now."

Domaren looked at his friend and nodded to confirm his correction.

"But I was wrong before," he continued. "They betrayed me before."

"Well, let's go find out what's going on," Brikana replied.

Domaren patted his horse on the neck and tapped

Wiggly on the nose before turning back to his dragon colleague. He cleared his throat.

"When I spoke with him last, I told Crizichial that I would make for Gru Glech and assist him with whatever might be going on there. Want to join me? If all goes well there, we can search out the others."

"What did he say was happening?" Brikana asked.

"There's an army of some kind, not sure how large, making their way to the calling tower there."

"So, we've lost contact with the Grove," Brikana sought to confirm, "and it's been suggested we not use our knight calling stones, while at the same time, a force is supposedly marching on a tower."

Domaren extended his hand and bowed his head.

"Okay, right," Brikana said. "Someone definitely doesn't want us talking to each other."

Domaren nodded.

"But, Gru Glech?" Brikana asked, her voice lilting in disgust. "I can't stand—"

"Oh please, spare me. I don't want to hear it," Domaren interrupted, turning back to check Munch's saddle girth.

Brikana scoffed.

"It's just so... bleak and harsh," she said. Domaren continued fidgeting with his horse as Brikana elaborated. "There's nothing redeeming about it. No beauty. No warmth. No soul."

"Kana," Domaren said with an admonishing bite, "the souls of the Redeemed are indeed where their beauty and warmth dwell. Not their home."

Brikana sighed.

"You know what I mean, Domaren," she said.

"Yes, I know," he retorted. "But it's better than being on the south side of the gap. There's no pain. No flame. The

Redeemed have turned their side into a home."

"After all this time, I still don't know that they should have been granted a knight of their own," she mumbled, mostly to herself.

Domaren spun around, but before he could respond, Brikana added a question.

"How do you want to travel?" She asked. "Did you want to fly with me?"

"No, I haven't really used my dragon form in months, other than those few minutes in Kimozoa," he answered. "I'd tire quickly, and I don't want to waste any time. No, I assumed you would fly, and I'll ride."

Brikana straightened up in rigid ferocity.

"No one rides *me*, Domaren!"

Domaren's face twisted in annoyance. He rotated his body towards Munch and extended his arms. His eyes stayed on Brikana.

"The horse, Brikana. I'll ride the horse," he said. He dropped one arm, leaving one pointing at the steed he'd been preparing in front of her.

Brikana's wings and neck relaxed.

"Oh, of course," the dragon said. Her eyes relaxed into a hint of humility. "Right."

"Sometimes you act like I haven't known you for however many generations it's been," Domaren mumbled, returning to his horse.

"Mm, yes, well, sometimes you treat me like I'm not just as much a godknight as you are," she snipped back.

Domaren dismissively but playfully waved her off as he circled around to the other side of the horse.

"I've told you millions of times that the dragons are lucky to have you as their godknight," he said. As he continued, his head popped up from behind the other side of the horse. "And *I* am privileged to have you as a fellow godknight."

Domaren leaned over and disappeared again to adjust a saddle bag.

"I still need some better bags," Domaren said to himself.

The gargantuan dragon rolled her eyes and looked down at the ground. Her wings lowered closer to her body.

"You're just hotheaded," Domaren said, muffled from behind the horse.

Brikana's wings snapped back up.

"I'm a dragon, Domaren. I'm *made* to be hotheaded."

He popped back up again with a wild grin.

Brikana snorted and set free another plume of smoke from her nose.

* * *

While the godknights usually traveled instantaneously by way of their grove calling stones, their individual powers, or their personal traveling stones, there were sometimes occasions that called for manual travel. And seeing that they currently had concerns surrounding their use of their instant travel methods, it was exactly those unknowns that inspired Brikana and Domaren to travel by air and land.

Whenever the knights required manual travel, the usual routine involved Brikana flying high, sometimes flying ahead to scout, before returning to whoever else she was traveling with to report on weather, terrain, or hostilities. Domaren rode his horses hard and frequently sold and bought extra horses—having them kept and tended to at various stables—so as not to harm one, and to keep Munch healthy. Through the ages, Domaren always kept a primary horse through their natural lifespan for consistency, but also, for companionship.

The two godknights set out from Kimoba along Foothill Road that ran along the western base of the Fi Mountains. Though there were initially no roads to Gru Glech prior to Wrathlore, a few major routes were established after the Kihdai forgave a segment of the demon population. These demons came to be known as the Redeemed, and were granted their own godknight. Settlements took hold as travel to, and trade with, Gru Glech increased. As a result, a road from Kimoba to Gru Glech became clear and well-beaten, but as it stretched through the human territories and farther south closer to Gru Glech, the route narrowed and its condition worsened.

After nine days of almost non-stop travel, Domaren and Brikana crossed the river near the outskirts of Hornercruck, the last human village before passing into Gru Glech. As Domaren prepared to rest Munch and rent a temporary horse, he tapped Brikana on the wing and made a request.

"It might be a good idea for you to fly ahead and see if anything sticks out," he suggested. "Crizichial didn't have too many details when we last spoke."

"Mm, I was planning on that. He said this army, or whoever they are, was going for the calling tower?" She asked rhetorically. "I'll fly southwest along the dwarf border and use the mountains for cover."

"How long do you think that will take you?" Domaren wondered.

Brikana shrugged her shoulders and wings.

"Depending on what I come across... I'm not sure. Maybe, a few hours?"

"Right, okay," Domaren said. "If you want to go

ahead and do that, I'll work on getting a fresh horse. Instead of coming back to Hornercruck, want to just look for me along the road?"

Brikana nodded and turned to launch into the sky.

"Hey," Domaren said, before she took off. Brikana looked back.

"Be careful," he said. Brikana tilted her long head, ready, Domaren was sure, to take umbrage with his warning.

"No, Kana, I just don't like this. It's been countless ages since, but I've felt like this before," he said.

Brikana released her partial scowl and nodded again.

"See you in a bit," she offered.

"All right," Domaren replied. "I'll be back on the road shortly."

After Brikana jumped and shot her wings back in their first powerful thrust, Domaren watched as she flew higher and grew smaller in the sky before letting his eyes fall back to the perimeter of the village.

There was initially no noticeable movement from Hornercruck as Domaren approached, but finally, a hefty figure stepped out from behind a humble shed. In his hands were a hammer and a glowing piece of metal.

Domaren glanced at the metal quickly, but soon raised his eyes to the towering creature in front of him. At about twice his height, with loose, grey skin sagging on his gangling frame and his back slightly towards Domaren, stood a Redeemed. As a demon outside the confines of Ba Glech, Domaren knew the demon was forgiven, and was forging a new life for himself. Indeed, Domaren assumed him to be a metalworker of some kind, forging something from the metal in his hand.

"Hello, friend," Domaren said. He spoke lightly and quickly. "You must be the village's blacksmith?"

The demon said nothing and did not try to acknowledge Domaren, but instead resumed tapping away slowly at the metal on his anvil. It had cooled slightly from a bright yellow to a washed out orange.

"Better get some more hits in. You're about to lose that heat," Domaren offered playfully.

The demon let his hammer fall, but instead of striking the metal, it landed on the anvil with a sharp, metallic ring. The demon let go of the hammer, letting the wooden handle smack with a much warmer thud, and turned towards Domaren.

As the Redeemed turned, Domaren caught sight of the forgiven—formerly evil—being's expression. Its mouth, locked and tangled in a twisted smile, appeared to simultaneously lust for and crave flesh. Bony pits for eye sockets stretched wide, housing sunken and puny eyes, as if in perpetual shock. A narrow and pointed tongue dangled out from a side of its mouth, unable to be reeled in. As it replied slowly to Domaren, its mouth only partially moved, making it hard for Domaren to distinguish between sounds and syllables. Its voice was a mixture of whispers and hisses.

"How cah aah hewull you?" It asked.

Domaren repeated the greeting softly to himself as he tried to understand.

"How cah aah—" he started. "Oh! How can you help me? My apologies. Yes, I was wondering if you know where I might be able to find a stable? I'm afraid I haven't been here in..."

Domaren trailed off as the Redeemed slowly lifted a shriveled arm and hand. It pointed down the village's main street.

"Stahbul thah weh," it said.

"Ah! The stable? Perfect. Thank you."

Domaren walked closer, but fanned out past the creature's work area and entered the main street, leading Munch off to his side. As he walked by the demon's blacksmithing booth, Domaren considered the former evil entity further. After passing in front of him, the demon reached out for his hammer, and picked up the metal, which had cooled to the color of a ripe cherry. With its grotesque face frozen in place from its former days as a doer of evil, it turned back towards the forge for a reheat.

After joining up, Domaren and Brikana hadn't come across any Redeemed prior to reaching Hornercruck. In fact, it was rare to hear of any Redeemed traveling outside of Gru Glech, much less Hornercruck. And even though Domaren had engaged with plenty of them in his time, he always found something unsettling about his encounters with the Redeemed. They had been forgiven by the Kihdai long ago, but being physically trapped in permanent physical reminders of their deviant past was a reminder to the world, as much to themselves.

And like most other villages and cities close to various borders, Hornercruck was a host to residents and merchants of all kinds, intermixed with dwarves, humans, elves, seavers, and more. The streets teamed with raucous laughter and lively debates. Drunken belligerence and vicious insults. Shouts of wares and goods mixed with rolling wagons and giggling children. And while most everyone else walked quickly or ran from one side of the street to the other, one's eyes could always quickly pick out the Redeemed with their extreme height and slow movements.

"Hello, there. I need to get my friend here some rest," Domaren said, walking up to the stable. "Could I house him here for a few days and borrow a fresh one. I can pay, or perhaps trade something? Whichever might be best for you."

The orc behind the stall's counter grunted and looked up at the godknight.

"Coming from Kimoba? You don't look like you're the type that needs a horse," the orc said.

Domaren tilted his head.

"You mean I don't look like a *customer?*"

He shook his head and looked around before complaining under his breath.

"Really, what is it lately with the resistance to making money?" He said. He swung his head back towards the orc.

"Interesting thing for a merchant to say to a potential... customer."

"You asked for a trade," the orc said. "There's no money in trades, friend."

The orc chuckled at himself as he hung some tack up on the wall.

Domaren rolled his eyes and lifted his hands.

"Fair enough," he said. "I can respect that. Besides keeping my friend for a few days, how much would say, that horse over there cost me for the same amount of time?"

The orc turned back for a quick glance at Domaren once again. Domaren assumed the orc knew who he was, or at least that he was high born or nobility, and well to do, so much so that he was expecting a less than fair response.

"How far do you need to go?"

Domaren couldn't help but chuckle this time.

"That's my business, friend," he replied. "How much?"

The orc tossed his last piece of gear onto a nearby shelf and stepped back to the counter.

"*Where...* do you need to go?"

Domaren quickly rubbed his face.

"How are you able to run a business and be so

disagreeable and nosy?" Domaren wondered.

"I'm only nosy when I need to be," the orc answered. "And by the looks of you, I think I need to be."

Domaren took some slack out of Munch's reins and turned to lead his horse away.

"Mm," he hummed quickly. "Never mind."

"Okay, okay," the merchant shouted. "Okay, I'll trade. No extra fee."

Domaren looked back at the merchant with dubious eyes.

"Come on, come on," the orc said, waving Domaren back. As Domaren walked back over, the merchant leaned in even more and spoke with a hushed intrigue.

"Just looking for a little news or gossip," the orc said. "Come on, I'll trade you."

Domaren looked around and down the street before settling back on the orc.

*Maybe I can get some information out of him, too,* he thought.

"All right, fine," Domaren said, handing the merchant his horse's reins. After waving Wiggly down, Domaren unstrapped his saddle, Wiggly's smaller saddle, tack, blankets, bags, and obliged the curious stable master.

"There's apparently a force marching on the calling tower just east of here," he said. "I'm headed that way to investigate."

The orc listened intently. His eyes popped wide and his jaw dropped as Domaren spoke.

"You're off to investigate?" The orc asked. "By yourself?"

Domaren said nothing.

The merchant looked Domaren up and down before settling on the pommel of his sword.

"Looking in on a calling tower... Wait... That sword! You're Domaren! The human godknight!"

Domaren grinned and let his head tilt towards his shoulder as the orc enjoyed his epiphany.

"Sure! Well, it all makes sense now," the merchant said. "Yes, that's very interesting. I heard about an army of dwarves making their way south out of the heart of their lands about a week ago. You think that same group is marching on the calling tower?"

Domaren's brow wrinkled.

"Dwarves?" He asked. "Are you sure? Dwarves?"

"That's what I heard," the merchant said. "I heard a mention of seavers, too, but nothing very specific."

"What? Seavers? Interesting. Any word on which dwarf clans? Any affiliations?" Domaren pressed.

The orc shook his head and shrugged.

"I didn't hear any more than that. Just that they had been spotted."

Domaren rubbed his chin and, after looking at the sky and considering what Brikana may have found, walked behind the counter and into the corral.

"How's this one? Is this okay?" Domaren asked, pointing at a horse.

"Sure," the merchant said. "Go ahead. That one will serve you well. Been trained."

Domaren nodded and reached for his saddles, blankets, and tack.

"Actually, no, wait," the merchant said, shuffling over. "This one's a good bit sturdier. Take this one."

The godknight offered the slick merchant a grin and went to work prepping his temporary mount.

## Six

Domaren made quick work of the saddles and harness and returned with Wiggly to the road in the direction of Gru Glech. With the distance between Hornercruck and Gru Glech a much shorter ride than the journey so far, and then only a day from the border to the Redeemed city of Vordzinad, Domaren rode somewhat leisurely to give Brikana ample time to finish her scouting mission and meet up with him.

The first portion of Domaren's ride was quiet and uneventful. There was a long stretch of not seeing anyone on the road, but just as the first plumes of smoke from the homes of Gru Glech appeared on the horizon, Domaren finally ran into fellow travelers. But unexpectedly, they were riding away from Gru Glech in unexpected numbers. He stopped and tried to start some conversation as scores of Redeemed rode past.

"Hello, respected Redeemed," he said.

No one looked up. Whether they were walking, leading draft animals on foot, or riding in wagons, they paid Domaren very little attention. Normally, their warped forms and grotesque faces instilled fear in those unfamiliar with the history of the Redeemed, but instead, the fleeing convoy meandered silently as if they themselves were fearful of something.

"Is everything all right?" Domaren said, trying to strike up a conversation again. "I'm hoping to meet with..."

Domaren's attention snagged on a small part of the caravan, which had come to a halt. Most of the Redeemed continued their slow trek, and the wagon wheels kept turning. But as the stream of forgiven demons passed by Domaren, a lone Redeemed came to a complete stop. Other Redeemed at the end of the marching column turned back toward the front after watching the single Redeemed pause, apparently unsurprised by the odd development.

Domaren watched the column creep farther into the distance, but spun a suspicious eye back to the Redeemed across from him.

"Hello, friend," Domaren said, turning to face the demonic straggler. "What has so many of you leaving your home?"

Rather than the type of response Domaren expected, such as a warning about the rumored armies nearby, or maybe something related to the weather, the demon widened its stance and spread out its arms. Its brown skin, appearing painfully taut, rippled and bulged with movement before cracking, splitting, and oozing bits of white and red puss. Horns, only partially visible at first, sprouted out from its cheekbones and skull in a startling asymmetry like wild roots hunting for nutrients. It then lifted its head to the sky and uncurled its tongue, some three feet in length. A long and scratching hiss followed.

Domaren's hand shot to Verikta's handle as he shoved

his other hand forward in an attempt to first calm the situation.

"Wait! Don't! I'm here to talk and help!"

The Redeemed's hiss quickly crescendoed while it lowered its head to face Domaren. As it caught Domaren's eye, the gnarled demon scooped up its outstretched arms before struggling to push them up farther against an unseen resistance.

*Looks like a young one,* he thought. *Almost completely immobilized while it's summoning.*

Domaren drew Verikta and whipped his head to the left and right in an effort to determine who might be joining the impending fight. The column of Redeemed that had passed continued on their way, leaving only the last few visible.

*Doesn't look like any are coming back.*

He looked to his right.

*Another column is heading this way,* he thought. *But not moving quickly.*

He brought his sword up in a defensive stance.

"You really want to do this on your own?" Domaren asked. It did not answer.

The lone Redeemed's hiss transformed into a screech as its arms shook. Through a dense rumble, the ground shook and tore. From the creases and folds of broken ground stretching out for thousands of feet, decaying corpses and skeletons of dead beasts and former members of the world's races clawed their way to the surface. Hooves, hands, feet, claws, and paws punched out from the world's depths and sent clumps of soil shooting into the air as the Redeemed returned the dead to life. Each abomination shook loose of the soil and twisted and writhed as they looked for their target. One by one, they crawled out of their earthen tombs to secure their footing and stare down the godknight.

"I guess a conversation is out of the question," Domaren said. "Very well, my young demon friend."

Domaren raised Verikta and immediately ducked under the vaulting attack of a dead bear. Its dangling flesh and detached sinew, drenched in bloody and rotting filth, brushed across Domaren's helmet as the undead beast passed overhead. The sour sting of decomposition, tempered slightly by the smell of disturbed soil, poured into Domaren's nose.

Immediately following the bear attack, the skeleton of a crocodile finished wrangling free of the ground and snapped at Domaren. As he lunged back, he jumped up and lifted his feet out of the way. At the same time, he sliced downward in a circle and cracked the crocodile's jaw bones off its skull.

Domaren landed with an armored thud. He poked at Verikta's brown handlestone as his feet hit, before thrusting the point of his blade into the body of what seemed to be the remnants of an unearthed demon, if not a Redeemed. With its head and half of its upper torso missing from one shoulder down to the opposing hip, Domaren shoved the point of his sword into its distended navel area. With the brown handlestone pressed, Domaren's next strike slowed the surrounding scene down. The black energy flowing into and out of the attacking demon in the form of smoky, silent lightning, pulsed and streamed noticeably slower. The speed of the attacks from the reanimated creatures decreased as well.

Another bear, with clouded eyes but less decayed than the first, stumbled awkwardly on hind legs towards Domaren. Its jaw hung low in the silent memory of its horrifying roar, but threatened him with the same sharp claws and teeth as its living cousins.

The bear raised an arm and brought a swiping set of claws down at Domaren which just brushed off of one of the godknight's pauldrons. As Domaren pulled his shoulder out of the way, the bear brought its other arm down. But Domaren had anticipated the bear's second attack and brought his sword up in an upward block, slicing cleanly through the bear's arm at the elbow.

Domaren spun in a circle to gauge the next closest threat as the encroaching mobs of dead beasts slowed a bit more.

In an interesting but unsurprising sight, Domaren watched as two undead demons and the animated corpse of a dwarf exchanged unspoken gestures and approached him in a coordinated effort. The two dead demons, one mostly decomposed, and one mostly intact, stayed close together and moved towards Domaren. The dwarf darted away in an attempt to flank him from the rear.

Domaren shifted his feet and struck out to regain the initiative. In a violent burst, Domaren shot towards the two dead demons with his sword raised overhead. As he drew closer, he jumped and spun, and prepared to bring Verikta down into the skull of one of his latest attackers. But just ahead of making contact with the demons, the controlling Redeemed screeched a howl of terror and sent a shock wave of energy out into the controlling threads of smoke. As the pulse of energy reached out and extended through the demon's energy, extensions of the smoke rapidly flew out from the main arm of energy and exploded into thousands of smaller bursts of something resembling black mold. Completely surrounded by thick clouds of matter that reminded Domaren of a blown dandelion, though larger and putrid, the spores of horror set loose curtains of blackness and painful cracks of excruciating sound. Not only did these rob Domaren temporarily of his sight and shatter his concentration, it threw his attack off track and caused him to miss the undead demons.

The hazy explosions of smoke that smelled of burning vegetation stung Domaren's nose. Temporarily blinded, he blinked repeatedly to clear his eyes, and shook his head from the painful blasts of sound. And though he maintained calm enough to push through his momentary disabilities and listen or watch for what he could, he stepped back repeatedly and swung his arms in cautionary blocks, hoping to avoid any incoming attacks.

After what he felt were hundreds of blinks, Domaren's vision improved. From seeing nothing but a void of blackness, slivers of the landscape seeped in before finally, the lone Redeemed and his animated mob emerged from the dissipated smoke.

The godknight squeezed and stretched his eyelids and, after a twirl of Verikta, prepared to re-engage. But a puzzling distraction gave him pause.

The surrounding undead beasts were no longer slowed. Their movements had returned to their original speed, and the swirling storm of the demon's magic had also been restored to its original power.

*It canceled the effects of my handlestone?* Domaren questioned internally. *A common Redeemed? And one this young?*

Domaren stepped farther back and took stock of the fight within its new context. With a brow weighted in suspicious intrigue, Domaren scanned his surroundings again.

"Still alone," he said to the demon. "But, I'd say you've been given some help! I can accommodate you."

The beasts continued approaching at their normal speed, but Domaren's defensive retreat gained him a few extra moments. After pressing Verikta's purple handlestone, he picked up a palm-sized rock from the ground, tossed it into the air, and with a one-handed swing, struck it with the flat of Verikta's blade.

A sharp crack erupted from the collision as the rock splattered blinding light into the vicinity and hurtled through the air with exponential, kinetic energy. The stone sailed through stomachs of beasts and ribs of skeletons before finding its way to the troublesome Redeemed. When the shining wave of energy reached the young demon, the kinetic force knocked the creature down flat on its back.

Domaren shot off. He raced straight down the path he had cleared towards his Redeemed foe. As he ran, Domaren stabbed through the wounded undead or sliced through the disoriented skeletons. Additional decaying and reanimated beasts rushed him as he closed in on the Redeemed, but they too were dispatched with Verikta's overpowering fury and Domaren's ancient skill. Any who weren't engaged were skillfully deflected or avoided so Domaren could get to the Redeemed necromancer.

But Domaren was delayed enough for the demon to regain much of its connection to its evocation. The godknight watched as the attacking Redeemed rolled over and scratched up to its knees. It then outstretched its arms and resumed its dark attack.

Domaren continued tearing through the surrounding army of decaying dead. Over the cacophony of hissing, growls, and groans, a new, louder and more violent rupture of the ground shook up through Domaren's legs as he raced towards the demon. But he remained focused on the Redeemed ahead of him.

As he grew closer, Domaren heard the beast's hissing morph into a grave chorus of multiple voices. What began as its initial hissing and indistinguishable syllables swelled in volume and complexity. Domaren raced closer and closer and easily made out the demon's words spoken in the ancient demonic language of Demith.

*Like the wakening at the beginning,*
*Like the birth of the virtues,*
*So let the ancient dead wake.*

Upon hearing the start of the Demith words, a sharp pulse of confusion gnawed at Domaren's focus, but he dug in harder and pushed himself to prevent the creature from completing its spell.

*Let an original monster rise.*
*Let it wield its darkness once more.*

The demon had spoken too quickly, and Domaren had been too late. To prepare for a killing blow, Domaren flipped Verikta over with the point down and cupped the pommel with his other hand. After closing to within a hearty leap's distance to the Redeemed, Domaren jumped up, the violent shaking of his armor falling silent as he ascended into the air. As he sailed forward through his arc and fell towards the Redeemed, he watched it look up to meet him with a smile of decaying fangs and diseased gums. Now that it had successfully uttered its spell, the creature silently mocked Domaren from below.

Even so, Domaren pushed Verikta out in front of him as he continued to fall. Blade pointed down. One hand on the handle. The other on the pommel. As he practically landed on top of the demon, Domaren thrust the point of the blade down through the length of the creature's torso and forced Verikta down until Verikta's hilt met the creature's collarbone.

The mortal Redeemed collapsed to the ground on its knees as its body remained impaled by Verikta's metal. As they both came to a rest after Domaren's landing, he pulled Verikta out and finished the demon off with a clean severing slice to its neck.

But the continued rumbling of the ground demanded Domaren's attention once again and reminded him that the demon had finished speaking its last spell. After a final, focused glance at the Redeemed, Domaren spun around. With a rapid calculation, he estimated the distances between the remaining undead creatures, but also desperately searched the field for the target of the dead demon's final evocation.

The ground continued to shake and threatened Domaren's balance. The resumed fight was manageable and Domaren made quick work of them. One moment, a freshly risen wolf would crawl from the ground and attack, and then more humans or more bears, the next. After only a minute of solid attacking, Domaren had dispatched the entirety of the demon's initial conjurings like a village's rat catcher swatting a broom at a room full of rodents.

Just as Domaren killed the final reanimated creature, an unnaturally large plume of debris exploded up from a spot in the field about a mile away, accompanied by shoots of mostly stone and dirt, along with a few spurts of bright red lava. From the center of the tons of ejected earth and molten material, emerged the cracked, broken, but mostly intact, animated carapace of a Bainidon.

Domaren stood frozen as he watched the gargantuan figure bust out from the final streams of soil, rock, and fire still falling back down to the ground. After quickly scanning the area to make sure the immediate fight was concluded, he shot his eyes back to the Bainidon. His arms sank slightly as he took in the harrowing scene ahead. With a jolt of disbelief at how the ancient horror had been summoned, he glanced back to the dead Redeemed.

*You shouldn't have been able to call this,* he thought, *before focusing entirely on the Bainidon.*

Domaren took a massive breath and forced it out, as if resetting his thoughts and strategy. With a forward and violent thrust of his sword hand, he shook the bulk of the blood off his blade before bringing it up to wipe it on an exposed piece of linen.

The Bainidon slithered out of its crater. Its huge head, flat at the top and narrowing down to a pointed chin, was bathed in antennae with eyes extending out from each. It turned its gaze and methodically searched the area after being awoken from oblivion. Its dozens of legs rippled along and helped it completely pull itself out of its resting site while it stretched its two wings and tail. The stinger at the end of its tail glistened and reflected the falling lava like a distant beacon atop a vaulting lighthouse.

The resurrected Bainidon continued to look for its target. Its head whipped from side to side as it crawled farther away from where it emerged. Its various lengthy antennae and extended eyes flitted back and forth casually before settling straight ahead. It finally locked onto its prey.

Domaren spun Verikta and took in another steadying breath. The Bainidon replied with a high-pitched screech that seemed to reverberate for miles in every direction. The massive creature beat its wings once to help its lengthy body jump and close the distance between it and Domaren. A slap of wind on the ground rolled out from under it and rolled over him, requiring him to widen his stance and confirm his footing. Domaren then watched as the Bainidon grew even closer and partially surrounded him with its significant and long body.

*Okay, a bunch of opportunities here,* Domaren considered calmly. *Which is the worst threat? It could chew me, trample me, or sting me. Hmm, haven't fought one of these in a very, very long time. Legs make the most sense, I guess. Easiest to get to.*

As Domaren evaluated his options, the Bainidon continued forming its circular perimeter around him. Its screeches grew louder and scraped harder, changing from something resembling an expulsion of air to a sucking in of air. Violent sounds clashed together as though they became stuck on something, just to rip loose again into another hateful sequence of sound. The scarred yellow of its body contrasted with its many black legs and black wings. The matte, dirty appearance of the beast's yellow body transitioned to a cleaner and shinier yellow up to the top of its pincer up high on its tail, with the color growing darker and blacker towards its face.

Domaren found it uglier than he found it scary, but he knew that was primarily due to the nature of who *he* was. While analyzing the pace and gait of the Bainidon's legs as it continued enclosing him in, he recognized his appreciation for the fact that the sight and presence of a Bainidon would more than likely drive any other being to a horrific death caused entirely by fear. Allowing himself a moment to respect the monstrosity, he looked up at its face.

The Bainidon's eyes, extending out from its head on sinewy and muscular antennae, and together with its head which tilted in slightly, kept a constant watch on Domaren. The many mandibles and antennae chomping and dancing about, alongside its extended eyes, created a vision of what appeared to Domaren as a jumbled throng of eerie appendages, twirling and waving about as if each had a mind of its own.

But despite taking a quick moment to review the entire beast, Domaren paid most attention to its feet.

*Need to immobilize it first.*

Domaren held Verikta up and loosened all but his thumb and index finger to study the handle. Despite knowing the placement, function, and feel of every handlestone as well as he knew his own mind and body, he considered which stone would serve him best with the Bainidon.

Almost as quickly as his eyes landed on the handle, he brought his other fingers back around and pressed a stone. As he did, he looked up and smiled at the Bainidon. Its intelligence had been reanimated as well, apparently, as it didn't seem to care for Domaren's flippancy.

The Bainidon stopped its circular posturing, reared back, and thrust its massive head towards Domaren. The godknight sidestepped and ran backwards just in time to miss a targeted bite from the gigantic creature's mandibles. Having just avoided the attack, Domaren heard the efforts of the Bainidon's exertions seep out through its teeth. Its smell of sour rot followed almost immediately.

Taking advantage of the momentum of the Bainidon's attack, Domaren took off running down the remaining length of its head and beginnings of its thorax. As he approached the first pair of legs, Domaren raised Verikta up over his shoulder, not so much out of a preparation for exerting a particular amount of force, but to prepare for his placement of the blade.

Once he was within close enough proximity to one of the massive legs from the first pair, Domaren swung down with little effort and sliced cleanly through the huge, unnaturally armored leg. Even a godknight normally had to give their all, and possibly needed to make several hits to sever such a beastly leg. But, Domaren had enabled the appropriate handlestone to allow for such effortless attacks.

The first leg plopped to the ground. As the Bainidon finished following through with its own attack and registered the pain of losing a leg, it slid into a skid and spun around before unleashing its loudest and most hateful screech yet.

Domaren spun Verikta in one hand before brandishing the blade in an 'X' pattern to his front.

The Bainidon dug in and flapped its wings again before initiating a more violent charge. It lowered its head as it raced forward, protecting the rest of its body. Grasping his sword with both hands, Domaren brought Verikta up to his side in a preparatory posture.

Domaren stood his ground as the Bainidon sprinted for him once more. The beast's head hung low to the point some of its antennae and eyes grazed the ground. Its wings folded back against the length of its body. With a quick change of strategy, Domaren switched sword hands and repositioned, hoping to take the matching front leg.

"I'll take one at a time if I have to," he said to himself.

It was almost time. Domaren crouched slightly to center his gravity and raised Verikta up over his shoulders again. After rocking on his feet some to anticipate another quick dodge, Domaren's eyes shot open wide. In an unanticipated maneuver, the Bainidon dug into the ground with its multiple rows of legs and slid to a halt. Instead of another full charge at Domaren, the Bainidon rapidly skidded into a violent stop and, as it slowed, whipped its long, plated tail up and over its body and head.

"Look at you acting like a seaver!" Domaren said.

Domaren looked up and watched as the massive tail

whipped over the beast and came arcing down towards him. Without a thought, Domaren pressed the amber stone on Verikta's handle. And just before the Bainidon's terrifying stinger impaled Domaren's body from head to toe, Domaren raised Verikta over his head, hoping to block the strike.

When the stinger was a second from contacting Domaren's blade, a boulder three times Domaren's height faintly popped into view. Rather than sinking into Domaren, the stinger collided with the temporary boulder, causing a horrible crunch of sound and sparks to fly out hundreds of feet in all directions.

While Domaren was unaffected and unharmed, the impact shocked the Bainidon and sent it stumbling backwards as it lost its balance. The monster lost control of its enormous body in the rear first, before rolling into an uncontrolled and chaotic tumble. The force was too much for it to regain control. As it continued sliding backwards, the center of its body, followed by the front, continued rolling backwards and off its feet until it had completely landed on its side before coming to a rest on its back.

Its legs, minus one, squirmed helplessly high in the air.

Both the godknight and Bainidon knew how vulnerable the resurrected beast was as Domaren shot off in a sprint to take advantage. The Bainidon slapped at the ground with its wings but was unable, while upside down, to exert the force needed to right itself. Its head thrashed about from side to side as well and punched down at the ground in a desperate attempt to adequately protect itself from the charging godknight. So too, did the Bainidon's tail try to swing back and forth in an attempt to upright itself.

In a sight that resembled the combined chaos of a supernatural hurricane and earthquake, the helpless Bainidon stirred and flung acres of rock, soil, and vegetation into the air across hundreds of feet.

Domaren had no desire to show it mercy or give it a chance to get back to its feet. If anything, his speed increased, as did his focus to determine the quickest method of dispatching the abomination. Through short, guttural bursts of pitiful bleats, the Bainidon pleaded helplessly for aid. But whether it was howling its needs to someone, something, or argued with itself over its inability to right itself, no salvation would come.

*Your summoner is dead, old one,* Domaren thought.

Domaren's unnatural speed closed the distance quickly. In an equally powerful jump, Domaren launched up and towards the head of the Bainidon. Just as he had with the demon necromancer, Domaren landed on the underside of the Bainidon's head and into a clump of the beast's wildly flailing antennae.

Domaren pivoted on his feet, ducked, and dodged the many pairs of mandibles. And at his earliest opportunity, Domaren plunged Verikta into the soft underside of the Bainidon's head. It let out a sharp screech but quickly focused its various appendages as it tried to unbalance the godknight or catch it in a pair of its pincers. But Domaren had already withdrawn Verikta. As if slashing at a wild forest to clear vegetation for a path, Domaren hacked at many of the beast's extremities. Increasingly blind, and losing additional senses from losing antennae, Domaren met less and less resistance. He stabbed down into the soft underside of its head again.

The beast made no sound this time and continued to succumb to Domaren's attacks. Domaren weaved through the remaining appendages and jumped off before tucking into a roll and bouncing up to his feet. After a final spin to avoid another attempted chomp from its mandibles, Domaren ducked into a final roll up under the Bainidon's head and stabbed deep into the center of the top of the creature's head. The Bainidon screeched, but it almost immediately fell limp. Its last slashes and swipes carried through from their momentum, before the entire beast quickly fell still in a lifeless silence.

In an act of prudence, Domaren immediately pulled Verikta out of the beast's head and crawled out from under it. A small amount of blood escaped as the weight of the beast forced it to finally settle into the permanent position of its second death.

Domaren crawled until he was sure he was clear of the beast and teetered over onto his rear. He let out a soft grunt as he gently plopped down and welcomed a seat of dirt and gravel. While breathing only a fraction harder than normal, Domaren reached for a patch of cloth slipped under his belt. As he kept a glimpse of the Bainidon in the corner of his eye to confirm it was dead, again, he got to work wiping and cleaning Verikta.

"Are you going to stay down, my ancient friend?" Domaren asked. His voice was soft and respectful, but playful.

Giving the creature no time to answer his rhetorical question, Domaren focused on his blade once again. He looked down the length of the sword to look for missed wet spots before flipping the blade to inspect it and its edges for chips or other damage. As always, Verikta showed no signs of any cracks, chips, blemishes, or dull spots.

But Domaren always inspected his sword. He always tended to it as quickly as possible after a fight. Regardless of the time that passed with no harm coming to his blade, Domaren gave every regard and consideration to Verikta that anyone else would give to someone or something they have trusted through their existence. If Verikta were to ever need any repairs, Domaren would know about it within seconds of sustaining the damage.

Once again, Verikta was fine. Domaren wiped it until he could see nothing but the sword's uninterrupted shine. And after poking the cloth back under his belt, he twisted and reached for his pouch where he kept his wet stone—even though Verikta never grew dull either. But before he could retrieve the stone, a muffled series of agonizing moans caught Domaren's ear. After another check of Verikta's blade and the condition of its handlestones, Domaren rolled onto a knee, slid the sword into its scabbard, and stood up.

Domaren slapped at his rear to dislodge any dirt and pebbles before turning slowly to pinpoint the direction of the sound. After doing a full circle, he realized the sound was coming from the other side of the Bainidon corpse. He walked around to identify the source of the commotion and just as he identified it, he nodded to himself. When he walked around the Bainidon's head, his suspicions were confirmed.

*Ah yes, of course. Here we are. The other column of Redeemed,* he thought.

"Good," he said sarcastically. "There aren't any assassins hidden in *this* group, are there?"

Like the first line of Redeemed, this group also appeared weary and afraid. Many looked forward with their heads drooped. The few that looked at Domaren simply stared at him curiously as they passed. Domaren's face twisted with indignation.

"Oh, you can't be serious. None of you have anything to say about this?"

He turned and flung his arms out towards the dead Bainidon.

"I'm telling you," he said in a gentle threat. "If I hear even a rumor that any of you had a part in this..."

Domaren sighed and wiped his brow.

"No, no, I know. None of you had anything to do with..."

Domaren's voice trailed off, distracted by many in the new convoy of Redeemed who suddenly stirred and looked up. But they didn't look at Domaren. Instead, they turned their gaze above and behind him. They creaked and groaned with fear. Domaren turned to see what they had spotted.

It was Brikana. The silhouette of her imposing mass blotted the sun as she quickly approached.

"No, no, there's no need to worry," Domaren said urgently as he jogged over to the column. "That dragon is an ally. She is a friend. We agreed to meet each other on the road. You are not in any danger."

Domaren held his hands up to the Redeemed before spinning to meet Brikana. After whistling for and looking for his horse to confirm Brikana's descent wouldn't spook him, Domaren ran back and away from the convoy to meet her as she landed. Her eyes bulged and squinted in puzzlement.

"Just in time," Domaren said to his dragon counterpart.

As a fair number of skittish Redeemed started running away to rejoin their kin, Brikana ignored Domaren's passive aggression and instead extended her neck towards the resting Bainidon corpse. As she drew closer, her head shot forward and then back as her large nose unraveled layers of the dead beast's odors.

"What happened here?" Brikana asked coyly.

"Not too much," Domaren replied. "Decided to make camp. Roasted some rabbit."

After giving the remains of the Bainidon corpse a quick inspection of intrigue, Brikana turned to Domaren. With her massive closed mouth and weighted eyelids, Domaren assumed she was unamused. But it didn't stop him from laughing at his own comment.

"No, I was dealing with this Bainidon the whole time you were gone," he said, slinging his hand at the dead beast in frustration.

"What? How did it get—" Brikana said, before interrupting herself. "Where did it come from?"

"It was the last thing that dead Redeemed over there summoned," he said.

Brikana turned and the column of Redeemed stole her attention. Instead of replying immediately, Brikana lowered her head and neck and stared through a suspicious squint at the dwindling stream of Redeemed.

"Oh, stop it," Domaren admonished. "They're harmless. See the dead one over there?"

"Mmm, yes," she answered. "*It* summoned this Bainidon?"

"Yes, well, reanimated it. And that was after it reanimated almost everything else around here."

"Yes," she said quickly, scanning the ground. "I see all your litter."

"Not mine," he snapped back, playfully.

Brikana huffed. A puff of smoke escaped her nose.

"Kana?"

The dragon looked back at Domaren.

"That Redeemed summoned the Bainidon using Demith."

Brikana's long neck bent back in confusion.

"What?" She asked.

Domaren nodded.

Brikana looked to the dead Redeemed again before continuing.

"The dead one over there did?"

Domaren's eyes widened as he nodded slower, but more emphatically.

"There are so few that speak Demith, Domaren. Much less that know how to use it!" The dragon bellowed.

"I know, Kana."

"Yes, yes, I know you know," she snapped back, looking aimlessly around the landscape. "I'm thinking out loud."

Domaren tossed his hands up in confusion while looking back at the dead Redeemed.

"Right," he said. "The only ones that are skilled in Demith are the Kihdai, proxies—"

"And us, the knights," Brikana added.

Domaren looked down as his mind raced before nodding again.

Brikana's next statement was slow, and almost a whisper. It was fearful, but also sounded as though it was intended to instill fear. As she dipped her head closer to Domaren, her words grated along roughly like a knife's serrations digging into old burlap.

"If it's happening again, Domaren, and if you have anything to do—"

Domaren's head shot up as he cut her off in furious indignation.

"Don't you dare finish that," he said. "Don't. I'm the

only one left after it happened the first time. I didn't take part in the revolt then, and if that is what is going on now, I know nothing of it. If anything, you and the others are suspect."

Brikana pulled back from Domaren and noticeably assumed a more casual and relaxed posture.

"No," she said softly. "No, you don't need to be suspicious," she said.

Domaren's muscles loosened as her words allowed him to release his own tension.

"And like you said," she added. "What's going on now may not be a revolt."

Domaren's eyes darted back and forth as he thought.

"Well, we need some help. Some answers," he said. "Between losing contact with the Kihdai, not being able to connect with the Grove, and then, seemingly common mortals speaking in Demith to summon Bainidons..."

The two friends locked eyes.

"This isn't good," he added, shaking his head. "It isn't good, and we're completely in the dark."

"Cut off," Brikana said.

"We really need to check in with the other knights and find out if we're all in the same situation," Domaren said with rushed concern. "What about your scouting flight? Did you see anything?"

"Yes," Brikana huffed. "From what I can gather, the Redeemed are fleeing what looks like a battle that is about to start. At least that's what seems to be going on in the valley a few miles off."

"East of here?" Domaren asked.

Brikana nodded.

"So, it's as Crizichial said then," Domaren suggested. "There *is* an army marching on the tower."

"Right," Brikana said. "And I almost didn't believe it. Guess who it is that's headed this way."

"Dwarves?" Domaren said.

Brikana recoiled slightly.

"How did you—"

"Someone said back in Hornercruck they heard of an army of dwarves passing through the area on the way to Gru Glech."

"Hmm," Brikana mumbled. "Well, that is probably them."

"Could you tell who they were? Which clans?"

"No," Brikana answered. "I didn't get too close to them. I figured I could fly in closer again if needed."

"How far away are they from the calling tower?" Domaren asked.

"On foot, I'd say about a full day or day and a half if they stop tonight."

"All right," Domaren said, turning back towards his horse. "Let's get to Gru Glech and find Crizichial. Maybe he has some answers, for a host of things."

* * *

After returning to the road, Domaren rode towards town in a canter while Brikana only had to manage a moderate walk. As they drew closer to Gru Glech, the stream of those leaving thickened, consisting mostly of females, children, and elders.

"It is a terribly... curious sight," Brikana said. She spoke so that only Domaren could hear her.

He looked over from his horse.

"This," she said, dipping her head towards the column of Redeemed. "They're *demons*, Domaren."

"Shh," Domaren attempted quickly, while admonishing her further with a scowl. "Yes, and they're *Redeemed.*"

"I know," Brikana whispered. "But it's still odd... female demons. Children. The old. Does the world distinguish between them when they're on the other side of the gap?"

"It makes sense to, I guess," Domaren offered. "There are male and female demons. Young and old. It's how they were when they were made, or when they died. There are all kinds, good and bad."

Brikana continued walking silently, her eyes focused on the Redeemed.

"Have you encountered evil humans before?" Domaren asked.

"Of course," Brikana replied.

"Dragons?"

Brikana didn't reply.

"Dwarves?"

"I know, Domaren. I know," Brikana said, growing agitated. "The Redeemed forgave them, yes. I *know* they're a part of this world. I've just always felt uneasy. They come from an entire race whose roots are evil."

"Sure," Domaren said, weighing Brikana's words. He looked over again and waited to catch her eye.

"And the Kihdai made us all," he said.

Brikana could only return Domaren's stare until a sound ahead distracted them both.

A massive gate made of roughly hewn timber with tops sharpened to a point, slammed down and sealed the entry to, and exit from, Gru Glech. Having already seen the casually approaching human and dragon, the Redeemed who had exited before the gate closed looked back at the gate guards in confusion. Immediately following the falling gate, a scraping shriek erupted from inside the city.

With the speed and initial appearance of fireworks, hundreds of bright flashes shot into the sky. Each one rose higher and higher to the point they appeared as though they had ascended to the heights of the stars, but just before they fell back to the world, they exploded in blinding and hateful strobes devoid of pattern or sequence. Accompanying the initial explosion of light came screams and howls of anguish and terror. The massive curtain of explosions quickly subsided and gave way to the sight of countless demons as large as the heavens who then stepped down from and out of the sky, onto the face of the planet, ready to obliterate those who were not Redeemed—those unwelcome in the city of Vordzinad.

"Domaren," Brikana gasped in half anger, half fear. "What is this?"

The dragon godknight pushed up with her front legs and stood tall, unfurling her wings and stretching her neck as she did so.

"Redeemed of Gru Glech, city of Vordzinad," Domaren shouted above the noise. "We are Domaren and Brikana, godknights of men and dragons."

The massive figures continued walking, shaking the world with each step. Brikana stretched her mouth open wide as her long neck glowed red, then orange, and then with hints of yellow and white. Her wings spread out wider and higher behind her as she prepared to fight.

Domaren drew his sword.

"Get out of here! Go!" He shouted at the confused Redeemed. "Go!"

Domaren raised his sword to his side and prepared for another skirmish.

"If any of you can hear me, we are not here to fight!" He attempted. "We are here at the behest of Crizichial and wish to speak with him!"

With only a step or two before the giant nightmares would be on top of Domaren and Brikana, the dark monstrosities reached for their backs and produced swords, mauls, axes, and whips, each one larger than a city.

But just as quickly as the frightening entities retrieved their weapons, the entire wall of horror disappeared. Accompanied by nothing more than a muted and low hum, the towering demons evaporated into nothing.

Brikana remained standing as tall as she could without losing her balance. Domaren kept his sword up and to his side. But there was no longer an enemy. The column of fleeing Redeemed, previously confused and scared by their kin's illusion, resumed their shuffle out of the city after the wooden gate shot up once more. An armored Redeemed holding a spear approached the edge of the wall.

"You sssayyy you're godknightsss?" The guard said. His hissing syllables alternated between slow slithers and sharp snaps.

"We are," Domaren replied, still holding his sword in place.

"You were sssummoned here by Crizichial?" The guard asked in confirmation.

"Yes," Brikana responded.

Domaren released a hand from his sword and let his elbows drop. "Well, he should be expecting us, at least," he said.

"We will essscort you to him," the guard said. "You may passs through the gate."

Brikana surprised Domaren by being the first to move out of their defensive postures. She chuckled and fell back down to all four legs.

Domaren looked over at her as he sheathed his sword.

"This is starting off well," she said.

The two godknights weaved through the exiting Redeemed, and finally passed through the gate. Two columns of the forgiven demons stomped over and flanked Domaren and Brikana on either side. The spear captain who had addressed them approached.

"Follow meee," he said.

The two godknights exchanged quick glances before falling in behind the spear captain.

As they walked, Domaren was quickly reminded of the things that potentially lent to why Brikana felt the way she did about the Redeemed. Though he still disagreed with her fervently on her generalizations of the Redeemed themselves, the land this portion of demons was relegated to, after being forgiven by the Kihdai for their assistance during Wrathlore, was largely unchanged and unimproved upon from when it was still part of the original and single demon realm. Even after the Kihdai physically split the region in half with an eternal chasm known as the Vulgar Gap, the northern area given to the Redeemed—that part which remained connected to the rest of the world—has been largely avoided after Wrathlore.

Domaren hadn't been to Gru Glech in more years than he could recall, but the minute his gaze cut through the throng of departing Redeemed, the stark juxtaposition of a forgiven race living among the dead land they called home, washed over Domaren in a cold wave of restored awareness.

The path leading into the region from the gate quickly lost any definition and blended into the landscape as far as the eye could see. The ground was a relentless sea of grey powder, as if the region's plants, life, rock, and water had all been ground, crushed, dried, or burned into a finely grained ash.

Dotted all over the ground were long tubes made of a hardened form of the same ash on the ground, but instead of housing insects as one might expect, they were homes for single demons. Individual Redeemed. Every dozen paces or so, one of the pitiful creatures would emerge from one, grabbing at the tube's edges to pull itself out before making for the rear of the city, or before joining up with the line of those leaving the city.

As Domaren and Brikana walked farther into the demon lands, their visibility plummeted. Between the frequent patches of perpetually burning embers made of charred wood and vegetation, and the burned trees never to bloom or bud again, the area suffocated in a forever fog of dense smoke. There seemed to be no life to the air, no wind or current, but even so, the smoke shifted and wafted about in countless shades of slate, charcoal, and white.

Most times, they could only see the area within an arm's or wing's length. Other times, Redeemed citizens or guards inadvertently surprised and startled them. Occasionally, they passed small huts also made of hardened ash, which they assumed served some kind of civic function—whether operated by a merchant or some other type of trader or smith.

Deeper still, they walked into Vordzinad, the northernmost city in Gru Glech. And while the same spear captain and accompanying columns escorted them, Domaren noticed that they no longer saw any Redeemed leaving the city. Instead, all the Redeemed they encountered along the way, whether passing them from behind, coming in from another direction, or crawling out from their narrow tube homes, all joined a gathering force marching toward Vordzinad.

The Redeemed crawling out from the cramped holes in the ground did so with great effort. Almost every one exerted themselves with great effort to extricate themselves from their tight, claustrophobic homes. As their hands writhed up from their sides and past their heads to grab the edge of the hole's exit, they grunted and groaned disgusting sounds of agony and fatigue. Some had faces similar to the one locked in demented humor that Domaren first encountered on the outskirts of Hornercruck. Others appeared as though something had partially melted them before being rapidly frozen. Some had faces permanently stamped in horror or pressed forever into sadness. Indeed, they forever wore the expression they had in the last moments of their mortal life, or in the last moments before they were forgiven, and made a part of the Redeemed by the Kihdai.

Their march continued. Past more small huts of unknown purpose they walked, and past significant clusters of the narrow tubes that looked to be squeezing forth their Redeemed larva. But each was fully grown. A giant monster, forgiven and good.

Just as Domaren considered speaking out to the spear captain to get his attention and ask when they can expect to speak with Crizichial, the smoke temporarily abated and a feature in the distance distracted him.

"What is that?" Domaren whispered to Brikana.

"What?" She asked. "Where?"

"Up there," Domaren indicated with a flick of his chin. "See that? It looks like a drop off. Or a cliff or something?"

"Oh, that's probably the Vulgar Gap," Brikana said, straining to get her neck and head up above the sea of Redeemed as much as possible.

"Really? I don't remember having to swing so far south to get to Vordzinad. Anyway, I think there's something beyond it," Domaren said. "Yeah, there's something else."

"Yes, we're at the point where the path curves around the mountains," Brikana added.

Domaren had almost tuned Brikana out. Not out of disinterest in what she was saying, but mostly from being fixated. He knew something was different up in front of them, but he couldn't make it out. And before he had any ability to come to any meaningful conclusions, Domaren became flushed, and noticeably hotter than he had been only seconds before. The feeling never lessened and only intensified.

And then it became clear. The convoy of Redeemed guards he and Brikana were in slimmed down from approximately ten wide to four wide. The group was on a portion of the path that came perilously close to the edge of their side of the Vulgar Gap—the abyss that separated the forgiven portion of the demons from their still-forsaken kin. Those who retained their evil ways and who did not agree to help the Kihdai during Wrathlore.

"Brikana," Domaren whispered. "Look over there."

Domaren turned back and Brikana's eyes followed him.

There, across the expanse of the narrowest space in the Vulgar Gap was Ba Glech. The remaining portion of the original realm that was intended to contain all demons, forever. All of their evil. Their darkness. The rot of existence. The hateful.

But instead of a somber field of grey waste and tubes for homes, there was also an unending field of flame with no distinguishable breaks or relief. And instead of ash, there were only black, jagged coals, perpetually glowing with the heat of eternal fire. And as Domaren and Brikana continued walking, they caught sight of a lone demon staring back at them, forever damned, forever unrepentant, and forever lustful for inflicting pain and death on others. A portion of the demon was on fire as it hunched over slightly and held the stare of all those who passed by, across the way in Gru Glech. Included in the anxious gazes of dread were those of Domaren and Brikana.

"I don't know that I've ever seen Ba Glech, Domaren," Brikana muttered darkly. "No. I've never seen it before."

Domaren and Brikana continued behind their escort and kept their eye on the Ba Glech demon as long as they could.

It stood rooted in malevolence and never looked away.

# Part II

*"Too much credit was given. Too much leniency, and too much potential for triviality. Many chastised us for relocating to a new realm, but we did not care. The world had lost its right to a voice on such matters."*
*- Kihdai Reflections on Wrathlore, 564 ABV*

# Seven

The slow shuffling through the ash and smoking embers wore on Domaren's patience and allowed his mind to wander. Each step was an unasked question, and each look up to measure their progress was one less answer. *What's going on in the Grove right now? Is everyone okay? Was whatever happened an accident? How long until they communicate again?*

As the group walked deeper into Gru Glech, the silence between conversations grew. But, in-between bouts of frustrated sighs and the grunts of their labored march, Domaren and Brikana tried to take advantage of their time.

"I don't recall this area at all, Domaren," Brikana said as she made easier work of the terrain than the others. "How much longer is it?"

Domaren cleared his throat and squinted at Brikana through the smoke as he paused to survey the area.

"Well, I'm not sure how reliable my memory is. I didn't remember having to go around the mountains. And there isn't that much to see, but I remember a few features here and there. Maybe about an hour left?"

"Has it always been like this?" Brikana asked.

Domaren looked over.

"Like this," she continued. "Burned. Smoky."

"Um, yes," Domaren replied. "Even when Ba Glech was still a single region. It's always been a sea of blistered and burned land."

"There is absolutely nothing pleasant about it," Brikana said quickly.

"It was never changed. Nothing about demons or their lands were changed, except that some of them were forgiven."

"I know that," Brikana said. "But surely they wanted to improve upon their land, build homes, have something resembling civilized cities..."

"Well," Domaren replied. His tone was confident, almost defensive. "They did what they wanted to. Many wanted to live as they did previously, in the conditions they lived in, as a reminder of what they came from. Who they were. So that they would never take their redemption for granted."

While Domaren felt as though they were being escorted as prisoners and expected to be shushed at any given time, they were not. His and Brikana's conversation was met with occasional glances of suspicion and annoyance, but they were nevertheless allowed to speak. After a moment's break, Brikana resumed their discussion.

"But they're not all so... introspective now," she added.

"No," Domaren agreed.

As a fixed, dark shape started to emerge through the grey smoke ahead, Domaren pointed to it before continuing.

"There are some of the Redeemed that have returned to Ba Glech. Ones who have renounced their redemption and rejected having a godknight, but they are few."

Brikana snorted.

"Seems an odd way to show appreciation for recognition and forgiveness," she said.

Domaren laughed, causing Brikana to swing her head around. Domaren looked at her with playful contempt.

"What? It's a silly thing to say," Domaren said. "Do you mean to tell me you don't think the other races have those that spit in the face of the Kihdai? That haven't taken what they've been given for granted?"

Brikana sighed with a sharp frustration.

"No, of course not," she said.

The group continued walking while Domaren held a playful stare at Brikana, waiting for her to elaborate.

"I'm saying that after the Kihdai offered to forgive an entire race and bring them into the fold, that their knights and proxies over the years might have done all they could to instill as much appreciation and respect in their people as possible."

"Yes, I agree with that, of course," Domaren said. "I think all the knights and all the proxies could do better at instilling as much appreciation for what the Kihdai have done for us as possible."

Out of the corner of his eye, Domaren saw Brikana swing her head around, and anticipated her flippancy.

"Yes, including me," he said before looking at her with a grin. As his grin fell, he pointed again towards the black structure ahead that had emerged even more from the smoky fog. Just as Brikana thought the topic had concluded, Domaren spoke again, this time, in a whisper.

"We'll never fully understand what they've done for us."

Before Brikana could follow with a clarifying question,

the Redeemed spear captain shot an arm up and growled a comment to his countrymen. While the Redeemed exchanged orders and discussion, the two godknights took in the dark structure ahead.

The structure was massive. The portion visible to the godknights was wide and tall, with its full width and height obscured by the dense smoke. Its black material glistened, not from reflected light, but from moisture. It did not appear to be made of rock, stone, or engineered matter, but instead, a type of organic or biological byproduct, similar in appearance to the individual ash cocoons. The building facade resembled something akin to an organism's lone eye, flanked and topped by a pulsating skin of smoke and floating fire particulate. The entrance, with its definition hard to discern, did reveal edges, ledges, and various geographic shapes defined by varying lengths and widths of wetness. Catching Domaren's attention last was an odor of wax and sour milk.

"This building. This place," Brikana said, examining its features, "I remember it. I remember it now."

The Redeemed continued their chatter, sounding somewhat casual to Domaren's ears.

"Yes," Domaren said. "This is their primary civic seat. Now, that is."

"And this is where Crizichial is, right?" Brikana asked.

Domaren nodded. "It should be," he said. "I haven't been here in many centuries, though."

"Hmm, well," Brikana said, "I'm sure you have me beat."

As the two knights spoke, the spear captain broke from his countrymen at the front of the line and made his way back toward them.

"Okay, distinguished knights," the spearman said. His voice was still similar in texture and inflection, but his vocabulary and tone had improved. "If you come with us into center, we will take to Crizichial."

"Distinguished knights?" Domaren asked with a surprised lilt. "So formal! Such courtesy!"

The Redeemed spear captain closed his eyes and nodded before Domaren finished speaking.

"Yes, apologies, knights," it answered. "Lots of curiosities recently. Many strange activities nearby. We have been instructed to be careful and cautious. We were worried that something might happen before you arrived. We're here and safe, now. Please, follow us to Crizichial."

The two godknights looked at each other with shared looks of surprise and suspicion, but after smiling, Domaren extended his hand towards the entrance.

"Of course, please," he said.

A few of the Redeemed escort stayed behind and joined up with sentries outside an entryway that only became visible when extremely close. Domaren followed the captain up three large but shallow steps requiring multiple paces per platform. And after the captain disappeared into the structure through an opening roughly seven feet in height, Domaren was stopped by the exaggerated clearing of Brikana's throat. He stopped and turned around.

"Well, you're going to have to change," Domaren said to his friend.

Brikana tilted her head and sighed.

"I might just wait here," she replied.

"Um, no. Kana, come on. We both need to talk to Crizichial and hear whatever he might say."

The visibly confused Redeemed captain backtracked and reappeared in the threshold.

"Why have you stopped?" It asked with a hiss. "You said you wanted to see Crizichial—"

Domaren held up his hand to silence the Redeemed.

"Yes, we know," Domaren interrupted impatiently. "One moment."

"Kana," he continued, whispering. "Just shift and come on."

"Can't you just ask him to join us out here?" She asked.

"Now isn't the time to be proud. Just shift and come with us already."

"It isn't pride, Domaren," she snapped in return. "I just prefer to say in my natural form."

Domaren's shoulders fell as he let out a sigh. Brikana lifted and stuck out her chin.

"You didn't shift into your dragon form when we were in Kimoba," she said quickly.

"I didn't *need* to, Kana," he huffed in exasperation. He walked closer to her. As he continued, his voice dropped into an annoyed whisper. "Unless you're going to barrel through and knock the front of this building down, you have to shift!"

Brikana rolled her eyes and stared at Domaren who then turned to address the waiting Redeemed.

"No need to be alarmed, anyone," Domaren began as he raised his voice to the group. "Godknights can shift forms, as you all know, and the dragon godknight here is going to change so she can continue accompanying us."

Domaren then stepped back and locked his arms as he waited for the awkward silence to lapse and to encourage Brikana to get on with it.

"No hurry. Plenty of time," he said, for good measure.

"Fine, fine," she relented. "Let's go," she said, stepping back to put even more space between them. "I don't like not having my strength available to me in other forms, but fine."

"Yes, I know," Domaren replied sincerely, if impatiently. "But I don't think you'll need anything while we're here, and even if so, it takes just a moment to slip back. Now quit stalling."

Brikana snorted, shooting two rings of smoke at Domaren. He started wafting them away immediately, but didn't let Kana get the best of him.

"Any time," he added flippantly. "We'll be right here."

Brikana ignored her friend and stretched her wings before folding them back against her massive body. As Domaren watched her throat's firestone brighten while she began to shift, he took a moment to marvel at her singular, ancient form.

Sometimes referred to colloquially as the Black Dragon, by the older peoples and creatures of the world, the entirety of Brikana's massive body was almost completely black. After hundreds of centuries of heating and subsequently cooling her throat, and expelling fire at durations and temperatures hotter than any other fire dragon, her skin and scales heated and cooled, or charred and scarred, creating one of the most impervious natural defenses the world has ever known. And while other fire dragons build up similar scale and skin hardiness, only the Black Dragon—whoever the dragon's godknight is at any given time—can potentially live long enough and exude the necessary degree of flame to accumulate such natural armor.

The longer the Black Dragon lives, the more time the effect has to spread across its entire body. Due to Brikana's extreme accumulation of years, she had become almost completely encased in large, shiny scales of deep ebony. And in the few areas she had skin rather than scales, the charring black had spread there as well. From the tip of her nose and along the sharp angles of her face's edges, she mirrored the blackness of night. Down the length of her neck and under her throat, her scales reflected light from all angles, like thin sheets of water racing across mountain stone. Brikana's back, covered with overlapping spikes, was constructed with the same armored scales, though larger than the other areas of her body. Each spike, tipped with concentrated reflective material, danced along as she moved, appearing like dozens of miniature torches being held by small creatures heralding the impending doom of her would-be foes.

The blackening process gradually took over Brikana's wings as well. Her phalanges looked like long, articulated rods of shiny rock. And in-between the huge, dangling extremities were massive sheets of black, leathery webbing.

Her age and the centuries of expending her fire had ensured her legs and feet were covered in black skin and scales as well. The only remaining hint of her original reddish-brown began halfway down her tail, growing more vibrant and unaffected towards the tip.

As Domaren finished taking a quick moment to refresh himself on all of Brikana's imposing splendor, the Black Dragon folded her wings back flat against her body. After dipping her head and closing her eyes, her throat glowed brighter. And similar to when she prepares to unleash a torrent of fire like she had thousands of times before, her energy spread slowly and then quickly throughout her body. First red, then orange, before rapidly shifting to yellow and then white, her entire body was overcome with internal fire before flashing rapidly, blinding all of the surrounding Redeemed for just a moment. Knowing what to expect,

Domaren instead turned and shielded his eyes.

With his eyes protected and barely cracked open, Domaren waited for the flash to subside. Before it completely dimmed, however, he turned back to his friend with a slight grin.

"Great! Now we can continue!" He said.

"Hmph," Brikana huffed. Having shifted to her human form, she stretched her neck and flexed her fingers. "It always feels so strange," she said. "I feel so much lighter when I shift to my human shape, but it feels like I'm going to teeter right over when I only have two legs to walk on."

"Well, stomp your feet a few times and come on," Domaren said, teasing her while waving her over.

Brikana did exactly that, but looked up at him from under a brow of silly contempt.

"I don't do this for just anyone," she said.

"Kana," Domaren said, while gesturing over his shoulder. "You wouldn't have fit through the door."

"Right, right. Yes, yes," she said dismissively.

Domaren laughed as she walked to meet him.

"Even in human form, you're full of hot air," Domaren teased.

Brikana groaned.

After transforming to her human semblance, Brikana maintained many qualities and features similar to her dragon form's counterpart, though fewer or much smaller in comparison. And despite seeing her shift to her human form countless times, as well as those of the other races, Domaren always took a moment to appreciate her beauty that translated across all of her forms.

Her dark human skin held the hue of her dragon form's blackest scales. But unlike her dragon's many edges and ridges giving definition to her countless scales, her smooth skin looked similar to any other human. The only physical quality retained from her scales was the slight shimmer and reflection of light that gave her skin the appearance of being coated in a thin later of sand being kissed by the outermost mists of a waterfall.

The most noticeable difference between her human and dragon form, consolidated from the hairs and fibers from her dragon body, was her massive mane of thick hair. Dense and fluffy for a few inches out from her scalp, it then twisted into braids, forming many intricate locks. They dangled and bounced along as she walked, while the bright crystalline tips at their ends invited additional admiration.

While her body, hair, and skin assumed the colors of her blackened scales, her human form's armor borrowed from the size and shapes of her scales. Where her dragon form was adorned with hundreds upon hundreds of scales, only a few were needed to serve as her chest plate, back plate, and pauldrons. And though they were predominantly black as well, they exhibited a somewhat translucent quality. In the right light, they reflected the deepest hues of blood red and garnet.

The leathery material of Brikana's wings adapted to cover her arms. Indeed, rather than a form of plate or mail, her arms were wrapped in thick, shiny leather, articulating at numerous points to allow for ease of movement. Her thighs were protected by similar leather, though less articulated and in fewer, larger overall panels. And from her knees down, were the shiniest part of her wardrobe—long, smooth boots of obsidian, appearing to be holdovers from her massive dragon claws.

As a human, she wore a common sword as her primary weapon, which was as unremarkable as any blade crafted by the most amateur of smiths. She was adept at using it, though she had no enchantments on it or accentuated skills when using it. Whatever blade she carried in her human form at any time was acquired by her own means, as transforming from her dragon form provided her with nothing but her armor. And seeing that she was without the power of fire in human form, she acted primarily defensive in nature if thrust into combat. Nevertheless, despite her human armor not being the Kihdai-endowed wonder that her natural Black Dragon, godknight scales were, it was still substantial protection.

Brikana passed Domaren and stopped where the escorting Redeemed had paused before tilting her head impatiently. The Redeemed looked at Domaren in confusion, followed by Brikana's glance.

"Please, let's continue," Domaren said to the Redeemed, smiling. After a few additional puzzled looks, the Redeemed turned and marched back to the front of the line.

Everyone resumed their walk and entered the threshold of the massive structure. The smoke and particulate lessened noticeably once they were inside, but they could still see wisps and curls of smoke in the less disturbed sections of air closest to the walls. The halls were wide enough so that the smoke lingered, undisturbed, and was still thick enough in some spots to appear as though it took the shape of something as large as a human, almost like a smoky sentry guarding the paths.

Though there seemed to be no architectural planning or purposely shaped materials when it came to the appearance of the rooms and paths, they appeared to accommodate most creatures of any height and width. Other than perhaps dragons, it seemed most species could traverse the structure comfortably. Domaren considered it a highly practical building, if unappealing, though it lacked some of the adornments, fixtures, engravings, and carvings that he thought he recalled. The plain ceilings, walls, and floor were all seemingly made of a black tar and wax material, drooping and melting as if dripping in perpetuity from the drooling mouth of a grotesque and diseased entity.

The air quality improved, or at least became less smoky as they walked deeper into the complex, though an odor of mildew and mold wafted into prominence.

Lighting was surprisingly ample, and each of the party took their steps swiftly and confidently. Though there were no sconces, chandeliers, or candelabras, there were instead countless coals lodged into the walls of thick goop, each one no larger or smaller than the size of a human fist. Every few feet a coal sizzled and glowed brightly, and all together, provided more than enough light to *almost* counteract the dank atmosphere of the building's interior.

The group walked for many minutes. With each step, Domaren felt less and less familiar with the environment to the point he started to wonder if he had ever actually been in the strange fortress. Because of the lack of defining forms, features, or items in rooms, it quickly became a confusing labyrinth with no easily distinguishable exit or destination. And other than the coals in the walls, halls, and occasional cavernous room, only the cavities in the building's infrastructure gave their surroundings any distinction.

Like the holes in the ground outside, the recesses in the walls were just large enough for Redeemed to exit from or crawl into. As the escorted godknights walked, many Redeemed did just that—slipping into or out of their temporary places of rest. Each time one crossed the threshold of their confined cavity, the sound of sticky suction would puff out, signaling the pitiful creature's departure or tight confinement. Fueled by curiosity, Domaren came to a stop and leaned in closer to a wall and watched a Redeemed enter its home. Unexpectedly, a low and dense voice broke Domaren's attention, startling him, as well as Brikana.

"You must find this all a bit grotesque, no?" The voice asked.

Domaren shot up straight. Brikana turned and reflexively grabbed Domaren's shoulder before immediately pulling it away. He turned to her and grinned. Neither spoke.

"None of us have had to live like that since the split, but some nevertheless insist."

Domaren resumed a slow walk and craned his neck in an effort to spot the voice in the shadows, but quickly recognized it before closing enough distance to see.

"Crizichial," Domaren said with a smile.

The silhouette of the distant figure pushed away from the wall, instantly sliding into the healthy light of the corridor's glowing embers. As the godknight of the Redeemed walked towards his friends, most of the escorts disappeared down paths leading to other areas of the structure, leaving only a few to stand guard.

While Redeemed can walk or run as quickly as humans, and sometimes faster, Crizichial approached Domaren and Brikana at a leisurely pace. His long, lanky legs swung forward smoothly as his feet rose just enough to lift from the ground. His arms mirrored the casual gait of his walk for a few moments before bringing his hands together. He rubbed them and spun them within his palms. And while some might construe the mannerism as nefarious or something one might do while plotting against the welfare of their people, their neighbors, or others in the world, Domaren and Brikana both knew better. With the Redeemed and Crizichial specifically, the affectation was just something he did while thinking, considering, pondering one's position on something, or deciding on what to say—similar to how a human may place their hand on their chin.

As Crizichial grew closer, his features became more defined and sent a cold reminder through Domaren of how glad he was that Crizichial was a Redeemed, and not still a traditional demon.

Crizichial's legs and arms stretched out awkwardly, but only *just* out of proportion with his demonic form, which was some nine feet high in total. Suspended from the front of his waist, attached to a thick leather belt, was a collection of skulls that dangled on top of a set of femurs from many animals. Serving as armor, the femurs were bound close together and pierced at the ends so they could be connected with more bones. Numerous panels of bright burlap hung under the bones to further protect the front of his legs, with overlapping patches of leather protecting the back.

His bright grey torso could be seen through the mail made of dozens and dozens of other animal bones, like phalanges and small ribs. Though the godknight of the Redeemed appeared gaunt and weak, his skin was tight and defined, with hints of sores and cuts that became more exacerbated when he practiced his decay magic. A set of just-asymmetrical horns branched out from his head, with each horn having a half-dozen points. Together with the central horn, they sloped back gently over his head.

His overall appearance always struck Domaren as an enigmatic juxtaposition between his casual demeanor and the harsh shell of a former demon. An example of

Crizichial's set of awkward contrasts were the distinct features of his face, such as his eyes and area around his mouth which were smooth and taut. Yet, while those specific parts appeared youthful, his forehead and cheeks did not. The disturbing sight of seeping sores on his cheek and forehead complimented the various blisters and hints of blood all across his chest.

"I had forgotten about that," Domaren said. "That's right. The, uh, penance. Some, living like they did before."

"Perhaps if you had not let hundreds of years pass since your last visit, you might remember such details," Crizichial scolded gently. His voice, even in admonishment, coated the awkward meeting with calming reassurance. With warmly phrased shifts in pitch, he voiced his disapproval of his friend's long absence with softly accented consonants and drawn out syllables on words he wished to stress.

Many Redeemed had voices that most would find unsettling. Whether they scraped along and set someone's teeth on edge, or scratched and hissed, the tone and timbre of their voices remained similar to their forsaken kin on the opposing side of the gap. And while the deliberate—almost warm—qualities of Crizichial's voice were not reserved only for him, he did have a voice some might think was more befitting of a middle-aged human who had spent years singing jovial tune after tune at his local tavern. His was a type of reassuring voice that could lead one into a false sense of comfort, or perhaps encourage some to reveal their most guarded secrets.

Regardless, Crizichial's voice was still that of a demon. Redeemed or not, godknight or not, it was a voice that could lure you in, and put your mind at ease with its ability to adapt to what you needed to hear, and the way you wanted to hear it. Like a lilting jig that gave you a conjured notion of peace by wiping your heated worries down with a damp rag of nostalgia, it could then quickly modulate into a horrific rhythm of emptiness and despair. And in turn, never release you from it.

It was a voice that, centuries before, might have echoed through the halls of a home, driving a decent, hardworking man mad after being cursed by a hateful neighbor. It may have been the voice of a festering figure in the corner of a child's room, whispering to them nightly of their worthlessness, their meaninglessness, or their irrelevance. And even more, Crizichial's voice might have been the one heard whispering what it hatefully attempted to convey as the truths of nihilism to an aging and sick widow. The voice, or more accurately, the demonic speaker, would bombard her with doubt, with fear, with the insistence that she would never see her lifelong love ever again, and to spend the bit of remaining time she herself had, lingering in her memories that would mean nothing once she too slipped into eternal oblivion.

But while those types of motives, impulses, acts, or direction may have been part of Crizichial's existence before the redemption granted after Wrathlore, they had not been a part of his reality, his truth, or soul, for many centuries. And just as Crizichial was forgiven, other Redeemed continue to live in similar squalor as they did before the canyon was split, out of gratitude, respect, and penance.

"I don't think you've been to my neck of the woods in as long either, my friend," Domaren rebuked with a point and a grin. "At least my absence wasn't as lengthy a one as Kana's here."

Domaren's grin grew wider and his pointed finger shifted to a thumb gesturing towards Brikana.

"No, no, no," Brikana said with a chuckle. "Don't

either of you try to give me any grief over travel and visitations."

Domaren leaned over into a heartier, but stifled laugh.

"I was, of course, teasing, Kana," Domaren said, straightening back up. But Brikana paid him no mind.

"I've been dealing with centuries of political bickering and border disputes within the entirety of the dragon race while things have been mostly quiet for you two! When was the last time either of you visited the dragons?"

Domaren spun towards Brikana with his mouth open.

"Before this week," she whispered, without acknowledging him.

While Brikana took her counterparts to task for even joking, Domaren's laughter burned out. His grin fell. Crizichial's spinning hands came to a rest.

"I said I was joking, Kana," Domaren repeated, slightly annoyed by her defensiveness.

"Yes, there has been virtually no activity here," Crizichial said. "Living only hundreds of feet away at points, though across a chasm, from the majority of our world's darkest and most vicious evil has presented us with no challenges. Nor has trying to help maintain the morale and collective purpose of Redeemed who the world continually forgets was forgiven and blessed by the Kihdai themselves."

"Okay, okay," Domaren said, holding his hands up. "Kana, he was initially just giving me grief, and I playfully brought you into it. There's no actual argument here."

"Well," Crizichial responded immediately, "I was voicing a legitimate complaint about not having seen you, either of you, in some time, but I intended no resentment or anger with my words. As you said, Brikana, I have not been to Kimozoa in many years, myself. We all do, however, communicate regularly, and as we speak now, it is very nice to see you both."

A smile returned to Domaren's face as he bowed his head. Brikana gently released a reserve of air, which Domaren assumed was being stored for her next retort. But instead of a continued repartee, they had disarmed the tense moment.

In a subconscious effort to change topics, Domaren sighed lightly and walked towards the Redeemed godknight. Brikana took fewer steps and only partially followed.

"Crizichial, old friend. It is truly very good to see you." Domaren stopped within arm's reach of Crizichial and looked up with raised eyebrows and a sincere grin.

Crizichial blinked and nodded slowly in reply.

Domaren turned to Brikana as he collected his thoughts, but Crizichial beat him to resuming their discussion.

"Have you learned anything new since we last spoke?" Crizichial asked. "Any word from the Grove?"

"No, nothing," Domaren said. "Nothing new for you either, I take it."

"Nothing," Crizichial confirmed. He then looked over Domaren's head to Brikana. "Has your experience been the same as ours, Brikana?"

As she replied, she stepped closer, finally joining the others.

"If by experience, you are referring to no calling stones and no grove stones, then yes, it has been the same," she said.

Crizichial's eyes fell away from his friends. He stepped back and began pacing in deliberate glides as he whisked the knuckles of one hand up and down the rows of his bone chest armor.

"I have been thinking about this since you contacted

me, Domaren, and I can not recall a precedent similar to this. Can either of you?"

"Other than the events of Wrathlore, you mean?" Brikana sought to clarify.

"Of course," Crizichial responded. "I thought that was understood."

Brikana bit her tongue.

"There have been lulls in directives before," Crizichial added. "Times of prolonged peace and prosperity. Little need for the Kihdai to engage..."

"But, we have always been able to initiate communications with the Grove," Domaren said with a heavy note of concern. "That mechanism has never eluded us."

"And then," Brikana added, "there was the explosion you say that ended your last grove stone, right?"

Domaren nodded slowly at Brikana, before turning to Crizichial.

"Have you spoken with any of the others yet?" Domaren asked. Crizichial shook his head.

"No, I have not had a moment to even consider trying," Crizichial responded. "I have been busy coordinating efforts to temporarily evacuate my people while trying to determine exactly what is going on with the nearest calling tower."

"I have some news there," Brikana said, stepping ahead of Domaren. Crizichial stopped and, with wide, interested eyes, locked his attention on Brikana. "I flew ahead and scouted as we approached Gru Glech. There does seem to be a fight coming."

"Mm," Crizichial grunted. "Come, let us travel to Proxy Maphikim and continue our conversation there."

"Travel to?" Brikana asked, confused.

"Is he not here?" Domaren added. "In this structure?"

"Ah, no, not anymore," Crizichial said. Before continuing, he snapped and gestured at the nearby Redeemed guards. A few approached and received some whispered words from Crizichial.

"Like many of the others," Crizichial continued, "Maphikim has returned underground in an act of reverence. Of penance. He lives underground in what used to be part of Ba Glech."

"He lives down there?"

Crizichial paused between issuing whispered orders to his subordinates.

"Indeed," he said.

"I thought he abandoned it when the Redeemed were forgiven?" Brikana asked.

"That is correct. He did," Crizichial said. "But he is one of those who returned in recent centuries. If you are prepared to leave, we should set out now to confer with him and then determine next steps."

"Agreed," Domaren said. "Each additional moment that passes without clarity is an added moment of ignorance, which, in my experience, is rarely a good thing."

Domaren checked in silently with Brikana.

"Oh, absolutely," she said, "I'm for anything that keeps us moving forward. While I would like to be careful to avoid panicking or fumbling into an arbitrary response, I am always more prone to action rather than inaction. Let's go."

Crizichial gestured a final time at the Redeemed at the edge of the room and smoothly glided towards the room's exit.

* * *

The three godknights rushed out from the front of the civic tower with a dozen or so Redeemed guards in tow. Crizichial led the group while flanked closely by Brikana and Domaren. The guards followed behind in two columns. Crizichial set a surprisingly brisk speed, though it was easier for him to glide through the ash with his thin legs and while raising his feet only slightly. Though he sliced quickly through the ash, the speed caused Brikana and Domaren to hop and stomp awkwardly.

The initial hour of the group's trek was predominantly silent. Other than the *shoook shoook shoook* sounds the Redeemed made as they cut through the ashen layers with their almost elegant walking, there was only the occasional grunt of frustration at the terrain or an especially off-balanced footfall. But most noise was that of Domaren and Brikana coughing and clearing their throats due to being back in the dense smoke.

"It's times like these that I really wish I spent more time in my dragon form," Domaren said, complaining to Brikana. She jumped at the opportunity to commiserate.

"Why, so you could burn whoever decided against some roads in this place?" She asked.

After a quick chortle, Domaren clarified.

"No, so I was in shape to fly to more places," he said. "Speaking of which—why don't you? We could meet you there."

"Why, just to sit there and have tea with Maphikim while we wait for you lot?"

"Do dragons even drink tea?" Domaren asked, returning Brikana's flippant banter in kind. "No, you could go ahead and begin discuss—"

"I am afraid there would not be much benefit gained

from flying ahead at this point, my friends," Crizichial said, interrupting. "The next part of our journey is a trail just left of that boulder ahead. Do you see it there? There are a pair of barren trees between us and the boulder."

The thickness of the smoke, while mostly a hazard through the duration of their walk, had thinned substantially for the moment, such that the group could not only see the boulder, but could also once again see hints of the Vulgar Gap, and beyond, all the way to the horizon on the side of Ba Glech.

"Ah, we're almost there, of course," Brikana said, while wafting the latest stream of smoke from her face.

"Did you say you had been down here before, Kana?" Domaren asked.

"Their old part of Ba Glech? No, never. You haven't either, right? Even going all the way back to Wrathlore and the forgiveness of the Redeemed?"

"Never. I've only ever met up with any of them in that last structure we were in, in other spots above ground, or in other regions of the world. This will be a first for me," Domaren said.

"Yes. For us both," Brikana corrected.

"We are approaching our edge of the Vulgar Gap, where we will then take a path down," Crizichial said over his shoulder.

The group continued its march closer to the edge of the cliff. As they stomped and glided along towards the edge of the abyss, each member of the group risked unsound steps, and increasingly looked up and down to marvel at the sight of the approaching chasm. With each of Domaren's glances, he squinted and strained to see if there were any other tragic figures to be seen across the way, but he could not easily identify any. Together with the mountains that scrambled to the sky on Ba Glech's side, Domaren, and no doubt, Brikana, found relief in being spared further witness to the earlier forsaken sights that festered in perpetual torment on the other side. Indeed, those condemned demons festered in, and *caused,* perpetual torment.

Once the path began digging down into the ground, their march crept closer to what looked to be a sharp drop off as they approached the edge. The hardened tubes on the surrounding landscape became less frequent and the last hut or building of any kind hadn't been seen in some time. The powdery ash that made up the ground became thicker, however, from being traveled and compacted more, and developed into a smooth trail that allowed the group to speed up. But even with their quicker pace, the route of their path was still unknown to the godknights.

"All this walking isn't a terribly wise use of our time, Domaren," Brikana said.

A Redeemed escort hissed at them as they proceeded.

Domaren didn't immediately reply. Instead, he squinted and looked for any discernible markers or signs of life at the impending cliff edge. He cleared his throat and mentally shined up some charm. But first, he took an opportunity to playfully poke at Brikana's hypocrisy.

"Neither was wasting all that time arguing about shifting earlier..." he rushed to say. "Crizichial," he added quickly, raising his voice. "Is there not a quicker route to Maphikim? Why are there no other tunnels down, or paths closer to where we were?"

Crizichial sighed and replied in a soft, but quick stream of words.

"Maphikim wanted to keep our old home closed off to the surface," he said, almost as though he had been asked, or asked himself, the same question previously. "He wanted access to it to remain confined only to the entry available from the chasm—the entry we're heading for now. To preserve our old home, but also, to keep it sound tactically in case our people ever needed to retreat to it."

"Ah, I understand," Domaren replied. "That's a very wise consideration of strategy."

Brikana bristled with contempt and rolled her head closer to Domaren.

"I still think at least one other entrance or exit would have been prudent," she said.

"I definitely echo your concerns about timing, especially while flailing for information like we are," Domaren said in a returned whisper. "But we're almost there now, so hopefully something will come of this conversation with Maphikim."

As Brikana and Domaren spoke, the accompanying Redeemed slithered ahead and took point at the front of the group.

"What's going on?" Domaren asked.

"They are moving forward to lead us down," Crizichial said casually. His focus remained straight ahead.

"Why?" Brikana said, reinforcing Domaren's curiosity.

"To test the path," Crizichial answered.

A moment before, Domaren had prepared to voice a concern to Crizichial about Maphikim's ability to help or lend information, but after being taken aback by the guard's harrowing task, he was distracted. But after a quick silence, a sight out of the corner of his eyes flung his eyes wide open.

Domaren watched in horror as those at the front of the line dropped from view, their heads, torsos, and bodies slipping out of sight. Startled that his worries had already come true, Domaren realized it only appeared as though, one by one, each of the group walked off the cliff, in some type of enchanted suicide, with no hesitation. The only indication that gravity hadn't immediately sucked them down into the abyss was the comical bobbing up and down as they stepped along. And if Domaren had any doubt as to the trick his eyes were playing on him, it was immediately dismissed when he himself approached the edge of the cliff and saw the narrow trail descend sharply along the side of the cliff.

Far on the other side of the abyss loomed the matching cliff and mountains of Ba Glech. And while the area between the two sides had increased by miles, the scale of the distant mountains made it easy for Domaren and the others to judge just how far away they were from Ba Glech.

And to further assist with defining the sense of distance was the gap itself. Plummeting down to a lake of molten rock, the sheer faces of each opposing cliff framed it and reflected the light from the sun, as well as the bright glow of molten lava miles below. While most of the cliff faces were vertical and smooth, massive segments of stone the size of cities stuck out from parts of the cliffs, as if the roots of the world tore away from their ancient anchors as easily as ripping at the healthy bulk of a bothersome weed.

Domaren slowed before being overtaken by Brikana. As he leaned over and scanned the width of the lava lake visible to him, he instantly saw large swaths of land within the lava—some as large as a robust village. The lava itself was largely confined to the floor of the chasm, though its depth was unknown. There were points, however, where the lava found its way into ravines and crevasses that meandered their way into other areas, the extent of which could not be seen. The effect appeared something akin to a kind of lava lord who lay prone and held the depths of the world down, or held the living shallows of the world up. Its rivers of retreating lava stole their way into inlets and caves that no eyes had ever seen, and were like the imagined lava creature's pulsating and overtaxed veins.

Domaren's eyes finally made their way back to the path down where Brikana had turned around and stopped. She latched onto the opportunity to rib him the moment their eyes locked.

"Not afraid are you, Dom?"

Domaren rolled his eyes and resumed walking.

"Hey, if you misstep, you can fly out of here," he joked, giving Brikana a chortle.

"No, it's just that we've never seen this before," Domaren continued. "Even with who we are, and what we've experienced, it's quite something to see a... feature... on this scale, that the Kihdai caused."

"Mmm, yes," Brikana agreed.

"I can not recall. Were you not here when the Redeemed were forgiven, Domaren?" Crizichial asked. "When the chasm was made?"

"No, not for the chasm's creation," Domaren replied. "I was resolving a few bits of remaining revolt in Wattre at the time, at the request of the Kihdai. I visited soon after, however. When the Kihdai came, and for your elevation."

"Yes, yes, I remember now," Crizichial said. His eyes still focused forward. "So, this is your first visit to where we used to live?"

Domaren traded glances and smirked while recalling their earlier conversation.

"That's right," Domaren said.

"And you, Brikana? Have you been down here before?" Crizichial asked.

"No, never," she said.

"Well, I am glad you both will have an opportunity to see where we came from," Crizichial said. "It is regrettable that it has taken so long to bring you here, but I am glad it is happening nonetheless."

Domaren and Brikana didn't respond, but instead, focused on the narrowing path as it caused the group to slim down to single file.

"I would like to give you both some advanced notice, however," Crizichial added. Before continuing, he leaned into the cliff wall as he walked, and pressed against it with one hand for additional support.

"Much of our old home on this side of the abyss has been chiseled or cut out, leaving panels of clean rock..."

Domaren waited for Crizichial to continue, but enough silence passed to stoke his curiosity. He lifted his head up from the path and waited.

"You both should know there are still some areas," Crizichial continued, "which remain as they were from before we were Redeemed. They are untouched. Unmodified. These areas still reflect the... iniquity, of past ages. There are still some symbols and images you will see. Ancient implements and rituals... As well as other reminders that we have yet to remove or otherwise resolve. I would ask your forgiveness ahead of time for their presence."

Domaren said nothing at first, but instead resumed paying careful attention to each of his steps. Brikana was silent as well. Though, after quickly mulling over possibilities on how Crizichial's enigmatic warning made him feel, he decided a fairly neutral response was best.

"I understand," he began. "Thank you for sharing that with us. I'm sure we'll be able to overlook—"

Before Domaren could finish, a loud grunt and gasp

of breath towards the front of the group pierced the air. The sound of sliding gravel followed, and then, a lung-tearing male scream ripped through the gap, colored by the physical attributes of demonic deformities and mutations. One of the leading Redeemed had slipped. His feet whipped out from under him. After landing hard, he slid off the path and plummeted to the lava below.

No one spoke.

Crizichial immediately turned and reached into a pocket. After closing his eyes for no more than two seconds, his skin darkened and rapidly developed additional signs of decay and disease. As he opened his eyes, he pulled his hand out of his pocket and thrust his palm, and its contents, towards his falling demon kin.

The material in Crizichial's hand rocketed out quicker than the fastest crossbow bolt and raced down towards the imperiled Redeemed. The palm's worth of what looked like tiny black pebbles rapidly grew in size as they fell, swelling at first as individual pellets, before joining into a single mass of smoke. As soon as the pellets combined, the smoke took the shape of an outstretched hand. But it was no use. The demon was falling faster than Crizichial's magic could travel. The black hand formed from decay magic snatched its smoky fingers around nothing but air.

"Hold on," Brikana said calmly. "I've got him."

At almost the same time as she finished speaking, she leaned back into the wall and pushed off it, throwing herself off the path into a beautifully formed dive.

"Brikana!" Domaren shouted, his voice booming in startled concern.

After clearing the ledge where they stood and falling far enough away from the cliff face, Brikana spun in mid-air and in the time of a snap, blinded the group above with a flash of her firestone and exploded into her natural godknight form as the Black Dragon.

Domaren watched her head lower and her neck stiffen. She then flapped her wings twice before folding them back.

"She's trying to pick up as much speed as possible," Domaren said to the onlooking Redeemed. "I don't know if it'll be enough, but she's his only chance."

Domaren could tell immediately that she was making up ground with the falling Redeemed, but Domaren took the group's silence as justified uncertainty. They could only stand and stare to see if there would be enough time for her to catch him before the lava claimed their comrade.

"I do not know that she will be able to reach him in time, my friends," Crizichial said. "Should she be unable to," he continued, "I will be sure to thank her, regardless."

Domaren was unsure if he was talking to him, or one of the other Redeemed, or perhaps both. He couldn't take his eyes off the falling demon or the impressive black dragon shooting towards the chasm's molten bottom.

As the dragon and demon plummeted deeper and deeper into the abyss, they grew smaller and harder to see. Soon after, Brikana's shape could still easily be made out, but the Redeemed became too small for those on top of the ledge to discern.

"Can anyone still see him?" Crizichial asked.

The other Redeemed didn't answer.

"Domaren?"

"No, I can't, Criz. But Brikana's still falling, so I guess..."

Before he could finish speaking, the group watched intently as Brikana's distant form cut sharply to the side. Her pointed and efficient shape sprouted her two massive wings once more. She circled around and slowly but surely, beat her wings and began spiraling back towards the top.

Domaren rolled his head around slowly on his shoulders and sighed. While the fate of the Redeemed was uncertain, seeing Brikana beginning to ascend was a relief.

"Here she comes," one of the lead Redeemed said.

"Does she have him?" Another asked.

Domaren shook his head in ignorance.

"I'm not sure."

Little by little, the massive dragon climbed back to the top of the chasm in sharp, steady circles. With each circuit, Domaren strained to identify if the Redeemed was with her.

"I can't see him," one of the Redeemed said, panicking.

"Is that him on her back?" A different demon asked.

"Oh, I doubt that," Crizichial said flatly.

Domaren chuckled through close lips.

"No," he said, confirming Crizichial's statement. "Dragons are not ridden—least of all, Brikana."

Domaren, Crizichial, and the other Redeemed peered down into the chasm as Brikana continued climbing. Most of the Redeemed looked down while clinging to the wall, having found a new respect for gravity after their friend's slip. As the dragon climbed higher, those waiting on her fell silent.

Needing only a few more spirals, Brikana had almost returned to her friends. In one of her final passes, she looked up and found Domaren's eyes. She winked at him. Her old friend smiled and shook his head.

Brikana beat her wings another half dozen times and continued climbing, when at last, she rocketed past the onlookers. With a sound similar to wind slapping against a boat's massive main sail, she pounded her wings a final time and splashed her friends with an aggressive gust of wind, plastering them all up against the cliff wall. As she flew by, Domaren and the others spotted him. The Redeemed had been rescued and was secured tightly in the safety of her clutches.

Crizichial turned slowly to Domaren with a rare grin of his own and shared in what Domaren assumed was a mutual admiration for Brikana's actions and her enjoyment of resolving a scene, when not causing one.

The Redeemed guards shouted with joy and thrust their fists and spears into the air, though their reaction was not as lively as Domaren thought it could be. He assumed their newfound respect for gravity and the modest path beneath their feet had stymied their exuberance.

Brikana flew straight ahead for only a moment more, parallel to the cliff path, before swooping up and onto a large landing. From Domaren's standpoint, the roughly fissured opening looked to be the entrance to the half of Ba Glech on the Redeemed side of the gap, no doubt created when the Kihdai tore the area in half. Amid subsequent cheers and exclamations, the group shuffled along quicker than before the Redeemed fell, yet closer to the cliff wall. Some turned and faced the cliff as they continued, their palms and bellies scraping against the rock as they shuffled to the side deliberately.

Domaren focused on the landing where Brikana had landed and watched her transform back into her human form. The rescued Redeemed rested at her feet and propped himself up on his elbows before holding up his hand to acknowledge his friends. They bellowed in collective approval once again, and one by one, the group reached the end of the path and hopped down onto the landing. The Redeemed headed straight for their friend. Almost every one first slapped Brikana on her back or shoulder and thanked her before smothering their friend in relief and congratulations.

As Brikana stepped back from the group of relieved Redeemed, Domaren approached. She bent over casually and swung back up before taking a massive breath and releasing it.

"I didn't think you were going to be able to catch up," Domaren said.

"Mm," Brikana grunted. "Neither did I, to be honest. He had a decent head start."

"Well, that was impressive, Kana," Domaren said. "That should get you a bit of capital with the Redeemed, too."

"Perfect," she said. "Maybe they'll make my own dragon-sized hole in the ground or something."

Domaren grinned as Brikana added a sly wink.

"I'm glad you're okay," he added. Brikana nodded.

# Eight

Crizichial and another Redeemed slipped their arms under their friend and helped him up. He tapped his feet and stretched, and nodded at his friends, appearing to give the indication he was no worse for the wear. And while the Redeemed finished confirming their friend was okay, Domaren scanned the cavity in the cliff ahead of him as Crizichial approached.

"I assume this is our destination," Domaren said to his friend.

"Yes," Crizichial answered. "Our half of Ba Glech. Our only lingering tie to what we *used* to be."

Crizichial's words spit and bit into the air as he confirmed, surprising Domaren with his display of noticeable emotion and contempt.

"I would have the whole of it caved in if it were up to me," he added, "but like others, I understand the importance of preserving history, especially that which is... less than pleasant."

What struck Domaren first was the overwhelming

brightness of the large cavern ahead. The interior of the cave predominantly consisted of red sandstone and orange rhyolite which, due to the high silica content and glassy appearance, reflected light like a thin curtain of stars and shimmering sand stretched across the rock. Two lava flows provided large vertical beams of brightness, in addition to countless glowing boulders with exposed flames that scratched their way out through cracks and seams within the rock. In addition to natural light and flame, braziers of chiseled stone dotted the floor and gaudy sconces lined the walls of the natural hall. The varied shades of fire flashed and throbbed against the cave's floor and ceiling, creating the impression that traversing the cave was similar to living within the spirit of fire itself.

Drawing an additional contrast to the dark and damp facility above ground—which Domaren had attributed with the Redeemed for centuries—was the scale of the sprawling underground complex. It was some eight stories tall, about twice that wide, and stretched forward to such a distance that its full extent couldn't be determined.

As Brikana stepped forward into Domaren's line of sight, the accompanying Redeemed shuffled up from behind and rejoined the party. Brikana looked back at the other two godknights.

"Maphikim is in *here?*" Brikana asked, pointing at the cave.

"Yes," Crizichial answered.

Brikana turned back towards the cave with her hands on her hips before sniffing and huffing a breath out through her nose.

"Is seeing him really necessary?" Brikana asked.

Her question stirred Domaren's unease. He rubbed his eyes and leaned towards Crizichial.

"Have you not spoken with him since I contacted you? Since I reported the oddities with our grove stones?" Domaren asked.

"No," Crizichial replied. "I do not have occasion to interact with our proxy very often."

"Right," Domaren said. "It's the same with me and our proxy."

Domaren glanced back and forth between Brikana and the cave. His mind raced with decisions and indecision. Concocted scenes of destruction at the Grove trickled into his mind. The thought of becoming increasingly weaker and more worthless pinched at his pulse and stabbed at his nerves. With something not quite resembling a nod, his head bounced quickly but shallowly.

"All right, let's go," he said, as he exchanged glances with Crizichial and Brikana. "Let's meet with Maphikim and see if he has anything that may help us, and if not, we'll press on and check in with the rest of the knights. Okay?"

"Agreed," Crizichial said.

Brikana nodded.

"Sure."

"Okay," Domaren said. "Criz? If you would, lead the way."

He nodded slowly and looked over his shoulder to the other Redeemed. "Follow us," he said.

* * *

The group made their way off the wide ledge and passed under the shadow of the imposing cavern threshold. Brikana's head tilted back and forth as if trying to see something or decide how she felt about something.

"How far is it?" Brikana asked. "How far back?"

Crizichial met her with a cutting glance. But before Brikana could take him to task, he rolled his eyes and answered her.

"The full length of our half of the chamber is about twice what you can see from here," he said. He slowly lifted an arm and extended a long and emaciated finger. "If you look far ahead, you will notice a series of wide columns. Do you see?"

"Yes," Brikana answered immediately. Domaren said nothing as they continued walking.

"Those columns mark roughly the last third of the portion of the chamber we are currently in."

"And Maphikim is in the second half?" Domaren confirmed.

"Correct."

"I'm still puzzled as to why he would choose to live down here, way back there," Brikana said.

Crizichial huffed out sharply.

"Have I not explained it enough, Brikana?" Crizichial huffed in exasperation.

"You know what, just forget—"

"It is about penance. It is about remembering. It is about showing respect and gratitude for being made a Redeemed and being given the honor of being championed and defended by a godknight."

"Yes, you can stop repeating yourself, Crizichial," Brikana said. "You all can do whatever you want of course. I'm just curious why someone would choose to remain down here when there are plenty of options to show gratitude or remorse."

"Thank you for allowing us to do whatever we want," Crizichial said. "How kind of you. There are of course plenty that live in comfortable quarters, but some do choose to show their penance in these ways."

While Brikana and Crizichial continued picking at one another, Domaren examined the sprawling walls. As the group walked farther into the cave the chiseled and cleaned rock strata were devoid of features. Instead, as Crizichial had alluded to, sweeping sections of the primordial stone had been removed over time. At the base of each rock wall, Domaren noticed large piles of broken rock, pebbles, and dust, left from when the past carvings had been erased from the stone. As the knights and Redeemed continued their march, there was practically no stretch of clean or uncluttered ground. Whether the remnants were left behind in a hurry, or forgotten as an afterthought, Domaren couldn't determine.

The floor of the corridor was largely clear of obstruction, whether artificial or natural, and the support columns leading to the interior chambers were still ahead. But like the walls, the floors had also undergone a literal scrubbing of sorts. Where the floors had been scraped or scratched away, Domaren made out slivers of paintings and mosaics, though no portion of either was left intact enough such that Domaren could identify specific depictions.

"What happened when the Redeemed were forgiven, Crizichial?" Brikana asked.

There was no immediate answer which prompted Domaren to look back. He caught Crizichial's vexed glare.

"Quite a lot," Crizichial replied. "Can you be more specific?"

"Well, I was wondering what it was like internally, between the demons. Was it a clean break between everyone? Were all the demons who were forgiven and identified as Redeemed completely on board with the split? Were any good demons left behind in Ba Glech? Those kinds of things."

"Yes, it has been regarded all these years as a distinct split," Crizichial said. "The line between ideologies and choices was mostly drawn before the events of Wrathlore helped solidify it."

"That's right," Domaren added. "The disparate factions were identified early on in Wrathlore. There were some differing motivations, but those who eventually became the Redeemed were unified in leaving their world of perpetual darkness and evil behind."

"Differing motivations?" Brikana asked.

"Some wanted to leave for altruistic reasons, and those were mostly demons who were transformed, rather than natural demons." Crizichial replied. "Some were natural demons that helped the Kihdai due to epiphanies of morality, and others felt wronged by being condemned to a demonic existence to begin with, and felt as though they never should have had to experience it."

One of the escorting Redeemed let his curiosity get the better of him.

"What kind of demon were you originally, Knight Crizichial?"

Another escort scowled at the curious demon.

"Do you not know even the most basic of things about our godknight?" The admonishing guard said. As he corrected his subordinate, he flung and shoved his spear hand in animated annoyance. "Crizichial was, well, is, a natural demon. That's why I'm so honored to serve alongside him... a born and bread demon helping do the good work in the world. The work of the Kihdai."

"Now, now," Crizichial said, holding up a calming hand. "We all must remember that there are many throughout the world, of all races, who have far fewer years than others. Do not chastise one for their age, alone."

"Of course Knight Crizichial, of course," the senior guard said.

"So then," Brikana resumed, "what about the others?"

"Others?" Domaren asked.

"The ones who weren't chosen to be the Redeemed?"

"Other than the obvious you mean?" Domaren said.

"Well, of course, refusing to support the Kihdai," she said. "But what were *their* motivations? What was in it for *them?* Why hold onto that life?"

"Oh, that is a much more complicated answer," Crizichial answered.

"Oh, I'm under no illusion that it isn't," Brikana said.

Domaren looked back at Crizichial in curiosity. While he had his own thoughts and opinions on the primary reasons some demons resisted the Kihdai, he was more interested in hearing Crizichial's thoughts, than sharing his own.

"I believe the primary reason many did not relinquish their ways, is because to some—and this philosophy is not unique to demons—but to some, changing or evolving to anything different than one's original or current state, is to somehow become lesser. Changing at all, to any degree, on any given matter, is somehow abhorrent. Those demons who still dwell in Ba Glech hold to the ideal that their original, natural state and mindset is the perfect one. The right one. Deviating is wrong. Their power, magic, practices, and actions only serve them by way of their original means to their original ends. It never occurs to them that tormenting others and bringing painful life to the most vicious of nightmares, and executing despair on a level known only to the most horrific imaginations, might be a path of destruction or negativity. It is not right or wrong. It is original. And since that life is their original life, it is the only truth."

The group fell silent for a few moments, with only the sound of shuffling scrapes and kicked gravel to accompany their thoughts.

"I understand the philosophy of it," Brikana said softly. "But I don't understand the refusal to consider alternatives."

Domaren hummed a quick note of acknowledgment.

"That's exactly it," he said over his shoulder. "When the business of causing grief to others is ingrained to the point of being your reason for living, then the prospect of peace and goodness rots away like the peace of those who are tormented."

Domaren turned a touch more to catch Crizichial's eyes. The Redeemed knight took a moment before acknowledging him. Finally, Crizichial shifted his eyes and nodded slowly. There was no upturn to the corners of Crizichial's mouth, nor blinking or twinkling of his eye. Indeed, Domaren took the nod not as a note of satisfaction between themselves, but rather, a shared acknowledgment of the world's lingering shadows and the malevolence that dwells within everything.

After Crizichial and Domaren shared in their silent acknowledgment, Brikana's curiosity persisted to the next logical line of questioning.

"So, most of the forsaken demons were natural-born, and you say that most were unrelenting in their consideration of a different existence."

Crizichial met Brikana's continuation with silence.

"So, what was it for you then?" Brikana asked.

"What was what?" Crizichial replied.

"What was it that made you want to switch? What

made you want to change? Evolve?"

A new silence took over the conversation and was once more overtaken by the group's footsteps. While Domaren assumed Crizichial was taking his time with selecting the exact words he wanted to reply with, he didn't feel compelled to turn around and judge his friend's response speed this time.

The godknights and their escort stepped deeper into the underground cavity and closer to the massive stone columns that peppered the expanse ahead. As the entrance slipped farther and farther behind them, Domaren watched the distracting piles of rock dust and debris slowly decrease. With each dozen paces, the portions of intact etchings on the wall increased gradually in conjunction with the the decreasing debris. So too, the paintings and mosaics on the floor appeared less and less disturbed. Though no clear shapes or images could be made out just yet, it was clear the process of erasing the past had not been completed as they penetrated farther into the underground complex.

Though the floor of the cave was mostly clear of clutter—other than the rock dust at the base of the walls—signs of the space's hellish past crept back into sight. Forgotten or left behind iron fixtures dangled loosely from rusted anchors. Cracked segments of bars and brackets laid in various spots as if dropped or abandoned. It was as if the newly forgiven demons rushed, or were rushed, to hurriedly vacate the cavern before the land was ripped in two by the Kihdai.

The initial signs of worked metal consisted of hammered rivets and portions of braces. Strips and squares of larger items appeared more frequently as they walked. And as they finally crossed into the area supported by the sea of columns, even more intact hints of the old unified demonic culture took shape.

Where the ground had been scratched away to bare stone at the entrance and approach to the columns, there now appeared more frequent and unharmed patches of crimson, amber, and gold. The paints seeped into larger sections of undisturbed mosaics while sections of the tiled floor became more common and unified. With each step, the group was able to identify what appeared to be parts of characters, portions of the chambers, as well as tools, implements, and devices made of steel.

As the decorated floor revealed more of its original past, so too did the walls and columns. The walls, increasingly obscured by the columns and stretching out and away from the larger columned area, the group could still make out that their colors and carvings increasingly remained intact. The columns revealed hints at the types of designs and adornments that most likely carried out to the now-distant walls.

Farther the group walked. The countless columns surrounded the travelers and seemingly circled in behind them as they weaved through the stone structures toward the front. The tiled ground unfolded larger sections of the past with more complete glimpses into scenes of flame, beings, and creatures. Horns popped out above cracks or on sections of tile. Arms extended out from sections of stone that had been chipped away. Contorted faces of men, dwarves, dragons, and other races, stretched about in anguished despair. The nagging emptiness of abandoned hope took shape as the group passed undisturbed sections of the demonic lair.

Almost from the onset of the complex of columns, the towering stone pillars displayed far more complete paintings and engravings than the floor and walls.

Carved depictions of the world of the damned, and those condemned to it or made to suffer by it, adorned each column. Column after column showed demons stalking what appeared to them as souls of the living on the surface of the world. From casting magic and evoking rituals to aid in their unseen travel about the world, to the capture of spirits and consumption of living flesh, the stone pillars showed how the demons haunted and hunted. Together with the acts of physical pain, the carvings also included scenes of demons festering in the thoughts and nightmares of those who dwell aboveground—all representations of the ruthless horror demons inflict upon the living, detailed with sadistic precision.

"Again," Crizichial said softly to the group, "I would beg your forgiveness. These horrific scenes are as repugnant and foreign to you as they are to the Redeemed of today. This has been true going back to almost the day the Redeemed were forgiven."

"But, here they still are," Brikana grumbled.

"Kana," Domaren said in a hurry. He shot her a stern glance before turning to Crizichial. "Why has no one ever finished getting rid of all of this?" Domaren asked.

"Well, as you saw in the earlier sections of the chamber, there was an attempt to do just that," Crizichial said. "But soon after, guidance was given to abandon the area entirely, to reject everything this complex represented and turn our backs on what transpired here. And that of course leads us to where we are now, with the proxy returning to this area as a gesture of penance on behalf of the past—to memorialize those who were made to experience such pain here, and to remember that we can never return to this life in the future."

Brikana let a grunt slip, which sounded to Domaren

like a poorly suppressed sound of doubt. He braced for her subsequent comment.

"Seeing that the proxy hosts visitors from here, and plans to for the foreseeable future, I assume," she began, "perhaps it would be a worthy endeavor to resume the effort to remove these sick reminders of what you used to be from these chambers of prior deviance."

Domaren turned to scold Brikana once again, for instigating the verbal scuffle, but was distracted by Crizichial stomping to a stop.

"If you have something to say, dragon knight, I invite you to say it now," Crizichial challenged politely. "That is of course if it is not something you have alluded to and bothered me with countless times before."

Brikana approached Crizichial as her sparring partner spoke. She stepped slowly as a grin of agitation slowly expanded under a weighted glare of contempt.

"The other Redeemed and I have nothing to explain to you, and we have not had anything to prove to you since the Kihdai bestowed their grace upon us. As I have advised you before, Brikana, their judgment and actions should be more than enough for you."

"No, no," Brikana replied. "I have no desire to quarrel with you over the past. You and I have had our disagreements about the motives and future intentions of the Redeemed, yes, but strolling the halls of your half of Ba Glech, down here with the remaining vestiges, and well-maintained vestiges I might add, of what the Redeemed used to be a part of, compels me to take a moment of pause."

"Your pause is wasting ti—" Crizichial attempted.

"And seeing these *depictions* persist all around us, centuries after being forgiven, and despite your considerate attempt to anticipate our disgust, makes me wonder exactly how far removed from those old ways any of you really are."

As Brikana rattled off her doubt and insult, Crizichial closed the bit of distance between them. The Redeemed godknight's skin began to mold and tear, but only slightly. He replied immediately as his voice dropped into a thick rasp, dank and demented. The dense tone coated the air like a wealth of salt on a flayed enemy.

"How dare you even consider that your words might be said without consequence. We fought for the Kihdai. We fought on their side during Wrathlore. Where were you? You weren't even in the world yet."

Seizing the first opportunity to interject since the old argument was rekindled, Domaren sought an end to the quarrel.

"Brikana, Crizichial, stop this immediately. We do not have time for this bickering. At some point you both must find a way to end this baseless rivalry and tiresome squabble over ancient acts and second guessing of the Kihdai, but it is not now. Can we please press on?"

Crizichial and Brikana maintained locked eyes for a quiet moment but Crizichial's skin soon returned to its normal grey and clear complexion. Brikana's chest heaved with a hefty breath she let out as she turned back. Domaren resumed their march through the former segment of Ba Glech.

As the group resumed their march, weaving through and in between columns, no words were spoken for some time. There were no breaths or huffs, sighs, or any otherwise antagonistic sounds. Domaren found some relief in knowing that if there was any remaining hostility from the last discussion, it was being kept down under the sounds of footfalls, shuffling of armor and weapons, and the accompanying echoes throughout the chamber.

The complex of pillars continued long after the argument ended, and though Domaren made note of the increasingly complete mosaics on the ground and additional scenes on the columns, he worried a new argument could burst out at any moment. And as the work of the old demons pierced Domaren's thoughts with each passing mosaic and stone carving, he might have understood if it had.

Each carving chiseled into the stone pillars represented a method of inflicting pain, horror, and trauma. Below them, immortalized in each mosaic, colorful scenes represented the outcomes and accomplishments of their inflicted pain. Everything surrounding the group as they worked to reach the proxy, was a celebration of the worst of life, the best of death, and everything that brought either to fruition.

Column after column depicted what some might consider as the most tame methods of torture. Those means which superficially harmed or mocked the physical body. From the top to bottom of each giant pillar, were at least a dozen ringed sections, each roughly two feet in height, separated by ornate borders consisting of symbols and geometric designs. Within each ring was a series of images, similar to instructions, showing how a particular implement of torture was used.

Any imaginable manner of tool seemed to be depicted. From those that tore at the hair and scalp of a human, to those that separated or broke the bones of the living. Some scenes showed demons with tools specializing in the removal of parts of the human body, procedures that would not necessarily result in the death of a person. Related scenes showed organs and bones being removed and then put back, but only after the wound had healed. Some of the pillar sections showed this process being repeated to the same person in perpetuity. To amuse the demons.

Additional pillars showed what could be done to the other creatures of the worlds. In some scenes, dragons had their wings torn in half, sometimes length-ways, sometimes top to bottom. Other dragons were shown having their wings ripped off entirely. Additional scenes showed the demons removing the fire-producing organs from a dragon to be kept as trophies. In other depictions, dragons or members of the other races had their organs of reproduction mutilated, torn, injured, or ripped away in a number of ways.

A particularly rust-stained pillar caught Domaren's weary eye at one point, drawing him and his curiosity closer as they walked. As he grew nearer, he noticed rings hammered into the stone. Strung lengths of chain looped through them with iron shackles at each end. After closing to within a few feet, Domaren looked past the chains and to the stone carvings. In this pillar's rings, scenes showed victims chained up to the pillar as if being forced to hug it. Gradually, the chains were pulled to such an extreme that, depending on the type of race being chained up, their extremities would break. They might suffer internal injuries, and judging by some of the scenes, they would be pulled so tight, their chest cavity could collapse, causing fatal internal injury, should the demons of the time allow them to succumb.

Fire was a predominant factor in many sets of torture instructions. Dwarves' beards were set on fire. Or, over the course of multiple engravings, one could see a dwarf burning slowly between many separate engravings. Others were burned quickly and at a greater intensity over the course of only a few scenes. Seavers had their skin blistered and charred. Some beings of the world were fully immolated, often to be doused, saved and healed, only to be immolated again.

These were the most tame methods of torture. The scenes and practices depicted on the subsequent pillars were more abstract, though the means and end for each could still easily be determined.

In almost every frame of this new series of pictures, the target often stood apart from the other objects, beings, or action going on in the rest of the scene. Whether it was a dragon flying high in the sky looking down upon their family or village, a human sleeping in their bed, or a dwarf traversing a mountain ridge, they were separate. Far off by themselves, the victim was made to dream about or witness events unfolding in their mind, affecting them as individuals, or those whom the victim cherished.

Some victims, trapped within their own thoughts and souls, wallowed in the searing flames of inescapable nightmares, consisting of their most peace-killing thoughts and fears. Demons feasted upon dragon eggs, children, and other offspring of various races while their parents were made to watch. Again, with no way for the victim to escape the scene the demon had placed in their mind.

In some scenes, the victim appeared to wake up from the nightmare, crumble into tear-laden hysterics, only to be forced into another nightmare. Yet this time, they were allowed to recall just enough from the previous time to be driven mad at the prospect of having to see it again, but not the entire memory to prevent them from becoming numb to the shock of the sickening illusion.

In other scenes, victims were made to have a distant window into how their widows or widowers were haunted and taunted by what they thought were frequent visitations from their departed loved ones. A demon would appear to their surviving loved one and violate and feed upon the lingering trust and bond of their real relationships. The surviving kin or friend would at first find comfort in the hauntings. Eventually, the demon violated and betrayed their love and confidence.

All while the departed victim was made to witness it, the demon appeared more and more frequently, causing the old relationship to twist and devolve into a demented dependency. The demons warped the minds of the living. Their memories of the torture victim contorted into false scenes of contrived resentment and hateful encounters that never happened. The priests and healers of the living could sometimes discover and drive a demon out of such situations, but most times, the living endured endless suffering and were forever maddened into a such a state that happiness would forever elude them.

The mosaics along the ground celebrated the results of demonic torture, haunting, and possession. Many scenes consisted of tiles of few colors. These were smaller, but more frequent, and often showed large masses of people and creatures in collective pain and anguish. They were packed tightly together, humans, dragons, dwarves, seavers, and more. Some were shown being plucked out of the massive throng by the head, by a particularly large and tall demon, only to be thrown a far distance into a pool of magma. Others were impaled or stabbed by massive stalagmites broken from the cave floor, by spears, or in some cases, by appendages of some demons that resembled a stinger at the end of a tail.

But reserved for larger sections, dedicated to a single scene, were mosaics made of many more tiles and a spectrum of color. These grand panels were noticeably more important due to their intricacy and detail. Where the other mosaics were smaller and more common, showing general depictions of arbitrary victim selection and pain, these more prominent pieces involved only a few figures, sometimes labeled within the mosaic, and showed their involvement with events from the world's history. As the group continued to walk, Domaren recognized many of the figures and events and assumed the mosaics were intended to celebrate the former demons' influence over the person's or creature's actions, and the subsequent results of that influence.

A mosaic Domaren found especially disturbing was one that seemed to depict the actions of dwarf King Alberich. The legend told above ground of King Alberich is one heavily influenced by his rumored paranoia. And while paranoia typically has a negative connotation, King Alberich's paranoia was derived entirely from an immense concern for the safety of his people, and led to extreme acts of defense. There are some who would argue his acts were motivated by greed, but the predominant consensus of King Alberich's contemporaries is that he was driven by an obsessive desire to protect his wife, his family, and the lives of his fellow dwarves.

King Alberich was an accomplished and respected general who unified numerous clans of dwarves against a separate culture of raiding dwarves. Year after year the two sides fought and accumulated substantial casualties on both sides. Generations came and went knowing nothing but war and made no real progress towards a resolution to hostilities or hope for peace.

Late in King Alberich's natural life, he caught advance word of a planned attack upon his mountain city by the raiding Culloch clan. Weary of war and senile after decades of obsessive planning and strategy extrapolation, Alberich issued a flurry of commands to his commanders and lieutenants, instructing them to defend their city at all costs. His orders were dispatched via numerous couriers amid a torrent of chaotic hysteria. No one dwarf was privy to the scope of the king's entire plan. While none of King Alberich's individual subordinates knew the extent to which the king was closing off tunnels and passes, the few captains who voiced concerns were dismissed immediately.

One by one, Alberich ordered his men to block or cave in all paths leading to or from the center of their protected city. He'd had enough of war, enough of destruction, and enough death coming to his people, so in a stroke of irrational madness, Alberich entombed himself and his people inside the mountain.

The mosaic that referenced this event was thoroughly faithful, at least as far as Domaren could tell as he slowly stepped his ten wide paces over it. The only detail he had not expected to see, was that of a grotesque and prominent demon at Alberich's shoulder for each of the dwarf king's major decisions.

A bulbous, hunched figure of black and bruised sores followed Alberich closely in every frame on the mosaic. It walked on two legs and was roughly twice as tall as the dwarf king. It was in no way a symmetrical being, and lacked any hint of order and beauty usually found in nature. And while it had what appeared to be two arms that dangled to its front and right side, they hung loosely as if having no ties to the creature's thoughts, or at least had no muscle capable of moving the arms.

What did have movement however, were dozens and dozens of crooked and wispy appendages that popped out from the creature. They stretched out like pesky vines carried by the wind and encouraged by the sun, only to land on and wrap around their victim up like a young tree being consumed by intrusive weeds. Over time, the demon's dark feelers, these demented growths, steered their target towards dark destinations unbeknown to the pitiful captive.

# Nine

Following the mosaic showing the tragedy of King Alberich came a striking sequence painted mostly in verdant greens and hues of primordial stone and slate. Immediately evoking the steep and sharp cliffs of Tricca, the first frames of the mosaic depicted the moss-covered tops of the city's approach before it descended and switched back to and fro. The path cut into the rocks with precarious zig-zag patterns, down to the city's fortified and cavernous entrance. Standing at the top of the path working her way down—by herself initially—was the young seaver princess, Lilynia.

With each frame the young seaver queen progressively traversed down the steep path, following along the walls of sharp rock. Initially, the jagged cliff edges were bone dry as the higher areas received the majority of the day's sun. But as Lilynia descended and grew closer to wild waves and salty froth, the constantly wet rock glistened like black glass.

Bright moss and clumps of weeds triumphed through cracks in the rocks, providing flavor and character to the stone. As if wanting to greet or at least witness each visitor, ledges and cracks flaunted the persistent plants as they poked out in flagrant attempts to be acknowledged and appreciated.

Dry clumps of dead and hollow barnacles played neighbor to the blankets of moss. Appearing rarely and sporadically at first near the top of the path, the mosaic showed them increase in frequency as Lilynia continued. At first, there were few, and then many. The empty and dead casings filled up and showed additional signs of life. Eventually, large patches of moist and living barnacles covered sweeping sections of rock. Their small bubbles worked their way up to the surface before popping and announcing signs of life to the nearby onlooker.

Lilynia stepped farther down with each frame, passing by small, natural ledges, and paying no mind to some of the small hollows and chambers artificially dug out of the stone. Had the art only shown Lilynia, the cliffs, barnacles, and moss, each scene could have appeared almost serene, even mundane. But as one followed the progression of scenes, little by little, an attendant similar to the one in King Alberich's mosaic, played an increasingly involved role.

At first, there was nothing, but slowly through each frame, another demonic mass of blatant filth and raging malignancy took shape. But where Alberich's shadow was large and rotund, the one following Lilynia was tall and emaciated, though it had similar mismatched arms and stringy appendages.

However, soon after the appearance of Lilynia's first evil visitor, an additional shade appeared. And then another. Over the course of some ten frames of Lilynia's mosaic, a comparable number of new demonic attachments joined the panels—aligning faithfully to the majority of the ancient legend.

Lilynia was a jealous youngest sister to two sisters and their oldest brother. She was a resentful daughter of a respected king and queen who were in turn cherished by all seavers. At first, Lilynia suffered from a resentment and jealousy typical to that of any young sibling or spoiled child. The demons, however, ever vigilant and on the lookout for any unfortunate situation or arrangement they can exploit, saw an opportunity in Lilynia. As she grew older, the seaver princess took a daily turn out amongst the moss-covered landings outside the entrance to their cliff-sheltered caves. Every few days, she extended her strolls to the absolute top of the cliffs, before skipping back down.

On her climbs up and out of their rock and sea-locked home, she would dream of a life she would never have. She dreamed of diplomatic orders she would never issue, grand gowns she would never adorn, and rubies and sapphires that would never sparkle in her palm. There would be no political intrigue to the degree her brother and heir to their country would participate in, nor would there be consequential proposals or social excursions on the scale that her second or even third oldest sibling would enjoy.

Each walk up rooted her awareness that she would only continue to be looked down upon. She would be dismissed. An afterthought. The dagger she used to pop barnacles off the rocks before throwing them down into the water below was as common as any mediocre blacksmith's offerings. Except for a modest imprint of her father's seal on the blade, there was nothing special about it, just as there was nothing special about her. And as she made her way back down to her home after each walk, she increasingly thought of what her life would be like without the presence of her family members who held a higher station.

But her thoughts were rarely her own. Her innocent resentment and young jealousy had begun merely as pitiful roots, destined to shrivel and die once seeds of maturity and compassion were sown. But demons are the ironic water, air, and light that see to the prosperity of lesser life. With each of Lilynia's walks, the group of demons, just shy of a dozen, surrounded her and danced around her. One by one they ran up and whispered in her ear before darting back and letting another of their kind sneak up. With each whisper came a new tinge of doubt. A fresh wave of hate. Renewed paranoia. Each day brought new whispers. Each day brought new thoughts. Every walk brewed an ever-growing storm of unfounded rage and contempt.

Her walks and manufactured animosity eventually led to hushed conversations and clandestine meetings where she discussed her concerns with officials and captains within her father's senior ranks. The demonic deceptions fostered and nurtured during her walks provided her with the means to weave grand fictions. Over a period of years, she instilled paranoia and concern into her father's most trusted advisors. She laid the groundwork for schemes that would not only address the false betrayals she had convinced herself were true, but breathe life into her suffocated dreams of power and significance.

One perpetuated lie concerned her father's plans to invade neighbors, whether kin or not, in a grab for power unjustified in motive or capability. Another lie perpetuated whispers of her mother's infidelity and eroding moral bedrock. There was even a story she had concocted and woven throughout their people concerning her siblings being involved in an elaborate plot to assassinate and overthrow their father. Once dead, the rumor said, the sisters planned to install their brother on the throne.

Each story was as false as the others of course, but Lilynia took great care to spin and tend to the tales, each independent of the other. In narrow caves with low ceilings, she arranged to meet her father's captains and nurture rumors of her father's secret plans for invasion. And down where the sand of the city's approach met the rocks, she casually met other informants and let the spray and dense punches of waves conceal the conversations of her evil efforts. Or other times, at the top of the cliffs, she would place notes under stones, or retrieve them, in preparation of the execution of her accursed machinations.

At last, the day came that the demons' work was rewarded. Lilynia set out for a walk as she so frequently did. She blissfully ascended up from the base of the seaver beach, gliding her fingers along the wet rock and smiling at groups of bubbling barnacles. Closer to the top she climbed and into more of the penetrating sun. As she walked, she hummed one of the most beloved seaver folks songs, dating back to the settling of her people in the cliffs and lagoons. She repeated the melody countless times, sometime humming, sometimes singing the words:

*No one can go down below*
*Like the seavers of the old sea stone*
*No one can go*
*No one can go*

*No one can live down below*
*Like the seavers of the old sea stone*
*No one can live*
*No one can live*

*Wrathlore I*

*No one can rule down below*
*Like the seavers of the old sea stone*
*No one can rule*
*No one can rule*

After hours of carefree skipping amongst the dandelions and waving to bees and finches, she turned back towards home. She stepped onto the path for her return tip, immortalized in the demonic mosaic Domaren now found himself staring at. The emerald grass gave way to rock outcroppings, and then, instead of dandelions, moss and barnacles. Farther down the mosaic showed her walk past the caves and homes cut into the cliffs.

One by one the demons joined her.

But this time, rather than subtly whispering suggestions into her mind, they reassured her. They congratulated her.

Towards the bottom of the trail's end, next to a portion of rock wall with a particularly wide path, was a section of flat stone reserved for the punishment of criminals and thieves. Whether convicted of assault upon another seaver, or after being caught stealing food from a merchant, those miscreants of seaver society would often be chained up in punishment. For hours or days, they would be left strapped to the stone and made to suffer the elements without food or water.

And on that day when Lilynia returned, she saw her father, mother, and siblings condemned to the wall.

While on her daily walk, those with whom Lilynia conspired, captured her family and led them up to the narrow stone ledges. There, they were not only shackled in cuffs and collars of rusty iron, but they were also nailed and anchored to the stone. They were not there to be temporarily punished. They were to stay and suffer there, exposed to the frequent lapping of salty spray and punishing sun until dead.

Her father, mother, and siblings cried out in desperate confusion, pleading for Lilynia to help them. As their daughter and sister approached, they rattled about with wild assumptions as to what had caused this horrific fate to befall them. But only when Lilynia passed without comment or reaction did the shock and deceitful betrayal finally register. Their hearts hollowed with a cold throb of despair.

She had been the cause of their demise without any legitimate guess as to why she had done it. But it was of no consequence to anyone any longer. To the seaver people, and thanks to her fabrications, Lilynia's family was a hive of deceit and warmongering. She had done their people a service by putting the greater good before her family. Lilynia had purged the country of its disease.

And now, she would be queen.

"Crizichial?" Domaren asked softly.

The Redeemed godknight walked over and joined Domaren in looking downward.

Crizichial sighed as Brikana joined them.

"Yes, the twisting of Alberich back there, and Lilynia's manipulation here," Crizichial said.

Domaren lifted his head and looked forward, noticing additional mosaics for at least hundreds of more steps. He brought his focus back to Lilynia's story.

"I knew the demons influenced Alberich, but I didn't realize they had anything to do with Lilynia," Domaren said.

Brikana sauntered casually ahead.

"I don't see dragons in any of these," she said.Her voice was strong with confidence and pride.

"Oh, there are plenty," Crizichial said. "But unfortunately, there is plenty of evil done by all races without any assistance from the demons."

"Assistance? That's what you call it?"

"You know what I mean."

"How much farther until we reach Maphikim?" Domaren asked, hoping to prevent another biting argument.

Crizichial held Brikana's gaze for a moment before relenting.

"Once we pass through here, the Gallery of Memory, we need to go through the Hall of Patience, and then finally, the Nebulum."

Brikana scoffed and stuck out her arms, gesturing at the mosaics.

"You call this the Gallery of Memory?" She asked. Each word of her question grew thicker with fluctuating indignation. "How can you glorify this place?"

"How many times must I say that this is the ancient dwelling of a segment of our culture that no longer exists!"

"Then get rid of it, Crizichial!"

"It is not my place to do so, and any energy spent on this place is in my estimation, a waste!"

"Whose place is it?" Brikana fired back in a sharp whisper.

"If it is to be anyone's, it is probably Maphikim's. But frankly, I am tempted not to say or suggest anything else. We owe nothing to you or any race. The fact that we were forgiven by the Kihdai should be more than enough for you, Brikana."

An uneasy pause lingered between them.

"Well maybe I'll ask Maphikim about it anyway."

"Great, okay," Domaren said turning forward. "Let's

go see him and get this over with already."

Brikana squinted at Crizichial in disgust and shoved off to fall in behind Domaren.

Once the group resumed their trek to Maphikim, Domaren and the others traipsed over countless more mosaics. And as Crizichial alluded, scenes showing the corruption of dragons appeared quickly, and seemed to be just as frequent as the others.

Columns covered in sadistic torture techniques persisted as they walked. Mosaics, one after another, showed additional triumphs of the ancient demon generations. Human murderers. Seaver thieves. Dwarf extortionists. And yes, disturbing depictions of the world's harshest stories involving dragons.

A particularly wretched moment in dragon history appeared in the path of mosaics. Domaren saw it before anyone else did, and attempted to distract Brikana with gestures and rushed questions about her last engagement with the Grove.

The frames in question started out simply enough. The early days of Kimozoa were represented with new, grand construction. The sun shone vibrantly in every scene and where the land was not smothered in luscious forests and fields of farms and flowers, it was packed with stacks of wood and stone. Dragons peppered the sky and populated the busy thoroughfares. Also showing in the scenes, were thousands of human laborers, hired to assist in the construction of the city.

By all accounts, and throughout history, the amount of coin, gold, and other resources attributed with the dragons is extreme at practically any given moment in time. But contrary to various slander and lies from adversaries with a host of nefarious motives, the majority of dragon wealth has been accumulated by trade and treaties of protection. Various dragon broods were often hired out by the other races to provide protection to cities. Dragons are also keen negotiators in regards to sales of land and goods created by dragons themselves.

But grotesque greed can befall all, regardless of how much a society or an individual has. The mosaic now at the feet of the group reflected that, but greed was the least egregious tale captured in the mosaic.

An ambitious dragon named Parzidon had grown up mostly alone. While still a hatchling, Parzidon's father was killed in an internal dragon war. His mother died from disease only two years later. At a very young age, Parzidon found himself with too much money, too much time, and too little capacity for morality.

The demons latched on, and not just onto Parzidon.

Towards the end of the initial phases of Kimozoa's construction, Parzidon settled there. He brought with him a solid reputation for business as well as a respectable reputation for organizing and leading labor, whether dragons, humans, or others. He soon entered into agreements to provide human workers for much of the more intricate stone work, but very quickly, Parzidon began exhibiting curious behaviors for a dragon in his position.

Dragons had and have friendships and engagements with those of other races just as well as they do with members of their own race. There are of course disagreements, feuds, and even wars between dragons and other races, but there have been generations upon generations of peaceful and compassionate neighbors. They have shared in intellectual and civil achievements. They have thought together as well as fought together.

But the relationships Parzidon nurtured during

his time in Kimozoa made others uneasy. He spent an inordinate amount of time with the laborers he employed, flirting frequently with fraternization. It was reported that he would not only act casually with them as they worked, telling jokes and taking away from their progress on work, but would also spend time in social engagements with his employees.

Night after night, Parzidon led throngs of his employees to the massive social halls where dragons would drink. He invited them to drink and feast and would pay their bills. He gave preferential treatment and attention to those he spent time with, and would frequently dismiss better ideas or suggestions on how to accomplish their work, in lieu of those he spent time with outside their work. There seemed to be no meaningful explanation as to what drove their peculiar actions. But eventually, the reasoning would become clear.

Construction on the first iteration of Kimozoa had recently been completed. Weeks-long celebrations were held to commemorate the birth of the new city, its traditional beauty, as well as the overall majesty of dragon culture. But the revelry eventually ended. The visitors went home. The laborers moved onto projects in other cities. Large populations of dragons returned home to other cities, or followed work elsewhere as well.

It was then that the mobs of human hunters descended upon the new city and its inhabitants.

With streams of dawn's burned orange and bright plums rippling through the sky, legions of greedy and bloodthirsty men streamed through the city. The moments before the day's sun appeared were suddenly filled with the shrieks and guttural screams of dragons being attacked. When the whooping and screaming of men carrying out their coordinated attacks were no longer heard, sloppy slashes of deathblows were. And if the attackers couldn't land deathblows immediately, dragons scorched the early hours of the day with nauseating screams to match the terrors of having their wings slit, cut, and cut off.

Men, like any other race of the world, have the capacity for intelligence, strategy, and guile. But these attacks were more than the results of myopic greed after months of planning. This was more than alliances between disparate cultures of humans. This had the influence, suggestion, and inspiration from demons. And the fruits of their labors were depicted in the mosaic Domaren was desperately trying to keep from Brikana's eyes.

Domaren reviewed the remaining frames. Their violent chaos depicted men swarming structures and lighting structures on fire. Most men had spears and torches. Others wheeled about large bolt throwing devices that spun on bases so that their projectiles could be aimed. And only towards the end of the series, could Parzidon be seen celebrating in the streets with the hunters. The traitor dragon and dregs of humanity conspired to hunt and kill dragons that morning for profit, to teach the dragons a lesson in humility which was, more than likely, somehow conceived and encouraged by the demons. Regardless, the dastardly slaughter was championed by the humans and was sickeningly relished for mere sport. The few dragon carcasses that weren't loaded onto specially made carts were left to rot and clutter the streets of the dragon's new city.

Distracted by a sharp gasp, Domaren realized he had let his focus on distracting Brikana falter. As he lifted his head up from the final frame, Brikana erupted in a deafening fury.

"What is this? Is that supposed to... Is that Parzidon I

see?"

Before anyone could respond, Brikana swelled in size to within feet of the cave ceiling. Her tail unfurled and her muscles rippled into definition. The Black Dragon's throat began to glow.

"Brikana! Don't!" Domaren pleaded.

"The demons were involved with Parzidon's treachery? How else would you expect me to react?"

Her voice punched at the cave walls and reverberated back towards the group in a ripple of roaring echo.

"We don't have time for this," Domaren said sternly, slowly putting himself between Brikana and Crizichial. "And we definitely can't waste energy on this."

"They should have never been forgiven, and they definitely should not have a godknight of their own, Domaren. How can you defend these things when they won't even destroy these depictions they created to celebrate their evil?"

"There are things here showing the iniquity in us all, Kana!" Domaren shouted back, hoping to snap her out of her blind rage. "And as Crizichial has now reminded us numerous times, these are remnants. Reminders of what they once were. Not what they are now!"

Brikana's glowing throat maintained its color and temperature. Her whole body throbbed with seething hatred. Domaren continued, hoping to capitalize on her silence.

"And if you're going to judge Crizichial for the actions of these past demons, then you might as well hold me accountable for what the humans did."

"That isn't the same and you know it," Brikana roared back. "The demons manipulated your people, as well as Parzidon."

Domaren turned to Crizichial immediately.

"Were you involved with that deception, Crizichial?"

Crizichial, having maintained his composure from the onset of Brikana's fit of rage, looked up at Brikana, and then back to Domaren. The Redeemed godknight slowly shook his head.

"Do you see that? He had nothing to do with it. Now please, calm yourself, get back to your human form, and just let us talk with Maphikim. Please."

Domaren let his comment dangle at the edge of insistence, rather than that of a request, and waited on Brikana's response with a cold stare and tightened jaw. A brief silence followed, but Domaren then turned quickly and resumed his march across the path of mosaics. His patience was exhausted.

"Come on, everyone," he blurted. "Let's just get to our destination. No more arguing over or gawking at the past. And that goes for me as well. You coming Brikana?"

He asked his friend if she was coming without even looking at her. She didn't answer, but she did turn back to her human shape before jogging to catch up.

The columned chamber and their accompanying mosaics continued on for many minutes of irritating silence. When Domaren noticed a break in the columns ahead, he broke the silence with a question for Crizichial.

"All right," he said while continuing to walk. "What did you say is next up here? Something about patience?"

"Yes," Crizichial confirmed. "The last chamber before the Nebulum. Where Maphikim resides."

The group maintained their brisk march, following Domaren's lead, but it practically came to a complete stop when they crossed into the Hall of Patience. Their feet kept moving, but only in shuffled inches. With most of their attention on the sights in front of them, they mentally flinched when imagining further horrors of the past.

This new section of the sprawling underground complex vaulted up even higher, and simultaneously, plummeted lower. Only a path that accommodated approximately five redeemed at a time remained at the same height of their previous walking path. On either side below the path, were wide reaching seas of magma. The liquid flame bubbled and gurgled as if proud of its scale and energy. The heat produced by the fire pools floated up and stopped short of making the group turn back from excruciating heat.

"Do we have to walk this whole path? To the end?" Brikana asked. Her question slid upward with hints of what sounded to Domaren like aggravation.

Domaren looked at Crizichial, sharing Brikana's curiosity.

"Yes," Crizichial answered. He avoided making contact and slipped between the others and continued walking.

Brikana shook her head and stepped closer to Domaren.

"This is ridiculous," she said to him softly. "Literally having to take a tour of Ba Glech just to talk to the proxy?"

Domaren nodded in empathy, but tried to encourage patience.

"Maphikim is just at the end here. Let's just get there, speak with him, and move on."

"We don't have time—" Brikana started.

Domaren raised a friendly hand of interruption.

"Yes, I know," he said. "I've been alarmed from the start. If I remember correctly, you dismissed my concern when I originally reached out. Remember? I think your new-found urgency might be somewhat influenced by your distrust of the Redeemed."

Brikana sighed and stepped back in stunned silence. Domaren patted her arm and smiled.

"So, that's what we'll do," he said, beginning to summarize. His smile disappeared as he returned to a focused determination. "We'll speak with Maphikim and stress our need for more information and a new approach on how we should all proceed."

As Domaren continued, the tension in Brikana's face relaxed, even as she looked over and watched Crizichial continue along the path ahead.

"I'm with you," Domaren continued. "I have been uneasy from the onset. We don't need to be squandering time with traipsing through the world... visiting every country or proxy under the sun to solicit nothing but guesses and opinions. We must change course, and soon. I don't know in which direction yet, but we must."

The accompanying Redeemed escort slipped by Domaren and Brikana as they spoke, leaving the pair of knights at the rear of the group. After Domaren noticed Crizichial looking back, seemingly waiting for them to rejoin the group, Domaren patted Brikana's shoulder once again and raised his chin to the path ahead of them.

The magma on each side of the path stretched out to great distances, often meandering into natural recesses or coves. Like the worn ends of old nerves or tips of wilting plants, the magma chamber in the Hall of Patience appeared to have cut and burned its way to impressive extremes that stretched out far beyond its original constraints.

But the full extent and boundary of the magma's perimeter could never be quite determined. At almost every angle, every perspective, or every craning and positioning of one's vision, obstacles prevented a clear line of sight from any viewpoint, to the farthest stretches.

High above the magma and walking path, attached to the ceiling of the cave, were countless cages. Iron cage after cage dangled down at the end of immense lengths of rusty chains. Each one was suspended from the extreme reaches of the top of the caves and hung freely over the large pools of molten magma below.

Beginning in the shadows of the ceiling above, the chains swung down in sweeping swoops where the corresponding opposite ends then ran through massive pulleys. The pulleys were in turn hooked onto huge trunks of wood which laid horizontally and were supported by a constructed column of stone at each end.

These stations of anchored chains stood at the edges of the walking path and occurred at close, regular intervals as the group walked. There was little conversation as they passed the cage anchors. And as Domaren examined each station, he traced the drooping chains from the anchor stations to far up into the ceiling where they disappeared into the darkness, only to wonder which chains controlled which cages.

Had the cages been at the same height throughout the complex, one might not have quickly determined the purpose or function of the room, but there was little imagination necessary.

Each cage seemed to be at a different height. Some rested far above. Some looked to be equidistant from the ceiling and the magma pool below. Others rested just above the magma while others appeared partially submerged. Domaren could tell from his point on the ledge that those cages gently swung free due to their bottom portions being previously consumed by the magma. There were also some cages that had been destroyed entirely, with only the chains they had been attached to remaining.

There was no conversation. No questions. No banter or spiteful arguing.

The silence spoke on everyone's behalf. The quiet revelations conversed with themselves on everyone's behalf. Accompanied by the bubbling and gurgling of the magma, and infrequent creaks and scrapes of the chains and cages, the room told its story better than any discussion or recollection of history would.

This was where suffering was crafted. It was where pain was designed and executed. It was where agony was the goal and time provided an endless fuel to the machine of horror that the former demons operated. But in a moment of stinging realization, Domaren pondered.

*Are the demons over in Ba Glech still doing things like this?*

For ages before the Redeemed were forgiven, those demons fostered despair. The thousands upon thousands of cages held creatures, people, and beings, indefinitely. With no limit to how long the condemned could be held. Lives and souls, flesh and blood, scales and bones, existed in perpetuity in these cages. Domaren reluctantly dipped into his knowledge of history and involuntarily filled in any gaps with the hateful hues of his imagination.

In some of the cages of varying sizes, dragons were caged and held just above the magma. The size of their body in addition to their dragon scales protected them from immediate injury or pain. But after months and sometimes years, the heat would accumulate. It built up and consolidated. It would slowly spread and seep through. Like being suspended over a humble fire meant only to cook a rat, one might not feel anything for the longest time.

But as one log was added, one at a time over the years, the fire would grow. It became more robust and taller. Slowly but steadily, the fire evolved into an overpowering and malicious master that would consume you. These dragons suspended only feet above the magma pool surface would at some point over the inching creep of time be slowly roasted, if not to death, into madness. Little by little their scales would become betraying embers that would initially nip at their skin before the stinging and stabbing started.

Next, the dragon's internal organs would silently scream that the heat had broken through. The beast's pitiful nerves would send their messengers and couriers racing to its brain, begging for relief, pleading for reinforcements. But they would never come. The dragon would scream back that it's trying. It would ramble and rattle off a mental message that help was being conscripted only to immediately know that it was lying to itself.

Instead, the painful invader's siege raged and gained strength. It continued its approach. Unchallenged. Inevitable.

But just when the keep of the dragon's mental and physical fortification was about to fall, the pulleys shook. The chains clanked and rattled up. The cage raised, and the attacking heat abated. The suffering dragon raced towards the shadowed ceiling as demons below heaved down on the attached chains. In a blurry flurry, the magma below fell farther away. The dragon raced up and past other cages and other chains before being doused with falling floods of water dropped or released from the same shadows above by unseen attendants.

The sizzling sounds of crackling steam rang out and reverberated against the cave's rocky interior. The dragon shrieked in exponentially exacerbated pain, having been almost cooked alive, and then rapidly cooled. Sometimes the dragon would lose consciousness. A few succumbed from shock due to the rapid change in temperature. Most however, survived, and lived to go through the entire process all over again. Usually within hours. Sometimes minutes.

Forever.

And yet, there were additional variations on this form of agony. The demons of the times sometimes let loose a chain and dropped them in one fell swoop all the way down into the magma before being immediately pulled out. Some types of creatures survived. Others perished, but using healing skills or demonic magic, their victims were sustained or revived. Every time. There was no escaping the torment. Once a person or beast found its way in the clutches of the forever damned, there was no relief or escape, through death or otherwise. You were at the mercy of those whose primary motivation was to cause you perpetual misery.

The ingredients of the demons' sickening stew went far beyond physical pain however. Causing physical pain was merely one spice in their cupboard. Pain was a delivery system of horror's main dish of memory, reminder, and regret. Indeed, each time the condemned felt their cage shake, the initial fear of being plunged into the lake of fire was immediately followed by recollections of the event, or events, that sealed their fate to the depths of Ba Glech.

Even if it wasn't that particular individual's turn to suffer the magma below, the vibration of other cages falling set off a malignant vibration through their cage's chains, into the rock above, and back down to the others still suspended, waiting. Others watched and listened as the other chains raced through the pulleys. The fast and high pitched release of tension on the distant victim's cage sent a wave of relief through all the others, but then, their relief at being spared for the moment was superseded by an entirely different set of inescapable thoughts.

The crimes and sins were as varied as the races, cultures, and beliefs represented in the dangling rain of cages. Many of the condemned were deserters and traitors—those who had forsaken their brothers and sisters in the field of battle, or outright betrayed them and aided the enemy. And like so many others there for other reasons, after a time, the reason for their presence there escaped them. The memories of the war or fight in which they had committed their betrayal was forgotten. But still, they were cursed.

Some were the target of curses, hexes, and other forms of magic. This was sometimes also within the context of a battle or war, but oftentimes, it was the result of personal offense, or public offense committed upon a family or individual. The reasons were sometimes justified, but they could be subjective as well. Some of the condemned legitimately insulted a village's religious practices, as an example. Others insulted the honor of a family, their ancestors, or their deeds. Sometimes the offense was perceived, assumed, or acted upon due to anecdotal evidence. And of course, there were occasions that the curses were unjustified entirely.

And with each hint of one's cage rattling, or sight of a neighboring cage plummeting, those transgressions would shoot to the top of the mind of the condemned.

*That poor family. That poor, sweet family,* a cursed individual might think. *I ruined their reputation and saw to it that no one would ever do business with them again. All because of mistaking a conversation I thought I heard!*

*No, no, no! Not my cage,* another would say to themselves as they wrapped their fingers around the slats of iron. *That brood of dragons did not deserve that. I attacked them and killed their son, all over an argument about the costs of construction labor.*

Worse still were the wretched ones who were confined to an eternity of failing those who they loved, or loved them the most. The petty dwarf who turned his back on his brother when he simply tried to lend some advice on forging methods and techniques. At once he flew into a rage. He launched into a hateful tirade of insult and vulgarity, swearing off his brother and any interaction with him ever again.

But as is so often the case, the brother's reaction and escalation was born of something deeper, and much older. Over the years, he had grown resentful and jealous of his brother's success. He wallowed in a sea of bitterness and cynicism over what he perceived as his father's greater pride and love for his brother. And so it was that even decades before his death, when his life of anger and contempt would secure his place in a cage in the depths below, he had already condemned his heart and mind to an eternity of knowing only misery.

Others swore off their fathers or mothers for similar reasons. Rejection of love, advice, support, or concern was common among the condemned. But it was often not just the rejection, but the ensuing severing of ties or spiteful acts in return. Dragons, humans, seavers, and others. No race was exempt from the phenomena of personal failings. And where they all had opportunity for their personal redemption or changing of their ways, so too did they all have opportunities to stay their pitiful course until it was too late.

Spouses and partners were betrayed. Whether by causing harm, committing flagrant infidelity, or by willful neglect, so many had their love and loyalty spurned or rejected. Consideration and compassion were tossed aside or taken advantage of. The mental flames of failing those who had committed their entire existence to their prosperity and success eclipsed the searing flames of the magma below.

Domaren's imagination served him well as far as providing him a sense of the scale of horror and torment that had festered there. The continued silence of the group as they approached the Nebulum gave him reason to think the others were having similar thoughts. Pylon after pylon they passed. Still, the group said nothing. Brikana offered no additional observations of snide judgment, nor did Crizichial make any attempts to describe, explain, or ask for their understanding. The Redeemed guards kept their eyes forward, almost looking down, and never appeared to take in the scene around them. They didn't need to.

# Ten

The unrelenting march of endless pylons and echoed pain finally closed in on a massive structure of spiked rock. Soaring up through the molten flows below, was what Domaren assumed Crizichial had alluded to as the Nebulum. What looked to have begun as a series of natural bridges and ledges, extending out from the back walls of the chamber, organically stretched out over time from splashes, flows, and small eruptions of the underworld's magma.

The volcanic glass and obsidian exterior sparkled and shined wildly, like a broken kaleidoscope poorly reassembled by a simple drunkard. Consisting of eons of layer after layer of bubbled and cooled lava, it was without uniformity or symmetry. There was nothing clean or organized about it. Appearing as if underworld giants had haphazardly tossed handfuls of glass and stone into nihilistic piles, the Nebulum represented the nasty disorder of it all.

Domaren and Brikana continued their approach while the guards suddenly seemed to come to life having adequately shut out their surroundings. They slowed and lifted their eyes up to take in the sight before them. Crizichial stopped and turned.

"Thank you, my friends, for your patience," he said softly to his fellow godknights. "We have arrived." Crizichial then turned to look up towards the tallest of the spiny rock spires.

"Before we go in, Crizichial," Domaren began with a glance towards Brikana. "Can we talk about our intentions?"

"Of course. But, what do you mean by intentions?"

"We just need to keep moving forward," Domaren replied. "We've been out of contact with the Grove for too long. We definitely need to learn as much as we can, from as many of our proxies as we can, but we have less and less time to waste. It has been too many days now."

As Domaren concluded his statement, he reached for his grove calling stone. After quickly swinging his arm up, he tapped his calling stone and pulled his hand away. No light, no sound. Nothing. He tapped it again, and after a second, three more times in quick succession. Nothing. Afterward, he looked at Brikana who brought a hand up to just below her throat. After tapping rapidly in an attempt to connect with the calling stone in her human form's body, there was also no communications activity.

"Have you tried recently?" Brikana asked Crizichial.

The Redeemed knight dashed his eyes between his two friends before quickly shaking his head. He then breathed deeply and let it out as he took a step back. He clasped his hands together and closed his eyes. As he dipped his chin to his chest, his hair began to thin. His skin sunk in and small black holes began to appear. They quickly grew and revealed small grotesque windows into his mouth that revealed his jaw and teeth. Likewise, patches of decay elsewhere on his body appeared. The skin on his arms cracked and split. Not everywhere, however. Only in small hints of rot could portions of his bone and tissue be seen. But just as quickly as his demonic disgust began to show, it disappeared. Crizichial's eyes shot back open and his body stiffened. Though still gaunt and unhealthy in appearance, his physical form greatly recovered.

"No," he said, pensively. "Nothing for me either."

"Right," Domaren said. "After we speak with Maphikim, I would like to focus on less communication, and more action. We need to reestablish contact with the Grove, somehow."

Crizichial nodded and exchanged glances with Brikana before replying.

"Agreed."

"All right," Domaren said before quickly patting his friends on their shoulder.

The three knights turned and made for the glassy mountain's entrance. Having paused while their godknight spoke with the others, the guards fell in behind as they passed. Before passing through the threshold into the Nebulum, Domaren turned for a final scan of the nightmarish chamber.

Once inside, the narrow but tall passages echoed the shuffling of weapons and armor, and pounded the group's ears with their own footsteps. The cacophony of conflicting sounds clashed and fought against each other, and together with the accentuated volume of the noise, stung and stabbed at their ears.

There was no new light at first. The first many paces inside the Nebulum were dark and undefined. Only the dwindling light that crept in from the path outside and reflected off the group provided any sense of the hall's scale or dimension.

Just when the outside light was about to fail the group, tiny glints of amber seeped into view ahead. What at first appeared similar to the cracks and veins of light earlier in the cave, soon revealed themselves as distinct but simple lines. Delicate lines flowed along in shallow paths etched superficially into the stone. Small ribbons of flame and fire could be seen racing along them.

And though they started out as forgettable lines, they very soon grew in size. Additional lines appeared and ran in parallel with each other. Soon, the narrow tracks of fire split and twisted off to form simple geometric shapes. As the paths increased and became more involved, some also cut deeper into the walls to form recessed ledges. More and more light came to life and defined added dimension to the paths.

Recesses and shelves cut deeper into the rock, each with traced patterns showing exactly how far back the deliberate recesses went. The fiery outlines raced to the floor, under the feet of the group, as well as up to the towering ceiling. And while many of the patterns and shapes were already lit as they walked, many more shapes and characters flashed to life as they approached, only to fade as they passed.

Symbols and meandering paths gently combusted to life. Words and phrases of the ancient demon language wrote themselves into existence. But in reality, each image already existed. They merely throbbed alight with life as the group marched past. Symbols for dragons and demons outlined themselves with living flame. Other shapes of dwarves, seavers, and men sparked alight. And though Domaren felt confident he remembered stories explaining the function of what they were witnessing in the halls, he thought to ask a question of confirmation. But Brikana beat him to it.

"Crizichial. What is all this? What's going on?" She asked. Her voice was initially drowned out by the echoing sounds of metal and marching, but she quickly increased her volume.

"This is what the Redeemed used to call a filling chamber, well, before we were Redeemed" he replied with a booming reinforcement. "It's how some of us would commune with the old energies. Maintain our connection. Restore our powers."

A silence followed as Domaren's memory was refreshed, and Brikana, he assumed, was processing Crizichial's reply.

"Before you were Redeemed..." She repeated. "So why is it all still making this fuss? What is it doing?"

"It all still appears as it used to, but that is the extent of it. There is no energy or power behind it. Think of it like a painting."

"I understand," Brikana replied. Another silence followed, deferring temporarily back to the harsh clatter of armor and stomping.

"How was it stopped? The power or energy behind it, that is," she asked.

"The Kihdai stopped it," he answered. "Once those of us that were forgiven became the Redeemed, the Kihdai severed the tie with Ba Glech's energy. Afterward, they anointed me as the first Redeemed godknight, and anointed our first proxy. We have derived our power from the Kihdai ever since."

Domaren listened as Crizichial's explanation refreshed his own memory, and simultaneously felt an odd humor as the animated fire flashed furiously around him. The light had long been rendered pointless. Its intent had been supplanted by what most would define as the absolute antithesis of its original purpose. No longer would it help realize the most heinous procedures, horrors, and sickness upon the world. Now, it was all effectively nothing more than a series of elaborate torches and flickering sparks.

The group pressed on through the halls, and passed by an ever growing amount of flaming shapes, signs, symbols, and script. Step by step, there looked to be what Domaren roughly remembered or deciphered as instructions on how to either cause, enact, reinforce, strengthen, or commit all of the acts they had seen representations of on their way through the caves, and more. Some areas on the wall were covered in maps of cities, countries, or continents, all outlined by streams of flame.

Other sections of the walls had representations of the people and beasts of the world and how they should be oriented to properly receive certain punishments or spells. Whether it was the position of someone on a machine, the function of a torture device, or symbols and scratches of script arranged in particular ways around someone, the walls had not only previously been a source of demonic power, but provided instruction on how to accomplish some of their most profane work.

Some images showed mothers and offspring from various races. Images and text described various forms of blood magic, how to achieve the power of blood, and what could in turn be done after capturing the essence of the mother, the child, and their blood.

There were also large groupings of text from ceiling to floor, one after another, on how a demon could invade the heart and soul of their victim. Scenes showed demons doing the simplest, but still sinister acts such as manipulating the environment around their victim. They misplaced items, distorted how those around them appeared, or modified tastes, smells, or temperatures. Instructions then followed that delved deeper into the desired type of torment, whether exploiting the memory of a loved one, making someone relive a horrific trauma, or embellishing and remind the victim of embarrassment, humiliation, abuse, and pain. Indeed, the demons lived at creating a living hell for many during their mortal lives, in hopes of leading them to a path that condemned them to a damned hell for eternity, upon their death.

Nightmare craft was a major feature of the demonic culture and had a major section of the corridors devoted to it. Much of it was devoted to showing family and kin in violent situations, children being made afraid of everything from sleep, to death, their own family, as well as abstract fears like failure, and loneliness.

Domaren felt his interest in reviewing the imagery and information that surrounded them waning. When they first entered the Nebulum he was preoccupied with worry over losing communication with the Grove. Consumed by an urgent need to restore contact, find out what happened, and resolve the issue, he felt increasingly concerned about the speed with which they were proceeding.

But then the constant flood of old, demonic instruction took over his focus. What started out as a fuzzy memory shifted to a genuine interest and fascination about where the Redeemed came from. He even allowed himself to feel noticeable pride for the existence that segment of demons turned away from.

Each step, each symbol, each painful act, and each set of instructions that caused them carried on and on. Step after step. Panel after panel. Impotent instructions flourished with enduring fire seemingly enjoying reminding everyone that passed through the halls of what it brought to fruition all those ages ago. The evil information no longer instructed the Redeemed, and no longer gave them power, encouragement, or inspiration, but it was still there. Still seething with flaming light. Reminding. Finding new life in the minds of those who saw it. Taking up their thoughts and energy. Taking up their time. Wasting time.

Finally, Domaren's perspective shifted enough to the point he was almost as sick of their surroundings as Brikana had been hours before.

"How much longer until we see Maphikim, Crizichial?" Domaren blasted out in surprising frustration. An agreeable but confused Brikana looked over as they walked. "We've been walking for hours."

Taken aback by Domaren's unexpected outburst, Crizichial whipped his head around while also maintaining his pace.

"Why is it that some insist on asking such questions so close to the end? His working chamber is just ahead," Crizichial said. He spoke amiably, as if humoring himself with his rhetorical question and informative statement. "No more than an additional minute or two."

Domaren swallowed and dipped his chin quickly and sharply in acknowledgment. The subsequent minute was a quiet one, especially considering that the group apparently made an unspoken effort to lessen its metallic smattering and smacks. Domaren kept his eyes down, focused on his immediate next step and the feet in front of him, until finally, the narrow hall rapidly opened up, and Domaren's ears involuntarily rose as the acoustics of the much broader room caught his attention. He looked up.

"Please, please," a voice pleaded from the middle of the room. "Finish the terrain. Get the tower up."

Crizichial held his hand out to Domaren and Brikana.

"If I may present," Crizichial said softly, trying not to blatantly interrupt as he shifted his gesture towards the middle of the room, "our current proxy of the Redeemed, Maphikim."

Brikana and Domaren stood quietly while Maphikim continued barking orders at what appeared to be some Redeemed assistants.

"Yes, much better, yes," he said. "Time is not a luxury we have my friends, so we must proceed with all possible speed. The dwarves are hours within the calling tower. Please pay special attention to the scale of the surrounding farms and fields."

Brikana leaned over with a whisper for Domaren.

"He already knows about the calling tower?"

Domaren's shoulders and eyebrows shrugged.

"It appears so," he conceded before addressing Crizichial. "Criz. What are they doing?"

"They are preparing a battle map as far as I can tell," he replied.

But instead of a large sheet of parchment with scribblings made by ink and quill, two massive Redeemed stood at the far end of the room holding a gigantic slab of rock. Another pair of Redeemed stood off to the side. The separate pair worked through the task of using magic to etch fiery drawings onto the slab of stone, and create a representation of the area surrounding the calling tower, as well as the calling tower itself.

"Come now, we must be quick," Maphikim ordered. "Accurate, but quick."

While Maphikim spoke, the group's Redeemed escort broke off and stepped down three steps where they then assumed a sentry posture and three equidistant spots of the room's largest circle of flat floor.

The visitors had not been recognized yet, and as Maphikim fussed over the map, Domaren took the opportunity to take in the large room and the former demon that commanded it.

Unlike the approach to the room, the Nebulum's exterior, and each section of caverns all the way back to the entrance, Maphikim' primary working chamber was surprisingly welcoming.

Similar to the approaching halls, the center room had a far reaching ceiling that from what Domaren could tell, was almost as high as the ceiling of the primary cave. The walls, while still mostly black and reflective with volcanic glass and obsidian, also featured large columns and features made of quartz. And while all of the structures and features of the Nebulum seemed organic and naturally formed, the round chamber seemed to be carefully hollowed, and the quartz fixtures, carefully chiseled. Only the columns earlier in the cave showed signs of being worked and chiseled.

The floors were covered in rugs. Almost every inch of the bare floor was covered by mostly bright white rugs made from white lions and tigers, as well as various albino beasts such as camel, moose, and zebra.

Circling around the room were rings of shelves. Perhaps a dozen rings in total. Each ring of shelves were packed and stacked with overflowing books, papers, and artifacts, in addition to a few small creature skeletons.

In the center of the room, hanging down to within approximately a dozen feet from the ground, suspended from high above at the pinnacle of the ceiling, was a huge rod of cool white light. There were in fact, additional and smaller sources of light throughout the room. And they were all similar to the cool light of the chandelier rod. Nowhere in this chamber was there a sign of the abundant and ever-present light of the magma in the hall or outside in the Hall of Patience.

Maphikim was easy for Domaren to spot. Not by name, but by features, even when in a room full of former demons. The Redeemed proxy loomed over everyone in the room, even while standing in the lowest level in the middle of the Nebulum. He walked upright on four legs that branched out from low on his torso, with each one being a slightly different length than the other.

Unlike the spacing and length of a horse's legs, Maphikim's legs were grouped close together. And in addition to being different in length, no leg resembled another in size or shape or appearance. Three legs were a contrasting trio of skin tones from peach to ebony and most closely resembled human legs. One leg glistened and sparkled as Maphikim walked, wet with the moisture of blood from an open wound that stretched the length of its thigh. The other two legs, other than being different lengths, appeared mostly normal. All three of the human legs terminated at corresponding human bare feet. The feet were dirty to the point they looked as though they had been walking in ash for centuries, or as they they had been burned. Maphikim's fourth leg was oppressively weighted at the top. It's exposed skin was beige, wrinkled, and covered in shallow, sparse hair. At the end of this leg, was a cloven hoof.

Maphikim's torso was incredibly long and made up the bulk of his entire body's length, by far. The majority of Maphikim's weight had settled almost entirely at the bottom of his trunk of a body, right above his legs. Like a grotesque and exaggerated teardrop that gravity couldn't help but humiliate, his body radically slimmed from bottom to top. Having no elbows, his very long arms poked out from his narrow-set shoulders and were extended at all times when not dangling close to his body when not in use.

Domaren found his face and head as a whole the most unsettling. His smile was broad and out of proportion with his head. Despite being too big and though the corners of his mouth extended to the far sides of his head, Maphikim's smile was a perfect one when considered by itself. His teeth were a polished ivory and his gums were as pink as those obsessed with the best of hygiene. Oddly however, Maphikim never relaxed his smile as if something or someone wanted everyone to bask in how perfect a smile it was, if not Maphikim's own doing. It never wavered. It never shifted. The same, perfect smile was present at all times.

But everything else, whether chin or cheeks or any other feature on his head, was less than perfect.

Where one might have a chin, Maphikim had something close as far as how his head and skull seemed to taper down to one, but instead of a bone covered in skin, the small, blunt end of Maphikim's chin protruded out through the skin like a purposeful compound fracture. Absent of blood or infection surrounding the area, it was as if the exposed bone was as nature intended.

One side of Maphikim's face was smooth with no sign of a prominent cheek bone. On his right side however, a loose clump of skin hung down and bounced from side to side as he walked. It was very much a distraction that caught Domaren's eye frequently, as if an actual cheekbone had been slammed and broken free of Maphikim's skull.

The proxy's hair was long and the color of freshly drawn human blood. It sprouted out from his scalp in patches, separated by similar patches of nothing but skin. Some hair was straight, other clumps were curly. Some dry, some greasy.

While not as disturbing as some of his other features, Maphikim's nose was nevertheless jarringly peculiar. The foundation of his nose began like a human's might, but instead of quickly tapering to a point, his nose extended out and curved around before ending at a point that only just made contact with the smooth side of his face.

Finally, the feature Domaren tried to avoid lingering on for too long, was Maphikim's eyes. His left eye was proportioned like a normal eye with a perfectly ordinary iris and and cornea. On the other side however, Maphikim's face had a significantly larger eye socket. Inside it were two eyes which pressed up against each other. One the same size as the one on the other side of his face, and a much larger, second eye. The two matching eyes looked in the same direction while the larger eye seemed stuck looking slightly down and to the left. The larger eye socket was stretched and allowed the tender flesh and sinew of the socket to be easily seen.

Domaren was long accustomed to seeing the world's life, or death, arranged a variety of ways. Very little caught him off guard even when thinking back to when the Virtues were young. But Maphikim's features gave him a rare moment of pause. It was as though, Domaren thought, that something consciously picked the harshest combination of incomplete or incompatible features as possible. And seeing Maphikim almost made Domaren forget that when demons came into existence—Redeemed or not—that they were the physical manifestation conceived by the lingering energy from their ancestors' heinous acts.

"How long do we need to wait before we can talk to him?" Brikana asked. "Does he know we're here?"

"I assure you, I do know you are there," he said, without acknowledging them in any other way. He held his hand up to his assistants requesting silently that they pause briefly and looked back partially over his shoulder. He spoke to the group once again.

"Please bear with me while we get this map straightened out and I will be with you directly."

The godknights let their host get back to the business of building his map. While they did, Domaren took the opportunity to consider the map and ask his fellow knights some meaningful questions about what might be taking place.

"So, if he's only recently heard about the amassing army and is planning to meet them," Domaren began, "then it seems like we already have the most recent news. There must be something that has transpired even before the dwarves set off to war."

"It could be that simple," Brikana replied. "But I have to wonder why none of us can initiate a grove stone even if this one is still intact."

"They *all* have to be functional for our communication attempts to get out to the Grove," Maphikim interrupted.

Surprised by the proxy's addition to the conversation and hearty hearing abilities, the godknights turned to face their host.

"I don't believe that I knew that," Domaren said.

Brikana tilted her head at him.

"How could you not know?" She asked.

Crizichial beat Domaren to the answer.

"The towers were put up only after Wrathlore when the Kihdai separated themselves physically from the world."

"Ah, yes, that's right," Brikana said.

"Right. They weren't always around," Domaren added. "Back then, the Kihdai still lived here and we could visit and speak with them directly. I don't think any of the calling towers have ever been damaged before."

"I think you are correct," Maphikim said as he walked over to his visitors. "Upon hearing that the knights had lost contact with the Grove, and then confirming I and the other proxies had as well, I grew to believe that someone had already attacked a calling tower."

"Have you heard anything about any others being attacked?" Brikana asked.

"Nothing confirmed. Only rumors and hearsay regarding the outer towers. Unfortunately, as you know, not only is our ability to communicate with the Grove severed, the security of connecting with the knights and other proxies is in question, wherever they may be. What happens when you all try to activate a grove stone?"

One by one, the godknights went down the line and showed him. Domaren tapped his pauldron's grove calling stone. Brikana tapped below her throat, and Crizichial went into decay. Each time, nothing.

"Have you had any more luck than we have?" Domaren asked.

"No, the very same," Maphikim said.

"Would you mind trying?" Brikana asked.

Domaren turned towards him with eyebrows raised with curiosity.

Crizichial did the same as Maphikim replied.

"But I have only just said that I experience the same—"

"Yes, I heard," Brikana interrupted. "But we are extremely eager to find out what is happening, and any additional experience or insight would be extremely appreciated."

Maphikim tilted and bent his head back some and studied Brikana through a subtle squint.

"You are quite a bold one," Maphikim finally said. "Do you speak to your own proxy with such impertinence? You are aware of who directly selects us to represent them on this world, are you not?"

The sound and energy in the room immediately burrowed itself into a silent hole.

"Oh, I wasn't expecting such an odd reaction..." Brikana answered calmly.

"Brikana..." Domaren whispered.

She turned to her fellow godknight, then back to Maphikim.

"No," she resumed with a polite chuckle, "I only mean that I didn't realize I was being impertinent. He asked us what happened when we attempt to contact the Grove, and I was hoping we could share experiences."

Domaren tensed up as she spoke. His lips parted and opened more, in preparation for a reply. But instead, he deflated with a small sigh as Brikana finished speaking.

"Proxy Maphikim," Crizichial started. He moved slowly towards his race's proxy with his hands calmly touching only at their fingertips. "I am very sure that Brikana meant no—"

"No, no," Maphikim said, politely interrupting Crizichial. "Our dear dragon godknight has an excellent point. It is an absolutely fair and reasonable request. Shared information is definitely ideal, and I should have offered it without being prompted. Please, everyone, please. Follow me just over here if you will."

Domaren cut an angled look from his dipped head towards Brikana, his usual expression when he disagrees with her methods.

"Right this way," Maphikim continued, welcoming everyone over with wide, flowing arms. "If you would please wait a moment, I will attempt to contact the Grove."

Maphikim reached under a nearby table and fumbled around with what sounded like glass and metal containers as the others settled into spots at random intervals around his massive crucible. The large container stood approximately four feet high and was roughly twice that length in diameter at the top. The diameter narrowed from top to bottom before tapering back out drastically at its base.

Coming up empty with nothing from the shelves at the table, Maphikim made for the other side of the room, but not before stopping at a massive wooden rod that poke out from a slot in Maphikim's working chamber wall. The Redeemed proxy reached up above his head, grabbed onto the huge lever and started to pull it down.

He was met with initial resistance, but with a noticeable flex and pinch of effort, Maphikim pulled the lever down. As he pulled, a sequence of sounds were set off, one after another. First, the stretching of stressed ropes creaked from behind the wall. Next came slow bangs of slowly clicking chains as if huge links of metal were slowly slipping up and over a catch of some short. Lastly, two massive beams that extended from the ceiling above pushed down on two protruding lips on the huge stone crucible. As the counterweight back behind the wall shifted, the beams groaned with dense creaks and tipped the crucible over, spilling its previous contents out into a narrow but fairly deep path in the floor. Once the sludge of slightly cooled magma and long-consumed material finished pouring out, Maphikim released most of his tension on the wooden rod, and allowed the mechanism to return the crucible to its normal upright position. Once each piece of the assembly thudded and clicked into its resting position, Maphikim let go of the rod. He then whipped a finger in the direction of one of the Redeemed standing at attention, before darting over to a series of shelves carved into a section of the obsidian wall.

Without verbal instruction, the guard bowed his head at Maphikim, but the proxy had already begun poking and prodding at skulls of small animals and different jars filled with things like teeth and eyes. Nevertheless, the guard proceeded towards a wheel and much smaller lever, and via another, less substantial system of ropes and pulleys, the guard spun the rusted wheel by its humble handle that stuck out and sent a long and narrow trough into motion. With each rotation, the trough slid out from the wall and positioned one of its ends over the crucible, sending the visitors into a humorous dance to avoid it. Once in place, the guard slammed down the lever and opened a small door at the wall and let a manageable stream of magma flow in and down into the crucible. After the crucible was adequately filled, the guard cranked the wheel in reverse and brought the trough back to the wall. Crizichial, Brikana, and Domaren took their previous places back around the sides of the cauldron.

Maphikim found what he was looking for relatively quickly and turned back to the group, his eyes still on the jar as he walked. As Domaren tried to focus on what was in the jar, he half expected Maphikim to come back with a living rabbit or something equally as innocent. Instead, and Domaren confirmed as Maphikim grew closer, he seemed to be holding a jar of no more than ten stones, each one no larger than an acorn. To Domaren, they very closely resembled the brilliant, perfectly cut stones of remarkable clarity that the godknights use to maintain their connection with the Grove.

"Here we are," Maphikim said, still turning and

peering through the glass jar. "Thank you for your patience."

He tapped the side of its fragile lid and knocked it off into his other hand and placed it on the edge of the cauldron. Next, Maphikim looked up and offered everyone a quick smile before tipping the jar over to allow a single stone to roll into his palm which tapped and rattled the jar as it tumbled out. Almost immediately after it landed, Maphikim shoved his palm forward and tossed the stone into the collected magma.

Brikana's curiosity spoke up.

"Is this how you communicate with the Grove?"

Domaren shot Brikana another glance of disapproval, but Crizichial seemed to appreciate her curiosity.

"Yes, where each of us has our own method of communing with our stone to speak with the Grove, so too do the proxies."

Before Crizichial had a chance to elaborate on the Redeemed proxy's process, Maphikim began to speak, and commanded everyone silently to allow him to concentrate.

As the group turned back to watch Maphikim, they saw that his eyes were closed. His hands rested on well-worn and smoothed areas of the cauldron's edge. His hands were spaced far apart, but not so far that Maphikim had to bend or stretch his torso to accommodate the hand placement. Under the smoothed areas were carved symbols, but these were not symbols of the damned, nor the old culture of demons. These symbols were from the original root of all languages. The symbols of Soren.

Maphikim rolled his head around slowly and stretched his shoulders back. With his eyes still closed, he started to speak over the cauldron.

*Wrathlore I*
*Loaned to you, from the first riverbed*
*I return this stone, loaned to me.*

Maphikim's words rolled off his tongue like the most practiced of prayers by the most humble of aging priests. Standing in stark contrast to the sounds Domaren heard true demons spit and hiss, these words were rounded and spoken with a measured reverence. Each of Maphikim's syllables rose and fell deliberately in both pitch and volume. Nothing was rushed, and everything was respected.

After Maphikim began the first hints of the chant, the pool of magma started pulsating like an ocean finally disturbed by a distant storm. Pulses became ripples before widening and turning into subtle waves. With his eyes still closed and hands still in place, Maphikim continued:

*May this show of respect*
*Be an appropriate sign*

The waves lapped at the insides of the cauldron as he spoke. And while the waves never crested or grew in intensity, they increased in frequency. After a few moments, the magma belched and bubbled and settled into a rumbling boil. With the magma stirred and agitated to the appropriate degree, Maphikim completed his appeal to the Grove:

*That I come to you now in humble need*
*To speak with you, our Kihdai*

As he spoke the last sentence of his spell, Maphikim raised his hands off the edge of the cauldron, revealing the glowing trace of the etched symbols. The light sparked and sizzled within the symbols and raced down along the sides of the large stone bowl. After surging down to the floor, the light flew along etched paths on the floor before sprinting for the interior walls. Gaining speed each millisecond, the fire branched out onto patterns and flooded them with light. As the room was overtaken by amber light like the preceding tunnel and other areas leading to the Nebulum, this effect stood out as noticeably different to Domaren. Rather than looking like malevolent scratches of evil and horror, these fiery paths looked as if they were carved over, or on top of old patterns. These symbols and texts when lit looked nothing like the those of the former demons.

This new display was elegant. When text appeared, it seemed painstakingly crafted through centuries and centuries of practice and patience. Symbols and images were designed with a beautiful symmetry. Rings of concentric circles were perfectly round and equidistant apart. Edges and lines complimented one another with layered complexity, instead of clashing from random sharpness or careless placement. There was in fact, a craftsmanship in the energy being reflected in Maphikim's appeal.

The proxy's hands continued to rise and the light grew brighter. Each inch of fire had found the entire pattern necessary in the evocation of the Grove. At what felt to Domaren like the pinnacle of the process, Maphikim opened his eyes.

There were no additional words said, and the light engulfed the room in ribbons and beams of hearty oranges and yellows. Maphikim stared ahead, waiting, before looking to his hands, and then down at the roaring cauldron. And after approximately ten seconds, the light faded. Maphikim dropped his hands slowly. The boiling magma ceased bubbling and even quicker than when it was called to life, its waves receded to ripples, then to a gentle disturbance before settling to stillness.

Maphikim, the guards, and his guests stared blankly down into the lifeless cauldron and only offered a few, individual glances out of the corner of their eyes towards the proxy.

"And there we have it," Maphikim finally commented. "That is how it has been for the past two days. Three attempts, including this one. Three stones wasted."

"How does the connection usually become established?" Domaren asked before adding clarification. "What usually happens that didn't just now?"

Maphikim huffed out a quick sigh of frustration and explained further.

"As has been the case for these many years I have been proxy, once I complete the words of evocation, and the magma traces its ancient path, a curtain of transparent energy plummets down and penetrates through the roof of the Nebulum. It encircles me and the cauldron, creating a seal into the outer ring of that series of circles on the floor there. Once that seal is created, I am able to communicate with the Grove, and it, with me."

"I guess everything from our end is working," Brikana said, mostly to herself.

Crizichial stepped forward.

"That is what appears to be the case," he said.

"I don't know what troubles me most," Domaren said. "The idea that the Grove is unwilling to answer, or unable."

The proxy and other godknights looked at Domaren with widened eyes as if scared awake from a pleasant dream, but quickly set their sights back on the pool of calm magma ahead. As if looking at the magma instead of Domaren, it felt to him as if they found comfort and safety in the liquid fire than the possibilities he had suggested.

Before the silence consumed more of the room's nerves and set them farther down a path of worry, Domaren cleared his throat and stirred the subject.

"Well, regardless, thank you, Maphikim, for making the attempt."

"Yes, of course," the proxy said sincerely to Domaren.

Without expecting it, Maphikim then turned to Brikana who offered a nod to Maphikim, in appreciation for delivering on her request.

"Very well," Maphikim said. "Would you care to join me for a bit of strategy?"

"To what end?" Domaren asked.

"On developing a defense to protect the nearby tower," Maphikim replied. "Please... If you will follow me."

Maphikim led his visitors down to the bottom level, walking them past tables full of disintegrating tomes and piles of papers. Piles of small stones etched with characters from the old demon tongue rested next to dozens of jars filled with everything from rat teeth to pig eyes, to honeysuckle and thyme.

Chairs were pushed up against each other, sharing the burden of recklessly stacked piles of books. Leather trunks with loose locks sat under the shade of rickety tables. Their tops were flopped open with their small compartments in various states of being flung or pulled open as Maphikim no doubt went tearing through them over the years looking for that one herb or tincture needed to conduct a spell.

It was at once curious, yet a relief to Domaren, seeing no discernible signs of demonic life before their redemption. Nowhere in Maphikim' chamber were there any fiery symbols, or flaming shapes. No notes of torture or instruction on how to inflict the most horror upon someone as possible. There only seemed to be great efforts towards study, to history, to science, and to matters of improvement, whether one's self, or society. Scattered among the numerous documents and books, were specific items related to the history of the Kihdai, history of the godknights, the proxies, and the individual races and cultures.

Farther ahead on the lower level, stood the two Redeemed holding the slab of stone. The large sheet of rock looked as though it weight thousands of pounds—much heavier than two individuals could bear alone, especially considering the frail and weak appearance of the two demons holding it on each side.

Standing off alone, speaking to each other, were the other two demons who had the responsibility of filling out the features of the map. Having taken the opportunity to study the map's detail while Maphikim greeted Domaren and the other visitors, they took turns gesturing or pointing at areas of the map, and flicking their wrists and fingers to either add additional detail, or remove some. They increased the scale of the nearby forest, and decreased the amount of adjacent hills. With other points and gesticulations, they shot out beams of thin energy towards the map that struck and changed the fortification surrounding the calling tower, or modified the region's various borders.

"Before we begin," Domaren said. "I wonder if we should confirm what our priorities are."

After reaching down for a much smaller reference map of the region, Maphikim slowly rose and stiffened his posture. He turned around with the flimsy section of parchment dangling from his fingertips. His lips slowly parted while he squinted his eyes. His eyebrows crumpled in on one another.

"I do not understand," Maphikim said. "By priorities, plural, you imply that there is more than one."

Domaren started nodding, casually.

"Oh, yes. I do believe there are a few different ways we can proceed."

Maphikim relaxed his face some and slid his map back onto the table.

"I see," Maphikim replied. "But, alas, I am still confused. Having different methods to proceed with something is not the same thing as having different priorities."

Off on the edges of his peripheral vision, Domaren saw and felt Brikana look at him.

"Can you please clarify?" Maphikim prodded.

Domaren smiled as a sense of appreciation for Maphikim's semantics bubbled to the surface of his thoughts.

"My apologies," Domaren happily offered. "Regardless of any decision we make, there are of course different ways in which we might proceed, yes. What I intended to convey is the suggestion that we identify what we perceive the issues to be first."

"And again," Maphikim replied, "you are suggesting there are multiple issues."

Domaren sucked in a quick breath but let it out slowly through his nose.

"Yes."

"Very well," Maphikim conceded. "And what might those be?"

Domaren collected his thoughts and scanned the room while shifting his weight.

"Well, we mostly spoke to them already, but I think

it's important that we make the distinction between them, discuss them, and proceed deliberately."

Domaren clasped his fingers together and twirled his thumbs. As he continued, his eyes darted sharply from side to side.

"I think there are two primary issues, each one distinct from the other, at least as far as I can tell. There is obviously the impending attack on the nearby calling tower. But there is also the overall mystery of why we can no longer make contact with the Grove."

Maphikim tapped his chin quickly with alternating fingers but abruptly stopped.

"I am afraid I do not follow," Maphikim said. "Surely you must see that they are related."

"They might be," Brikana said, cold and snappy, "but they may not be. One might be a distraction from the other."

"Agreed," Domaren said. "They may very well be related, Maphikim, but I believe we need to confirm that before we react to anything."

Maphikim started to pace while poking softly at his chin. His head tilted side to side as he walked, but he quickly stopped and propped one arm's elbow in the opposite palm. His free fingers fanned out. Domaren felt confident of what type of tone to expect as Maphikim responded.

"So, in suggesting we confirm something, you are saying we should react with an investigation before we react to what the investigation yields?"

Domaren went straight into a direct retort.

"Before we head to the calling tower with an army, I'm suggesting—"

"Are you being like this on purpose, Maphikim?" Brikana interrupted with an abrupt bark. She then shot out an arm in disgusted awe at Crizichial. "This is your proxy?"

She shifted her attention back to Maphikim.

"We want to know what is going on," she continued in annoyance. "We want to know why the Grove stopped talking. And if the calling towers have something to do with it, then so be it, but the Grove's silence is the priority in my mind." Brikana then dipped her head and deferred to Domaren by extending her hand.

"Oh, yes, I agree," Domaren said immediately. "I just don't know that setting off straight for the calling tower is the best use of our time or energy at this juncture.

Maphikim resumed fiddling with his chin again, but now rubbed it instead of tapped it. Silently, he strolled around the lowest level of the chamber, appearing to consider his guests' comments.

After Domaren and Brikana exchanged glances, Maphikim suddenly stopped and asked a question that sounded like he was asking himself as much as the others.

"If there is a possibility of the different issues being unrelated, what might be the individual motives or causes for the two?"

"That is indeed a terrific question," Crizichial added, stepping closer to the group. "The answer to that is why I believe we are wanting to proceed carefully. It is entirely possible," he continued, "that the move on the nearby calling tower, or even any others if indeed others have been attacked, is the act of nothing more than raiders or rebels. There have been similar assaults on towers in the past."

"And the motives for those attacks were often no more than disrupting the communications of the Grove, or our own communications," Domaren added.

"In that case, if we have nothing but marauding barbarians attacking the towers," Maphikim asked, "and the Grove has gone silent for a different reason, then what might that reason be?"

The question was offered but there were no immediate attempts to answer. The group stood motionless, but shifted eyes to and fro awkwardly.

"I believe I am of a similar mind as Proxy Maphikim," Crizichial said. "I think regardless of potentially disparate issues, it seems most logical to begin investigations with what is happening at our nearest calling tower."

Domaren lifted his head and sighed.

"Is that the goal then?" He asked. "Are we agreed on that?"

Brikana crossed her arms and directed her frustration with her stare focused on the floor.

"At this point, I can't actually think of a better place to start," she said. "We just need to *start.*"

"What does everyone suggest as being the best manner in which we visit?" Domaren asked. "Do we go by ourselves? Do we attempt to reach the rest of the knights? Raise an army? Meet with neighboring countries?"

"I do not see how we can make progress in investigating the status of the calling tower while trying to reach the rest of the knights," Crizichial added.

"I'm just putting forth suggestions," Domaren said after a noticeably frustrated sigh. "They're just suggestions on what action we could take. If it is decided that we should make for the calling tower, I would prefer to move out sooner rather than later."

"Without raising a force?" Crizichial asked.

Domaren looked to Brikana and silently sought her agreement.

"Well, we could set out and do some advanced scouting immediately. You or Maphikim could begin gathering some forces here in the meantime. If needed, we can fall back and join up with the forces you gather."

After glancing to gather Maphikim's disposition, Crizichial proposed a variation.

"I would much prefer to investigate with you," he said. "If Maphikim is agreeable, he might assist with gathering the army in our absence."

Domaren's eyebrows lifted. He offered an open palm towards the Redeemed godknight.

"Would you be willing to assist us in that manner, Maphikim?"

The proxy rubbed his hands together before bending each set of fingers back with the other hand. One hand and then the other bent back, cracked as knuckles do, but Maphikim kept bending them back. They cracked more and shifted into a continuous grinding sound until the backs of his fingers touched the top of his wrist. Maphikim showed no signs of discomfort or blatant awareness of how unsettling his act might appear to his onlooking friends.

"That is a reasonable request," he replied as he dropped his hand. He then turned to look at the map which had not been modified in the recent minutes.

"What have the other proxies said about these oddities?" He asked. "Which others have you spoken with?"

Domaren's head fell to the side slightly as his chest rose and took a breath.

"The only other proxy I've spoken with was Vinlaza," he said. "That's what's so simultaneously worrying and frustrating. I... Well, we have been able to quickly communicate with the other godknights or the proxies like we normally would."

An ominous paused halted the conversation.

"The severed ties and subsequent silence is absolutely

concerning," Crizichial said.

A longer pause followed. Not only was there silence, but there was less shifting and shuffling. Less movement. Only the pops and cracks of torches and energy could be heard. Occasionally, the faint bubbles and flowing of material could be heard from outside the Nebulum.

"It must be said specifically," Brikana finally said softly, but firmly. "We might be up against rogue godknights."

Maphikim whipped his head up in surprise.

"Godknight betrayal? Treachery? Like the tales of the ancient Wrathlore?"

"Wrathlore isn't a tale. It was a fact that I was present for," Domaren clarified sternly.

"Yes, of course," Maphikim replied quickly. "I was only clarifying the possible supposition."

The clarification Maphikim sought only clarified a potential nightmare, but simultaneously introduced an entirely new dynamic. An uneasy silence settled into the room as everyone in it undoubtedly extrapolated various worst-case scenarios.

Domaren looked up with eyes petrified from pensive concern while making sure to make eye contact with everyone in the room.

"I am afraid, everyone, that we have run unrestrained, face first into a stubborn web of paranoia and suspicion," he said. "At least, I admit, for my part."

With each few words, his focus shifted to someone else. His words were calm, but dry, as if having to convince himself he was actually choosing to say the words he was speaking.

Even the Redeemed holding the fire-etched stone slab were caught off guard by the implications. Domaren saw them whip their gazes up from the floor or ahead where they had been blankly staring.

"But I wonder," Crizichial started. "How realistic might that possibility be?"

"What possibility, exactly?" Maphikim asked.

"Well, there are only two other godknights not presently here. Nanutsi and Kegli," Crizichial observed.

"Right," Brikana acknowledged. "Wouldn't any number of us be enough to be a cause for concern?"

"Sure, of course," Crizichial said in a rush. "But didn't the original Wrathlore involve all of the godknights at the time?"

"Yes," Maphikim answered.

"What?" Brikana barked.

Seemingly clueless as to his gaffe, Maphikim stood foolishly for a moment, staring blankly at Brikana.

"All but me!" Domaren shouted.

Maphikim grimaced immediately. He pulled his fists close and squeezed them.

"Yes, of course, of course!" Crizichial rattled out rapidly with closed eyes. "Please forgive me, Domaren. Please. I apologize. Yes, all but you."

Everyone kept their eyes trained on Crizichial and his slow release of his body's tense gestures of regret. Eyes wide with anger or disbelief at Maphikim's accidental insult eventually relaxed as well.

"I regret being the one to continue with this line of thinking and ask this, but I believe in saying or asking things that are necessary," Brikana resumed calmly. "But if there is something else similar to Wrathlore transpiring, how do we know for sure which godknights might be involved?"

Domaren slowly turned to Brikana and met her question with an expression locked in frozen staleness.

There was no sign of anger, nor any sign of confusion. There was at once disbelief and understanding. Domaren looked as if he had been punched in the gut while simultaneously sung and caressed to sleep. But this sleep was not a restful journey to peaceful dreams, or even irritating nightmares that threatened wakefulness. It was a catatonic deja vu that kicked and shouted at long-settled memories and pulled them up from the dirt of Domaren's mind and shoved their hungover irritation face first into the sunlight from a clear sky.

Crizichial watched Brikana deliver the sad correspondence of her suggestion and kept focused on her for many moments before letting his head dip, dip down, until finally it hung in what looked like defeat.

Domaren turned and put his hands down on a table. He moved slowly as if maintaining a stealth or trying to keep from waking a sleeping infant. With the hint of a burdensome memory weighing his head down, he drilled a stare into the table and addressed the others.

"I will not leap to that conclusion, quite yet," Domaren said. "We must continue as if that thought had not entered our minds."

Domaren heard a tongue click and looked up. Brikana's brow was dipped in confusion.

"Proceed? How can we proceed?" Brikana asked, puzzled. "Before we attempt to achieve any goal as a group, shouldn't we first attempt to uncover anyone that might undermine us?"

Domaren pushed off the table and rubbed his face.

"I don't know that it's wise to take a course of action based on an assumption," he said.

"What? Isn't it an assumption that the calling towers are being attacked?"

"Brikana, you saw the gathering forces for yourself. That isn't an assumption."

"Yes, but we don't know who all makes up that force."

"But the fact that we can't communicate with the Grove is a concrete issue we can respond to. The attack or attacks on one or more towers might be related. You're asking us to veer from that to look into something that isn't based in evidence."

"Yet," Brikana shot back firmly.

Domaren yelled back just as quickly.

"Right, not yet!"

Crizichial found a break to slip into.

"Friends. Domaren. Brikana. Please..." He began. "I would suggest for both of you, the three of us, actually, that we not allow any unknowns to cause animosity between you. Between us. Whether there is possible deception somewhere within the godknights, or the motive for any attacks on calling towers, there are questions to be answered for both topics."

Domaren and Brikana remained locked in a tense stare after either spoke last, and broke their focus only after Brikana rolled her eyes and spun away to pace her frustration away.

"I hear you, Criz, and I hear you as well, Brikana," Domaren offered. "Please know that I'm not rejecting your concern, nor am I refusing to pursue it."

Still pacing, Brikana snapped her eyes up for a few glances as Domaren continued.

"I just don't believe we should veer from determining what is going on with the calling towers until we know who is doing what to them and why."

Brikana stopped and took in a long breath, appearing to be processing Domaren's latest comment.

"And what if something, or someone prevents us from seeing that investigation through?" She asked, coldly.

"I will not arm myself for a fight with a what-if, Brikana."

"Fine, I understand" she replied, speaking more softly. Her face however, still maintained a tense sharpness. "Just don't tell me you didn't know the fight was coming when it does."

Domaren worked mentally on a reply, but didn't craft anything that suited him. Instead, he nodded slowly as if pulling down on a thousand pounds of resistance with his head. He then swung his vision towards Crizichial.

"Crizichial, I'd like to proceed with your earlier suggestion," Domaren said. Crizichial nodded. Domaren then turned quickly to Brikana.

"What was that plan again?" She asked.

"I believe you, Crizichial, and I will proceed to the nearby calling tower and confirm its integrity, as well as engage any hostile forces that may be causing harm, or attempting to cause harm. If necessary, we three will return here to join up with any conscripts Maphikim may help assemble."

Brikana scratched her face and rubbed her eyes, undoubtedly weighing her thoughts on the plan, as well as any counters she may have. Within moments, however, she responded.

"Sure, yeah," she replied. "Let's go to the tower."

"Good," Domaren replied in addition to a nod.

"Before you set out," Maphikim added. "Let me offer up one suggestion."

The three godknights turned to the Redeemed proxy.

"To Brikana's point," he began, "be cognizant of your surroundings. Not just of the environment, or those you seek out, but the surroundings of those and those areas where you normally feel the most safe."

As Maphikim completed his suggestion, Domaren felt his adrenaline boil to the top of his skin, though he was unsure of why.

"Call it prudence," Maphikim said.

# Eleven

The group thanked their host for his suggestion and willingness to gather forces in their absence. After a few head bows and parting sentiments, the three godknights exited the Nebulum and crossed over the bridge in the Hall of Patience at a brisk walk. By the time they crossed into the rocky chamber with mosaics and columns, the group was jogging. After a much quicker exit when compared with their entrance, the group found themselves at the top of the path, above ground, and in a much clearer place, mentally.

As the group slowed down to a brisk walk back towards the border city and huts of Vordzinad, the trio discussed how to proceed.

“What did you two think about Maphikim’s parting suggestion?” asked Brikana.

Domaren scoffed.

“You mean the one where he warned us to be paranoid around each other after you brought it up?” He asked in return.

"Oh," Crizichial said with feigned politeness. "I was hoping we might not return to this topic so soon."

"No," Brikana replied, chuckling. "I was thinking of Nanutsi and Kegli. Do you think either of them might be up to something? If not both of them?"

Instead of any immediate replies, the only sound created as the group quickly traversed northwest through Gru Glech was rapid rattles of metal and the occasional audible breath as the group began jogging again.

"Look, that's mainly what I was trying to get at when we were talking with Maphikim," Brikana offered. "The idea that those two might be up to something."

"They may very well be thinking the same about us," Crizichial offered casually.

"How do you mean?" Brikana asked.

"He probably means that since we haven't had a chance to speak with them yet, that it's logical to infer that they would make similar assumptions about us just as we have about them," Domaren said, rushing words out between breaths.

"We?" Crizichial asked rhetorically.

"I was being nice," Domaren offered.

"Listen, I didn't suggest what I did or bring it up just for fun," Brikana snapped. "Considering that we are on our way to investigate a dwarven march on a calling tower should be reason enough to consider it!"

"Kana, I hear you," Domaren said. "I do. I'm just afraid of the impact the idea might have if we three need to depend on each other. We might doubt or second-guess ourselves. Like Crizichial said. We just happened to connect with each other first."

A moment of jumbled jingling and jogging followed without comment.

"Well," Brikana finally added, "I have no problem focusing on the investigation ahead. I just want us three to be careful as we proceed, and until we meet up with the other knights and confirm their... situation."

Their jog resumed uninterrupted—by conversation at least—and the trio soon found themselves back at the outer Redeemed village. Their approach to the village was a quiet one, in that they didn't see any Redeemed. Not until they had entered the center of the village did they see any Redeemed, and even then, there were only a few. Most of the population appeared to have finished dispersing to more remote areas.

Once they returned to the gate leading out of Redeemed territory, Domaren reunited with his temporary horse and Wiggly, while Brikana watched the other two knights prepare to depart.

"So, I'll be flying there," Brikana dictated.

"Hmm," Domaren hummed. Distracted by Wiggly, he seemed to be only partially paying attention as he reached up to pet her. "I guess you should try to find a horse."

"Huh?" Brikana said. "No. I'm flying."

Domaren ruffled Wiggly's ears and shifted his attention to his saddlebags.

"Domaren," Crizichial prodded.

The human godknight slapped a flap closed and looked up.

"What?" He blurted. After catching Brikana leaning forward with a scowl of aggravation, Domaren raced to pay better attention.

"Oh, yes, of course. Sure. That makes sense," he added, after finally rejoining the conversation. "We can definitely stand to have some fresh information on what's happening and who is moving where."

Brikana rolled her eyes at the prolonged detour they took to arrive at her initial suggestion. However, her eyes found their way back to Domaren.

"Is everything all right?" Brikana asked.

Domaren pulled his hand out of another pouch and turned around. He huffed out a puff of air and let his shoulders slump.

"Okay," he said. "What? Out with it."

"It's just..." Brikana started, shuffling her feet and waving her hand. "We don't know what's happening. We don't know what's going on with the Grove. Can't communicate. Can't summon any grove stones, and we don't know who our friends are. Yet, here you are, carefree and frolicking with a dog..."

"Come on, Brikana," Domaren said firmly. "Where is this coming from? I had to come find you and drag you away from Kimozoa to even consider getting you to listen to me. And now you're the one most concerned about everything? You're setting the tone for everything?"

"No, I just don't think we have time to waste on—" she attempted.

"What? On taking three seconds to pet a dog?" Domaren said sharply. With a violent whip, he then slung the clump of rope he had pulled out onto the ground. "What is the real issue here? I've been saying this whole time that we don't have time to waste and that we need to give this the appropriate level of attention, but now you're apparently the authority on worry and suspicion. Now you're the one that seems to be the most concerned. What is your true concern?"

"Just forget it, Domaren," Brikana said. "I apologize for saying anything about the dog. You're right. I shouldn't have said anything."

Before she could even finish, Domaren shook his head.

"No, you can't get dodge it that quickly," he said. "We need to know what's really under your skin before we take another step."

"Never mind! I said I apologized. Now, let's just get a move on!"

"Are you afraid?" He asked her, stepping closer. "Are you afraid of the unknown? Feeling powerless?"

Brikana's throat started to glow. Though she couldn't exhale much of any fire in her human form, she wanted to shift, and Domaren knew she could at any time.

"Asking me that question," she began, softly, "that *stupid* question, just chewed a large chunk out of the foundation of our friendship."

As she spoke, her fists balled up and she settled into a wider stance. As if a subconscious posture took over, it looked as though she prepared to fight, regardless of her company. Domaren stepped back, in an effort to reduce tensions.

"I'll fight whoever needs fought," she finally continued. "Wherever the fight goes. I'll fight the newest stranger, the oldest partner, beast, man, or creature."

Crizichial listened intently, as he had from the start of the argument. Domaren placed his hands on his hips while Brikana continued. His shoulders went limp, and his head bent back slightly.

"I'm not afraid," she said, stepping towards Domaren this time. "I'm angry. I want to confirm whether or not any of our fellow knights have betrayed us so that I can unleash everything I can muster to burn those traitors."

This time, Domaren nodded.

"I understand," he said. "I apologize for the words

I said that wounded our relationship. And should it be revealed that we are in fact facing traitors, I swear to you now I will endeavor to cause them as much pain as possible, as a cost for their treachery.

Brikana stared at Domaren unwaveringly, with few other indications as to what she might be thinking, though she did finally nod in return. While Domaren returned to fiddling with his own gear and packs, Brikana looked up and scanned the sky. After noticing the mostly clear sky with approaching cloud cover in the direction of the calling tower, her mind returned to flying and traveling.

"How about you?" She asked of Crizichial. "Are you in need of some hooves?"

"No, I am not, Brikana," Crizichial answered. "But, I thank you for asking."

Crizichial's words trickled out of his mouth with a delicate kindness that struck Domaren as well as Brikana, he assumed, with a curious humor. Domaren's confusion quickly dissipated, however.

"May I?" Crizichial asked.

Apparently having little clue as to what Crizichial was asking, he turned to Domaren who had found a smile of his own. In his palm, he held a bright green apple which he had just pulled from his pack.

"Oh, sure, I have more," Domaren answered with a quick laugh. He then tossed the apple over to his Redeemed friend. Crizichial caught the apple and a mischievous grin accompanied his rising cheekbones.

"What exactly is this all about?" Brikana asked.

Domaren snickered. "Just watch," he said, before turning back to his saddle.

After whipping her head between her friends, Brikana settled her sights on Crizichial whose eyes were now closed.

CRIZICHIAL

Crizichial held the apple casually, almost innocently. With his eyes closed and head subtly bowed, it might have appeared Crizichial was offering a prayer in thanks for the apple. His other arm raised slowly, reverently. He rested his other palm carefully on top.

Crizichial cupped the apple for a moment, motionless and quiet. His eyes remained closed and he spoke no words. There was only stillness and nothingness. But soon after, a quiet but discernible sound could be heard emanating from the Redeemed godknight.

As a low hum grew louder, swelling from deep within Crizichial's chest, Domaren finished checking his packs and gave Wiggly a final ruffle of the ears. He then turned around and crossed his arms before leaning back.

"You sure you want to do that?" Domaren asked casually.

Crizichial didn't seem to acknowledge his question in any noticeable way.

"Do what?" Brikana asked, whispering from the side of her mouth.

"Use his power. Well, specifically, to summon his mount."

Brikana followed her question up with a silent look of confusion.

"Oh," Domaren said softly. "I only mean that I'm not sure how much longer we'll have to wait for a grove stone."

Domaren waited for a reply from either friend, but none came. Instead, Domaren watched Brikana's tightened expression slip away as gravity helped usher in a look of fortified uncertainty. As her eyes drifted down and past Crizichial, Domaren went back to watching Crizichial carry out his spell.

Crizichial's drone continued growing in volume before finally peaking. He supported the sound as if drawing from an endless supply of air while maintaining a low, dense, and rich timbre. Once he had seemed to build up to a certain threshold, Crizichial's hands, still cupping the apple like a cherished rarity, became encircled in slowly spinning circles of delicate energy. Crimson and plum in color, the thin rings spun within each other, and around each other. All the while, the series of rings spun around Crizichial's hands in wildly exaggerated patterns.

The longer Crizichial held his drone, the brighter the energy became. The spinning rings of light throbbed with growing brightness and flipped and rolled about with an ever-increasing speed.

While Crizichial continued humming and his magic thrashed about his hands and the apple, Crizichial's exhibited signs of the escalation in the spell's power.

The rings raced and the blood red light crossed and clashed with the purples hues of decay. With Crizichial's hum at its peak and the apple fully engulfed in the orb of magic between his hands, Crizichial's body began to yield to the next phase of the spell.

Crizichial's eyes remained closed, but with a slight twitch, he knelt down and placed the apple on the ground. As he stood back up, the apple remained engulfed in a pulsating orb of the same intersecting light that also remained connected with his hands. While slowly pulling his hands apart, he opened his eyes. His entire body was now primed to play its part in the process.

Crizichial's eyes, usually a shade of burned orange, quickly receded and appeared to be overtaken by a layer of clouded crust. Part scab, part film, and wholly death, his eyes helped commit the first growth spurt to the apple. Second by second, the progression of the spell sped up exponentially. Crizichial's cheeks sank, and the apple grew more. Sores appeared and grew. They festered and became infected. Sections of skin on his face thinned, tore, and slid back to expose bone.

Yet the apple grew that much more. Very quickly, the

shape of the apple transitioned from that of a mundane apple to that of a larger mass. The mass rapidly took a different shape, a longer shape. The shape soon sprouted four legs, and an elongated neck.

"Is he..." Brikana started, once Crizichial had captured her attention again, "growing... a..."

"Horse?" Domaren anticipated. "Yes."

Brikana's chin twitched out to the side. Her mouth hung open slightly.

"I didn't realize decay magic could do something like that."

"Mmm," Domaren acknowledge quietly. "Bringing something into being using the power of death. It's quite something."

The horse-shaped mass continued to grow, and Crizichial's body continued to wither. While the creature being conjured started to assume its final shape, more of Crizichial's skin tore. More blood seeped out and dripped down. His bones could be seen, and even small slivers revealed glimpses down to the surface of his internal organs.

As Crizichial's body rotted and gave itself to the energy of the spell, the rich and lush tone that had been sound out from the depths within him also began to falter. Starting out as a powerful and soothing, the sound eventually became softer. The sustained pitch also slid down and gave way to incremental dips. Down and down the note slipped until his humming voice cracked, grated, and crumbled into sputtering spits of desperation. As the conjured form grew closer to its final size, Crizichial's voice finally gave way completely.

With Crizichial almost spent, the spell approached completion. And as the final bits of red and purple energy spun about and put its finishing touches on the horse, it was revealed to not be a horse at all. It was in fact, a zebra. Or at least, what most closely resembled a zebra.

The zebra was intimidating in size and striking in appearance. As Crizichial carried out his spell, he had given rise to the large beast that upon first or even second glance, looked complete. While looking at it in passing, the animal appeared to be normal in regards to its charming clashes of black and white. But after additional inspection, one could see hints of ribs poking out from its chest. And the ribs could be seen in such a way that made them hard to distinguish at points from the creature's alternating white stripes.

It also showed signs of rot and decay, but nothing so far advanced as Crizichial when he was at the pinnacle of executing a spell. In addition to a few spots where ribs were only slightly exposed, it also had a small selection of cuts and sores, easily discernible by hints of their slight, weeping wounds.

Beyond it's decay, cuts, stripes, and ribs, alternating rings of iron armor also adorned the beast. Similar to its ribs aligning with a portion of its white stripes, these iron armor rings encircling its body also seemed to align with its black stripes. Its tail and mane flowed out freely in dense tufts of raven black hair. But it was not hair alone. Interspersed within the zebra's dry and coarse hair were long lengths of chains and spikes.

Its eyes were similar in appearance to those of Crizichial's dead eyes, milky, and textured. Its head, covered in the same black and white of bones and armor terminated in an ashen grey nose. At the front of its mouth, sharp fangs extended out from under its top lip, two unsettling pairs on each side.

Attached to the armor and protecting its legs, were four narrow shoots of draped mail. They were linked together tightly, and had articulated spaces to allow for free movement of the zebra's leg joints. And finally, each of the creature's hooves were covered and protected by a section of living magma, somehow contained and shaped to the contours of a hoof.

As Domaren watched Brikana watch Crizichial bring the creature into existence, he grinned. Brikana's eyebrows slowly raised throughout the entire process and her mouth slowly opened in an astonished synchronicity.

Finally, both Domaren and Brikana watched Crizichial's rapid progression towards decomposition cease. Once the zebra's form had taken its final shape, Crizichial completed the spell and healed quickly, returning to his normal, ghastly appearance.

"What... is this?" Brikana asked delicately.

"This is my Corpix," Crizichial answered quickly. He stepped over and tapped gently on a piece of its armor with a knuckle before rubbing the small patch of skin between its ears.

"You've never seen a Corpix?" Domaren asked.

Brikana stammered and uneasily shifted her feet. Domaren took the opportunity to playfully tease his friend.

"You've been a godknight for how long, and you've never seen a Corpix?"

"Okay, come on," she said. "None of us have an opportunity to spend a lot of time with the other races."

Crizichial continued petting the Corpix as he appeared to enjoy the bickering between the other two. Domaren winked at him.

"Sure," Domaren said. "But this isn't my first Corpix. Maybe once we figure everything out and get everything settled, Criz, we can all spend some time together down in Neceith? Get to know each other better?"

"Yeah, okay, that's enough of that," Brikana said. "I don't want to hear it. You've been around since the birth of the virtues. You've had a lot more time than any of us to become as worldly as you apparently are."

Domaren seemed to bounce as if hiccuping or holding in a huge laugh.

"Yeah, sure. You've still been around for centuries, though!" Domaren said before letting loose a cracking guffaw.

Brikana shook her head and waved him away before turning back to Crizichial. She stepped closer to the Corpix and took a discerning glance at the creature's fangs.

"So, is this the only Corpix? Does this one have a name?" Brikana asked. Her head tipped and rolled about as she studied the Corpix.

"There are more Corpix, yes, in the sense that we can conjure more than one," Crizichial replied. "Each time we conjure one, it is not the same beast, though I do have the ability to commit some of my energy to retaining the disposition and memories of one if I wish. The name of this Corpix is Grizara, and I have kept her personality and experience with me for many years."

Brikana pulled away from examining Grizara's head, and slowly stepped down the length of Grizara's body. She placed her hand on its neck and let her fingers dip down and jump up as they glided over Grizara's armor.

"Are these Corpix, um, immortal or, invulnerable, or..."

"They can be destroyed, or maybe a better term is, extinguished, yes," Crizichial replied. "They are quite hearty creatures with an incredibly old root in advanced decay magic. It takes quite a catastrophe to destroy a Corpix, but they can be destroyed. If they are killed, to use that term, it is usually due to neglect while summoned, or abandonment, on the part of the one that conjured it."

"Neglect?" Brikana asked.

"If I may," Domaren interjected. "Let's continue our discussion on our way to the calling tower, shall we?"

Crizichial bowed his head. "Yes, of course."

Domaren had a final note for both of his friends.

"The only thing I need to do first is swing through Hornercruck to return this guy and pick Munch back up. We'll be quick."

As Domaren and Crizichial stepped into their stirrups, Brikana stood where she was, looking up at her two friends under contemptuous eyes.

Domaren flicked the reins and tightened their slack. He then caught sight of Brikana.

"What?" He asked.

"I won't be able to continue the conversation from the sky," she said flatly.

"Ah, right," Domaren acknowledged. He bowed his head and extended his hand. "Please."

"Yes," Crizichial continued. "By neglect, I meant that though they require no sustenance or water while conjured, they can be harmed and killed if they are left susceptible to attack or injury without supervision or support."

"Oh, I suppose that makes sense," Brikana offered. Turning to Domaren, she then began walking back to give herself some space. "All right, so—" she started. But Crizichial wasn't finished.

"I hope, Brikana, that I can soon ask you some questions as well, about the wonders of being a dragon. I have myself always been fascinated by your kind."

While the sudden exchange of pleasantries and curiosities was not in itself peculiar to Domaren, he found himself warmly surprised by the conversation. It seemed to him, that judging by Brikana's widened eyes and slight smile, that she was as equally surprised.

"Absolutely," the disarmed dragon knight said. She then turned to Domaren a final time. "Right then. We're heading for the calling tower, right?"

"Yes, the one on the dragon-dwarf border just outside of Bundinul," Domaren confirmed. "We'll be right there after that stop at Hornercruck. Kana, you'll be able to spot the area long before we can. If something seems vastly different from what we're anticipating, you can find us and let us know."

"That should be fine," Brikana said. "And back to something Crizichial said... Since we'll be arriving at different times, we should agree where to meet as a final staging point."

"Agreed," Domaren said. "Suggestions?"

Brikana thought a moment as her eyes danced from side to side before she turned to Crizichial. "You are much more familiar with the geography of your borders than I am."

Crizichial let go of his own reins and caressed his face with the back of a long talon.

"Hmm... I think that if you will be in the air, Brikana, that it might be best for you to stay back as much as possible and remain undetected by anyone so that we can then gather and make the final approach with as much surprise as possible."

"Right, and where should we gather?"

"My apologies, yes," Crizichial added. "The dwarf-Redeemed border cuts through the center of a valley, which is just south of the ridge that separates it from Bundinul. There is a tree line that extends out into the valley there that might make for a good gathering point and provide us with cover while we prepare our final approach."

Domaren and Brikana looked at each other, silently checking the other's opinion. Domaren nodded. Brikana shrugged.

"Sure, that should be fine," Brikana said. "I should be able to make it out fairly easily from the air."

Domaren tightened his reins and pulled to the right and brought his horse up closer to Crizichial.

"I know that valley," Domaren said. "Plus, I'm riding with you, so... shouldn't be a problem."

"Very well, then," Crizichial said.

The two mounted godknights looked to their friend whose firestone had already begun glowing. By the time the energy of her stone's heat glowed to the point of being noticeable, Brikana's body had already morphed into a figure three times her normal size. Then, in as much time as it takes a minuscule drop of pine rosin to pop in a raging bonfire, Brikana's legs and body exploded in size. Her wings sprouted and unfurled like hefty tapestries being beat against the side of a castle tower by a team of servants. They beat the air once and washed her friends over in a wave of wind that send their horses skittering back a few steps. Like Crizichial's Corpix, Brikana's neck elongated and her harrowing head of dragon likeness flowed into final form, only on a substantially grander scale.

The stone within Brikana continued to grow, and glowed brighter. As she settled back into her natural form, she beat her wings once more and stretched backwards, and then forwards. She arched her neck and head up to the sky and stuck her wings straight out to their farthest span. With her stone having realized the most brilliant and powerful levels that it can, in conjunction with shifting into her dragon form, Domaren thought for a moment that she might erupt in a torrent of fire towards the sky, if not them.

Instead, the dragon godknight relaxed and brought her massive head down to look upon her now, much smaller friends, at least from the perspective of her own eyes.

"See you there," she said. Her natural dragon voice punched the air in a solid but gritty alto. The last syllables smacked up against the mountains far behind them, and seemingly came back to reiterate just how extraordinary a being she was.

After pausing a moment for any potential reply and hearing none, Brikana jumped and beat her wings in a full ranged beat of significant power, followed by another one. Slowly at first, and then faster, the entirely unique dragon rose into the sky. Domaren and Crizichial, her two friends bound to the land below, watched in awe as the mighty figure of blackened scales gave way to the blackness of an ascending silhouette.

As Brikana's shape grew smaller and smaller in the sky above, Domaren waited to see if Crizichial would turn to face him. He did, and Domaren offered him a smile.

"After you," he said.

* * *

The human and Redeemed godknights set off through the gates of Vordzinad. It was still quiet and desolate as they left the city. Where there had previously been bustling activity of defense and teeming throngs of Redeemed moving about, or out, of the city, there were no signs of civilization other than the empty huts and chrysalises. As if the city had been abandoned centuries before, if not hours before, Domaren could not help but weather an unfounded fear that no one may ever routine to the city again.

The area surrounding Vordzinad was largely still as it was from before the time of Wrathlore, before some of the demons decided to assist the Kihdai in exchange for their forgiveness and redemption. Sprawling acres of ash and sand with small plumes of smoke and fire escaping out to the surface occasionally.

After the events of Wrathlore settled, and the Redeemed were forgiven, those demons involved pleaded with the Kihdai for a sampling of the rest of the world's geography. It was then that the city of Neceith was founded, and with the direct involvement of the Kihdai, was settled amongst a newly created forest and lake. As part of their gift, the great dragon Kihdai also thrust his claws into their section of the continent and ripped a great canyon into it. This also contributed to the creation of what came to be known as the Forgiving Ocean.

The canyon, which quickly started being referred to as the Vulgar Gap, was a means for the Kihdai to permanently segregate those demons that contributed nothing to the benefit of the Kihdai during Wrathlore.

As Domaren and Crizichial rode towards Hornercruck, and Brikana flew north, life trickled back into view. Ash and sand transitioned to soil. Stubborn flowers of yellow and orange defied the edges of the dead land and demanded life. Flatness turned into rolling hills of lush grass, which then gave way to the border mountains in the south of dwarven land.

The two godknights rode silently for the most part, at least as they approached Hornercruck. There were a few quick and casual questions of animals or suspicious of others at the horizon, but not until they had picked Munch up and made their way back east towards the valley did either re-engage in deliberate conversation.

"I'm finding myself going back to our conversation with your proxy," Domaren said while craning his neck up to spot Brikana.

Crizichial's position in his saddle remained unchanged.

"Oh?" Crizichial replied.

"Well, actually, I've been thinking about the conversations with both your and the dragon proxy," Domaren clarified.

Without speaking, Crizichial turned and prompted him to continue.

"I don't know. I just wish we could get everyone together immediately. Knights and proxies. I can't get over the feeling that there is a considerable opportunity being squandered while not being able to put our heads together."

"Hmm," Crizichial mumbled. "I guess that is why we are doing what we are doing at this moment. Working to check in with everyone so we can assemble sooner rather later."

The riders had slowed their horses to a trot upon nearing the valley, and for a moment, all that was heard after Crizichial's comment was the hollow stomps of rhythmic horse hooves.

"How do you feel about Maphikim's reaction?" Domaren asked.

"To what?"

"Our concerns. Our worries. The interrupted and lack of communications with the Grove."

"Ah, well," Crizichial replied, "Redeemed are a very calm group. demons as a whole are. We have traditionally made it our business to cause hysteria in others."

"Mm, that is true. I hadn't considered that," Domaren

confided. "But still, any thoughts?"

"I did not think much of it. I found his suggestions to be fairly logical. What did your proxy say about it all?"

"He reacted in a similar manner, honestly. He mostly just advised we continue looking into it and update him when possible."

Whether from the lack of a revelation in their conversation, the sheer size of Brikana's shadow, or a combination of the two, Domaren and Crizichial were suddenly distracted. Having come within a few minutes ride of the valley's northern forests, Brikana flew down and returned to her friends. As she landed, her firestone flashed and in the tiniest pinch of time, outshone the light of sun's most oppressive rays. Almost instantly, it subsided, and revealed Brikana in her human form.

"See anything interesting?" Domaren asked.

"Not much different from when we first approached on our way down," Brikana said. "The tower seems to still be intact and operational."

"What about the belligerents?" Crizichial asked.

"Belligerents?" Brikana mocked playfully. "Again, similar. A small group appears to be surrounding the calling tower. I would imagine they're waiting to gain entry."

"Size?" Domaren asked.

"No more than a few hundred, I would say."

"Are there are no more?" Crizichial asked.

"There are. They just aren't here yet," Brikana replied. "There are a few thousand marching south. I'd estimate they're roughly a day out."

"Does it still appear to be dwarves?" Domaren asked.

Brikana nodded.

"I still do not understand the potential motive for this action," Crizichial said, partly to himself. "How can they think they would be successful as one people in destroying the towers?"

"Well, I did a lot of thinking up there," Brikana started. "Time in the clouds, the temperature, and the wind currents flowing over me always give me time to think, and I vowed to myself to not give in so quickly to paranoia. Like we had discussed. Let's look into this and go from there."

Domaren crossed his arms while Brikana spoke, mostly to settle into a comfortable stance, but also to ponder on her words.

"I wouldn't consider any past concerns or worry as anything but a good thing," he said to her. "I'd much rather you, Crizichial, or I think through any contingencies than not, and be unprepared for what may lie ahead. Now, I'd suggest we take advantage of the smaller numbers and introduce ourselves well before that larger group arrives. What do you two think? Should we cross over the ridge where it dips down over—"

In a heart-bursting explosion of unexpected sound, streams of jagged rock shot down from the sky and pierced themselves deep into the soil. The curtains of sandy energy sank into the ground, tearing the soil with a violent shake and excruciating sound. The shaking continued for a moment and the clapping rips of sound and roaring of the land reverberated out and back between mountain ridges. In seconds, massive rings of stone reached up from the depths of the world, immediately next to the three godknights.

"Grove stones?" Domaren said. His voice gasped for urgent air as he spoke. "Go, go!"

Brikana sprinted between the horses. Flat out, she raced towards her stone on the far side of the surprise complex of grove stones that had appeared, while Domaren and Crizichial slid out of their saddles with a chaotic clumsiness.

After crashing to the ground in a jumble of rattling and stomping, they dug into the ground and clawed their way towards the stones.

With their questions and worries renewed by a fresh confusion, each one found themselves centered and situated in their stones as they had countless times before. Domaren slapped his hands into their recesses with a desperate force, as if it had been years without contact, rather than weeks. Once the others had done the same, the indentations below their hands glowed to life and an unexpected voice rang out from the stones.

"Knights! Knights! Are you there? Can you hear us?" The voice asked.

# Twelve

The three godknights paused for a shocked second and looked up at each other with eyes widened by conflicting stings of fear and hope. Each knight instinctively looked back down to where their hands rested.

"Yes!" Domaren shouted. "We hear you! Is this a groveknight? Wait... I don't—"

"Domaren, listen," the voice said. Their voice was firm, but measured. "This is the human Kihdai."

Domaren's eyes widened again, but stayed trained on his glowing stone ring.

"Not sure how long—" the Kihdai attempted. The message crackled to silence. An odd mixture of sound overtook the communication that Domaren couldn't quite place. Sounding something like a combination of churning brush and rolling boulders mixed with a windy rain, the Kihdai's voice only occasionally made its way through.

"What's he saying?" Brikana asked in a whisper.

At a loss, Domaren shook his head.

"...somehow found a way here," the Kihdai said.

"They're keeping us..."

The friends looked up while the strange noises flooded over the Kihdai's voice once again.

"...routes have been fortified."

"They are being held captive?" Crizichial wondered, while squinting and trying to make out each audible syllable.

"We can hold..." He continued, before immediately breaking off. "...you must protect the towers."

"Kihdai," Domaren yelled. "Please restore us. While we have our stones, can you restore us?"

As if Domaren's question went unheard, the Kihdai continued.

"...a new betrayal."

Domaren's eyes went from dancing aimlessly as he worked to process the messages, to being focused with a horrified clarity on the glowing stone. He felt frozen, trapped in his inability to understand. While he wanted to shout for help again, or lash out in anger, he couldn't.

"Domaren!" Brikana yelled. She gave him a moment but couldn't wait any longer.

"Kihdai! Please, can you hear us?" She asked, her voice weakened with desperation. "Can you send us a pulse of restoration? Kihdai?"

Domaren's eyes unfocused and his ears focused on the rumbling stone and windy rain sound which had returned.

Crizichial made an attempt.

"Are you still there, Kihdai? Please restore us," he pleaded.

But the noise only continued.

"Who exactly is involved in the betrayal?" Brikana asked.

But as the seconds accumulated without answers to

any of their questions, and no sign of a restoration, their hope dwindled. And like their individual grove stones that soon pulsed with light and crumbled to pebbles and soil, so too did their hope.

For a moment, the three godknights remained stunned in place and in silence. Each one leaned forward slightly, their hands still in the spot they had been in while attuned to their stones. But one by one, they let their arms fall and dangle uselessly by their sides. Domaren was the first to look up at the others, with Brikana and Crizichial following almost immediately after.

"I knew it," Brikana whispered. She raised her hands again and looked at her palms before rubbing them together. "I knew it."

Domaren turned away. After starting a slow, circular path around his friends, he brushed his hands over his eyes and down his face.

"I think I did, too," he muttered. "I didn't want to, but I think I did."

Crizichial sighed.

"That was a remarkably frustrating experience," he said.

"Well, of course it was," Domaren said. He stopped pacing and addressed his friend. "Well, wait a moment. Frustrating how?"

"In numerous ways," Crizichial said. "I have more questions now than I did before."

"I do as well," Brikana said with a stinging bite.

"All I gathered from that," Crizichial started, "was that the Kihdai are somehow being threatened inside the Grove. That notion lacks any sense to me. I do not know how anyone can enter without the explicit involvement of the Kihdai. Secondly, who might be involved with that or the betrayal here that they referenced?"

As he spoke, Brikana nodded continuously.

"Did you notice how he didn't respond to you," Brikana asked, "or any of us, for that matter? It was as if he was communicating widely because it was his only option. As if that was the only option available to him and hoping we would hear."

"Yes, possibly," Domaren said, his voice soft and ominous. "I can only hope that they had only intended to communicate with us three, and that the others aren't aware they made contact with us."

"As I said," Crizichial added, "I have more questions now than before."

Domaren rolled his shoulders and then rolled his head around in a stretch.

"I'm not sure what to make of all of that, to be honest," Domaren said. "There are too many gaps, and yes, Crizichial, too many questions. All I think we can do at this point, is protect the towers. I don't care who's attacking them, or how many of them there are, we need them all safe and functional. We depend on them, the Kihdai told us to protect them, and having them all working will get us one step closer to reestablishing our permanent connection with the Grove and the Kihdai. Agreed?"

There was no immediate reply from his friends, but after exchanging looks, they replied.

"Yes," Crizichial answered.

"Agreed," Brikana said. "It seems to be our only path. If anything, I at least feel better about our next immediate steps."

"I feel the same way," Domaren said. "Now how shall we proceed?"

"Like you had said earlier, I recommend we make

our best possible speed to investigate as quickly as we can," Crizichial said. "There could potentially be time to engage with those at the tower now, gain some information, and then pull back to gather additional forces if necessary."

"I think that will work," Crizichial said. "Yes, we must be quick. What do you think, Brikana?"

"Yes, we can start with that," she answered. "We can use the forest for cover while we cross over the ridge. Hopefully the trees will get us fairly close once we're on the other side."

"I agree with you," Domaren said. Before continuing, he pointed up towards the ridge. "If we head up in that direction, we won't have to deal with the steep climb for too long.

"Mm, yes," Brikana said in agreement. "From what I remember while I was flying, the forest extends over the ridge with the bulkiest portion on the other side being closer to the mountains, rather than towards the end of the ridge. If we went around, we'd be out in the open. They'd see us coming long before we reached the tower doors. And beyond that, it would take another day to go around."

"Up and over seems to be our agreed upon task," Crizichial said.

Domaren agreed.

"Right. Let's get a move on and see what we can see."

* * *

The trio of godknights took off for the mountain ridge, and more specifically, a small section that dipped in elevation a helpful thousand feet. At first, no one spoke and focused on their footing.They crunched leaves and slipped on sticks buried beneath.

After an hour, the climb leveled off if just for a moment before tapering down on the other side. They had reached the top.

"Can anyone spot the tower?" Domaren asked.

There were no immediate confirmations, but Crizichial made a different observation.

"Be careful not to make too much noise," he advised. "They may have sent scouts into the woods or stationed guards."

The three of them fanned out to cover more territory. Crizichial went to the left, Domaren to the right, while Brikana stayed in the center and descended down the other side some. All three took turns bending and craning their necks to try and spot their destination through the trees. Finally, someone spotted it.

Domaren clicked his teeth once and then again. When Crizichial and Brikana looked, he waved them over and pointed ahead through the trees. They rejoined Domaren and peeked out.

"See it?" Domaren asked. "It's a lot closer than I thought it would be."

Brikana stepped down the slope a few steps.

"I see some tents around the base of the tower, but I can't see the whole camp," she said. "It extends behind that hill over there."

"There does not appear to be anyone in the valley between here and the camp," Crizichial added.

"Well, the approach seems clear and easy," Domaren said.

Brikana turned back and put her hands on her hips. "I'd almost say too easy," she said. "If it wasn't for those reinforcements we know are on the way. It may not get any better than this."

As he knelt down to one knee, Domaren looked up at Crizichial.

"What do you think?" He asked.

"Given the information we have at this moment," he answered. "I am inclined to agree with Brikana's position. Time is most likely of the essence."

"How should we approach?" Domaren asked his friends. "Out in the open and casual? To try and see if some conversation will yield or anything, or sneak as best we can and attack?"

"Do any of us think a conversation will accomplish anything?" Crizichial asked. "I honestly can not decide."

"Listen," Brikana said. "After what the Kihdai said, I'd have a perfectly clear conscience if we attacked first and asked questions later."

Domaren rubbed his chin and scanned the forest. His eyes glided over the patches of emerald moss and ambitious saplings.

"Hmm," he mumbled. "I agree with you Kana. But I'd like to see if we can get them to spill any information before we fight them. I'm fine with fighting them and removing them from the the tower, though. And honestly, I think we'll probably have the same success if we surprise them or if we engage them after whatever conversation we have goes sour."

"Sure," Brikana said with a shrug. "I don't really have a preference."

"Criz?" Domaren asked.

"I will defer to you. I am also fine with either tactic."

Domaren tossed a twig he had been fiddling with and leapt to his feet.

"Right, okay," he said. "Let's go then."

He stepped down past Brikana and took the lead. With

the impromptu plan decided, the group made no effort to conceal themselves or to step softly. Though nothing was said as they finished their descent, they made plenty of noise while making their best speed down the other side of the mountain.

After reaching the valley floor, they continued walking through a broad section of forest that extended out into the valley. There was once again no sign of any guards or scouts, but as the forest started to thin out and give away to additional openness, the trio slowed their pace and looked up to the tower and surrounding hill.

"I can't see as many of the tents now that we're in the valley," Brikana said. No one replied.

Their trek continued until they finally broke free of the trees. Once they were within half a mile of the tower, they were completely in the open, exposed, and without much of natural cover.

"What's next?" Brikana asked. Her voice was louder than a whisper, but only just.

Crizichial added to the questions.

"Straight to the gate or veer towards the camp?"

"Let's go straight for the gate," Domaren answered with his eyes glued to the approaching hilltop. "If it gets as far as a discussion, we don't owe them an explanation, but we can say whatever we have to."

"Like what?" Brikana asked.

"Do we want to try the truth?" Crizichial suggested.

"Crizichial," Brikana began, scoffing, "we know you're Redeemed and scrupulous and all that, but—"

"I was not proposing that due to any moral obligation or guilty compulsion, Brikana." As he spoke, he looked away, dismissively. "I simply suggested it as a potential best topic to illicit the most meaningful dialog for our purposes."

"All right, fine," she said. "So, what exactly do we say to them when they notice us? 'Oh, hello. We've heard there are some shady types about. You boys better not be up to anything—'"

"Okay, okay, Brikana," Domaren said, interrupting with a wafting hand. "Just let me do the talking, you two, and we'll go from there. Count on ending up in a fight, regardless."

Brikana waved a hand of her own back at Domaren.

"I don't think they've been in the tower yet," she said, squinting up at the massive cylindrical turret. "At least not yet, it looks like. They don't seem to have severed the tower's connection with the Grove. I can still see the light from the roots shining through the window. Why would they just be camping out here like this?"

"Likely waiting for their reinforcements," Crizichial offered.

Domaren worked to extrapolate possibilities..

"If it is indeed a knight behind all of this, they would be aware of calling tower defenses. Waiting for the larger force makes sense."

"Should I go ahead and shift?" She asked.

"Not just yet," Domaren replied. "It might buy us some extra—"

"You there!" A voice at the top of the hill shouted. A dwarf had crested the hill just below the tower and caught sight of the approaching godknights. Another dwarf ran up to his side.

"Stop where you are right now!" The same dwarf ordered.

Domaren rushed a last comment under his breath for his friends.

"Just keep walking casually," he muttered before

yelling up the dwarf. "Apologies!" He yelled kindly. "What was that you said?"

"Quit playing stupid!" The dwarf yelled. "Stop!"

Domaren held his palms up in an effort to diffuse the rapid escalation.

"Master dwarf," Domaren resumed. "We are three godknights, friends to the dwarves. We approach without malice or hostilities. Are you camped here? Can we be of assistance?"

The dwarf didn't answer. After another half dozen dwarves ran up, the second dwarf ran off. After he disappeared behind the hill, a harsh and wooden horn sounded. A first pitch. A higher pitch, and then an extended low pitch. It was then repeated at what sounded like the rear of the camp the knights had originally gotten glimpses of.

"Hmm, well, this is providing us with a wealth of information," Brikana mumbled.

"Okay," Domaren conceded softly. "Let's go ahead and stop here for a minute."

As the three came to a stop, they watched as a modest group of dwarves assembled, but upon further inspection, the knights were surprised by an unexpected sight.

"Who is..." Brikana started. "Are those—"

"Seavers," Crizichial answered.

Brikana shifted her feet and flailed her arms in annoyance.

"Seavers? All the way over here?" She said.

Domaren rubbed his eyes and rested a hand on Verikta's pommel but immediately removed it.

"Yeah, they probably swam out from Andein and down through the Okinsoba Sea," Domaren said. "Anyway, that would make sense, I suppose. With us three here, that would only leave Nanutsi and Kegli to go against the

Kihdai. It would then follow that they would unite their forces towards their ambitions."

While demons don't sigh, necessarily, they are known to express frustration in other ways. Some slide and dig hooves into the ground. Some cause the grasses and flowers of the ground immediately around them to wither and die. Crizichial was one that did the latter. When Domaren noticed the ground dying, he turned to his friend.

"What is it, Criz?"

With the Redeemed knight's mind distracted, the ground was spared and it quickly recovered.

"Oh," he started. "I was just holding onto a slim possibility that they were not attempting a full on betrayal. Much less both of them.

Brikana said nothing. Domaren assumed her silence was an agreement of omission.

"It is quite something," Crizichial continued. "Something terribly unfortunate."

Domaren and Brikana looked over, waiting for Crizichial to complete his thought.

"To potentially have to fight a second time, against those who so flagrantly reject the gifts and blessings of those who granted me and my people redemption."

Brikana's eyes lingered on her fellow knight as his comments took hold in her mind.

"Some people will never be happy, Crizichial" Domaren said. The ranks of dwarves and seavers at the top of the hill settled. As they waited to see what actions the group might take, Domaren continued. "They can be given things. Gold. Land. Rank. It doesn't matter. Some will never be grateful. Some will never be content. They will fight for things they don't have no matter what, and will never allow themselves the rich rewards of peace, and allowing themselves to be at peace. That's a lot of what we saw when you and some of the demons came to our aide. The life of this world never learns."

"I appreciate the insight, my friend," Crizichial whispered. "Nonetheless, it is no less discourag—"

"It must go without saying," a dwarf shouted, "that we can not allow you to approach."

"See?" Domaren said in a hushed voice. "Discussion."

"And why is that, exactly?" Brikana yelled back. Her voice was bold and confident, but amiable. "Who has given you this directive?"

The dwarves didn't answer, and the gathered force on the hill tightened up. A dwarf and seaver could each be seen speaking with another dwarf.

"I'm sure they're discussing options and weighing their chances while they wait to be reinforced," Domaren said. "If they don't reply soon, I'm going to keep going."

"I might try some additional diplomacy for good measure," Crizichial said.

Domaren playfully presented the dwarven and seaver force to Crizichial by extending his open palm.

"Please..." Domaren said.

"Dear friends and allies," Crizichial began. "As I am sure many of you know, I am Crizichial, Godknight of the Redeemed, and proud defender of the Kihdai and their lands we currently inhabit. Next to me are of course Brikana and Domaren, Godknights of the Dragons and Humans, respectively. We have no desire to engage in battle with you. As you can see, we have no accompanying forces, and simply wish to enter the calling tower. A calling tower, I would remind you, is the responsibility of all godknights to protect. Surely you would not hinder us from our duty in that regard."

"You may say what you like, traitors," the dwarf yelled in disgust, "but you will not advance freely. Your being without any attending forces is of no concern to us either. We are fully aware that godknights operate alone."

"Traitors?" Brikana repeated under her breath.

"Now we have tolerated your facade long enough," the dwarf continued fiercely. "Say nothing more and take your leave of us and this tower!"

"Wait a moment," Domaren muttered to his friends as he stepped forward. He shouted his following question.

"Why do you call us—"

Domaren couldn't finish. The dwarf leader stepped out a few paces and looked down to the end of the front row. He waved his arm and signaled. A dwarf at the end lifted a horn and blasted out a different series of tones. Once again, a much fainter repetition sounded out from farther back. The dwarves and seavers set off down the hill.

"They called us traitors, Domaren," Brikana reiterated. "What do we do with that?"

"I don't know," Domaren said as he stepped back towards his friends.

"Are they here to attack the tower, or defend it?" Crizichial asked.

The three knights stood their ground and continued trying to decipher what was transpiring. As Domaren considered strategies, a few dozen dwarves and seavers broke off for the tower.

"I'm not sure," Domaren said. "Not enough to on. They were waiting on the reinforcements for some reason, but we don't know why. Either way, they may be trying to move on the tower now while the larger group distracts us." As he finished outlining the plan, he gestured at Crizichial to back away.

"Might as well shift, Brikana. Crizichial. Let's me and you engage this larger group. Kana, will you strafe that group nearest the tower?"

Rather than answer, Brikana instead proceeded to heat up her firestone. It once again burned bright and blasted a wave of light across the field. When the flash had dissipated, the Black Dragon had returned.

"Wait, strafe was a bit much," Domaren added. "Just steer them. Get them away from the tower. Send them our way, or wherever else, just away from us."

As soon as Brikana shifted, the marching dwarves and seavers sounded a charge and raced down the hill. Brikana lifted off with furious energy and quickly climbed to gain elevation.

"Unless we absolutely have to, Crizichial, let's try not to land killing blows," Domaren said.

"Agreed."

"And try to conserve whatever energy you can. Let's just try to... dissuade them from continuing their attack," Domaren added.

"Understood. Should we attempt to make our way to the tower?"

"Yes. They really won't want us to, but yes."

Domaren pulled Verikta and positioned himself in a defensive stance. He whipped his head side to side to gauge the approaching group's velocity and timing. When he felt his thumb slide over one of his sword stones and thought to press it, he pulled the sword down to his eyes and examined the handle. His eyes blurred and his awareness of his surroundings temporarily evaporated. He had never had to second guess pressing one of Verikta's stones before and he found himself locked in a flurry of confusion. Having completely become disassociated with the moment, what he was preparing for, and what was coming, he simply stood there as if trying to remember why he was holding his sword.

"Domaren," Crizichial attempted.

Still, he simply stood there, motionless and dumbstruck.

"Domaren!" Crizichial shouted. "They are upon us!"

The words *upon us* stirred something up within Domaren to snap him out of his mind's sedentary fog. With stunned eyes wide, he looked over at Crizichial who had initiated fighting hand to hand with a spear he had relieved a dwarf of. Crizichial had refrained from using any of his energy as suggested. Combined with the blunt end of the spear, kicks, and shoves, Domaren saw Crizichial use primarily defensive attacks to subdue or disarm the swarming force.

Anxiety scratched at Domaren's nerves. From losing touch with reality, to being late to engage the attacking mob, a foreign discomfort soaked into his limbs like a glue made of fear. But in hopes of slapping some of what he knows back into his mind, Domaren spun Verikta in his hands. Domaren then lunged towards an approaching dwarf to join his friend in the fight.

Domaren also kept to defensive tactics. He also kicked, punched, or slapped, but in addition to blocking with Verikta, also used the flat of his blade to beat and bash. Painful, but not lethal. Dwarves flew back, stunned and irritated. They hurled curses and yelled at the godknights in frustration. The dwarves weren't holding back, and even with the knights doing all they could to avoid killing blows, the dwarves still found themselves unable to land anything meaningful against Domaren and Crizichial.

The seavers provided a different, but similar challenge.

Roughly the same height as humans, the evolved race of seavers—a humanoid creature with a combination of beaver and seal features—met Domaren on a similar footing. Their smooth heads and short noses were protected by a rounded helmet. The lack of edges encouraged incoming slashes to glance or slide off.

Their torsos resembled the shape of an inverted avocado. Seavers stand on two feet and though their long torsos start out broad and rotund at the shoulders and taper down to a slightly slimmer waste, their chests are typically muscular and strong. Similar to human armor, their arms and torsos wear similarly designed mail or plate. Like their helmets, their chest pieces, pauldrons, and other pieces are rounded as well. Where there might be any articulating edges or rivets, the edges are often layered over one another or are covered with additional flaps of layer tied by connecting strands that are woven through small holes in various pieces of armor. But the most distinguishing feature of a battle ready seaver, is most often their most deadly and feared by those who encounter them in battle.

Their long and flat tails are very often covered in small segments of plate and arranged like scales. They are often simply covered and protected while the particular seaver has a specific role and does not depend on their tail too often. Other seavers use their tails as their primary weapon or use it for other means.

Some seavers are heavily armored and carry no weapons. These seavers use their tails similar to a sleigh, and carry supplies or other needs for war on their tails, darting about across a battlefield. When there is no active fighting, or before or after a fight, these seavers will also transport items throughout a camp.

Other seavers are known to accompany carts filled

with projectiles. These projectiles can range in composition from water to combustible oils ignited by distant archers, poison, tar, or sometimes, they're merely large stones the size of a seaver or human head. In a fight, attendants who ride along with the carts will toss these projectiles onto the tails of the beavers to be launched towards their enemies on the opposing side.

Lastly, the most challenging seavers to fight are the ones who march into war with weaponized tails. These tails can be adorned and configured in a host of ways. Many seavers enter battle with rings of iron attached to the bottom of their back piece of armor. Attached to the rings are short chains that dangle freely with extremely small morningstar heads on the end. In a fight, the seavers will spin their tails around and around, or spin their entire body around and use their full momentum to bash their approaching enemies with the full force of their flurry of maces. Even a moderately timed hit with moderate force will cause significant damage to most plate.

Another option for seaver tails are large single spikes meant to impale and kill enemies quickly. Though it takes years for a seaver to train and learn how to master how to control its single and significant mass, the results can be devastating.

The tools and weapons that have been arranged for seavers throughout the ages are numerous. A tail's adornments can vary from something as innocuous as food or supplies, to the most obscene of weapons. There are countless more, and one of the biggest advantages for a line of seavers is having the advantage of knowing what their tails carry and keeping their adversary in the dark for as long as possible.

Domaren dodged a rushing dwarf at the last moment

possible, and let his momentum carry him right by. He then weaved the other way and only just missed a swinging seaver tail, slicing low at the height of his shins. The sound of the seaver's tail chains clinked as they clashed against each other and tore at his nerves like a knife cutting a piece of linen in two. The seaver spun again. This time, he accidentally swiped and made contact with one of his allied dwarf.

A bright orange plume of light caught Domaren's eyes. He turned and saw Brikana circling down and launching streams of fire in the direction of the dwarves and seavers at the base of the fire. As Domaren had requested, she seemed to be steering them. Short bursts to encourage their movement, and hopefully change their course when necessary.

"Crizichial!" Domaren shouted. "To the tower! Go! Get some distance on me. We need to thin the group out some."

Without looking back at Domaren, Crizichial nodded and rebuked the attacking seaver by batting its tail out of the way with his spear. Domaren held his ground while Crizichial made his way farther up the hill. And in between blocks and parries, Domaren watched Crizichial eek his way toward the tower.

Brikana was clearing the way for Crizichial to approach. Slowly but surely the dwarves who had spears gave up on trying to hit her, or simply ran out of spears. Regardless, without outright running away, they shifted their position to stay away from Brikana's fiery streams.

In a careless tick of time, while Domaren was assessing Crizichial's and Brikana's position, a seaver tail struck him in the leg. Without giving it any immediate attention, Domaren pivoted to anticipate the seaver's follow up attack and instead of dodging, brought up his foot to step on it when it made its way around next. The seaver spun and brought its tail around. Domaren lifted up an extra inch and prepared to stomp.

Domaren slammed his foot down. But instead of landing his stomp and sticking in place, the seaver immediately pulled on his tail and sent Domaren flying backward. He stumbled and tried to hold his balance, but was unable. He teetered, tripped backward, and tumbled down to his rear. But before he had a moment to to instinctively defend himself, he was already being shoved back up to his feet but an unknown force. After ducking under a dwarven ax and hopping over a seaver tail, Domaren smacked a spear away and darted over towards a clearing. As he gained some distance between himself and the fight, he looked over his shoulder and saw the translucent shapes of the assisting apparitions Crizichial had conjured to help get him off the ground. Crizichial found a second in his own fighting to nod and raise his spear to his friend. Being far more appreciative than disappointed that Crizichial used some of his power, Domaren smiled and nodded back.

While enjoying a brief reprieve from pursuing seavers and dwarves, Domaren took in the state of the fight. A combined hundred or so dwarves and seavers had crested the hill and appeared to have no other immediate numbers to add to the fight. Crizichial was succeeding at thinning the main force out by artfully withdrawing from the fight's primary concentration while Brikana continued her rapid ascents and descents in randomized circles to predict and steer the movements of those near the tower. A number of dwarves and seavers had fallen. But while Domaren was confident most, if not all, should still be alive, they were at least unconscious, or wounded or pained enough to be out of the fight.

Domaren broke off into a sprint back towards his pursuers.

As he approached, he caught sight of a dwarf off by himself. Standing separate, still, and not wielding a weapon of any kind, he knelt to one knee and raised his hands as if holding something, but there was no object between his hands. Instead, a pulsing ribbon of orange light pulsed to life which then grew brighter and larger between his hands.

Just as Domaren identified him as a warlock, the dwarf had seized the presence of boulders and stone underground and thrust them up through the ground.

A few shot up in Domaren's vicinity, but they weren't close enough to cause any concern. Very quickly after, a pointed boulder that fattened rapidly towards its base shot up and tore the ground enough to knock Domaren off his feet, but he managed to roll out of it and back to his feet. After sprinting another fifty paces and weaving through the field of conjured rock, Domaren reengaged the dwarves.

"Warlock!" Domaren shouted at Crizichial. Intended more as a point of information than a warning, Domaren didn't bother looking to confirm Crizichial had heard his observation. Regardless, it was the warlock he headed towards next.

The warlock was noticeably more heavily armored than the other dwarves. Without a need to move as often or as quickly, dwarven warlocks were intended to enter into battles with their dwarven brothers and sisters and aide their fight from a distance. Just as this one was doing now.

Domaren watched as the warlock summoned energy to harness another boulder. And as the dwarf rapidly tore his hands away from each other, the massive impediments shot up through the ground. While continuing to watch the ground for rips or tumbling piles of soil in anticipation of the next stone, Domaren maintained his path towards the warlock.

Other dwarves and seavers flew into that path, in defense of the warlock. With additional bashes, back-handed punches, and blocks with the flat of Domaren's blade, he either deflected the warlock's defenders or knocked them out of the fight. Until finally, he was upon the warlock. He pointed Verikta at him.

"Enough with the stones," Domaren said.

The warlock held the latest batch of conjured energy in his hands, poised, ready to strike. But as he replied, he released his contained energy and pointed back at Domaren.

"I have more than stones at my disposal," the warlock said with contempt. "Plenty of tools to deal with traitors." As he finished speaking, he brought his hands back together and this time, rather than a sphere of orange energy, it was green.

Domaren had forgotten about the initial mention of being labeled a traitor when they first came upon the tower, and the repetition of the term caused his eyes to squint in confusion. But instead of dwelling on the implications, he launched back off towards the dwarf.

As he ran, he noticed new sounds emanating from the grasses and ground around him. With sounds of delicate whipping and rustling blades of grass, large ropes of grass weaved together and strung themselves into thick lengths. Like the jumbled limbs of an octopus, the long grass fingers then fanned out and worked together to lash out in an attempt to capture and grab Domaren. And though he was able to slap a few away or slice them all together, replacements took their place.

"All right, Verikta," Domaren said to himself in disappointment. "Time for some heat."

With a press of his thumb, Domaren pressed the stone amber stone on his handle. After a second, Verikta's blade had heated up to a glowing orange with hints of yellow.

Domaren immediately started slashing at the dozens of grass ropes. He cut off sections and sent them tumbling worthlessly to the ground where they collapsed into a harmless pile of grass once their magical cohesion had been severed. Others were stabbed or slapped and instantly burned. Their ends burned and shriveled up, rendering their parent length of grass rope harmless as well. After slashing through the sea of thrashing grasses, Domaren closed to within a few lunges of the dwarf warlock. Having momentarily misplaced his notion of non-lethal fighting, Domaren raised his sword for a killing blow.

Before Domaren brought his sword down, a rumbling groan seeped out from low in the ground. It moaned deeper and carried longer, and seemed to affect more area. But unlike the warlock's magic, this geologic disturbance snatched the attention of godknight, dwarf, and seaver alike. The fighting quickly ground to a halt as the entire field of battle stopped to look about in confusion.

Domaren's hands slipped apart as he unconsciously lowered Verikta. He struggled to make sense of what was transpiring.

*What is this?* He thought. *The only thing that would—*

Feeling a sharp twinge of dread, he interrupted his own thought process and whipped his eyes up to the tower's portcullis. They shot open wide when he saw a seaver standing beside the entrance with its hand pressed into the tower's defensive activation stone. Once a hand is placed on the activation stone, the stone surges with energy and awaits instruction on who to defend against.

*They activated the tower's defenses?* Domaren asked

himself in frustration. *Why?*

After hastily scanning the field and skies, Domaren caught sight of his fellow knights. Crizichial directed a cluster of undead apparitions to chase and threaten some of the dwarves and seavers away from the tower, while Brikana flew back after forcing another group away from the tower. She beat her wings twice before folding them tightly against her body to minimize resistance.

"Criz, Brikana!" He shouted, before turning to block an ax. "They're bringing the wall up! Watch out!"

The ground continued to growl but the sound soon morphed to crunching and tearing. The few dwarves and seavers still fighting were sent teetering. Domaren and Crizichial also found themselves fighting to retain their balance. The moment the ground finally cracked apart, Domaren remembered but was still stunned by how broad the walls were.

With no recollection of the last time a tower's additional defenses were activated, Domaren paused for a moment in exasperated awe to watch the wall ascend from the continent's depths. The ensuing chunks of soil tumbled over and cascaded in chaotic waves, sending those fighting and wounded tumbling.

Domaren wasn't immune to the tumultuous rippling of the terrain and crashed to the ground after an especially violent rupture. After landing, he rolled through the momentum and spread his arms and legs in an X shape before laying prone long enough to sheath Verikta.

With a moment to watch the defensive wall climb into place, Domaren saw Brikana circle around, undoubtedly to wait for the defenses to settle. Domaren noticed Crizichial for a moment, but as the huge wall stretched farther and farther up, the wall cut them off, leaving Crizichial stuck between the tower and the wall, and Domaren outside.

"Ugh," Domaren sighed as he scrambled up to his feet. *Of course,* he thought.

The newly raised wall appeared structurally sound, though it was wet and covered with dirt and moss. Clumps of both materials crumbled off and fell to the ground. When the remarkably broad wall first broke ground, Domaren not only noticed that the walk was some ten feet deep, but also watched as the walk populated with dozens and dozens of translucent archers that spanned the entire length of the circular wall.

Instinctively, Domaren slapped a shoulder stone to make sure his friends saw the archers, but of course, nothing happened. Before he could shout another warning in hopes they would hear him, he jumped to the side and leaned back to dodge an arrow.

Still intending to defend the tower, now behind the wall, and also wanting to regroup with Crizichial, Domaren shot off in a zigzag toward the wall. As he took advantage of the break in fighting by sprinting through the subconscious and simply running around the sparse remainder of dwarves and seavers, Domaren frequently glanced up to anticipate as many of the archers as he could.

He swiped a dwarf's buckler off the ground and continued his run towards the wall. With the goal of finding a gate, he avoided blocking and fighting as much as possible and continued running with the buckler held up at an angle to protect his head and neck. After many minutes of running and feeling confident he had made a complete circuit around the entire length of the wall, he sighed in disbelief.

*I don't remember these not having gates,* he thought. With arrows flying and the remaining dwarves and seavers regrouping, Domaren sighed and pressed one of Verikta's stones as he pulled her from her scabbard. *I don't want to, but I have to.*

He pressed the stone and felt the sword pulse in his hand. The blade flashed a rapid hue of orange and signaled its kinetic energy had been increased exponentially. Domaren pulled back and brought Verikta crashing against the wall.

While still holding the buckler over his head, Domaren stepped to the side and hacked at the wall like the sharpest of axes against the wettest of wood. Palm-sized chunks of stone flew away and quickly sent larger stones tumbling off. Domaren was making quick work of the wall and creating just enough of a path through, but just as he thought he was making good progress and turned to judge the proximity of the dwarves and seavers, he saw a group of a half dozen curiously stopped in the middle of the field and no longer pursuing.

They stared at him.

He squinted.

A few smiled back.

# Thirteen

Domaren had as long as a blink to think.

*What are they doing?*

*Just keep hacking at the wall.*

*Or should I call out to them?*

It was too late. He was out of time.

With no warning or hints of sound or sight, Domaren's entire awareness flooded over. In what seemed like the entire Akänse Ocean being poured onto him, an unnaturally torrent of water had been unleashed at the wall, washing him out and away from it. He couldn't help but swallow and choke. Razor thin hints of air gave his lungs hope as he tumbled and rolled about in the water. Glimpses of light flickered in and out of sight as he thrashed helplessly. He paddled and kicked and tried to slash the water with Verikta to try and get his bearings, but before he knew it, he landed on the ground. The overwhelming body of water finished washing over him and quickly soaked into the broken and parched ground.

Body and pride bruised, Domaren reached for his

eyes. Before he could wipe and open them, he heard a new rhythm of a horn blast.

After choking and forcing a round of coughs to clear his throat, he whispered to himself.

"Reinforcements..."

Domaren wiped his eyes and opened them. A blue sky greeted him, and for a moment, he wanted to stay right there. But instead, he took a deep breath and huffed it out. He leaned up and rolled onto his right elbow where he once again saw the towering wall. The conjured archers stood still with knocked arrows. The wall looked pristine. He had seemingly been washed far down the length of the wall. After continuing his roll, he flipped onto his knees and looked up. A few thousand paces ahead, stood the massive throng of dwarven and seaver reinforcements. After registering that Verikta was still in his hand, he rolled his fingers in a stretch along the handle and saw the additional army resume their march.

A gentle waft of wind and what sounded like dense curtains being beaten announced Brikana's landing. Domaren looked over his shoulder as she stepped closer.

"Where's Crizichial?" Brikana asked.

Domaren kept his eyes on the approaching reinforcements.

"On the other side of the wall. It came up between us."

The two knights watched some of the initial dwarves and seavers jog over to meet up with the new, primary force. Some helped others to their feet.

"I still don't understand why they ran up the defenses," Brikana said.

Domaren maintained his focus to the front.

"I'm not sure either," he said. "Unless they wanted to

do something with it before disabling it."

A silence fell between them as they kept their sights focused forward. Out of habit, Domaren squeezed Verikta's handle again, which reminded him that his other hand was empty.

*I lost the buckler,* he thought. He scanned the ground for another one, but there wasn't one nearby. He then looked up to the wall. The archers continued to hold their posture. Though they still had their arrows trained on the two knights, none were launching them.

"Shouldn't they be charging us by now?" Brikana asked.

Domaren didn't answer. His eyes rapidly jumped between the marching force and the wall.

"Well, I'm going back up. I think we'll need to be more forceful this time around," she added. "This is a far larger group."

"Wait," Domaren blurted. His eyes darted to the marchers and back to the wall.

"We need to find good positions before those archers start back up," she insisted. She relaxed her wings off her back.

"No, hold on a moment," Domaren said.

Domaren looked back to the army, still marching at a steady pace, but they weren't charging.

"You're not going to like this," Domaren said, "but shift back to human."

"What?" She barked. "No!"

"You said it yourself. There's something odd about all of this," Domaren replied quickly. "They raised the wall and aren't charging... and those archers aren't attacking. Please shift back!"

"All right, all right," she said. After another stunning

pulse of her firestone, she returned to human form.

"If this is some kind of trick on their part..." She complained through a whisper.

"Yes, you can blame me," Domaren replied as he slid Verikta into her scabbard. "Just hold on a moment."

The dwarf and seaver army marched closer. The few stunned or wounded remaining on the field finally made it to their feet and simply stayed in place as their allies approached.

"Good," Domaren said. "It looks like everyone is okay."

"Mm," Brikana grunted. "Everyone I was toying with should be okay, too."

When the approaching force grew within a few hundred feet, Domaren thought to address them, but before he could, there was yet another ground disturbance. Domaren looked up. Though this rumbling of the ground beneath was the most gentle so far, those across them stopped in their tracks.

Sounds of ripping roots and shifting soil accompanied a new ruptured blister of rock and dirt. But instead of constructed defenses, or summoned boulders, a skeletal hand shot up through the ground, and then another. Two skeletal arms reached up and grasped farther out to lift a quickly regenerating body up from below. Fat and tissue rapidly grew into place, followed by a rapid glimpse at organs, veins, and blood. By the time the figure had reconstituted enough to have skin, it lifted itself up and flopped onto its stomach before shoving up to its knees. Finally, it stood, fully clothed with its recomposed clothes.

It was Crizichial. He had used decay magic to decompose into the ground and exploit his drastically reduced mass to travel through the already-loosened terrain. His humble remnants crawled under the wall before scratching up and out to return to his friends. Domaren smiled at him while Brikana and the gathered forces across from them appeared locked in disbelief. After a dismissive glance over at the additional gathering, Crizichial casually walked over to his friends.

"It appears our fight will continue, then," Crizichial said.

"Possibly," replied Domaren.

Crizichial looked back across the field, and then turned to look at the wall.

"The archers stopped?" Crizichial asked.

Brikana hummed her reply.

"Mm hmm," she said.

Crizichial looked back to his friends before settling on Domaren. He tilted his head and looked Domaren up and down.

"Why are you wet?" He asked.

But instead of speaking, Domaren tossed up a pointing finger. Crizichial turned to look and scanned the front line ahead.

"What am I looking f—" Crizichial began. "Wait, is that Nanutsi?"

The lone three godknights exchanged glances of confusion and stared back at the one. Nanutsi, Godknight of the Seavers harnessed control over water and had manipulated it into flooding Domaren away from the wall.

Domaren started to speak again, but was once more interrupted by a commotion from behind. The dragon, human, and Redeemed knights turned.

Before anything was seen, barked exclamations and rhythmic chants rang out from around the wall. Brash melodies with simple harmonies seeped onto the field, followed by the clatter of shaking armor. Finally, marching quickly at half time, a broad contingent of dwarves arrived on the field.

“Ah, perfect. This must be Kegli,” Brikana said.

Domaren spun to look at Nanutsi’s forces, and then back to the dwarves.

“If we want to withdraw temporarily,” Crizichial suggested calmly. “Now might be our last opportunity.”

Domaren looked up to his friend and pondered the notion, but said nothing.

“There he is,” Brikana confirmed. “Kegli.”

The dwarves continued marching and reached the cadence of their tune. After another thirty or so steps, the dwarves stopped. Now surrounded on three sides by Nanutsi’s seavers, Kegli’s dwarves, and the wall, the three grouped knights took turns silently observing the disposition of the two large groups. But the fourth and only open location would soon close in around them as well.

“Domaren, they’re swinging out from the rear ranks to close us in,” Brikana said. “I’m shifting back.”

“Wait!” Domaren said with a bite.

“No, we’re just sitting here while they close in!” Brikana snapped in retort.

“Kegli!” Domaren bellowed out. Brikana sighed and stepped back.

“Nanutsi!” He yelled after looking back. “What an interesting situation, hmm?”

The flanking dwarves and seavers continued closing out the only easy escape route. Kegli nor Nanutsi spoke.

“Let us at least decide what to do should they charge,” Crizichial suggested calmly.

“There are three of us, and two of them,” Brikana said.

“Yes, but they have armies as well,” Domaren rebutted.

“Have we ever given much thought to fighting mortals?” Brikana asked rhetorically.

Domaren looked down at his leg where the seaver struck it. A trickle of blood had found its way down the punctured and creased armor.

"For now, I do," Domaren said, his words fell off quickly, supported barely more than a whisper.

"Perhaps they will meet with us," Crizichial suggested.

"Where?" Brikana asked, scoffing.

Instead of replying, Crizichial addressed their estranged, fellow knights.

"Kegli? Nanutsi? Would you be willing to speak with us?"

"I have no words for traitors!" Kegli shouted in response. "Only blades!"

KEGLI

The dwarves blasted out collectively in an antagonizing series of chants and slapped their bucklers with their axes.

"There they go with 'traitors' again," Brikana said.

Once the dwarves calmed down, Domaren seized the opportunity to challenge the notion.

"It might be possible, old friends, that we are all here for mistaken purposes."

Once again, no one replied immediately. Instead, Domaren, Brikana, and Crizichial looked back and forth between the seavers and dwarves, and saw Nanutsi and Kegli leaning over to confer with their captains.

"And what exactly makes you believe that, Domaren?" Nanutsi asked.

"We came here to defend this tower," he said. As he continued, he gestured at the wall. "And by the looks of it, you did as well."

Nanutsi and Kegli leaned in to speak with their people again, but this time, segments of the gathered armies broke out in murmurs and conversations. The leaders within the ranks tried to quickly silence them with sharp jeers which echoed humorously off the wall.

"All right," Brikana said. "We've come to it at last."

"With any luck, they will speak with us now," Crizichial added.

With eyes squinted from the setting sun low on the horizon, Domaren nodded at his friends in agreement.

Finally, after a period of silence, the three knights standing alone were pleasantly surprised. Nanutsi broke out from her forces with five guards in tow and marched forward. Nanutsi weaved back and forth to make eye contact with Kegli and gestured for him to meet. With a pair of his own guards, Kegli also approached.

Domaren, Brikana, and Crizichial waited silently for the other two nights. As they grew near, the flanking seavers and dwarves finished filling the gap.

Brikana forced a scratch of her face to shield her mouth. "Here's hoping this goes well," she said, under her breath. "I'm shifting the moment things go poorly."

Even if there had been an objection, there was no time for Domaren or Crizichial to voice it.

"It has been a very long time since we were all together," Nanutsi said flatly as if thinking out loud.

"Yes, quite some time," Domaren replied. "Probably not since," he continued, turning in Kegli's direction, "Kegli was knighted."

Hearing his name, Kegli took the opportunity to blurt his first question.

"Yes, fine. Why did you three attack the camp?" He asked.

Domaren took a quick breath and let it out before settling into a cold stare.

"We were led to believe you two were going to attack the tower," he said. He spoke confidently and sternly as he felt his softer approach wasn't being appreciated.

Kegli returned the stare but then let his eyes drift over Domaren's shoulder to Nanutsi.

"And we were under a similar impression about you three," Nanutsi replied.

Brikana leaned into the conversation.

"What? That we were attacking towers?" She asked.

"Yes," Kegli replied. His words were quick and impatient. "Nanutsi and I were in Naucra—"

"Ah yes," Crizichial interjected. "Your meeting with the elves."

"Aye," Kegli said. "When our discussions concluded,

we tried to make contact with the Grove and couldn't. We've been out of contact ever since."

"It was very similar for us," Domaren said. "My last grove stone was severed by sounds of horrific destruction."

Kegli shifted his weight.

"Destruction?" He repeated. "In the Grove? How?"

Having no answers, Domaren could only shake his head.

"What made you believe we were attacking the towers?" Nanutsi asked.

Domaren's eyebrows jumped. He looked about aimlessly while trying to decide where to start.

"At first, we were unsure of what was happening," he began, "or who may be doing what. When I lost contact with the Grove, I contacted Criz and Brikana but then lost the ability to use the calling stones. With news of towers being attacked, we started visiting proxies to seek their guidance."

Crizichial spoke next.

"We had little information, and made no assumptions," he said. "We decided only to seek you and the other proxies out, but—"

"But what?" Kegli asked. His voice shifted slightly towards curiosity, rather than aggression.

"The Kihdai finally made contact," Brikana added. "Warned us of another betrayal."

"Another betrayal..." Nanutsi said. She looked at Kegli and then back to the others. "We received a similar message, though it was broken, and rushed. We believed them to be referring to the events of Wrathlore, like *some* of the knights committed all those ages ago."

Nanutsi lingered on some of her words, and nodded in deference to Domaren. "We had some difficulty in trying to believe that you, Domaren, much less all three of you, would turn to treachery for *any* reason."

"Our message was also broken and incomplete," Crizichial said.

"It was probably the same message," Brikana offered as an afterthought.

The group fell silent as each knight seemed to chase their own trails of thoughts.

Kegli turned to his army of dwarves and gestured with a pat of his hand at the wall. After a blast of a horn toward the back of the dwarves, the defensive wall dislodged and shook the terrain once again, before slipping slowly back into the deep places of the world. The conjured archers popped into a puff of dust and disappeared.

With the horn blasted and the tower defenses deactivated, both the gathered army of seavers and dwarves relaxed. The flanking segments of both armies made their way back to the primary groups, and bits of chatter and relaxation filled the air. Domaren dipped his chin at Kegli.

Kegli slapped Domaren heartily on the arm while Nanutsi, Crizichial, and Brikana reached out and placed hands warmly on each other's shoulders. And after Domaren and Kegli exchanged smiles, Kegli's smile fell. He retreated into his thoughts.

"But that means..." he started. "Wait. If none of us are the traitors... Who is?"

Each knight stared back at the other. With heavier breaths and concerned eyes, they waited for someone to offer an explanation. But none came.

"I'm afraid we, all five of us now, are still no closer to clarity than we were just hours ago," Nanutsi said.

Domaren let out a huff of exhaustion.

"Let's see to a proper camp for everyone," Domaren

said as he rubbed his forehead. "We can continue this once we have everyone settled."

* * *

The day's sun completed its customary descent and handed the exposed camp over to a cool and gentle wind. The spot in the shadow of the tower was that much cooler. But as the camping dwarves and seavers made several trips to the nearby forest for wood, several fires sprouted up and took over heating and lighting duties throughout the camp. Domaren approached with an armful of firewood and plopped it down next to the fire Brikana built. In addition to the fire, a conversation had already been kindled.

"So, how much of your energy have you two used since we lost contact?" Brikana asked. Kegli and Nanutsi looked at each other.

Kegli blew up his cheeks and puffed out a sigh while Nanutsi shrugged.

"Oh, um, well," Nanutsi said with a shrug. "It's hard to estimate."

"What do you mean?" Brikana asked. Nanutsi gestured silently with her hands as if trying to explain it to herself mentally.

"I only mean that I've never gone very long without being restored," she said. "I don't know how much energy I have left at my disposal."

"Same with me," Kegli blurted while holding a small skinned creature over the fire. He dangled and bobbed a long makeshift skewer over the tips of the flames. "I don't know what I can compare energy stores to."

"Well, could you tell us what types of things you have had to use your magic for since the Grove went silent?"

Crizichial asked.

"A number of small things," Nanutsi said, still gesturing in an attempt to help herself remember.

"But those add up," Domaren said as he poked at the fire.

Nanutsi looked at Domaren, not quite understanding Domaren's implication, and went back to her gesticulating.

"A few skirmishes we got dragged into in Nekhsemn and Naucra. Disturbances the elves asked for our help with."

Kegli nodded and pointed his skewer at Nanutsi.

"Right. Squabbles and disputes between some of the elven territories," he said.

"And you used your power while helping?" Brikana asked in confirmation.

Nanutsi slowly dipped her chin. She dipped it again and then let her head hang for a bit before finally looking back up. She spoke with an ominous regret.

"I'm so sorry, friends," she began. "We didn't know we wouldn't be restored soon."

"No, no," Domaren replied. "There's no need to apologize. We all felt the same way. I only started being truly cognizant of my power usage during the fight at the wall."

A natural break in the conversation fell across the group of knights while the fire at their center crackled and popped. Kegli's modest catch occasionally sizzled. Behind them, dwarves and seavers laughed and cooked around their own fires. And as if begging Domaren to tackle Kegli to the ground for his pitiful bite of food, Wiggly sat next to Domaren and looked between the dwarf and human godknights with eager eyes.

"We were initially suspicious of each other," Brikana said with a smirk. Nanutsi and Kegli glanced at her.

Kegli waved his suspended skewer at her. "You mean, *you* three suspected each other?"

Crizichial looked to see if Brikana was going to elaborate, but when she didn't, he answered.

"Yes, since we three were separate when all of the oddities began, we were not sure what to think when we first reunited."

"What made you resume trusting one another?" Nanutsi asked.

Domaren looked at Crizichial and Brikana.

"Time, I imagine," Domaren said. "Things kept happening to us as a group, and then of course, the message from the Kihdai."

With the meat of the small rodent looking just shy of burned, Kegli brought his skewer closer.

"So, how do you know you can trust me and Nanutsi?" He asked, before stretching his lips to safety and biting into the hot meat.

Nanutsi's eyes widened slightly.

Domaren laughed, partly at the sight of Kegli attacking his meal, and at his question.

"Besides all of us knowing each other for thousands of years? The result of the fight at the wall earlier helped me rule you out," he said.

"Which of course leads us back to our current problem," Crizichial said.

Brikana restated the group's collective question.

"Who are the traitors?"

"I have been pondering this to quite an extreme degree," Crizichial said as he grabbed his chin and stared into the fire, "and I believe we should discuss what might be the most complex and difficult possibility."

Those who weren't distracted by Kegli's noisy eating

listened intently to Crizichial continue.

"We must consider the populations of the world being the traitors," he said. "Not necessarily all of them, but only that they may be the source."

"The regular mortals?" Brikana asked. "How could they ever be in a position to confine the Kihdai? To render their powers useless?"

Crizichial's eyes remained on the fire, but sighed.

"I am not suggesting this as fact, Brikana. I am merely proposing possibilities."

While Crizichial looked at Brikana with a glare of frustration, Nanutsi extrapolated on the notion.

"I imagine something like that may be possible. There is a lot of power and magic across the countries and histories of Stä Bläsjä," she said. "There is no one or nothing as powerful as a knight or what we have at our disposal, but..."

"Right, it's far more diluted and spread out," Brikana added, "but there is a lot of knowledge out there. A lot of superficial magic. Enchantments. Enchanted weapons."

"Could any of that rival the power, knowledge, and mechanisms of the Kihdai?" Crizichial asked.

"It was your idea, Criz," Brikana said, dismissing him with an eye roll.

"I am not challenging you, Brikana," he snapped back quickly. "I am pursuing this line of thinking."

"I don't care if every man, woman, child, beast, and dog, knew a book's worth of spells," Kegli said as he tossed a bite to Wiggly, "or had an indestructible sword—but I don't see how any of it could overcome the power of the Kihdai. Even the proxies pale in comparison."

A subconscious smile slowly slipped onto Domaren's face and his eyes blurred over in relaxation as he watched

Wiggly enjoy her bite of food. As his dog made him think of Munch, he turned to his other side and found the horse chewing on the thick patches of thin grass blades. But his eyes suddenly sharpened and his smile fell.

"The proxies," Domaren whispered.

The others barely stirred. Brikana looked over and squinted as if it made her hear better.

"What?"

Domaren looked at her, but away again while formulating his idea.

"Kegli mentioned the proxies," he said. "What if someone is using the proxies?"

Brikana's squint shifted from one of trying to hear to one of confusion.

"*Using* the proxies?" She asked. "How would anyone be *using* the proxies?"

"I don't know," he said. "But if the people of Stä Bläsjä can't overcome the power of the Kihdai on their own, they might be able to with the proxies."

"That doesn't make sense," Brikana objected lightly. "If we're having trouble thinking the various nations could overcome the Kihdai, then we should have trouble thinking they could overcome the proxies."

Nanutsi shook her head.

"The proxies are mortals just like the rest of the continent," she said. "They are appointed as representatives of the Kihdai, help communicate the intentions of the Kihdai, but are essentially clerics."

"Hmm," Crizichial muttered. "I do not know that I would distill them into such a harmless label. While they do not have the degree of strength or power that we do, they are very fluent in the ways of the Kihdai nonetheless."

"All right," Domaren said impatiently, "we can come

back to the overall strength of the proxies later, but let's consider they're involved for a moment."

The group thought quietly for a moment, but Brikana needed more.

"To what end?" She asked.

"Well, I want to be careful with getting too extravagant with any hypothetical possibilities," Domaren said, "but two primary motivations come to mind. Political and financial."

"But what might they be up to specifically?" Kegli asked.

Apparently following Domaren's line of thinking, Crizichial lifted his head and looked to the dwarf.

"The motives could be many," the Redeemed knight said, while taking a moment to look at each knight. "We have seen several before. There could be alliances in trade and war. Promises of goods or influence in exchange for support or favor."

"Have either of you spoken with any of the proxies recently?" Domaren asked Kegli and Nanutsi.

Both shook their heads.

"Which ones did you see?" Kegli asked. "What was their... disposition?"

Domaren, Brikana, and Crizichial took turns looking about to see who would speak first.

"Domaren spoke with the dragon proxy, and the three of us spoke with Maphikim," Brikana finally answered.

"Yes. I spoke with Votazzin, who seemed... concerned. Cautious," Domaren said. "He suggested another possible godknight revolt, but again, he was the first, and I hadn't spoken with anyone else so I didn't have many details to provide. And then, Maphikim..."

"Maphikim was also slow to assumptions or

conclusions," Crizichial said, "but he worried that another rebellion might be taking place."

"Neither really gave the impression that they suspected us, or were necessarily up to anything nefarious," Domaren added.

"I don't know that I would go that far," Brikana countered.

Domaren looked at her, puzzled.

"What does that mean?" He asked her.

"I just don't know that I'd go so far as saying they didn't seem to be acting suspicious, Maphikim at least."

Crizichial extended his long arms towards the fire and rubbed his hands together.

"What are you attempting to imply?" He asked her calmly.

Brikana opened her mouth uttered the beginnings of a syllable, but tossed her hands up and shook her head instead.

"Never mind," she said. "Never mind. I... I don't know. I just didn't like the way the conversation felt."

Domaren looked over to his friend from under disapproving eyes.

"That's two proxies any of us have spoken with since the Grove went silent," Kegli said. "Should we try to talk to the others? Revisit Maphikim or Vinlaza?"

For a moment, the camp's background sounds crept to the forefront. Muffled conversations hinted at assumptions as to what was happening. Scrapes of sharpening blades and the light tapping of blades being repaired meandered through the tents.

"I don't know," Domaren finally said. "I'm not sure what might be waiting for us if we show up to a proxy as a full group."

"What does that mean?" Brikana asked. "I've never known you to shy away from a fight."

"That isn't what I mean," Domaren said sharply after cutting a spiteful glare. "I mean that we don't know who our friends are."

Nanutsi looked up from the fire with relaxed and kind eyes.

"There are at least five friends gathered here, that I can tell," Nanutsi suggested.

"Yes, of course, I know that, I do," Domaren said. "That isn't what I meant."

The others leaned back and looked over or settled into their patient stares.

"A better way to put it is," he continued, "is that we don't know who our enemies are."

"So?" Kegli questioned.

Brikana held her arm out towards the dwarf knight in agreement.

"Okay, fine," Domaren conceded. "But whether it's a king, their country, some proxies, all of them, whatever our adversary looks like, we need to be extremely careful about what we spend our energy on. As we've all discussed, there is no telling when we will get restored, and we have all used a lot of energy already. Agreed?"

No objections were made.

"So with all of that said," Crizichial started, "what should our next course of action be?"

"Are there any legitimate options other than speaking with the proxies again?" Kegli asked. "I can't think of anything."

Having experienced an epiphany of some kind, Domaren started waving a finger.

"I was thinking a bit more on that," he said. "Time

is still of the essence, and assuming for a moment that the proxies are not involved and that all of the others are as equally puzzled as the two we've spoken with, then I don't know that visiting the proxies would contribute much."

Brikana leaned over. Domaren noticed her encroaching with increasing obnoxiousness.

"Well?" She asked.

"Well what?" Domaren asked in response.

"If you're saying it's not worth visiting the proxies, what are you saying we should do instead?"

Before Domaren could answer, Kegli suggested something.

"We mentioned countries and politics earlier," he said. "Perhaps we could split up and speak with some of the most prominent houses."

Crizichial wagged a finger.

"Oh, I do not believe that would be wise. To Domaren's point, that would take far more time that revisiting the proxies."

"And I think splitting up is a bad idea now that we're together," Brikana said.

"Agreed," Domaren said.

While Domaren was distracted by the ever-increasing brightness emanating from the tower's windows, he asked the group for help in making progress in their planning.

"Then how do we proceed friends?" He asked. "There is no clear path, but we must pick some kind of path. A delay in acting still eats into our time."

Kegli slowly stood up before bending back in a stretch.

"Is there really no one else that could help?" He asked. "No one that could shed some light on any of this?"

Silence was the response, though Domaren found himself locked in an ominous gaze with Nanutsi. Though they couldn't hear each other's thoughts, Domaren had a sense that she wanted to propose a final option. An option that both had little faith or hope in, but one they both knew deserved discussion.

"We may want to consider seeking out the Stäld," Nanutsi said. She blinked to break the silent stalemate with Domaren and looked around to the group. Some had turned to her, stunned by her suggestion, while others watched Domaren for his reaction.

NANUTSI

"I have to admit," Domaren said softly, "I have considered a few times that their involvement may be a possibility."

Kegli took turns jerking his head between Domaren and Nanutsi, before including Crizichial and Brikana. He burst out into laughter.

"The Stäld?" He said after gasping for breath.

Crizichial had not yet responded or acknowledged the idea and resumed staring at the fire. Brikana's face contorted in a mixture of mysterious disgust and confusion.

"I had only thought about them as an option," Nanutsi said. "What reasons might they have, Domaren?"

Domaren shifted where he sat and collected his thoughts.

"Well, it is known that they have harbored a deep resentment for the Kihdai since the birth of the virtues. Perhaps they have decided to exact some form of revenge."

"But do we know if they even exist still?" Kegli said, slowly settling from his chuckling. "And why? Why after all of this breadth of time would they decide to act?"

In what sounded like a huff of concern, Crizichial exhaled slowly.

"I had not considered them," Crizichial admitted, "but after hearing the idea, I believe their involvement is a reasonable notion to pursue."

"What would their role in all of this be?" Kegli asked, having returned to a demeanor of a constructive participant.

"They're practically a myth at this point," Nanutsi said. She then looked at the others with a silent look of asking for assistance. "Right? I don't really remember. No one has seen them in eons. Shortly after the birth of the virtues. Is that right? I've never seen them, much less met them."

"You're right. I don't think anyone knows if they even exist anymore. The Kihdai granted their requests to gave distinction and definition to the various forms of life, as far as everything I've ever been told."

"Yes," Domaren said, his eyes drifting to the fire. No one else spoke, and as they waited for Domaren to continue, they made no effort to rush him. He was there. He was there some 272,000 years before.

"The Kihdai met with us," he continued. "Well, they agreed to meet with those we chose to represent us. We were all fragile nothings at the time. We were all the same, nothing and everything all at once. We simply existed and persisted. We grew weary of what we new life to be at the time and asked for meaning. We wished for variety. We craved something to set the days and nights apart. We imagined experiences and dreamed of memories that would never come. But the Kihdai recognized our need for complexity, and granted it."

"That's pretty much what we all already know," Brikana said, looking around the group. "What does that have to do with those left over?"

"It's what isn't told or remembered," Domaren answered. "Or, what's conveniently forgotten when told. It's what happened after the Kihdai created the virtues and bestowed the complexity of life upon the world. There was a price for the request. A price no one wants to recall."

"Yes, and what was that?" Kegli prodded.

Domaren didn't reply. His gaze, and apparently his tongue, were trapped by the fire. Nanutsi continued for him, but maintained a stare at Domaren.

"In what was intended to be an unbiased lesson in fairness and repercussions, the Kihdai agreed to grant the Ställd representatives their requested variety, but the cost of their request was that they themselves would not be able to experience the complexity of life that we all desired."

The knights took turns looking at each other, or at the fire. Most wore stoic expressions of misplaced regret, or empathy for those they had never met. And where the background sounds were previously those of an active camp filled with dwarves and seavers, sleep had now claimed most of them. The night was now mostly filled by the sound of crickets and the failing fire in front of them.

"I must say," Kegli began. "That is regrettable for the few, but not all together inappropriate."

"No, not at all," Domaren replied quickly. "Virtues were born. The first godknights were chosen. The world filled out in wondrous dimension and richness. And he rest of the world's population thought nothing of the sacrifice of those five Stäld for the longest time. The Stäld themselves didn't seem at all bothered by the fact for an extremely long time as well. Generations of mortal races came and went with no signs of displeasure. Though finally, after some thousands of years, the Stäld grew disillusioned with the rest of the world. They grew weary of watching the rest of the world develop and change and squander, until they chose to leave."

"Leave?" Crizichial asked. "I do not remember hearing the details of that."

"Yes," Nanutsi resumed. "Please, correct me if these details are wrong, Domaren."

He gestured in deference with an open hand.

"It was sudden, and without notice or warning. But in complete peace and quiet, the remaining Stäld simply left their homes at the time, and other than a few sightings from or conversations with travelers, their location and fate faded into memory."

Brikana tapped a finger to her lip and sat back.

"My... I wasn't aware of all of that," she said mostly to herself.

"One could see how they might want to... do something to the Kihdai at some point," Kegli said.

Letting go of his chin and turning to Nanutsi, and then Domaren, Crizichial found himself hung up on a curiosity.

"But even so," he began. "How would the Ständ, the proxies, or any of the mortals detain the Kihdai? I still can not imagine any means by which that is possible."

Nanutsi replied first.

"Well, I think we're equally dubious of the proxies and the rest of the continent having the ability to do that, but..."

Following Nanutsi's thought, Domaren continued.

"But there's no telling what the Ständ might have the ability to do," Domaren said. "They had some level of primordial energy, just as all of us did before the virtues. They may have evolved that somehow, I don't know."

"So, what do you think we should do?" Brikana asked him. "Proxies again, tour of the continent, or look for the Ständ?"

Domaren looked at her and sighed.

"I don't know, Kana," he said. "Any of those options could yield something. They each might yield nothing."

After tossing a twig into the fire, he asked the others.

"What do the rest of you think?"

"So, our options are traveling the countryside aimlessly," Kegli began. "Visiting the other proxies and possibly getting no new information, or seeking out the Ständ and being attacked?"

Though Kegli seemed pleased with his humorous

appraisal, Nanutsi's lifeless expression appeared less enthusiastic.

After standing minutes before and pacing slowly around the outside of their circle, Crizichial stepped back towards his friends.

"I think the option that has the most potential for yielding additional information is indeed to visit the Stäld," he said.

"You sure?" Brikana asked with a silly wave towards Kegli. "Even if we're at risk of being killed by them?"

Crizichial shook his head and tapped his fingertips together.

"I am unable to say that I am sure, but I am confident. We have not spoken with them yet, and their has never been any evidence that would indicate they are are violent or malicious. The risk of conflict with the Stäld is, I believe, low," he said. "As previously discussed, their ancient animosity, is not only ancient, but it was also directed towards the Kihdai. Again, I believe our risk to be low."

The group of knights silently reflected on Crizichial's words. Kegli sat back and fiddled with his cleaned skewer while Nanutsi and Domaren stared contemplative holes into the fire. Crizichial resumed his slow walk around the fire pit while Brikana shook her leg and tapped her knee.

"Well, listen, I'm fine with seeking out the Stäld," Brikana said. As she continued, she motioned at Crizichial. "We need to do something," she continued, "and seeing if the Stäld can shed any kind of light on everything going on is worth gambling on them."

Domaren listened to Brikana and watched the others as she spoke. In addition to their reaction to Crizichial's logical justification, it seemed the group was of a similar mind.

"I'm of the same mind, Kana," Domaren said. "Nanutsi, and Kegli. Are you okay with that?"

The dwarf and seaver knights exchange glances quickly. Kegli shrugged while Nanutsi offered a nod to Crizichial who had stopped to measure each of his friend's sentiment.

"Very well," Domaren said after scanning the faces of his friends.

The group fell silent having made their decision, and Domaren found himself once again watching the dying embers cling to life.

Domaren laughed gently to himself.

"What?" Brikana asked softly.

After snapping out of his self amusement, he looked at Brikana but quickly turned back to the fire. His laugh had given way to a smile, which in turn gave way to uncertainty.

"I just hadn't ever imagined I would see the Stäld again. It should be an interesting reunion."

* * *

A reluctant sun rose the next morning behind a veil of dense clouds which appeared to delay its typical punctuality. Overnight, the crickets gave way to silence before being taken over by the earliest of the early birds and only their most delicate and considerate birdsong.

The dwarves and seavers struck camp before dawn. By the time the sun's searing orange finally peaked out from behind the clouds, packs were filled, carts were loaded, and a convoy of warriors streamed out through the valley towards their homes. Seeing no need to wait until the departing forces had dispersed completely, the knights prepared to depart as well. But first, they made their way up the hill to the tower.

"I honestly can't remember the last time I was in one of these," Brikana said. And while the group stopped at the gate and bent their necks back to peer up to the tower's soaring reaches, she amended her comment. "Actually, I don't know that I've ever been in one."

"I know for a fact that I have not," Crizichial said

Kegli said nothing, but Nanutsi spoke.

"I have," she said. "It's been a very long time, but I have. There isn't all that much to see," she added.

Domaren nodded and gestured up towards the top.

"Yeah, she's right. They aren't all that complex or anything," he said. "Their main purpose is to allow us to stay in touch with the Grove, no matter where on the continent we are."

"I don't usually hear a lot about these," Kegli said, pointing an axe at the tower. "Never had much of an occasion to need to visit one. They're essentially larger versions of our personal grove stones, right?"

"Yes, very similar," Domaren said. "Well, let's go in and take a closer look."

Domaren waved his fellow knights closer to the gate and placed his hand in the recessed access stone. Once again, light pulsed from underneath. The light flashed and clung to Domaren's hand and with his other hand, he reached up just beneath and pressed one of the stones with Soren symbols. Where the seaver had pressed the stone to activate the defenses the day before, Domaren pressed the stone for entry. After tapping the entry stone, he pulled his hand away and the light dissipated. The gate then ratcheted up and as Domaren stepped in, he beckoned for the others.

"Follow me," he said.

Domaren walked in and headed straight for the wide

spiral stairs at the center of the tower, his head already filled with thoughts about what they might find at the top. But before he took a second step up, he stopped. After being distracted by the silence of no footfalls behind him, he turned to see what was holding his friends up. When he looked back, he saw them standing frozen, their mouths agape.

Lining the interior of the tower walls, massive stone rings pulsated with a fiery energy. Like a stoked blacksmith's fire, they radiated and coursed with white hot light. Almost appearing as though they were floating, each stone ring attached to the tower walls and extended out for many feet. One after another, stacked on top of each other with a space of only a foot or less, dozens upon dozens of rings stretched up to the heights of the ancient fortification.

Domaren swung his head up slowly and joined his friends in a moment of reverent awe. The rings pulsated with mesmerizing light just as they had going back to the time the virtues were created, the knights were anointed, and the world was at its peak innocence and excitement.

The small grin that had found its way onto Domaren's lips, inspired by the remaining sliver of an ancient memory, fell as it gave way to the burden of uncertainty. Regardless, he took an extra moment to admire the ancient structure and its part in helping transmit the communications between the knights individually, as well as the Grove through the ages.

"All right friends," he finally said, as he turned back and took a step up. "Let's get to the top."

With their focus and admiration disrupted, each knight stepped away from the group and shuffled over to the stairs, while occasionally sneaking an extra glance up in wonder.

With Domaren in the lead, the other four knights followed behind in pairs. Each step up was a step into brighter and brighter light the farther they got from the entrance. After a steady pace of uninterrupted climbing, the knights ascended the hundred steps and reached the upper landing.

At the top, the steps connected to a massive platform that spanned across almost the entire circumference of the tower. Close to the wall, the platform had four separate gaps where the highest ring connected up to a final ring above the platform. That ring in turn connected to burning stones that ran vertically along the walls, to a smaller ring at the top, before running down to a hexagonal bank of stone surrounding the step landing. A small gap in the hexagonal stone allowed any who ascended to step up to the large platform. And while the bank of stones were not lit, two smaller and thinner sets of stones connected to the top of the primary stone podium pulsated with energy similar to that of the series of rings below. One set represented the connection between the world and Prumo Hald, while the other represented the connection between the knights.

One by one, the godknights stepped up and walked through the gap in the upper stone bank and spread out across the upper platform. While moving about the space slowly and in silence, each knight inspected the stone bank and the vibrant stones running up and then back down.

After a few quick moments, the group collectively stopped in their respective spots on the platform.

"This seems odd, but at the same time, reassuring," Crizichial said.

"What do you mean by that?" Kegli asked.

As he gestured at the various rings below and those around them in the top chamber, Crizichial elaborated.

"Well, the stones signifying each of the other towers

is illuminated," he said. "Meaning, they appear to be operational. The stones for our personal communications between ourselves are lit as well."

"No, I know that," Kegli fussed. "Why does it seem odd and reassuring?"

While studying the bank of stones at the center of the room, Nanutsi twirled some of her whiskers.

"I believe he's saying that since we can't communicate with the Grove, that he had expected some of these not to be lit."

"Precisely," Crizichial confirmed.

Domaren approached the stone hexagon for a closer inspection.

"Right," he said. "If all the towers are functional, then we should be able to initiate grove stones."

"We know that, Domaren," Brikana said. "So why can't we?"

"Kana, I don't know yet, obviously," he said calmly.

As Domaren spoke, he reached out for a set of indentations.

"If we can't use our grove stones, maybe we can use the stone bank directly," he said.

He reached out slowly, ready to place his hands in the stone bank, but before his hands made contact, the light corresponding with the tower that section of the stone hexagon was attributed to, flashed, flickered, and then went out.

"What... What was that?" Brikana asked.

No one replied.

Domaren went through with placing his hands on the stone anyway. With nothing more than the futile sound of skin slapping against dense stone, nothing happened.

"Which tower is that for?" Kegli asked.

"Looks to be the easternmost tower outside Beybluff," Crizichial answered.

With Domaren's hands still on the stones for the Beybluff tower, another tower's connected stone flickered next to him. While it didn't go off and stay off, it continued to flicker on and off at random intervals.

"And there's the one near Grat," Domaren said in a defeated whisper.

As Domaren slowly pulled his hands away and let them fall, another tower's stone connection flashed. And then another. One went off and stayed off.

Domaren sighed and looked around to his friends. Each knight's eyes were wide with worry and weighted down by confused brows.

"What?" Crizichial asked to the room. "How is this possible? All of them are disabled?"

Brikana looked at Domaren in a rare concession of concern.

"I thought we had only heard of one being tampered with," she said. "But all of them?"

Domaren looked ahead, silent, his eyes dancing about as he worked through thoughts.

"All but this one, it would seem," Nanutsi said. "But yes, I don't believe we had any indication the disruptions were this widespread. This... extreme."

Without commenting, Domaren began to pace around the bank of stones, their lights flashing and strobing at aggravating intervals.

"What is it Domaren?" Crizichial asked.

He continued pacing, staring intently at the stones, transfixed by their hypnotic and nauseating patterns.

"I'm trying to determine if there is at any point they are all lit at the same time," he said. "Maybe if so, we can get a message out to the Grove, or to the proxies. Let them know what we've found and what we're going to do next."

"I don't think that's possible," Brikana said as she flicked her hand out towards the bank of stones. "I believe one of them has only lit up once since we got here."

"If we were to get through," Nanutsi began, "what would we say we've discovered anyway?"

As he stroked his beard and scratched his neck under it, Kegli offered an answer.

"Well, we could at least tell them we're off in search of the Stäld," he said.

"But, even if we were to get something through," Crizichial added, "we still do not have much to report as to what has caused the situation we find ourselves in. We've ruled ourselves out."

Brikana reluctantly nodded at her Redeemed counterpart.

"I'm beginning to wonder if this is evidence towards the notion that this is a wider problem of politics and nations." As she continued she shook her head at the chaotic lights in front of her. "This is just too... too... big."

"Maybe it's worth trying to get something through anyway," Kegli suggested.

"How?" Brikana asked, flailing and annoyed by the panel's disarray. "None of the other towers are functioning. Look at this."

Domaren returned to the stone indentations and placed his hands in them.

"Well, it's worth trying anyway," he said as the stones lit up.

The light pulsed brightly, casting a shadow in the shape of Domaren's hands on the ceiling above.

"How can anything make it through?" Kegli asked.

"With their connection fluctuating so wildly like this?"

"That's just it, my friend," Domaren replied. "We don't know that it will. I'll just attempt a few things, and then we can be on our way."

Kegli nodded and walked over. The others gathered around Domaren as well.

"Hopefully there's someone at the other towers that will hear this," the human knight said.

"And if they all light up, the Grove could hear as well, right?" Nanutsi asked.

"I believe that is how it works," Crizichial answered. "But I am not sure that any of us have experienced the towers in such a state of disarray before."

Domaren looked back at his fellow knights and shook his head.

"That's right. This is something new all together," he said in agreement. "All right. Let me try something."

He turned back to the stone slabs and looked down to the bright energy that gently warmed his hands before looking up to their silhouette above. After bringing his eyes back down, he glanced about at the random patterns of chaotic flashing and focused.

First, he spent a moment examining each tower's corresponding light for any predictability in their connection. One flashed erratically with frequent but extremely short pulses. Another flashed brightly and held for a time before dissipating and remaining dormant for anywhere between ten to thirty seconds. The others shined on and off at even less predictable intervals.

"I do not understand how they can come and go like this," Nanutsi said with soft confusion. "Off and on. Why isn't it one or the other?"

"It has to do with the rings in each of the towers,"

Domaren answered, still focusing on the stones. "If any of them are destroyed, or if the path in which they normally route energy to the arrays of stones at the top is disrupted, their connection is intermittent or takes longer to generate the energy needed to establish their connection."

When the other knights ran out of questions or stopped asking, Domaren focused. He leaned down closer to the slab of stone and let his eyes blur as he monitored the various tower connections through his peripheral vision. Finally, he spoke to anyone who could listen.

"Knights together," he began. "Knights together. Repeat. Knights together. Knights together."

Despite not knowing if there was any point, Domaren paused to listen for any return sounds to ring out from the stones. They heard nothing.

"Knights together. Knights together," he said again. "Proxies consulted. Investigating disruptions. Proxies consulted. Investigating disruptions."

After another pause and a look over his shoulders, Domaren attempted to continue. But before he could speak again, Brikana posed a question.

"Why are you speaking in these choppy fragments?" She whispered.

"Really, Brikana," Crizichial said, exasperated. "I would imagine it is to try and get messages through in the limited segments of time that the towers might be connected."

"Shh," Domaren said before continuing. "Investigating disruptions. Unknown cause. Knights together. Proxies consulted. Investigating disruptions. Unknown cause."

Domaren and the group maintained their silence yet again and were met with only complete silence in the wake of the continuing flurry of random flashing light.

"Knights together. Proxies consulted. Investigating disruptions. Unknown cause. Seeking the Stäld... Will seek the Stäld for help. Knights seeking out the Stäld."

The entire summary was repeated three more times before Domaren pulled his hands away. He bent back up and stared at the stone array as it continued with its flashing patchwork of disorder. The others joined Domaren in staring ahead. Waiting. Listening. But nothing changed. No messages were returned. No confirmations of receipt of Domaren's messages were heard.

"Well... Okay," Domaren said. "Anyone want to say anything else?"

The others shuffled their feet or shifted their weight.

"No?" He asked.

"I don't know what else we would say," Brikana said.

In apparent agreement with Brikana, no one offered a rebuttal.

"Right," Domaren said. "Well, if the Grove heard any of that, they'll know we're together and that we're trying to help. And if anyone else heard, perhaps we'll meet them on our way to the Stäld."

## Part III

*"After Wrathlore, the petty beings that roamed the world—almost as helpless as they were at the birth of the virtues—could continue roaming aimlessly without our guidance, as far as we were concerned. Our desire to support a world that so willingly rejected us became our lowest priority for many an age."*

*- Kihdai Reflections on Wrathlore, 564 ABV*

# Fourteen

After the disappointing attempt at communication at the top of the tower the knights descended and prepared for their next journey. There were no remaining signs of the previous night's camp of seavers and dwarves, and the valley had returned to its typical serenity of unoccupied lush fields and prancing pockets of game. Deer loped casually across the landscape and finches sang songs as they excitedly shot through the sky on their way to a nearby, warm bath.

"So, the idea is to head east, Domaren?" Nanutsi asked as she poked a blanket into a saddle bag.

Domaren replied as he patted Munch's saddle and waved Wiggly up.

"That's right," he said. "Until we can confirm where the Stäld may be, we can head for where they used to reside—in the direction of the abandoned citadel. There's never been any indication they relocated too far away, so with a little luck, I'm hoping we'll be able to find them."

"What if they don't want to be found?" Brikana asked

while tightening the girth strap on her own horse.

"That brings up a good point," Crizichial said. "We will need to discuss plans and contingencies should any potential encounter go badly."

"I have to say, Criz," Brikana said as she turned around. "You and I are agreeing quite a bit lately. It's quite a refreshing change of pace!"

Crizichial, who had completed his packing and preparations before the others, stood calmly next to his cow and looked at Brikana with an expressionless face.

"I am overjoyed at the progress we have made in our interactions recently, Brikana, yes," he said flatly.

In preparation for riding, Nanutsi removed her tail armor and placed it in a special leather case and draped over her horse. As she did, her curiosity bubbled up.

"Why is it you two bicker as much as you do?" She playfully asked Brikana and Crizichial. "You both have had centuries to work out any differences or quarrels."

Crizichial looked about the group with a dubious eye as if doubting none of them didn't already know.

"Come now," he said. "We all know there are those who feel the Redeemed should not have a knight. And that demons shouldn't be trusted at all."

"And no one amongst this group thinks that!" Domaren insisted amiably.

Having finished his own packing, Kegli tied his final bag closed and stepped over to join Crizichial. The dwarf knight slapped his much taller Redeemed counterpart on the back.

"Not even Brikana?" Kegli prodded.

Domaren looked over his shoulder at Kegli with disapproval as Brikana spun around hastily.

"What is that supposed to mean?" Brikana asked

angrily, the glow of her firestone growing brighter.

"Oh, Kana," Kegli replied through laughter. "I'm only teasing with you!"

The dragon knight squinted at the dwarf knight as her mouth hung open slowly as if trying to decide which of her thousand thoughts would leave her lips.

"You should watch what you say, Kegli, joking or not," she said. While she brought the temperature down on her firestone, she continued. "I don't disagree with the Redeemed having a knight, and I trust many of the Redeemed as I trust anyone else. It's just that I haven't known him as long as the rest of you, is all."

"That's still thousands of years you've known him," Nanutsi teased.

Brikana whipped around towards the seaver knight with a face mixed in legitimate and feigned indignation.

"No, no," she said. "I see what this is. No, I'm not going to abide this hypocrisy!"

The others were now laughing or at least smiling by that point.

"We all know we don't get to interact as much as we would like! Our various cultures and obligations keep make it extremely hard to stay in frequent contact!"

"Oh, come now. They're just joking, Brikana," Domaren repeated.

"Joking or not," she retorted, "I don't appreciate the insinuation!"

Kegli raised his hands in playful submission and walked back to his horse. And after Domaren finished his own preparations, he stepped into Munch's stirrups and also mounted up.

"All right, everyone" Domaren said from atop Munch. He reached over and ruffled Wiggly's ears while scanning the horizon. "We'll head west out of the valley before turning north to go around the mountains before heading east. After that, we'll continue east towards the old citadel, hopefully finding the Stäld first."

"The population is pretty sparse between here and the citadel," Crizichial said. "I worry that our opportunities to gain information will be few."

"I'm worried about that too," Nanutsi said. "Hopefully we will have gleaned something well before we reach the Pass of Finjara or it'll be a long walk to the citadel without anything else to go on."

"That's a good point," Domaren said. "And before we go, I want to say again, that I highly suggest we do anything we can to make sure we reserve as much of our power as possible. Each of us has been using it off and on since the Grove went silent and we should try to hold on to everything we can until. There's no telling who or what we'll run into before we get restored again."

"If we find the Stäld," Brikana began, "do they have any means of restoring our energy?"

Each knight stopped their rustling and messing about and turned to face Brikana and what they must have considered an excellent question. They then looked at Domaren.

"I..." He started, at a loss for words. "I don't... I don't know. That's a very good question. I can't speak for certain as I haven't seen them since shortly after the virtues. I don't think they had any means to then, and I doubt they would know. But, that would definitely be a pleasant surprise."

Discouraged, but not surprised at the lack of an answer, the others finished preparing and mounted up.

"Okay," Domaren said. "Let's head out."

* * *

The sky remained clear and the verdant land presented few challenges through the rest of the morning and into the late afternoon. The knights didn't speak much as they exited the valley, and the few words that were spoken were usually relegated to small exchanges about letting the horses rest or get a drink. There were times where the knights saw riders at the horizon or small groups in the distance, but their paths never converged, and that's the way Domaren and the others preferred it. It was only when the sun slipped below the western sky and rapidly took the day's light with it that the knights found their first major topic of conversation since earlier that morning.

"Were we going to set up a camp soon, or..." Brikana asked. "Not a lot of light left."

Domaren did a quick scan of everyone's faces.

"Good question," he said. "I'm fine with continuing on, but what does everyone else think?"

Kegli twisted and turned in his saddle.

"Ah, there it is," he said whispering. As he continued, he spoke louder for the benefit of the group. "If the weather holds and we can hang onto this moonlight, we could probably ride straight through and reach the forest by sunrise," he offered. "The terrain is fairly easy between here and the border. Even if we had to use torches."

"Would we want to do that?" Brikana questioned.

"What? Use torches?" Domaren asked.

Brikana mumbled in the affirmative.

"It would probably be wisest to minimize calling attention to ourselves," Nanutsi proposed.

"I agree," Crizichial added.

"I'm fine with continuing on in the moonlight,"

Domaren said. "We'll save time and can stay concealed."

"If the weather turns, we can slip into one of the caves on the northern edge of the mountains," Kegli proposed.

"Yeah, that's fine," Brikana said.

Having settled the matter while continuing their walk, the group pressed on. But the distraction had caused Brikana's mind to wander and settle on something becoming increasingly irritating. In the fading light, Domaren and the others humorously watched Brikana contort, roll her neck and shoulders, and twist awkwardly in her saddle.

"Is there something the matter?" Nanutsi asked their dragon counterpart.

"This isn't working quite correctly," she said.

"What? What does that mean?" Kegli asked.

"This. This saddle. This seat," she said while becoming increasingly perturbed.

"I do not understand," Crizichial said. "Is the saddle failing at holding you somehow?"

Domaren tried to stifle a chortle but it snapped out through his nose in a cracking snort.

"What are you laughing at? This is causing me to experience unpleasant physical phenomenon, I'll have you know," she said.

"I think you're just getting sore," Nanutsi said dryly.

"Sore? What are you talking about?" Brikana said, bitingly.

"Soreness," Crizichial began. "It is the physical trait of being in pain or experiencing a sense of discomf—"

"No, I know what it means," Brikana said. "But I don't get sore. I don't feel pain from simply sitting!"

"It's because you're usually flying!" Kegli belted before a hearty laugh. "Don't your wings ever get sore?"

"No, my wings do not get sore! They've never gotten

sore. Dragons don't get sore!" She snipped back.

Before she finished her rant, Domaren had doubled over in his saddle, breathless in silent laughter. One of his hands held onto Munch's mane while Wiggly licked his other.

While the others chuckled and snorted in various fits of laughter, Crizichial perpetuated the humorous situation in his own way.

"Pardon me for saying so, Brikana," he began, "but it does indeed appear as though dragons are able to get sore."

"Listen... All right..." Brikana started, growing tired of her friends' playfulness. "I'm just going to shift and fly ahead while you all get this all out."

"No, no," Domaren said as his laughing subsided. "We're just giving you a hard time."

"I'm starting to get somewhat stiff as well, now that you mention it," Kegli said.

"As am I," Nanutsi added.

After a final big sigh to expel the remaining laughter, Domaren felt a bit of empathy for his friend.

"Yeah, I'm feeling weary as well, Kana," he said. "I'm not sure if it's from riding, or the fight at the tower, or both, but it seems to be compounding as each day goes by."

With the sun's light just about exhausted for the day, all that could be seen in the sliver of bruised blue light were silhouettes of large trees and the base of the northern mountains. The conversation ended for a moment and allowed the area's frogs to take over. But soon, the knights had more to discuss.

"It's worth mentioning," Nanutsi said with soft pensiveness, "that we should be more cognizant than ever of the amount of energy we use. We don't know when we might be restored again."

"If ever," Crizichial added quickly.

The frogs seized on the following silence while the group wrestled with Crizichial's insinuation. Domaren spoke next, his vocalized reflection rolled off his tongue in a dark reflection that seemed directed at the trees and grasses as much as towards his fellow knights.

"During the fight back there at the tower... I got hit by one of the seaver's tail spikes. A spike punctured through my leg armor and poked a hole in me. It bled badly for a bit, but it's fine."

No one but the frogs replied.

"I've never had a wound stay with me for too long," he continued. "I usually, just, fight fight fight, get cut, sliced, wounded, and then, I get restored. The Grove sends a stone, and just like that, I'm brand new. My blood never has a chance to dry like this did. It was warm, then cold, and now it's dry. And it itches."

The small caravan of godknight riders continued to ride in silence as they, Domaren assumed, considered the significance of their own wounds and fragility, and even possibly, the notion of mortality.

"Is it really possible we'll never be restored again?" Kegli asked.

"I think that we should each prepare ourselves for that exact possibility," Crizichial replied.

The conversation fell quiet once again but the frogs didn't fill the void this time. Something had spooked them. Something had frightened them. The implications of a possible void, far removed from any of their prior considerations, exacerbated the silent void that only allotted for the occasional shuffling of grass as the horses trudged their slow steps. It was a dense smack of the unknown that sent everyone's minds racing through possibilities and worries. And everyone knew it.

No one spoke. No one could. For a time, it was as if each of the godknights had the power of telepathy for each knew the others were extrapolating hypothetical fears and nihilistic possibilities that stunned each of them into silence. The notion of never being restored, and potentially being nudged towards frailty and death after hundreds of thousands of years of assured existence put teeth and horror into the void. It made the night that much darker and the stars that much dimmer. The forest thinned in their mind's eye, and for a time, all signs of life withered to naught. For a time, they weren't walking towards hope or to the idea of a positive resolution. Instead, they merely slogged along on the way to futility.

But like a diseased drifter begging for water and gasping for breath on the side of an abandoned dirt road, one of the knights finally lashed out at fate and stole themselves from fear to put some sound back into the world. But rather than spoken words, the first sound was that of a violent rip of cloth that jarred the others, followed by a knight's voice that floated over from a distance.

"There isn't a way to prepare," Brikana said casually. With her next breath, the firestone in her chest grew bright and swelled up, and before anyone could remind her to save her energy and not to shift, she instead stayed in her human form and shot out a plume of fire and ignited a makeshift torch she had made.

The others brought their horses to a stop and stared in silence.

While standing next to her horse a few dozen paces away, Brikana looked back at her friends. She stood in the middle of a gently swaying prairie and held a makeshift torch proudly, her chin elevated slightly in defiance.

"We don't know what may or may not happen," she continued. "We don't know if we'll be restored or not, and if we are to run out of energy and die a victim of mortality, we don't know when that may happen. For now, I have life, and I have fire. We have each other and I have the ability to see where I'm going, and I want to see."

Rather than a conversation or reply of any kind, Brikana stepped into her horse's stirrups and mounted back up. After walking back over, Domaren gestured for her to take the lead. As the group resumed their trek, Kegli couldn't help but grumble a comment.

"I could see just fine with the moonlight."

* * *

After increasing their pace to a slow trot, the five knights settled into an efficient rhythm of silent travel. While taking advantage of the peace found at the height of the night, the knights allowed themselves to drift into waking dreams, or thoughts of future resolutions or the clarity of the past, and anything else beings hundreds of thousands of years old ponder.

Over the course of many hours, the knights rode across a variety of grasses, flowers, and trees whose presence were mostly determined only by the scents wafting through the wind as they traveled. The sweetness of dropseed grass permeated the air first, followed by marigolds. And as the riders grew closer to the forests, the night air was overtaken by the ancient innocence of honeysuckle. Finally, once they rode under the canopy, the comforting warmth of pine, pine needles, and rosin took over.

The current ride was the longest the knights had gone without talking ever since reuniting at the tower. And in addition to the variety of natural fragrances floating through the air, so too were a variety of thoughts flowing in and out of the minds of the knights—to the point that they found enough to occupy their thoughts by their lonesome. But after hours of riding, the forest grew thicker and the knights slowed back down to a walk. The pine trees that had enjoyed being in the majority gave way to an increasing number of birch and sycamore. And just as the first hints of the coming day's sun seeped through the trees, a need to leap back to reality presented itself.

"Domaren, are we supposed to keep to this path?" Nanutsi asked.

Brikana, still in the lead, came to a stop and brought her horse around. All eyes turned to Domaren.

Domaren sighed and rubbed his forehead before looking over to Wiggly who met him with a pant and wag of the tail. Domaren clicked his teeth at her and then swung out of the saddle. After landing and taking a moment to take in the faint hues of the forest being revealed by the pinch of light, Wiggly ran off to take care of some dog business.

"Well, yeah, I thought so, Nanutsi," he replied. "I expected the road to be grown up, but I also thought we would have come across the old Fimham Way by now. It started at the edge of the forest. We should have come across it by now."

Kegli leaned over in his saddle.

"Fimham Way?" He asked in a whisper.

"Yes, it was one of the main roads that led to Prumo Hald," Crizichial answered, making no attempt to whisper.

As Kegli and Crizichial discussed the history of Fimham Way, Domaren asked Brikana to bring her torch over. He borrowed it and knelt down to a knee before holding the flame close to the ground.

"Right," Domaren confirmed loudly, before drifting into a quieter mumble of his own. "I haven't been here since just after Wrathlore."

As he continued inspecting the ground, he occasionally plucked up clumps of dirt and grass. At times he stood up and kicked at the ground with his heels until finally, he swatted the fire at the top of the branch out and poked at various points in the ground.

"What are you doing?" Brikana asked with an amused huff.

"Looking for the road," Domaren said.

After a few additional pokes, Domaren repeatedly struck hard objects that the others assumed to be any variation of common stone, but Domaren suspected differently. He poked and slung more clumps of grass out of the way until finally, he seemed to have discovered something the others couldn't see from atop their horses.

"Ah ha!" Domaren exclaimed.

"Yes? What?" Nanutsi asked.

Instead of answering, Domaren stood up and tossed Brikana's branch to her.

"Well I don't need this now," she said, before tossing it off the trail.

Domaren darted back and forth randomly in the space in and around his friends before stopping and locking eyes on an unassuming moss-covered rock.

The others could only watch the humorous display unfold. Domaren leaped over to the stone and poked at the moss and peeled it away. After he scraped, wiped, and brushed off the moss and dirt, it was revealed to be a chiseled stone, rather than a random rock. And in the stone, was an indentation, much like their grove stones, and the rock arrays in the tower. By this point, the others had dismounted and walked near.

"What does that do?" Kegli asked.

"Maybe nothing," Domaren said. "But seeing the energy at the tower, maybe something."

As he uttered the last syllable, Domaren placed his hand in the indentation. With a flash of warm light, the stone came to life and beamed up and around Domaren's hand. Once the light of the stone flashed quickly to its brightest level, it subsided, but then receded back down into the stone, through it, and down into the ground before weaving its way under Domaren and the other nights before rapidly racing out in a wild web to illuminate the grown over road stones below the superficial layers of moss, grass, and soil. Though mostly covered, their shallow depth allowed the road's original, ornate pattern to show, outlined in a crisp white with hints of turquoise.

"Oh, my..." Brikana said softly.

"I can't believe that worked!" Domaren said as he jogged a few feet down the road. "It still works! It still illuminates!"

"What is this for?" Crizichial asked in a rare gap of knowledge. "What is its purpose?"

"The light?" Domaren said, turning back to the group. "It's to simply allow for easier travel in the dark. It'll stay illuminated for a time, and then fade until its needed again. Those trigger stones are placed every so often along the road. And now that I think about it, the last I heard, the Ständ were rumored to live not too far from..."

With only a word or two left to say, Domaren cut himself off. Distracted first by a distinct and sharp jumble of light off to his side, Domaren slowly turned towards it. Before he could finish the motion, the forest floor trembled from a grating and gravelly rumbling growl that permeated from all directions. The sound faded but sounded again. The second rumble skipped along in a jagged bass that scratched at the knights' ears and harassed the whole forest's serenity. If not for the light, the knights would have felt completely surrounded by the sound, and whatever was making it. As he finished his rotation, a long-forgotten memory tore itself back to the forefront of Domaren's mind. Everyone froze.

"Domaren?" Nanutsi asked softly.

Brikana added to the questions.

"What is this?"

"The Rifren. Don't anyone move," Domaren replied.

After emerging from the black abyss of the deep woods, a massive four-legged creature defined by loose and smoky beams of crimson and yellow stood before the group of knights. Immediately after, two more walked up to the left side of the first, and then two more to its right. Five wolf-like beasts, roughly twenty feet high, stared down the knights. Translated from old Soren, their name means fang gate.

Their entire shapes were made of the smoky energy. Their fur was perfectly patterned and defined and appeared to have coarse texture similar to that of their traditional cousins. There was no drool, but their teeth were prominently displayed as they growled. Their most menacing teeth were the length of Crizichial's legs. All five creatures stared down the knights, ready to attack.

"What do we do?" Kegli asked in a whispered rush.

While staying still, Domaren involuntarily squinted.

"Just wait a..."

The first beast's growling vibrated the ground and haunted the forest. All five growling was a deafening and intimidating tactic for which no one had a response.

"What should we do?" Kegli asked louder.

Domaren didn't reply, though he heard Kegli this time. He couldn't. He didn't know what to say. He didn't understand.

"Hello my friends," Domaren said gently, to the Rifren. "I remember you. Do you remember me? You used to."

The five beasts gave no indication they knew or much less understood Domaren. Their growling continued, and at times, seemed to mesh and synchronize, compounding into a disorienting and disturbing series of rippling pulses that seemed to beat from inside the chest of each knight. Each of the knight resisted the urge to grab their ears and protect them from the blanket of rupturing sound that surpassed pain and went straight to the abstract lack of discernible sound caused by volume. Soon, the painful noise grew fainter as their eyes were being temporarily damaged.

"Domaren?" Crizichial asked, even louder, in a noticeable attempt to speak over the Rifren.

"Hold on!" He shouted back. "We can't afford to fight with them, for a host of reasons."

The back and forth agitated the Rifren. They looked from Domaren to Crizichial and back as the knights argued. They stepped closer and lowered their heads.

"We've got to do something, Domaren," Brikana said as her firestone started to glow.

"No! We don't need to fight them, and we can't waste our energy!"

"They're going to jump any second," Nanutsi blurted quickly.

"No!"

With no indication that they would, the Rifren

stopped growling. The knights' ears emptied out the hurtful growling and were left with a subtle muffle. Their chests fell still and the ground's vibrations ceased. After a shuffling of leaves stole the knights' and the Rifrens' attention, they all turned to see Wiggly casually running back to the group. For the first time in months, Munch stuck out his leg without being prompted and let Wiggly run right up. As usual, she bounded in one leap from Munch's rear over and into her saddle. She then barked and waited with an excited pant.

Domaren's eyes cut from side to side as he considered what was happening.

"Why did they stop growling?" Brikana asked.

Rather than answering, Domaren stepped slowly towards Munch.

"Domaren?" Nanutsi asked. "What are you doing?"

"I think I know," Crizichial commented gently. The Redeemed demon grinned.

After his careful and deliberate approach to Munch, Domaren read over and slipped a hand into a pouch on his saddle bag. After pulling out a piece of dried meat, he offered it to Wiggly who promptly snatched it. As she always does with her usual treats, she held it in place between her paws and enjoyed her snack.

With Wiggly enjoying her treat, Domaren slowly turned to once again face the Rifren. As he settled his feet, the forest was once again blasted with a booming sound. But rather than the sound of growling this time, it was a thundering voice but smooth and measured. Its low pitch rang out through the woods with boundless reverberation.

"That canine you just fed," the Rifren began. Their collective voice was sturdy and confident and emanated from the grouping of Rifren as a whole while none of their mouths moved. "Who is that?"

Domaren swallowed not out of fear, but as his mind transitioned from uncertainty to enthusiasm at the opportunity for dialog. He looked back at his friends in reassurance before answering.

"Oh, this... This is Wiggly. Well, Wiggly IV, to be accurate," Domaren answered.

The Rifren looked at each other.

"What do you mean, 'the fourth'?" They asked.

"Um, yes," Domaren said, laughing to himself. "That's mostly for my amusement only. This is the fourth dog I've named Wiggly. I tend to name my animal companions after..." Domaren paused to consider his word choice. "... physical traits or behaviors they exhibit."

"And you, canine," the Rifren said, looking to Wiggly. "You approve of this name? You approve of this human's methodology for how your name is decided?"

With a slight tilt of his head and brow wrinkled in confusion, Wiggly looked over to Domaren, and then back to the Rifren. The dog then, to Domaren's surprise, casually whined and barked at the wolves.

"We see," the Rifren replied.

Domaren's head jerked back in humorous surprise. He directed his next question at both Wiggly and the Rifren as he shifted his eyes between them.

"Did you..." He started. "Did you just speak to them? Did she just speak to you?"

The Rifren replied matter-of-factly.

"She said she enjoys her name, and confirms you are companions," the wolves said.

Domaren laughed and stared at Wiggly before scratching the top of her head.

"You called us friends a moment ago," the wolves continued. "We are not familiar with you, or at least can not recall you, much less recognize you as a friend. How do you know us?"

"Oh, yes," Domaren said softly, turning back. He took a few steps closer to the wolves, his facing taking on more of the crimson and yellow hues from their bright, smoky energy.

"It has been a very, very long time," Domaren said, "but I used to know you well. I am Domaren, the last of the original knights anointed by the Kihdai to help maintain order, oversee human dealings, and to enforce the will of the Kihdai. When the final destination of this road, Prumo Hald, was populated and active, I used to travel it and other connected roads frequently. The time since I've seen you last was so great that I had forgotten about you. I regret that, but having seen and remembered you again now, is a very welcomed memory."

The Rifren turned and exchanged glances and shared a variety of subtle growls and whines between themselves.

"It seems that you are not alone in having forgotten and then remembered," the wolves replied.

A pause followed, their words drifting off into the depths of the woods and stubbornly dissipating.

"We were once tasked by the same Kihdai you spoke of to guard the roads. To watch the roads. To keep the roads to Prumo Hald clear of any unwelcome or threatening travelers," they continued. "We had long forgotten that we were tasked with anything specifically, as well as those who tasked us. For these many, many thousands of years, we have lingered and waited for the roads to once again have travelers, having forgotten why."

Another silence followed as the other knights gathered closer to Domaren.

"We thank you for helping us remember this,

Domaren. We have now not only remembered that history, but we now remember you," they added. "We do not however, recall those in your company," they added with amiable curiosity.

"Yes, of course," Domaren replied, turning towards his fellow knights. "These are my fellow godknights representing some of the other races of the world. For various reasons they have replaced those knights who came before them, or as in Crizichial's case here, was newly anointed long after the birth of the virtues."

As the Rifren nodded in apparent understanding, Domaren gestured for them to step forward even more.

"Allow me to present Crizichial, Brikana, Nanutsi, and Kegli," he said.

The knights each offered a friendly bow as the Rifren also bowed their heads.

"It is very nice to meet each of you," the wolves said, "and it is very nice to have activity on the roads once again. Why did the roads become vacant, Domaren? Why did traveling along Rifren so abruptly cease?"

"Ah, well, yes, that is quite a long story," Domaren said. "I'll summarize it by simply saying that the Kihdai abandoned Prumo Hald after a rebellion of some godknights threatened their rule. It was more a punishment to the world than a necessity. They abandoned the fortress and retreated to a domain removed from this world. Separated. Apart. Once they left, trade and commerce in around the citadel quickly ceased and the need to travel there ended as well."

"We see," replied the wolves. "We of course welcome you to travel anywhere on these roads as you wish, like you did so long ago, so frequently, but we are curious. What brings you to the road now if there is nothing left at the end of it?"

Nanutsi stepped forward to volunteer an answer.

"Mm, yes," she said. "We're afraid there has been another rebellion. It seems there are some who once again seek to rebel against the Kihdai, and in turn, have somehow impeded our ability to remain in contact with the Kihdai and have our energy restored."

"We see," the wolves acknowledged. "But this revolt does not appear to be one led by the knights."

"Correct," Brikana confirmed with a scoff of frustration. "We unfortunately don't know who is behind it."

"Until we united again as a group, some of us thought other knights were involved," Crizichial added, "but that is not the case."

"And you're hoping to travel to Prumo Hald to... see if there is any activity there? We do not understand," the wolves said.

"Oh, right," Kegli said, stepping forward. "We may possibly, potentially end up there, but we are actually in search of those called the Stäld first for any potential guidance. We believe they may dwell near Fimham Way. Is that right, Domaren?"

Before Domaren answered, the wolves exchanged glances between themselves.

"Um, yes, Kegli, that's correct," he answered. "Is there something the matter, my friends?"

The wolves settled their sights back on the knights.

"Well, that is not exactly how we would describe it," they answered.

A brief silence followed and piqued Domaren's imagination.

"Wait, the Stäld. Do you know the Stäld? Do you

know where they are?"

The Rifren conferred with each other silently once again with another series of nods, but then added some additional whines and warm growls. Wiggly lifted her head and her ears straightened.

The wolves shared an additional few whimpers between each other but looked back.

"My friends, please," Domaren implored. "Is there anything you might be able to share about the Stäld?"

"You are correct, Domaren," the wolves replied. "The Stäld do dwell near here."

"They do?" Brikana shouted in excitement. "Can you please tell us how to find them?"

"I am afraid we can not," the wolves replied.

With her reply, Brikana's voice scraped with a note of agitation.

"What? Why?"

While there were no signs of anger or animosity, the slight shift in the conversation's tone seemed to irritate some of the Rifren. A pair of them took a slight step forward while their collective voice offered a reply.

"In the very long and ancient span of time that the Stäld have lived in their current home, we have come to know them. We have developed a friendship with them, and we are stewards of each other's interests. In that time, following their abandonment by the Kihdai, the Stäld have asked us to keep their location secret and to stand watch over a large area surrounding their home. In return, they are friends to us, welcome us, and provide assistance to our natural, living kin. In a way, both of our groups were abandoned and we found friendship in our mutual experiences. We had merely forgotten that shared quality until now."

Domaren turned and looked at Brikana and dipped his chin, hoping she'd understand it as a request to wait. After a few rubs and scratches to his face, he turned back to the Rifren.

"But is there no way to see them?" Domaren asked.

"We said a moment ago that there is not," the wolves replied.

"Perhaps there is a way we could ask?" Kegli attempted. "We could dispatch a request?"

The wolves' voice grew louder, noticeably closer to the volume when the knights first arrived.

"We will not repeat our answer again," they said firmly.

"Friends," Domaren replied, hurriedly trying to disarm the escalation in the conversation. "We mean no offense, and respect your words as well as the wishes of the Stäld. Just please let me explain our motive, and urgency. I only ask now that you hear this last bit of information."

The five wolves looked at each other but this time, exchanged no whimpers, whines, barks, or growls. Instead, they looked back at Domaren in silence. Domaren seized upon the opportunity they seemed to present.

"As we mentioned before, someone is trying to subvert the Kihdai, or their influence, or both. Now, we know there is very little motivation for you or the Stäld to concern yourselves with the fate of the Kihdai, but our present concerns are much broader than that. Being their primary means of enforcement in this world, we are very obviously wanting to find out what this effort has in store for the Kihdai, yes, but we also are very worried about what this will mean for the inhabitants of the world. All races. All creatures. Everywhere."

The Rifren looked straight ahead.

"I believe we adequately understand your implication," the wolves said.

"We have no desire to disturb them," Domaren added. "If anything, warn them, and seek any guidance they would be willing to lend. If they wish to lend none, we will proceed accordingly at that time."

"We could warn them ourselves..." the wolves said.

Crizichial spoke a syllable, but Domaren shot a hand up as the wolves continued.

"But we do not have the capacity to pass along any of their potential guidance."

Domaren lowered his hand while the Rifren communicated between each other. As they spoke between themselves, Wiggly barked. One of the wolves whipped its head around as they continued their conversation in their canine language.

Being the closest to Munch at the moment, Brikana flicked her hand up in anticipation towards Domaren and reached for a hunk of meat for Wiggly. The wolf whose attention was snagged by Wiggly and her request for another snack turned back to his pack. Their conversation continued. The other knights walked closer to Domaren and faced away from the wolves.

"What's next if they won't assist us?" Brikana whispered.

Domaren pinched at the bridge of his nose and rubbed his eyes.

"I don't know," he said. "I imagine we can only press on and continue slogging through the brush."

"That is assuming they allow us to," Crizichial said.

Domaren reared back in surprise at the suggestion, but quickly relaxed after recognizing the truth in his statement.

"I really doubt they would prevent us from continuing," Nanutsi said. "They know we mean the Stäld no harm."

As Kegli started to provide his feedback, he stood an ax on the ground and leaned on the handle.

"If the Rifren do not assist us, I don't know that there will be many other opportunities to source out information," he said. "My people's lands border this entire area, and I have no knowledge of a potential location for the Stäld. Not even rumors. The land south of the our borders and over to the orc border has been largely uninhabited as far as we have ever known."

Domaren grunted in acknowledgment.

"Well, that may only mean that the Stäld and potentially others, have done a fine job of staying hidden," he said. "Something tells me we may not yet be out of op—"

"Knights?" The booming Rifren voice interrupted. The knights turned to face their massive canine apparition friends.

"We have discussed this situation, as you have presented it to us, and considered your request, as well as the ramifications of our potential responses. Our decision was not unanimous, but as a group we have accepted the majority suggestion."

Other than Crizichial and Brikana, each knight's head drooped from what they imagined was inevitable disappointment after such a considerate and informational preface.

"We will provide you the assistance you have requested."

Domaren's head jerked up, his eyes wide with surprise. Kegli and Nanutsi both jumped and hugged each other from the side. Crizichial and Brikana traded optimistic grins.

"Thank you," Domaren said with hearty appreciation. "Thank you. I don't believe any of us expected that result. Thank you. Even those that disagreed, thank you for considering our request."

"We will make every effort to make sure you do not regret this," Crizichial added before offering a bow of the head.

"Please ensure you do," the wolves replied. "And know this. On the whole, even those of us that disagreed with assisting, believe you and believe in the honor and goodness of your motives and intentions. The treatment of your animal companions while we have been speaking also worked to your benefit."

The knights laughed at the humor in the revelation and prompted Domaren to walk over and ruffle Wiggly's ears before giving Munch a snack of his own.

"So now, hear us knights," the wolves continued. "We will share with you the location where the Stäld dwell, and guide you in the initial starting direction, but we will not accompany you. We have our obligations to the forest, as well as the Stäld, and will remain on guard to continue our hunt for those less friendly than you. You will make the journey on your own."

Domaren took a quick look at his friends and replied for the group.

"We understand. The information and directions are all we could have hoped for, and we are grateful."

"Very well," the wolves said. "Follow us and we will guide you around this thick brush that obscures the road and set you on your way to the Vale of Kalndaia. When we take our leave of you, you must remain vigilant. In addition to the Stäld, there is knowledge and danger out there as old as you, Domaren."

# Fifteen

The Rifren made quick work of guiding the knights to the northern tip of the forest. Whether by following naturally unobstructed paths or by trampling brush down as they stepped, the wolves accommodated their friends' urgency with ease. The sun spilled slowly into the forest, its full prominence delayed and hampered by a clouded sky of ashen greys and festering blues. When the forest began to thin, and the base of the northern mountains could be seen, the wolves stopped to reiterate the final set of instructions and returned south.

With a plan and directions, the knights resumed their journey. The wolves had instructed them to stay in the thinner part of the forest, following it due north. If they exited the forest completely, they had gone too far east. If it grew thick again, they had gone too far west. Then, once they met the base of the mountains, there would be a trail head hidden and protected by a noticeably large outcropping covered in moss and vines. Once on the path, they were to follow it up a winding, and sometimes narrow trail until they encountered what the wolves said would be the unmistakable home of the Stäld.

The cloud cover was such that the amount of light they would have on the day's journey was moderate and disappointing. Though none of the knights necessarily concerned themselves much with the state of the weather, they did however collectively wish there was more light to accompany their journey into unknown lands.

"Looks like we have some rain on the way," Brikana mentioned in passing.

Kegli peered up.

"Good," Domaren said. "I normally prefer it overcast and cooler. The armor gets hot."

"It might make the ride up the mountain trail a little interesting," Nanutsi said. "I can probably come up with something if it gets too wet, but, I'll have to use some energy."

"Let's hold off on that for as long as we can," Domaren said.

"Yes, we should all agree to reserve our strength as much as possible," Crizichial suggested.

"Agreed," the others said.

"So, what else can you tell us about these Stäld, Domaren?" Brikana asked, changing the subject. "I've never met them. Have any of you? I can't remember any of you referencing them before."

Domaren waited for others to respond before replying. Each knight shook their head.

"There isn't a lot more to say that we haven't spoken about recently," Domaren said. "We were all Stäld at one point. You all know that already, though. We were essentially the same. Bland. Fragile. No real variation or dimension to life or existence."

"And that's what inspired the request for the virtues," Kegli said, stating, more than asking.

"Right," Domaren said. "We started to consider the notion of *more,* being more, having more, before we even really knew there was a word to describe it, or what it might even mean."

"What would you attribute that to?" Crizichial asked.

"Well, I think it was just something that happened naturally," Domaren said. "All of the life at that point existed in an identical state. With unchanging surroundings. We just eventually... thought all there was to think about existence, if that makes sense. I think our minds just collectively started to wander. I guess before the world was given any added definition from the Kihdai, our imaginations were the first to develop, and they developed, initially at least, on their own."

"Hmm, yes," Crizichial said as he pondered. "I simply find the notion of such primitive life developing a want for more, and in turn knowing how to voice it in order to request it, fascinating."

Domaren leaned back in his saddle a bit as he continued reflecting.

"It was an extraordinary time," he said. "So many memories have come and gone. Many experiences lost to time, or are well on their way. But I remember that early period and the birth of the virtues very well."

After a fairly long silence, and once most of the other knights thought the topic had reached a natural conclusion, Domaren had yet another reflection to share.

"You know, as we're talking about this and as I dwell on it all a bit—thinking about the early period and the virtues, and all that... I find it kind of odd, almost sad, really... There hasn't been any real shift or growth like there was then. We grew. The world blossomed. Life, passion, thought, and aspirations were sparked, kindling a massive bonfire of wonder and potential. But it's almost as if, at some point, the world stopped throwing logs on the fire."

"Do you mean, everyone stopped caring?" Kegli asked.

"No, not so much that they stopped caring," Domaren said. "It's that for whatever reason, they stopped dreaming. They stopped considering that there might be more. And what's funny but also somewhat sad, is that they gave up on the idea of making their own strides, building upon their own experiences. It's as if they thought they were dependent on the Kihdai to become something greater."

"Are you talking about the Stäld or the world in general?" Brikana asked.

"Oh, the world at large, definitely," Domaren replied. "The Stäld never had a chance to become apathetic. They tried to hang on for a while. They lived amongst the other races for ages—humans, orcs, elves, dwarves, dragons, seavers, everyone. They were able to look past being left out of what they asked for the whole world, for a time. But after a long time, longer than one might expect, they could no longer abide what they felt was an arbitrary sacrifice. The majority of the world today doesn't know what happened to them, and not just now, but then. Most of the world considers their story a cute mythology. It even took me a bit to consider they would actually still be around for us to visit."

"Do you have any idea what we might run into when we meet them?" Nanutsi asked. "Any actual chance of having them help? Right into a fight? Or something in-between?"

"Hmm," Kegli began. "Between what the Rifren shared and what we've discussed previously, I wouldn't expect all that much."

Domaren whipped his hand towards Kegli in agreement.

"You're right there, definitely," Domaren said. "At this point, we just need to save everything we can until we absolutely need it."

As the knights continued their philosophical conversation and discussed their meet with the Stäld, the terrain started to slowly ascend. The soft forest floor which consisted of grasses and laurel soon gave way to rockier soil, boulders, and outcroppings sticking out from increasingly steeper slopes. And as they continued, the sky began to clear. The colors of the land turned more vivid, and the sun's presence beat down with greater intensity.

"Great," Domaren said with feigned optimism. "Here comes the heat."

But while the others teased Domaren for his complaint, he found his gaze turning upward. He watched as the clouds high above shifted quickly to a lighter white and moved through the sky quicker than he would normally expect, but on the ground, the trees stood still without any hint of being bothered by wind. Domaren stopped while the others walked ahead. Eventually, Kegli noticed their group had lost a member. Kegli stopped and turned his donkey.

"Domaren? What is it?" He asked.

The others followed suit and looked back.

"Domaren?" Crizichial also asked.

Domaren raised his hand slowly and pointed up.

"Do you see that?" He asked. "See the sky? That looks like there's about to be a—"

Before Domaren could finish, the sky exploded with five separate bolts of rock and sediment shooting down in single, rapid bursts. One by one, they pierced the ground and as the land absorbed their strikes of rock, they left behind a standing ring of stone, similar to the ones used by the Grove to communicate with the godknights. But when the stone lightning dissipated and the stone rings crumbled, standing before the knights, were each of the five proxies. Each of the knights immediately shoved themselves off their mounts.

Each of the proxies stood still, expressionless, almost casual. Maphikim and Vinlaza in her dragon form were there, as well as Midovin, Tobati, and Bitano. While no one stood in any particular stance of defense, offense, or other noticeable demeanor, Domaren, and no doubt some or all of the other knights found the proxies' arrival and initial silence odd.

"Proxies? All of you? Here? How?" Domaren asked.

The human proxy, Midovin, spoke up first. The tips of his loose and wavy blonde hair flipped about as his leather and mail clinked as he gestured.

"Knights! All of you together!" Vinlaza said. "I am very glad to have found you all together. We weren't sure if you were still traveling as a group."

"I'm sorry, Vinlaza," Brikana replied, "but what do you mean you weren't sure... How are you here?"

Midovin replied to her dragon kin.

"We heard word of your communications from the tower," she said. "We worked to meet and come to you as quickly as possible."

"That worked?" Brikana asked in a gasp of surprise. "That's amazing. We had no real hope that any of that was going to get through.

"What's this about a revolt?" Midovin continued, seeing additional updates. "A rebellion? What have you discovered?"

"Very little, I'm afraid," Nanutsi offered. Crizichial then stepped forward to contribute.

"We have not been able to correlate a great deal, especially considering our lack of communication with the Grove or ability to restore our powers."

Tobati stepped forward and cross his arms.

"Well, we have recently heard rumors of a substantial build-up of a force in the region northwest of Greyley that we need your help investigating."

"It may be nothing. Maybe just a rumor. But if it is something, we need to look into it. With any luck, we might be able to uncover what has led to this disruption."

The knights exchanged silent glances as both they and the proxies considered the rumored news. Some of the knights studied the ground aimlessly while others rubbed their hands or faces. Domaren's eyes settled on Munch and Wiggly.

"I think that would definitely be prudent," Domaren said, still holding his eyes on his horse and dog. "But before we leave, I want to confer with the Stäld. If they will see us."

"The Stäld?" Maphikim said, his voice leaping in shock. "You've found them? They actually still exist?"

"We believe so," Nanutsi responded. "We were given some information from the Rifren that will hopefully lead us to them."

"Well this is astounding," Bitano said, almost breathless. "Two groups of the world's oldest beings confirmed to still exist."

Being a stickler for details, Crizichial spoke up. "One confirmed," he said. "One rumored."

"Right, of course," Vinlaza said. "So, of course, it goes without saying, we would highly suggest we proceed together," the proxy said. "Perhaps we can seek out the

Ställd together, see what information or assistance they can offer, and then look into the gathering forces in the east?"

The knights didn't immediately answer but instead gauged each other's disposition by surveying body language. Finally, Domaren replied.

"I'm not sure that would be wise," Domaren said. "We committed to visiting the Ställd by ourselves after making an extremely delicate agreement with the Rifren. Our chances of having an audience would be drastically reduced, I believe, if we were to arrive with an even larger group."

Maphikim looked around to his fellow proxies before nodding quickly to himself as he thought. His head then popped back up with an idea.

"I can definitely appreciate an agreement, especially with the sensitive notion of encountering the Ställd," he said. "I would think however, a simple doubling of five visitors to ten would not affect our odds of a successful meeting."

Brikana glanced at Domaren quickly.

"To give our shared concerns and needs the best chance of being resolved, I would recommend we continue on our way to the Ställd alone. Maybe we can in turn maximize having two groups coordinating by having the proxies go to Greyley. After we meet with the Ställd we can then meet you there."

The rate of silent communication and shared glances increased, on both the proxy and godknight side.

"I think that sounds like a very wise and strategic idea, Brikana," Kegli offered.

As the conversation continued, the questions, statements, or answers grew shorter. The silence between each increased.

"I'm not sure that I agree," Bitano said. "There would be sizable strength in a combined group. I believe we would prefer it if you we were to travel together."

Crizichial took a step forward and relaxed his arms. As he replied, he lowered his head.

"The proxies have never dictated instruction to the godknights, Bitano. You know that."

Tobati matched Crizichial's step.

"But we represent the Kihdai," Tobati said. "And this is what they want."

Domaren immediately replied.

"And we represent the strength of the Kihdai."

Each of the proxies said nothing, but shifted their eyes slightly for a new angle on the knights.

"You said this is what they want?" Nanutsi asked. "Have you been in contact—"

"This is what they would want," Maphikim interrupted in a rush. He repeated himself with a forced smile. "We're sure this is what they *would* want."

Domaren continued darting his eyes between the proxies and his fellow knights. A crinkling itch started to irritate his skin as an undefined denseness seeped into his mind. His eyes kept moving until they fell once more on Munch and Wiggly.

Wiggly hunched down in her saddle pouch. Her head hung low and her ears were pinned back to the sides of her head. There was no panting or wagging of her tail.

Domaren's head whipped back towards the proxies. He drew in a large breath and closed his eyes. As he exhaled, he grinned and narrowly shook his head. A wave mixed with realized foolishness and the relief of clarity washed over him. His eyes popped open.

"Of course," he said, loud enough only for his benefit. As he drew Verikta, he turned quickly in a complete circle and locked eyes with each of his fellow knights. Crizichial's decay had already begun spreading. Brikana's firestone had already begun to glow. Just before Domaren lost sight of Brikana, her stone flashed, revealing her in her dragon form. Domaren completed his silent readiness check and faced the proxies once again.

"We will not be complying with you today, nor the Kihdai, I'm afraid—though I am glad to know that they are not under duress. Instead, I believe the other knights and I will proceed to visit the Stäld on our own," he continued, his voice shifting from conversational and cooperative, to one of confident and powerful defiance.

While Domaren spoke, the proxies spread out slightly before settling into rigid postures. They stared back at Domaren.

"We have been instructed by the Kihdai to prevent that, Domaren," Midovin said.

"So, the Kihdai are at war with us?" Kegli asked flippantly.

"You are an obstacle to the execution of their plans," Maphikim answered.

Brikana's long neck bent up into the trees as she erupted in laughter.

"Well, that sure was delightfully vague," she guffawed, her volume comparable to that of the combined Rifrens' voice. "What could possibly make them think they would succeed in fighting us?"

"They don't want to fight you," Vinlaza shouted back. "They need to be rid of you. They want to recreate their world and start anew, and in order to do that, you cannot be permitted to disrupt that goal."

Crizichial, now in his decayed state, stood puzzled in the circle of blackened ground and dead vegetation.

"They want to recreate the world... arbitrarily?" He

asked.

"Stop being so naive," Tobati roared back. "Ever since Wrathlore, and from the birth of the virtues really, the citizens of this world have squandered their existence. Year after year, their failures and disappointments far surpass any gains or honor. They kill, steal, take, and take for granted everything around them. Each of you are increasingly tasked with having to subdue or rectify petty wars and prevent ridiculous wastes of life. The world has failed, its citizens are undeserving, and the Kihdai want to make something more deserving. And in order to do that, they can't have you resisting them. So, we have been merely waiting for you to exhaust your power so we and the Kihdai can proceed unchallenged. The other proxies and I are here now to help expedite that."

A flash of worry raced through Domaren's mind.

*How much energy do we have left? How much time?* But his thoughts quickly turned back to defiance.

"Oh, we can oblige you," Domaren said. He spun Verikta in his hand and slowly brought his hands together for a double grip. "I don't know what we have left in us, but we all know that while you may have the support of the Kihdai, and while your powers may be more varied, we are not yet mortal. You are. And the pain we can deliver has much deeper dimension than anything you can muster."

Maphikim, Vinlaza, and Bitano smiled and offered variations of a head bow while the others stood their stoic ground.

"That may be the case," Maphikim replied. "But it is also—"

Rather than finishing, Maphikim's words were blasted to silence by a torrent of Brikana's flames rupturing out at the proxies from over Domaren's head. The proxies were sent diving out of the way or scattering away like exposed cockroaches to hide behind nearby boulders. As Domaren shot away towards the nearest proxy, Nanutsi's spheres of protective water popped to life and encompassed him and the other knights. The thin film of water resembled a translucent waterfall that, while not entirely impervious, drastically slowed any projectiles or penetrating blades and doused incoming flame.

Leaves crunched and the ground pounded as Domaren sprinted towards Midovin. As Domaren approached the human proxy, a dark anticipation shoved its way up to the top of his nerves. After Midovin jumped up and out of his defensive roll after dodging Brikana's fire, he pivoted and swung his own sword up and blocked Domaren's downward slice. The blades slammed together in a cataclysmic crash that sent shards of metallic sound into the forest. As Domaren pushed closer, he and Midovin locked eyes while straining against the other.

"Only one stone on *your* sword," Domaren goaded. Midovin didn't bite.

"I truly regret this, Domaren," he said. "None of this is the knights' fault. The Kihdai simply didn't want to bother with seeing if you'd go along with it."

Domaren stepped back slightly to confirm his footing before heaving forward again with an upward slice. Midovin's blade slid off as Domaren brought the upward deflection around and down to his side.

"This is ancient betrayal and murder on a worldly scale," the godknight said. "I have no need for your words and I will make them your last."

Midovin initiated the next attack and marched over with his blade out in a defensive, piercing posture. After closing to within the range of a lunge, Midovin brought his sword over his head and raced it down at Domaren's side where the knight's protection sphere slowed the human proxy's sword. Then, with the flat of his blade, Domaren pushed up to shove it out of the way with his cross-guard. While Midovin used the momentum to bring his sword back down on the other side, Domaren pressed the stone on Verikta's handle for added force on impact. When Domaren stepped back and swung up to block, Midovin's blade was smacked away with a hateful exacerbation of Domaren's strength, sending Midovin's arm and sword swinging back in a rapid arc. Midovin stumbled back.

"Just... abandon all life because it hasn't turned out perfectly? No," Domaren said.

He stabbed his foot into the ground and tore off in a sprint. As he raced towards Midovin, he left the impact stone pressed, but at the expense of more of his energy, he also pressed the speed stone. In a blur of movement, Domaren jumped at Midovin in a fresh attack.

Domaren's protection bubble quickly burst from all of his disrupting movements and splashed to the ground. And while Midovin's attacks and blocks would no longer be slowed, Domaren was able to attack three times as fast. In a further equalizing note, Midovin had pressed his sword's one gem, which accentuated Midovin's overall command of combat with a sword. And though Midovin's sword, or any other sword for that matter, was not as powerful or versatile as Verikta, Domaren did face a bit more of a challenge.

More slicing followed heavy slices, which were all met with dodges and parries. Sidesteps avoided thrusting moves, and hectic bends backward saved proxy and godknight alike from quick one-handed swings on the diagonal.

After a particularly sly jump to the side on Domaren's part, Midovin raced past and found himself in a moment of pause. Midovin tossed his sword away which disappeared before hitting the ground. After tracking the sword and seeing it evaporate, Domaren looked back at Midovin just in time to see him pull a long handled mace from his back. The handle ended with a stubby spike while the head was formed from a massive ball of iron covered in obnoxious ribs of steel. A moderately sized oak shield with steel braces and horizontal spikes at the center had appeared on Midovin's opposite arm.

Domaren subconsciously nodded, as if switching his combat mindset and rather than racing towards Midovin again, marched over in a measured steadiness. Midovin held the mace out to his side and brought his shield forward.

As Domaren walked closer to Midovin, he heard a noise and in a splinter of time realized it was his own heavy breathing. He knew it was attributed to fatigue, but only then realized *he* was fatigued. He cursed himself silently for acknowledging it but focused on Midovin's mace ahead.

"Swing it," Domaren prodded. "Swing it!"

Midovin remained frozen in his stance. His eyes stared ahead without a blink. His face maintained a relaxed and focused disposition and showed no signs of labored breathing.

Domaren walked closer. A wave of fire caught Domaren's attention off to the side. The red dragon, the proxy, had unleashed it.

*I've got to help the others,* Domaren thought. *This is taking too long.*

But instead of continuing his measured approach, Domaren rushed Midovin again. With Verikta slightly off to his side and pointed forward, Domaren raced ahead. Midovin shifted his feet in preparation.

Domaren brought his sword up, ready to slice down

at Midovin's mace arm, but Midovin anticipated it by dropping his shield, which evaporated it, and rolling forward. While Domaren swung and Midovin rolled under it, Midovin swung at Domaren and smashed into Domaren's calf. Domaren sucked in a sharp breath of pain and fell to a knee. Midovin then continued around and swung the head of his mace with all of his might into Domaren's chest. Domaren's armor crunched and creased immediately, the spikes of the mace lodged partially in Domaren's armor, and partially in his chest. Blood crept out and dripped down his armor. Midovin dipped his head down and stared at the wound with satisfaction and flicked a few fingers to make the mace disappear. Domaren's wounds were no longer blocked by the mace's ribbed blades and the exposed cuts bled that much faster. As Midovin reached back once more, his original sword reappeared. He pulled it and stared ahead at his former friend. Domaren could only return his gaze, with noticeably more labored and muddled breath.

"It has always been a curse and a blessing," Midovin said with ironic reverence. "You knights have always been nothing more than pure power. Pure force. Unparalleled strength, but never much for strategy, sadly. You just receive your orders and—"

Before he could finish, Domaren shoved up from the ground in an explosive thrust, avoiding Midovin's breastplate, and plunged Verikta through his belly, up to the hilt. The godknight immediately jerked out the blade, sending Midovin to both knees.

Domaren stumbled slightly as he stood up completely, but quickly found his footing after assessing the strength of his leg. He shrugged at it after stomping the ground a few times.

"How valuable the most powerful sword and a bit of

acting can be," Domaren said as he walked around behind Midovin. "I used a third stone, you see, my sight stone, to anticipate your next attack. And as you can see, I'm not as hurt as I made out to be."

Once Domaren was completely behind Midovin, he leaned in to whisper another comment.

"Also, I think you forgot to reactivate your sword's stone when you re-summoned it," he said.

With only garbled gasps, Midovin had no retort. No comment. And after a quick lunge up and then back down, Domaren shoved his sword into the back of Midovin's neck.

Domaren put his foot on Midovin's lifeless shoulder and as he kicked him away, pulled Verikta out before wiping his blade on his legs. He turned and took in the state of his friends and their encounters.

Everyone was still up, to Domaren's relief. And though he wasn't surprised, he quickly assessed who appeared to need to he most assistance.

Brikana's and Vinlaza's fight had sent them tearing the farthest away from the rest of the fight, leaving burning trees and scorched ground in their wake. Large splotches of sunlight found paths path straight to the ground after the two dragons alternated between shooting up through branches and limbs and chasing each other into the sky, before racing back down to find cover in the woods. Domaren watched as streams of fire cut through the sky, always able to tell Brikana's apart. Hers shot wider, hotter, and longer, but each blast took that much more out of her energy stores. The noticeably smaller proxy was able to dodge and dart about, avoiding many of Brikana's flames, and making the dragon knight use that much more energy.

*They'll be in the air too much,* Domaren thought, dismissing Brikana's fight as an option he could help with.

Looking to Kegli, Domaren watched the dwarf battle his proxy's counterpart with constant adaptation, though each attack often led to a stalemate. Tobati raced back and forth, using his throwing axes to keep Kegli off-balance and keep him from approaching slowly. As a means of directing and steering the fight, Tobati threw axes at Kegli, and as he sprinted to retrieve them for another throw, he brought his battle hammer down in a devastating downswing. But Kegli was able to dodge or counter the threat with his own threat of his gigantic battle ax.

Where the proxy had throwing axes, Kegli had powers similar to that of the dwarf warlock at the tower. But Kegli's were much more powerful. In-between flying axes and swings of hammers, Kegli harnessed the strength of the massive boulders in the area and summoned them to life in his defense. When he could, Kegli would race to a boulder and slam the butt of his ax upon a clear face and kneel. After closing his eyes and a rushed invocation of the ancient dwarven language, the boulder would rumble and roll to life, attracting smaller stones like magnets to its larger torso, before clomping clumsily at the dwarf proxy.

*Kegli's more than holding his own there,* Domaren thought.

Nanutsi appeared to be stuck in closer quarters combat, and didn't seem to have had a chance to take advantage of any of her water magic. Making the most of the flail attached to her armored tail, Nanutsi stayed low to the ground and swung about, keeping Bitano at a distance.

*Nanutsi could use some help,* Domaren thought. *Wait... Where's Crizichial?*

Domaren jumped away into a jog, but didn't have a direction decided and stopped after a few steps. He scanned the area again. He spun around. After making a complete circle, he spotted him.

Crizichial had also become separated, though not as far away as the dragons. Looking on, Domaren watched Maphikim and Crizichial trade distanced projectiles of fire and swarms of shadow as their fight brought a similar path of destruction to the forest, but rather and burns, their path was made up of rot and decay.

*They're keeping us apart intentionally. Not fighting to win, but to make us waste our strength.*

Domaren looked back at Midovin's body.

*They're down one,* he thought. *We need to get back together.*

Domaren sprinted out for the nearest of his allies, Nanutsi, who was still embattled with Bitano and only had her tail's mace at her disposal. He lifted his sword hand up and slapped the pommel stone with his other hand, resetting the gems on the handle. With Bitano's back to him, Domaren sliced down at Bitano's back as he ran by before running to Nanutsi.

"We need to group back up. They're just wasting our energy. Midovin is down."

Nanutsi nodded and gestured at Kegli.

Domaren slapped Nanutsi on the back and took off with her towards Kegli. As they ran past one of Kegli's animated stone beasts, and then another—both of which were keeping Tobati busy—they saw Kegli kneeling down on another boulder, preparing to create another.

"Wait! Kegli!" Nanutsi shouted. His eyes shot up. After tilting his head in confusion, he jumped up to meet his friends.

"We have to stop the one-on-one business. They're just wearing us down," Nanutsi said.

"Aye," Kegli barked. He looked around quickly and

suggested their next move. "Brikana?"

"Right," Nanutsi replied.

The three regrouped knights sped off towards Brikana who was still on the ground after a recent landing. She and Vinlaza ripped through trees and sent them splintering, cracking, and falling to the ground in ferocious destruction.

Domaren looked over his shoulder as the three ran towards Brikana. Bitano was just now stumbling to his feet. Tobati had broken free of his struggle with the stone creatures and was chasing. Crizichial was still off by himself, but they would gather him soon. For now, it was Brikana they must reach.

Once the three grouped knights got within a dragon's wingspan of Brikana's fight, they slowed down, being careful of sudden movements from either dragon. With their wings tucked in close to their bodies, the two dragons leaned over close to the ground, occasionally lashing out in rapid attempts to bite their opponent. After facing off with her foe in a rotating circle, Brikana's three allies came into view. They said nothing, and neither did she. With no indication it was about to happen, Brikana mustered the longest, hottest, and broadest flame she could, and unleashed it at Vinlaza. She held the flame, and sustained it as she moved. While moving next to, and then past Vinlaza, Brikana maintained her fire on her enemy and provided cover for herself and her friends to make a run for it.

Next, they were on their way to Crizichial.

"We were just wasting time fighting—" Domaren said as they ran.

"Yes, fighting alone," Brikana finished. "I surmised."

Domaren couldn't help but smile at Brikana and her sharp wit, despite the situation.

"Criz!" Nanutsi shouted. "Criz!"

The group raced towards their demonic friend while he continued to fight, unable to hear, or unable to respond. They then watched as Crizichial held his arms up high over and conjured between his hands an orb of reflective black and burned orange, which as he lowered it, tore and shuffled the ground beneath Maphikim. With each inch of descent of Crizichial's orb, the ground grew that much more turbulent, and soon, revealed dozens of hands in various states of decay, clawing at Maphikim's feet and legs. Within seconds, they had brought Maphikim to his knees, and them made him fall prone before tugging and pulling him down below the surface.

He then turned immediately and raced towards his friends, closing the bit of space left between them.

"That won't hold him long," Crizichial said. "He'll be back."

"That's fine," Domaren said. "We just needed to regroup. We can't let them separate us again. Midovin is down. Are any of the others?"

As Domaren posed the question to his friends, he motioned them to back up and get the remaining proxies all to their front.

But before anyone answered, the seaver and dragon proxies ran over to Tobati who appeared to have been caught on the edges of Brikana's last eruption of fire. With half his body charred, Tobati stumbled through a few more steps, visibly shaking, before crumbling to his knees. Soon after they reached the dwarf, a path of disturbed dirt tore itself from close to where Crizichial had buried Maphikim, closer to the other proxies where the Redeemed proxy then scratched his way out from underground. As the proxies leaned over the dwarf and mumbled to each other, Vinlaza swung his huge dragon head around and snarled at the knights.

"That should do for now," Vinlaza said with a hateful slither. "See you again soon, knights."

"Don't forget to take Midovin with you!" Brikana shouted back. But after the surviving or wounded proxies were summoned away one by one with rapid strikes of rocky debris, there was indeed one proxy left behind. The lifeless corpse of Midovin.

For the first time since the fight began, the forest was mostly quiet, save the few additional cracks of trees succumbing to their burns and bashes from the fighting dragons. A few small fires added the occasional pop or fizzle.

The knights said nothing. Most were too busy collecting their thoughts or like Domaren—legitimately this time—were trying to catch their breath. After pulling at a thick piece of linen stuck between his belt and his armor, Domaren wiped Verikta clean and placed her in her scabbard.

Brikana's firestone flashed and upon seeing her human form, Domaren walked over and grabbed her shoulder in relief. But his eyes were cold and conveyed a silent hesitation. Once additional embraces and taps of backs and shoulders were shared between everyone else, Domaren looked back over to Midovin and stepped towards him.

"Domaren..." Brikana started, but said nothing else. She said his name and let it linger, not quite as though she was hesitating to continue out of fear of how it might be received, but more with a lilting declaration. It was as if she had made the decision to address Domaren's approach, but hadn't determined how she herself felt about it.

The other knights fell in quickly behind Domaren, some jogging a few steps to catch up. Brikana exchange glances with Crizichial, while Nanutsi and Kegli did the same. The walk over to the dead proxy was quiet, and tempered. No one made any effort to walk alongside Domaren, or overtake him. There was no talk of time, urgency, or strategy. They simply let Domaren lead them.

When they reached Midovin's body, Domaren stopped and knelt down to one knee, still visibly working for breath. The others looked at each other and shrugged, still silently trying to decide how they should act, not act, support their friend, or leave him alone. Eventually, the others fanned out to either side of Domaren and silently took in the scene for themselves.

Domaren kept his eyes ahead and said nothing for as long as he caught his breath. He and his friends said nothing as they each took their time with what had just happened. What was said, and what was was coming.

Kegli took in a breath and and shoved it out through his nose and dragged his face down his face and down his beard. When his eyes settled, they landed on a spot just in front of Domaren. There, accumulating in a tiny pool, was a slow but consistent drip of blood falling off of Domaren's armor. After looking across and drawing some of the other knights' attention to it, Kegli prepared to insist his wound be looked at. But before he could, Domaren uttered something.

"This isn't right," he said.

"What?" Kegli asked, straining to hear.

Domaren shot up to his feet and looked over at Kegli before screaming.

"This isn't right!"

Kegli raised his head to meet Domaren's eyes. Domaren's head shook in anger as the two stared at each other. Kegli knew Domaren wasn't angry with him however, and he calmly stood his ground.

"Domar—" Nanutsi attempted.

"No!" He said, whipping around. "No. This is obscene. This is grotesque. Eon after eon of life and development and progress and they just want to stop and start over? What? They got bored? They grew tired of having to work on what they brought into existence?"

As he continued, he flailed wildly and spun about berating the Kihdai by way of shouting at the other knights. They let him.

He turned back to Midovin and addressed the dead proxy.

"And then they send you all along to waste our energy by wasting your lives? What twisted malformation of thought made the Kihdai think this was acceptable? What could they have possibly said to you that made you think attacking us was a wise decision?"

His anger raged and his screaming scratched at the heights of his voice's capacity.

"So we had to fight the proxies today? I had to kill one of you?"

Domaren stormed off around Midovin's body, shoving his hands out in dismissal at the betrayer's corpse. He then spun back around to continue his tirade.

"I've carried out every whim asked of me. Everything they've asked of me since the beginning of time. The beginning! I was there for them when the world wanted to overthrow them. To kill them, and they didn't take it upon themselves to share one concern with me? One plan? One hint of the deception to give me a chance to talk them out of it?"

As if desperate for a reply, an answer, a plan, or something to make sense of the chaos in his mind, Domaren searched the faces of his fellow knights. Finding no solace there, he spent just a moment looking at Midovin's corpse once again before scanning the wounded forest and finally landing along the slopes of the mountains ahead. But just as it seemed to the others that he may have determined an idea on how to proceed, his head fell once again.

"Domaren," Crizichial offered, with a gentle reassurance. "You should take a look at that wound there," he said, pointing at the crinkled and punctured dent in his armor.

Domaren's head continued to hang, but his chest heaved up, full of air, before releasing it in a disappointed sigh. In a surprisingly quick response, he then flipped off his outer wardrobe and began fiddling at his armor's straps and buckles. With an aggressive tug and impatient pull, Domaren tore off his chest plate and threw it over onto a nearby boulder.

While the others watched Domaren tend to his armor, Brikana and Kegli found nearby rocks to sit and rest on. The said nothing and stared ahead blankly as if putting the world on hold while Domaren saw to his armor.

Crizichial turned to Nanutsi and whispered.

"I was more concerned about his wound than the armor..."

After searching the ground for an adequate stone, Domaren returned to the boulder where his armor rested, face down, and began beating on it. The force of Domaren's bashes increased rapidly with each hit, the volume and frequency growing louder and faster.

"Doma..." Brikana started between bashes. "Domaren!"

He pulled his hand back and paused.

"What?" He shouted without looking back.

"It'll take you centuries to do anything to that armor

with a rock."

"Well, time is evidently of the essence now," he said with a subtle bitterness. "Kegli!" He hollered. "Can I borrow your hammer?"

Kegli stood up and glanced at Brikana as he reached back for his hammer. He pulled it out and walked over to Domaren who had turned slightly to wait for his friend.

"Might want to clean that wound first."

"Yes, I will, Kegli" Domaren snipped. "After I work this out."

After reaching out and snatching Kegli's hammer, Domaren went right back to beating on his armor. Kegli stood at his friend's side and watched as he pounded on the armor.

"That would go a bit faster with a bit of heat," Kegli casually offered, turning back and gesturing at Brikana.

"I understand, Kegli," Domaren said, keeping his eyes ahead and the hammer in the air long enough to respond. "But we can't waste energy on something like this."

Domaren returned to banging, and slowly but surely—longer than it normally would have taken—the steel relented and assumed a shape that its owner was happy with. After reaching out it touch it and then flipping it over to inspect it, Domaren offered the hammer back to Kegli.

"Thank you."

"Of course my friend," Kegli replied. "Now before you put that back on, go clean your wound."

Domaren grunted and waved him away but immediately followed it up with a smirk and a nod.

* * *

After another silent session of the rest of the knights

sitting and contemplating their options and potential fate, Domaren approached with a cleaned chest wrapped in loops of torn linen. One end of the makeshift bandage tapered down over his shoulder with the other end under the other arm. Dangling loose from one hand was his mended armor.

"It wasn't bad at all," Domaren said, sounding and appearing much more calm. He spoke quickly however, as if unconcerned with it and wanting to move past the inevitable discussion about it. But the others didn't bother him.

After slinging the breastplate and its straps over his head, he shoved the straps through the buckles and began fastening them.

"Nice work on that," Nanutsi offered.

Domaren looked up from his buckles and gave her a nod. Once his armor was back in place, he stood in front of his friends with his hands on his hips, as if they had only had a casual delay in their journey.

"Okay, let's continue on before they come back," he said.

The group didn't move or speak. Other than a few lazy glances, there was no reply or rousing cheer to resume their journey.

Rather than addressing the lack of optimism, Domaren found within himself a matching dread. A matching disinterest.

His eyes glazed over and his gaze drifted around the small, makeshift camp before settling on Crizichial who was seated and giving Wiggly a snack. Crizichial looked up.

"From your saddlebags," he said to Domaren.

Domaren felt himself grin and didn't fight it.

He walked over and knelt next to Wiggly. He ruffled her ears as her lips smacked and as she chewed the jerky.

"Good 'ole Wiggly Butt IV," Domaren said with a chuckle through his nose. His tone then fell to something softer and pensive.

"I hadn't really been able to..." He began as he tapped his forehead. "...make sense of it. I didn't put together what they were saying until I saw Wiggly's ears. They were down, you know?"

As Domaren looked at Wiggly and recalled the events before the fight, he mimed his ears being flat.

"They were down close to her head," he said before looking back to his dog. "You tipped me off. Thank you for that."

"And thanks for that initial wave of fire," he said with a glance to Brikana, before looking back down to Wiggly. "That gave us some time to get situated."

"You really didn't know?" Brikana asked in return, rapidly changing the subject.

Domaren turned with a look of disgust.

"What?" He said, shocked. Brikana looked around at the group.

"None of you knew about this?"

The others stirred and began grumbling. Kegli stood up.

"None of you heard any rumors, idle chatter, or hushed secrets about how the Kihdai wanted to rid the world of all its life? That seems as improbable to me as fighting the proxies would have seemed only days ago."

"Now listen," Kegli said sternly. "Domaren walking around shouting at the world is one thing, but you need to take a moment and consider what you're implying."

Brikana slung the pouch of jerky back in Munch's direction and launched to her feet.

"Come on, Kegli! Does it make any sense to you that

five of us, with thousands and thousands of years between, can exist without having any hint of what they were planning?"

Nanutsi replied calmly.

"There's no telling how complex or old their plans were, Kana. With them living in the Grove for all these centuries..." Nanutsi shook her head as she continued. "There's no use in accusing anyone or getting angry over hindsight."

"Don't dismiss my anger, Nanutsi," Brikana said as she waved a finger. "We're on the verge of weakness and mortality here, with not so much as an intercepted courier or warning from a clandestine ally. I'm right to be angry."

"Be angry," Crizichial suggested. "But do not blame us."

"I am still having trouble believing this is happening as well," the Redeemed knight continued. "After considering it might be knights deceiving the rest of us, or the proxies acting on their own... I never thought the Kihdai would be behind it. I never thought they would want any part of something like this."

"So, where does everything stand?" Kegli asked the group. "I know they're waiting for us to grow weak, but do we have any options?"

"Other than visiting the Städ to see if they can help, I can't think of any," Domaren said. "We're essentially back where we were, only weaker."

"Why don't the Kihdai fight us themselves?" Nanutsi wondered. "They could wear us down as well as anyone, if not better."

"That goes back to the birth of the virtues," Crizichial said. "Part of the Kihdais' agreement with the Städ when bestowing the virtues and creating the knights, was that they would not be able to attack the knights. It was intended to ensure the ability of the knights to protect their respective cultures. At least that is how I understand it."

Domaren grunted and offered a single nod.

"But at the same time, the Kihdai and the Grove control the mechanism by which the knights are restored? Seems to be a bit of a conflict there," Brikana said.

"Just a bit," Kegli replied flippantly.

"Well, let's get out of here," Domaren said. He shoved himself up to his feet before kicking and shoving dirt onto the fire. "Let's see if these Stäld can do anything, if they don't kill us first."

# Sixteen

"I don't understand," Kegli said, slowing his donkey. "This is it?"

The rest of the knights brought their horses to a stop. Nanutsi and Crizichial looked at Kegli while the others craned their necks to look deeper into the trees ahead ahead.

"This is what?" Domaren asked in return. "The Vale? Yes, according to the Rifren, this should be the Vale of Kalndaia."

"No, I know that," Kegli huffed. "I meant, this is where the wizards live? These Stäld?"

"It looks fairly serene," Crizichial added. "Not quite where I would imagine a group of primordial beings to dwell."

"That's precisely what I was getting at," Kegli said. "I was just expecting the vale to be somewhat more... foreboding."

"Well, enchanting or foreboding," Brikana said, "this is the way we need to go. Let's get on with it. And who says the wizards can't live here, or on an island, in a forest, or anywhere in particular?"

Kegli's expression crunched towards his nose, squinting one eye significantly. His head and beard shook side to side.

"Yes, I understand," Kegli said with exasperation. "There's just something odd about it. Are we sure this is the right cove? We've been in this valley for days and all the ridges and coves look like the others."

Domaren turned around and sighed before spinning off his horse.

"We all heard the same instructions from the Rifren," he said dryly after landing. As he looked up to the peaks behind Kegli, he pointed at features and landmarks.

"We followed the river through the valley until it turned sharply," Domaren said, pointing behind Kegli. "And then they said continue through the valley for two days by horse. And once a waterfall pouring off an escarpment comes into view, look back and try to spot the two peaks that form Bondollan's Saddle. See? There it is. Just up there."

As Domaren finished turning and pointing, he approached Kegli and slapped him on the shoulder. He then turned once more and while staring down the path that cut through the vale, he addressed the entire group.

"And once you can see Bondollan's Saddle," he continued. "Turn left into the Vale of Kalndaia. Shall we?"

"Before we proceed," Nanutsi began. "I think Brikana was onto something a moment ago."

Domaren wasn't sure what was on Nanutsi's mind, but he and the others waited silently for Nanutsi to elaborate.

"Some of the most lethal things in this world are beautiful." she said. "Plants with beautiful colors and patterns. Predators with mechanisms or disguises to blend into the landscape. Others sing serenades or display physical performances to entice would-be prey. They seduce. Disarm. Reassure. And as soon as their victim's guard is let down... That's when they strike. The enchantment becomes your doom."

The group's initial response was silence as they collectively looked back down the path into the Vale of Kalndia. Finally, Kegli spoke up.

"Exactly. Exactly that," Kegli said softly.

"I'm sure we all agree," Domaren said. "I'm sure we're all of the same mind on our intentions. And we need to remember that all we have right now, is each other. And while I would normally call that enough on any day in any century, we can not trust to that entirely anymore. Our strength is dwindling, and whatever amount we have left is unknown to us. We must be extremely vigilant and extremely selective of what we expend our efforts on."

A gentle wash of wind crept through the valley, sending swarms of leaves twirling through the air and skittering along the ground. Domaren watched them pass before looking up to a layer of soupy clouds that had settled into the mountain slopes.

"Might we... review our plans, should we have a poor encounter with the wizards?" Crizichial asked.

Nanutsi nodded as Domaren shrugged and tilted his head.

"My biggest hope is that we can simply get them to speak with us," Domaren replied. "And in order for that to happen, I'm confident we must never at any time give the impression we are here with any ill will. I would suggest we make ourselves seen and heard at all times."

"And if we succeed in speaking with them?" Kegli asked. As Domaren answered, he stretched, stomped his feet, and climbed back onto his horse. He then rubbed at his sore chest.

"I think we need to find out if they're involved with the Kihdais' plans," he said. "Which, if that's the case, will quickly escalate any conversations we may be having, I'm sure."

He sighed as he pulled the slack out of his horse's reins.

"Friends. Again, I don't know what to expect. I haven't seen them in ages. They were half a world away at the time. They resented me and the other knights, and hated the Kihdai. They stayed wrapped up in their cloaks and kept to themselves."

"We still need a definite plan if they're not willing to talk," Brikana said.

"I don't know that there are many options beyond fleeing," Nanutsi replied.

"Agreed," Kegli said. "The question is to where?"

"Well, all right," Domaren began. "Let's commit now to not initiating any kind of a fight. If anything violent happens, we must let the wizards start it. And should that happen, that will be our signal to flee."

"Again, to where?" Crizichial asked, nodding at Kegli.

"Let's say, the river." Domaren suggested.

"Back where it cuts out of the valley?" Nanutsi asked.

"Yes, and if we get split up, we'll wait for a day for everyone to return?" Domaren asked the group.

Brikana snorted. A few, slight but noticeable smoke rings slipped from her nose.

"And what if some don't show up after a day?"

Domaren dropped his chin but looked up at Brikana and what he perceived as her pessimism.

"Contingency, Domaren. Just need a contingency,"

she said.

He nodded in hesitant agreement.

"Kimozoa," he suggested.

The group exchanged glances. Domaren saw no discernible disagreement and heard no counter.

"All right," he said softly. "Though I sincerely hope there is no need to backtrack to Kimozoa, or even the river for that matter."

Some of the others took a moment to stretch as well, while others scanned their surroundings in the valley. Domaren and Brikana looked forward and down the trail into the vale.

* * *

The valley and its swaying trees settled into a rhythm of innocent bird calls and cutting chirps from arguing creatures. Swells of autumn winds carried the comforting smells of damp leaves to the godknights' senses, threatening to chip away at their heightened awareness. Mile and subsequent mile of the vale's entrance was covered by thickening forest and bright canopies. And though enough leaves had fallen to reveal patches of the blue sky above, the knights and the trail they traveled, were basked in crisp pigments of yellow, orange, and red.

If the vale had any negative or enigmatic reputation, the local wildlife seemed either unconcerned with it or ignorant to it. Kites called out, piercing the relative hush of the forest with their metallic calls. Deer dipped their heads and chewed on the vegetation at the tops of hills just within sight on the edge of the knights' periphery. Munch appeared jealous and watched them closely. Chipmunks and squirrels raced along or across the path as they built up their winter stores.

The trail was an easy one. It was clear of stones and lose soil, and was almost wide enough for three riders to ride side by side. Any curves in the trail's direction were slight enough to not be noticeable by the naked eye and there was no meaningful ascent or descent to the terrain. The group traversed the trail slowly at first, but after a few hours, the godknights quickened their pace.

As their speed quickened, their assumed burden of the unknown weighed less on their shoulders. Their vision darted about less frequently and their attention was stolen less by the scurrying about of the forest's creatures. And after hours, even their silence was interrupted. Crizichial spoke up.

"I have to say," he started. "If we had not been told to look for the wizards in this vale, I would not classify this area as anything but a common plot of land in a common mountain range."

"It's actually quite beautiful," Nanutsi retorted.

"Well, yes, that is not what I mean," Crizichial replied. "I meant only that it does not seem to be the what I had envisioned as being the location of the world's oldest beings."

"What are we actually looking for, anyway?" Brikana asked. "I'd like to have some kind of indication, rather than simply stumbling upon them."

Domaren gestured ahead, but looked partially over his shoulder.

"All I know is that they are said to be here, and in my mind that means all we can do is follow this trail until its end or until we find them."

The first conversation since the godknights entered the vale ended almost as quickly as it began. And while silence took over their travels once more, the trail stretched farther ahead. They trotted deeper into the woods and rode in increasing silence. The day crept along just as the godknights crept. And once the sun slipped farther behind the mountains which were slowly closing in on the trail, the silence was broken once again.

"I haven't heard any birds in a while," Kegli said.

"They're probably preparing to settle for the night," Brikana replied.

"No deer, either," Nanutsi added, ignoring Brikana's dismissal. "Or squirrels."

"I supposed we could just be in an inactive spot," Kegli said.

The godknights continued riding, but the trail became less accommodating. It narrowed, and grew littered with loose stones and crumbling edges. Clumps of ground had washed into the path and dried, forming additional obstacles. The condition of the trail was not the only changing element of their surroundings.

"Looks like we're nearing the back of the vale here," Domaren suggested. "Starting to go up."

Kegli brought his mule to a stop and peered up at the converging mountain ridges.

"Heading for a pass, it seems," he added, before kicking the mule back into a walk. "Have any of you noticed the trees are thinning? I didn't think we've climbed high enough to reach the tree line."

"No, I don't think we have," Domaren said as he spun and slid off his horse. "But even so, that seems an odd looking tree."

Domaren hopped up and off the trail which had become increasingly dug into the ground.

"See it?" He asked, pointing as he walked. The others

dismounted and joined him in traipsing into the woods.

The others jogged ahead and after catching up with Domaren, encircled the odd sight that had caught Domaren's eye.

"This is a tree?" Brikana asked doubtfully.

Nanutsi walked closer.

"Well, it seems to be, if only in... shape and features," she said. "Pine."

"It almost looks to be made of stone," Crizichial said.

"What, petrified?" Domaren wondered.

Nanutsi swiped a quick but hefty swipe at it. A dense scraping sound rang out.

"I don't think it's petrified," she said. Before she finished, Domaren was already sliding his bare hand along the trunk.

"I think you're right, Criz," Domaren said. "This feels just like stone." As he continued staring at it through a curious squint, he tapped it with his knuckles.

Kegli pointed up.

"Look at the branches and needles. They're stone too."

"Same with the pine cones," Crizichial said.

Domaren's eyes widened into a blur as he scratched his forehead.

"Well, I'm not sure what to make of this, but—"

"Hey, there's another one," Kegli said, pointing back to the other side of the trail.

The group instinctively started scanning and searching for more. While others stood in place, Nanutsi and Crizichial stepped away from the group in the direction they had been traveling.

"I see a few grouped together farther up the trail," Nanutsi shouted back.

Domaren sighed and waved the others back to the horses.

"I don't know what the wizards would have to do with these trees, but I can only imagine they're related somehow," he said as he stepped into the stirrups. "Any objections to continuing on?"

A silence followed, combined with exchanged glances of raised eyebrows.

"All right, what are they?" Domaren prodded. "Speak your mind."

Crizichial looked around the group as if checking for horse traffic on a busy village path.

"I do not believe any of us are loathe to continue," he said, "but rather, are only unsure of the best manner in which to proceed."

"The best manner?" Domaren repeated. He dipped his head and looked to the ground as if already considering options.

"I suggest we simply continue along the path," Nanutsi proposed. Brikana shook her head.

"While maintaining human forms?" She asked before pointing her chin at Crizichial. "Well, most of us? I'm not sure. It may be time to shift and be ready."

"Remember," Domaren said. "We need to appear as though we're not ready for anything. If we encounter the wizards in our full armored, beastly, demon, ax-wielding, and dragon glories, we may walk right into a fight that exhausts our strength. And that's if we survive. I think we should continue as we are. Whoever may need to can shift in a blink."

Brikana rolled her head around on her shoulders.

"Okay, yes, I agree. It's the most prudent option," she said.

"Right," Domaren said. "Are we all agreed?"

He took a moment to look each of his friends in the eye and waited for a nod of acknowledgment, and once the decision was made, he returned to the trail.

The group of godknights mounted once again and pressed on, returning to the silence previously employed. And now that it had been discussed, the knights were collectively cognizant of the lack of life—wildlife or otherwise. No birds. No deer. No squirrels. The thinning trees no longer swayed, and their leaves hung motionless. And as the riding knights ascended the still-deteriorating trail, the stillness grew more apparent. The lifelessness increased. The color drained out of the trail, out of the forest floor, and out of the trees.

As the trees continued thinning, the amount of Ställd in the world increased. Where the ground had been blanketed in bright emerald mosses, wild lilac, and clover, the swaths of vegetation also gradually transitioned into patches of slate and stone. With each dozen strides of the knights' horses, the colors of life gave way to patches of colorless life halted forever in stone. Once there were no pockets of color anywhere to be seen, the physical representations of flora and forest decreased until finally, the knights saw no trees. No flowers. No hint of anything that may remind one of what life might have looked like. Whether the godknights looked to the trail just off their side, or peered far across to the opposing ridge, there were no longer any discernible signs of trees, plants, or soil. There, at the towering elevation the knights had reached, was nothing but step after step, and stride after stride, of smooth, ashen rock.

The trail meandered farther up. The noticeable indentation in the path, which until then had indicated an immeasurable amount of use, slowly filled in—not with soil or other loose material, but merely raised to be flush with the surrounding ground.

The knights, while not quite intimidated, slowed their ascent. The horses were still climbing confidently, but the stone ground became increasingly smooth. The amount of cracks decreased. Their length, width, and depth lessened until finally there were none. The surrounding stone ground contained fewer elements of texture or features of depth. And just as any hint of the day's remaining amber brightness gave way to the evening's charcoal-stained sky, the trail leveled off.

As each knight reached the top, no one said a word. Each knight walked their horse next to another and dismounted. In calculating silence, Domaren stared ahead and evaluated the new location.

The steep path's climax ended at a sprawling, flat, and featureless expanse of smooth rock beneath their feet. One side was open to a truly straight cliff, thousands of feet high, other than the connecting trail that winded up to it. As the open side, shaped like a crescent, curved around, it ended at a wall of rock that stretched up to a mountain peak. Straight ahead of the godknights along the base of the towering rock face, were five doors. The size of their openings varied noticeably in size.

Each door seemed fairly indistinguishable from one another, at least from where Domaren and the other knights stood. No carvings could be seen. No etchings. No paint or symbols. The rock face that the doors were cut into was just as smooth as the ground beneath them. It appeared that the mountain and the carved out area the knights were at now, was a single piece of gigantic stone. Domaren scanned the area quickly and saw no strata layers, discolorations, seams, or cracks.

The only other item visible to the godknights, other than the stone ground, immense wall, and humble doors, was what appeared to have once been a towering bonfire, carved out of, or long turned into stone. Even in the dwindling light, Domaren could see the distinguishing features of what seemed to represent orderly stacks of wood towards the bottom, which hadn't caught fire yet. On top of those were solid depictions of charred wood, followed by pitiful bits of burned logs and embers strewn all around. All, frozen in stone.

Atop the imprisoned fire were frozen flames. Each whip of fire without color or life extend out into the sky and reached for the heights of the mountain. Dozens of flames, each as tall as Crizichial or taller, roared out high as if trying to singe the stars, only to be stone-flashed into a snap of time and held in place indefinitely. Domaren found it exquisite and unnatural all at once. He found it relaxing and unsettling at the same time. Fortuitous or ill-timed, he felt as though they had reached their destination.

A faint drone of chirping crickets stole Domaren's attention. As he became aware of it, he turned and looked down towards the shadowed origins of their path before the reminder of a distant rumble of thunder brought his focus back to the mountaintop doors.

*No rain, yet,* he thought.

"I don't remember any mention of doors leading into a mountain," Kegli said.

Domaren shook his head in agreement.

"Who's taking which door?" Brikana asked.

Nanutsi replied while keeping her eyes on the doors. "Perhaps we should agree on whether or not that is our plan?"

Brikana huffed impatiently and pointed an open hand

towards the doors.

"It appears as though that is our only next step in searching for the wizards, Nanu," Brikana snapped.

"But, need we split up?" Crizichial asked gently. "Dividing a force is rarely the best option when there are so many unknowns and variables. And, I would surmise that these individual entrances lead to the same destination."

"There's also no way to be sure when we may start running out of energy," Domaren said, quickly checking the others' dispositions.

"Yes, everyone, I understand. Pros and cons," Brikana said. "Risk and reward. But let me remind you all, that we need assistance sooner rather than later and I believe we have a greater chance of finding the wizards sooner by splitting up."

Kegli turned to Brikana and slung an arm out in exasperation.

"And what if you're alone, following a tunnel, by yourself, find yourself in a fight, and the moment you shift, you find that you can't because you're out of power? Hmm?"

Brikana widened her eyes and shrugged.

"Well, I believe I *just* mentioned risks and rewards. I'll risk it." She replied. Her and Kegli's voices rose as they argued. "We can discuss hypotheticals all night. Here, I have one. What if we group up and keep reaching dead ends for each tunnel and have to retrace our steps out and follow each entrance individually? We don't have time for that."

"There is a difference between being efficient, and being reckless, Kana."

"Are those our only two options?" Nanutsi asked. "Proceeding in a group or individually?"

After a break to consider the implications, Domaren started to reply.

"What do you have in mind? A group of two and a group of three? Split the difference between a single group and individuals?"

Nanutsi nodded and started to reply, but Brikana interjected.

"Staying stagnant and discussing every possible approach is foolish, Domaren. I can't stress enough how each minute that we linger here is a minute we could be spending searching for the wizards, restoring our energy, and bringing the fi—"

Before Brikana could finish her latest volley in the group's stalemate, a crunching rip of thunder blistered the night sky. Lightning flashed behind the mountain and cast the shadow of the peak's silhouette upon the ledge's stone floor.

A second flash of brightness blanketed the sky but pulsed again and concentrated down into a strike upon the mound of petrified fire. When it was hit, the bonfire appeared to gasp for life and consume the sky's fire, injecting every thread of wood, chunk of ember, red, orange and yellow flame, and the burning bits almost too small to see, with life. The power and light surged through the fire and as it roared to gigantic life, streams of unrelenting light dripped out of the base of the flames and into previously unseen channels along the stone arena's floor.

"Hold on, everyone. Wait," Domaren ordered quickly.

The tiny rivers of molten light raced along, outlining what at first appeared to be random and undefined shapes. Pulses of fire from the bonfire flooded even more flame into the ground and branched out rapidly like expanding roots and fingers. But as more of the rock became etched with additional lines and patterns, deliberate and recognizable patterns took shape.

At times, the energy rushed ahead and receded, leaving designs behind. It then rushed along elsewhere and remained in place only to have other streams of fire branch off elsewhere. As the fire continued to race along, concentric rings emerged, rippling out at great diameter from the bonfire. As the rings came into being, the streams of energy darted in-between and across them, carving symbols and characters. At an accelerating rate, the fire etchings shot farther out from the bonfire until, once an enormous symbol had carved itself into the floor of stone, the veins of flame branched out and made their way to the doors leading into the mountain. They then struck the wall and shot up, framing the doors in flaming boundaries. Once they had accentuated the doors with a few symbols of their own, the invisible quills of fire scratched symbols into the stone above each door. When the door symbols were complete, the fire's exercise of etching came to a halt, but left all its work alight and emboldened.

After the rock floor and wall on the side of the fire opposite the godknights were tattooed by fire, a third ripple of concussive punches followed and accompanied another punishing flash of excruciating brightness. The light bathed the mountain top of stone in energy and as much time as it took for the lightning to flash, the central bonfire raged even brighter, even higher, and revealed five previously absent figures standing around the mystifying bonfire.

Domaren heard a rustling off to his side followed by a significant vibration under his feet.

"Kana! Stop!" Nanutsi whispered with a dense scratchiness. But it was too late. Their dragon counterpart had shifted to her natural form.

"Wait!" Domaren urged.

She acknowledged no one, but remained motionless

and stared ahead, waiting to pounce.

"Everyone, wait!" Domaren said to the rest of the group. He looked to each side to confirm no one else had shifted, and that they were holding in place.

"I would say we found our wizards," Kegli said with a frosted resolve. He suspended his hand over his shoulder, ready to expend just a pinch of energy to grab his ax.

"Wait," Domaren whispered again, holding his arms out at his friends. As he pleaded with his friends a final time to resist reacting, he strained his vision to gain an idea of who or what exactly had appeared ahead of them.

The figures stood motionless around the bonfire and made no effort to interact with the godknights. They looked as though they had been plucked out from the depths of the mountain while asleep and set around the fire, standing up. The only aspect that made them seem alive, or at least aware, was their collective postures of appearing to look into the fire—peering into the fire as if waiting for an indeterminate amount of time to be warmed by it.

Domaren looked around at the beings, trying to settle on what he thought they were or who they were, and which he may want to address first. They seemed to have a semblance to various races. If these were the Stäld, the wizards, they should have no semblance to anything. And if they were members of the world's races, they shouldn't have been as haphazard or large as they were. None of the figures around the fire were shorter than Brikana in dragon form.

Domaren's eyes raced to examine the faces of each figure before settling upon the one closest to him. On one end of the semicircle, stood something that had the shape of what Domaren determined to be the closest representation of a human. As with the other strange beings, its head was titled down towards the fire. The towering flames danced and stretched up, bathing the oddity's face in oscillating shades of yellow and red.

Its eyes couldn't be seen. It didn't appear as though it had any. Though Domaren and the other godknights had not yet moved, the fire allowed Domaren to see its features well enough that he was extremely sure there were no eyes. Only black recesses. It did however generally have a face. But where Domaren expected to see skin, he instead saw cheeks and a forehead made of moss. A nose in the form of a portion of a bent branch had been fashioned, along with a chin made of old, soggy leaves.

Very little of what Domaren thought was a face could be seen. Covering the majority of what he thought was a head were large sections of shaped bone and bark. This helmet of sorts, had been fastened by draping sections of bark over the top of the head with additional pieces attached to antler and bone which wrapped around the back and sides of the head.

Continuing down from the head, the startling likeness appeared to be adorned in additional armor, though Domaren was puzzled by the material. Though it was deep charcoal in color, it was extremely shiny and reflected the bonfire in such a way that the figure seemed to be alight in flame itself. The crudely configured breastplate, backplate, and armor for the legs and arms had the appearance of sheets of brittle rock, unblemished and smooth towards the center of various sections, but broken and rough at the edges. And rather than armor-clad hands or feet, the constructed warrior had extremities made of twigs and bones of rodents and similarly-sized woodland creatures.

Next to the fabricated knight was a replica Domaren recognized quickly. The largest of the beings around the fire, the imposing creature stood on four legs with sprawling wings outstretched as if shielding the others from a violent wind, though there was none. The body of the dragon was constructed from shards and plates of semi-transparent crystal and glass. Most seemed pristine, while a few were missing, some were cracked, and older ones were smudged or foggy.

The wings, and the area under the dragon's chin, along the bottom of its neck, and down under its belly, seemed to be made of a variety of animal skins. The wings were made of countless quilted sections of short and medium grey and spotted brown deer skins, which were fastened together next to fewer bear skins. Smaller game, such as rabbit, squirrel, or gopher had been given their skins to dress the dragon's neck and stomach.

The dragon's head, also missing discernible eyes, was made from small shards and pieces of opaque crystal. Its rows of teeth consisted of stalactites and stalagmites of varying lengths. Some appeared to be missing, possibly from chewing on the people, beasts, and lands of the world. And what Domaren found the most unsettling of the features as he looked around the fire, was the dragon's mouth, frozen open as if smiling at its next meal.

Though the dragon was the largest of the bonfire beings, it was not the tallest. The height of the figure between the brittle-armored one and glass dragon was second only to the peak of the mountain. It stood awkwardly like a diseased tree, which had either grown too far and too quickly, or an ancient tree that had lived and swelled to a ripe age, but then started to wither away to emaciated sickness. It's wobbly height reminded him of a drunken elf.

Rather than being pieced together from old leaves, bones, or stained crystals formed at the creation of the world, the lanky creation, also without eyes, was dressed in the flesh of the world's creatures. But while some of the other beings had dried and cleaned skins or animal bits, the tall one's borrowed flesh glistened brightly in the presence of the bonfire. They shone wet and bright red as if freshly skinned off of animals who had met a hurried and unfortunate fate. Oddly, Domaren thought, the creature had for some reason determined it could not proceed through its existence naked in its borrowed flesh and instead had tattered pants of a crude black fabric and shirt of worn burlap. Its stringy arms dangled like beheaded snakes dangling from hooks, and the gaunt giant's meaty chunk of a head rested on its shoulder as if it had no skeleton. Something that resembled a pointed ear had been stitched into place on one side of its head.

The fourth figure was roughly the size of the constructed knight. Standing on two legs, the fierce form created almost entirely of dense bundles of moss and dried mud resembled a diseased human, but with branches protruding from its head, and long bones extending from its mouth area. Its feet and hands with disproportionate claws—each one looking to have been claimed from various types of animals were large and extremely pronounced. Its legs of branches and dried grass shot up vertically to a massive body made of similar materials, but where the bulky creation could be seen through at various points, this being was packed densely like an unbridled yew bush. It was full of dimension, full of depth, but like the others, showed no signs of life.

As Domaren traced its features and studied its material, he realized that it was intended to resemble an orc. Though, like the others, this one also lacked eyes. Additional strips of grass and twigs stuck out from the center of its face and wriggled out to a nose tipped by a shiny rock, similar to the material that formed the armor of the first being.

The rocky armor material made another appearance as it was also used by the fifth figure standing around the bonfire. But what caught Domaren's attention first were what he assumed were intended to be axes, which quickly led to the notion this figure was intended to be a dwarf.

But the fake dwarf didn't have one ax, or two. It had at least nine different axes that Domaren could see from where he stood. Sticking out from behind the facsimile's back upon crooked branches of various lengths, were nine ax heads, poorly hewn and shaped from a variety of stone. As with many of the mystical group's adornments and armaments, the axes didn't look practical or functional. They were not uniform in size and were not arranged in a meaningful way that no one would be able to access one, let alone nine. Also impractical, was the armor strapped to or draped upon this figure. Like the first entity, the pitiful dwarf's armor was also made primarily of jagged sheets of shiny, but useless, fragile stone.

The eyeless dwarf figure had a similar face construction as the initial being. Its small cheek areas and forehead were made of moss, with a large nose feature created by a single, small branch with a warped knot on the end. And like its nearby godknight counterpart, the unnatural dwarf representation had a beard, but where the real dwarf's beard was made of long and tended hair, the fabricated dwarf's beard was made of old cobwebs which had, it appeared, become an eternal home to hollowed beetle exoskeletons and detached moth wings.

As Domaren finished examining the figures, he found himself surprised that no one had darted forward yet. No one had spoken or shouted. No one had made any attempt to engage the odd group ahead of them. They simply watched and waited as the fire waved and prodded at the deepening and solidifying night. And while the etching fires of the symbols and symbols persisted along the ground and wall, the gigantic bonfire easily claimed the majority of the dense evening's blackness for its own.

"What are these?" Domaren asked.

Kegli turned his head only enough to realize he shouldn't move. He instead tried to spot Domaren from the corner of his eye.

"What do you mean?" Kegli replied in a whisper. "They're the wizards. The Ställd."

"I do not believe so," Crizichial added in agreement. "Those beings ahead of us resemble races of the worlds. They have description. They have form and exist physically."

"Resemble?" Brikana asked. "Is that what you call resemble?"

"Exactly, Criz," Domaren said, ignoring Brikana. "The Ställd are just that. The Ställd. They are fragile and featureless. I've seen them with my own eyes. These are not the St—"

Before Domaren could finish, a tearing chorus of voices, louder than the previous explosions of lightning, interrupted. And though the voices were not animated to the point of anger or fury, their unbridled volume caused pain to the supernatural knights.

"Do not presume to speak of us with such certainty, knights."

# Seventeen

As the knights instinctively closed their eyes and turned their heads, or clawed desperately to cover their ears, the previously frozen figures stirred. One by one, the haunting warrior, glass dragon, spire of elven flesh, clumsily armed dwarf, and orc of dead vegetation lifted their heads. The primal curiosities raised their heads and gazes to glare at the trespassing knights.

As the threatening group's command finished being spoken, Domaren let go of his ears and relaxed from his reactionary cringe. He then feared an immediate reprisal from Brikana and turned to her where he found her frozen in place, just as the group around the bonfire had just been. But rather than frozen in her previous posture of attentiveness or readiness, or a posture of pained reaction to the deafening command, he instead saw Brikana stopped in time where it appeared she had just begun to unleash a torrent of flame in a defensive counterattack that the imitations stopped mid-stream.

"Kana," Domaren attempted. "Kana?"

"What happened to her?" Crizichial asked.

Domaren looked back and saw the others relaxing and securing their footing once more.

Though none of their respective mouths moved, the beings spoke again, but not as punitively.

"We have the ability to release her," the voices said. "Do not jeopardize her release with your next actions."

The godknights didn't reply immediately, though Domaren didn't care for his friend being imprisoned within herself. He took a moment to consider his options for action, inaction, what to say, or what not to say, while the bonfire took the opportunity to fill the silence with its sparking pops and crackling wood.

"If you will not harm my friends," Domaren said quickly, "I would speak with you as friends as well."

The large, cobbled-together faces of the enigmatic beings maintained their eyeless stare. Their mouths remained open and still as the voices responded.

"We will return your dragon's freedom," the cacophony of voices said.

As they spoke, the stream of fire Brikana had initiated continued shooting out but was immediately deflected out into the sky above by an unseen barrier.

"Kana! Brikana! Wait, wait," Domaren pleaded as he placed his hand on her nearest leg. "They're talking. They're talking with us. It's okay."

The godknight of all dragons rolled her shoulders back and stretched her wings. She breathed in slowly and deeply and after craning her neck up to it's great height, brought it back down to Domaren's height. After a parting and furious glare for the mystery beings, she turned to Domaren.

"I told you not to do anything," Domaren whispered.

Brikana, usually argumentative and combative, said nothing in response. Her eyelids hung low with restrained fury, but not enough for her to provoke the strange entities any further.

"Who are they?" Nanutsi quietly asked her friends. No one spoke, and all, including Brikana, remained fixed on the bonfire figures.

"They must be the wizards," Kegli insisted. "Who else would they be?"

"If you have questions for us to consider," the group of voices said, "you can pose them directly to us."

Domaren took a step forward and examined the faces in front of him once more. Not knowing who to speak to or what to look at, he looked mostly at the fire.

"We do have a question," he started. "We have been traveling in search of a particular set of beings we were told resided in the Vale of Kalndaia. Are you these beings?"

For the first time since the godknights arrived, a lone voice replied, though the owner could not be determined.

"We are indeed a group of beings that dwell in the Vale of Kalndaia," the voice answered. "But, what sets the particular group you are in search of apart, Domaren?"

Domaren's surprise at hearing his name made him recoil, only if slightly. His eyes squinted and his face tensed.

The thin being made of old cloth and bloody flesh caught Domaren's attention. It lifted its head off its shoulder and offered Domaren a grotesque grin from the area it's mouth generally might be.

"You know my name?" Domaren asked. He looked back at his friends, trying to recall if he had spoken his name to the unknown creatures, or if his friends might have said it loud enough for them to hear. Regardless, something gave Domaren the feeling they knew it already.

"Of course," the grouped voices replied. "You are known to us."

Puzzled, Domaren tilted his head and pondered a moment.

"I don't understand," he said. "You're *aware* of me, or do you *know* me?"

The chorus of unsettling voices exchanged lazy laughter between each other.

"Forgive me," Domaren added, "but the source of your amusement escapes me."

"Now, now," a few of the voices responded, becoming stern again as they spoke in response to Domaren's tone. "We know you, and you know us!"

Domaren looked away in an effort to bite his tongue, or at least tame it. He sighed and spoke again.

"I have never seen you before. These..." Domaren said, pausing to search for a mild term, "...forms are unknown to me, or at the very least, I can not recall them."

"Are you sure?" the voices asked. "Can you not pierce the superficial, Domaren? Can you not see beneath?"

Domaren lifted his hands and looked back to the other godknights who returned shrugs and gestures of confusion on their own. Except Brikana. She stood poised, and as far as Domaren was concerned, annoyed.

"Truly Domaren," the voices said, reclaiming Domaren's attention. "There may be more to us than you realize."

Domaren looked away to think, but then locked his vision back on the odd creatures. He squinted again, but quickly relaxed his eyes and unfocused. As his eyes blurred, he let his head fall back, but only a pinch. He let his hazy vision take in the entire surroundings so that he could examine it in whole and without the distraction of focusing on what might not be right in front of him. As he settled into the scene of smudged sight, he saw it, or more accurately, saw them.

Throughout each fabricated being, creature, and entity, Domaren was able to make out blotches of smoothly shifting movement. Whether it was the stone-armored warrior, the glass dragon, the flesh elf, overly armed dwarf, or orc of twigs and straw, each one had pulsing masses of grey contorting slowly between arms, legs, bodies, and heads.

Domaren's vision shot back into focus.

"The Stäld?" He gasped. "How? Wh..." He continued, lost for words. "Why are you in—"

"Yes," a different, singular voice replied after a quick laugh. "Yes, we are indeed the Stäld. It's been an immeasurably long time, Domaren."

"What are these strange representations? These costumes?" Kegli asked after stepping up to Domaren's side.

Domaren looked back at the others and held up a hand requesting Brikana's continued patience.

"No," the voices immediately boomed. "No. It is our turn to ask some questions of you and the others."

The godknights maintained their positions and waited while the fire whipped about and snapped at the air.

"We of course would like to know why you are here," the Stäld said together. "Why are you? What unworthy reason would you think justifies disturbing us?"

Domaren swallowed and struggled to find words adequate words. Instead of providing an answer immediately, regret and primordial nostalgia overcame his thoughts. While it had not yet started to rain, distant flashes called his attention to remote mountain ridges. A crisp and biting wind further humbled his response.

"I have not sought you out in ages," Domaren said softly.

"You have never sought us out," a Wizard voice replied.

"Not after the virtues were bestowed, that is true," Domaren acknowledged with a tip of his head to the side. "I have never attempted to find you or maintain contact, because I thought it was what you wanted."

Domaren expected a response, but received none. Seizing on their hesitance, he continued.

"Was that an incorrect assumption?" He asked. "If so, I apologize. But it would seem by your relocation to this area, and the remoteness of this area, that there was some element of seclusion desired."

"We did not desire seclusion, Domaren. You know this."

"I do know, old friends, yes. I remember. We were there, together as Stäld. Though I was made a godknight and have had to fulfill those duties ever since, I never felt right about how the Kihdai left it. Left you."

Domaren used the following silence to shift his feet and check in with his friends by way of subtle and short glances. He planted his feet and addressed the Stäld once again.

"I felt they had betrayed you in a way. And they have now betrayed us all."

The angry baritone of a singular Stäld voice bit fiercely in response.

"There was no betrayal originally, Domaren. It was abandonment. We were used to harness the collective power of our singular race to create the virtues, and transform you and the other original godknights, and then abandoned. We were not betrayed. We were abandoned!"

Domaren raised his hands, palms facing the Stäld as the agitated entity raged.

"Yes, I agree," Domaren replied. He looked down as if searching the ground for the grain of a memory within the mountain. "I remember you," he added in a whisper.

"What?" The furious Stäld snapped.

"I remember you. I remember your," he said, trying to find the right word, "presence. I remember you. You're the Stäld that helped make me."

One of the other gentler voices replied, agitated, but fatigued, Domaren thought.

"None of us here *made* anyone," she said. "We just helped transform you."

Domaren nodded.

"What were you referring to a moment ago," the unified Stäld asked. "The Kihdai have betrayed us all? What do you mean?"

"Yes," Domaren replied. "It is why the other knights and I are here. It is why we were looking for you. The Kihdai have decided upon a malicious and sickening course to destroy all life in the world."

The Stäld, or at least their false suits of deception did not move. Their eyes remained empty. Their mouths remained agape. Nothing was said.

Domaren heard a huff of frustration come from behind him. Without looking, he assumed it came from Brikana.

"Stäld? Friends?" Domaren asked.

"Do not presume to call us friends just yet," they said flatly.

"What would you have us call you, then?" Brikana asked casually.

Domaren whipped his head around, scowling at his

friend.

The silence and stillness of the Ständ persisted, creating an uneasiness within Domaren. But the lack of comment on the notion of the Kihdai ending all life in the world mutated the uneasiness into the beginnings of anxiety. The Ständ did not appear to reciprocate the knights' sense of urgency, causing Domaren's anxiety to diverge into streams of frustration and impatience.

"So yes, that is why we have come to you," Domaren said. "I would please ask that you provide us guidance, wisdom, or outright assistance in answering the Kihdai' efforts to destroy and recreate the world."

An unconcerned Ständ answered the proposal with a question.

"What is their reasoning for this action?"

Nanutsi let a whisper slip out from behind Domaren.

"The reasoning behind a desire to destroy all life seems irrelevant."

Domaren swatted at the air behind him.

"Irrelevant or not," thundered the combined Ständ, "answer our question."

Domaren took another step forward and immediately replied.

"It is said that they have grown tired of their creation being taken for granted," Domaren said. "The world's races wage war, generation after generation, for petty and meaningless reasons. They squander and hate. Regress more than grow. Destroy more than create."

Domaren searched the absent expressions of the Ständ as he waited for a response. His inability to distinguish expression or discern disposition continued to chip away at his patience and though Domaren found the measured and subdued timing of their responses inappropriate given the discussion, they finally replied once again, in unison.

"We find nothing disagreeable in that position," they said.

"How can those be your thoughts on this?" Brikana erupted. "Wouldn't the destruction of all life include you as well? You would do nothing while all that exists is destroyed, as well as welcome that fate upon yourselves as well?"

As Brikana finished her tirade, the bonfire, which had been calm and reserved for the course of the conversation to that point roared back to violent and obnoxious life. A wave of thunder punched the sky, and bolts of lightning shot up *from* the fire before tearing into scratches miles high across the sky. The symbols, circles, and symbols swelled in brightness from a faint yellow to a glaring crimson.

The mountain groaned and scraped like timber settling under autumn's first frost. The ground shook and tilted, sending the godknights teetering and stumbling, though they quickly secured their footing. As they regained their stability, they watched as the Stäld stirred with life.

Their open mouths closed and their empty eyes filled with what resembled the cores and souls of individual amber flames. Their stationary legs and paws lifted and smoothly shifted the Stäld in their disguises around and out from behind the fire. The Stäld had full movement and control of their creations and approached the godknights with deliberate stomps of furious disgust.

"We owe this world nothing," the approaching Stäld roared, their mouths slowly and then quickly moving to crudely match their words. "We owe nothing to you, or anything in it. We have grown tired of our true selves and have grown tired of you. It is time you and this world, were gone."

Domaren backed up as the Stäld approached. He saw

Crizichial nod quickly at Brikana.

"We tried it your way, Domaren," she said.

"Everyone, no! Don't! We can't afford to spend our ener—"

Domaren searched the faces of his friends with eyes wide in panic, but they were all focused on the Stäld who continued their march to confront the knights.

"Leave us now, as you left us ages ago, Domaren," they said together, their voices grating harshly.

The Stäld orc crouched slightly before taking off in a charge towards the godknights while the fake dwarf reached back and grabbed a handful of throwing axes. As it grabbed one with its other hand and began to throw it, the fleshy, Stäld elf reached behind him at the bonfire as if grabbing onto a rope. As it swung back around, a cascading wall of fire arced out at the godknights.

But Crizichial had already put an initial defense into place.

When the fire, axes, and charging orc came within feet of the godknights, a row of demonic apparitions with shields and weapons shot out from the rock and blocked or deflected each attack. Like Brikana's earlier fire that was blocked, the bonfire's extension whipped out into the sky. The charging orc was slammed in the face with a shield, sending it tumbling back before rolling onto its side, with the thrown axes clanging and crashing off the summoned demons' shields and swords. As Crizichial's defending apparitions were struck, they collapsed and disappeared back into the ground.

"Stop!" Domaren yelled as he grabbed Verikta's handle. "We will leave! Knights, the Stäld are not our enemy!"

Domaren ran in and out of flying axes, orcs, and fire,

and attempted to steal his friends' attention, but it was too late.

A familiar sound rose up and over the sound of the fight, crushing Domaren's hopes for tensions to abate. A rugged and harsh scrape of massive air being sucked in noticeably disturbed the surround pressure behind Domaren. As he turned too late to urge Brikana once more not to attack, he watched as her unmatched onslaught of fire launched over his head and blasted into the Stäld. Domaren lost sight of the Stäld, except for the upper few feet of the Redeemed impostor which he saw quickly claimed by Brikana's fire.

But Domaren had missed one. The armored human duplicate had rolled under the flames before jumping up in front of Domaren.

With his hand still on Verikta's handle, he quickly slid it into position to tap her purple handlestone before drawing the sword and brought it up over his head just in time to deflect the Stäld's downward slice. Domaren slid the attacking Stäld's sword away, down Verikta's blade, and ran past. The foes both turned to face each other once more.

"We will let you leave," the Stäld knight said to Domaren, "if you leave *now.*"

"We?" Kegli mocked. "It appears you are the only one left," he said.

"Kegli, and the rest of you," Domaren admonished. "You're exhausting whatever we might have left. Quit acting like fools and try to grasp the severity of the situation."

The Stäld knight laughed and made no effort to acknowledge Kegli while Domaren took a moment to stare directly at his flippant friend. After addressing his friends, the real and fake human godknights stared each other down, but the Stäld's mossy expression quickly gave way to an enigmatic grin.

Brikana brought her flames to a halt while they finished washing across the rocky terrace, stealing Domaren's attention. As the flames extinguished, Domaren was equally surprised, and not, to see the Stäld's true formations of energy still present around the fire. Ashen piles of debris with bits of straw, vegetation, bone, and other animal matter, laid still at the base of each Stäld. The still-intact armored wizard addressed Domaren once more and regained his attention.

"As a gesture of deference for our shared origins, Domaren," the Stäld said darkly as if instructing, rather than proposing, "we will let you and your friends leave. But you must leave now. We will not offer this again."

Through noticeably heavier breathing, Domaren acknowledged the truce.

"I understand," he said, gesturing at his friends to stand down. As he sheathed Verikta, he prepared to make his parting words to his ancient Stäld siblings. "We understand. We will leave."

While Domaren caught his breath and watched the bonfire recede back to its previous calm, the group of godknights waited for the next word or signal. The featureless group of Stäld also waited as the light within the rock etchings faded to an almost comforting level.

"As we prepare to go," Domaren said, "might I ask a final question?"

There was no immediate response, whether by an ambiguous response out of thin air, or from the armored one, but quickly after, it turned towards the others as if silently conferring.

"Ask your question, Domaren," multiple Stäld voices said.

Domaren nodded quickly while mustering a particular

type of hope in what the response to his question might be.

"I understand your position" he said with a weighted sincerity. As he spoke, the armored Stäld turned back towards the fire and rejoined the others. "I understand why you feel the way you do," Domaren added. "Upon hearing about what the Kihdai are doing, there must be a fairness and sense of justice you're feeling that I hadn't been able to even adequately appreciate until now."

"Pose your question, Domaren," they said.

"Right," he said. "I just have to ask again, and will of course accept any answer you provide. But while it would be justified, and while it would be understood, I feel like the other knights and I must continue our efforts to stop this."

The Stäld screeched with anger, sending the bonfire stretching once more into the sky.

"The question, Domaren!"

"It is our duty to defend the survival of our races," he replied quickly.

"Go try!" They yelled back. "Just leave!"

"We will, but if you will not join us, will you at least tell us if there is a way for us to regain our full strength and refill our energy?"

Domaren hung desperately on his last syllable and dangled helplessly in the following silence, but in it, was able to find some hope to grab onto.

"What do you mean, refill your energy?" A lone Stäld asked.

Their ignorance of the situation confused Domaren and sent his eyes looking for clues in the faces of his friends. Crizichial shrugged.

"Aren't you routinely contacted by the Grove and regenerated then?"

"Normally, yes," Nanutsi answered, "but our ability

to communicate with the Grove was severed. We're not sure how they accomplished that."

"Wait a moment. If we understand correctly then," the Stäld voices said, "the Kihdai want to destroy life and begin anew..."

Nanutsi nodded.

"The Kihdai knew you have the power to fight back and would resist, but they control the source of your power. They then cut off the source of your power and waited until they could enact their plan without interference from you."

"Exactly," Crizichial confirmed.

"Then, it seems," the Stäld continued, "that the Kihdai are manipulating and controlling all variables without giving the world any significant opportunity to defend itself. They're waiting for your energies to be exhausted."

"Yes," Domaren answered. "And again, I promise you, I understand your desire to remain uninvolved. I only ask you help us regain our full power so that we can make a legitimate stand on behalf of our races."

Domaren's final request had been proffered and he rejoined his friends while they waited for a response. The armored and other Stäld grouped up next to the fire and communicated silently. Domaren had his own conversation with the other knights.

"I'm not sure what options we'll have if they turn us down," he said.

"Well, we never really had any other ideas to begin with," Kegli said.

"I'm beginning to grow tired of having to scrape for help and conserve my energy while waiting for the real fight," Brikana said. "Let them decline. Let them refuse us. I'll happily wait for the Kihdai to arrive and fight them until I can't fight anymore."

"We're all of the same mind on that point, Kana," Domaren said. "If a fight leading to an inevitable loss is what fate has in store for me, you, the world, then so be it, but I want to exhaust every option, opportunity, and chance, not only for our own survival, but for the survival of everything else in this world. All living things should be able to exist until their natural conclusion, whether by their own hands, or from the world's reaction to them."

"Hmm," Crizichial started, pondering. "It seems as though the Städ are trying to decide if they think the Kihdais' plans could be considered, in your words, a reaction of the world."

"Knights," the Städ interrupted.

Domaren and the other turned and waited.

"Please, follow us," they said together.

Crizichial's eyes shot open in surprise before looking at Domaren in relief who huffed out a sigh through puffed cheeks. The godknights stared in astonishment at each other, unsure of what the Städ intended for them. And before they speak to any ideas, they were distracted by the sound of a stirring wind coming from the bonfire.

The human-looking Städ had already started for one of the doors into the mountain, but the other Städ remained behind. An invisible force stoked the bonfire once again and stirred the etchings to brightness yet again. As the light and fire roared back to life, the burned piles of their former likenesses launched up and for a moment, hung motionless in the air. Seconds later, they stirred and spun in place before being joined by streams of energy which launched up from the fiery etchings. As the burned material spun and mingled with the conjured energy, each disguise reconstituted, reformed, and returned to their previous state. As each bit and piece was completed, they drifted over to their respective owner with increasing quickness and reattached to the appropriate Stäld. One by one, the Stäld finished returning to their prior appearance and walked towards their entrance in the stone wall of the mountain.

"Where are we following you to?" Kegli asked.

"We're considering your request in light of this new context," one of the Stäld responded, "and wish to speak with you further."

"Into the mountain?" Kegli pressed.

Before anyone replied, Domaren started towards the mountains.

"Please be patient," Domaren insisted. "This is good. This is a good sign," he said.

"Is it?" Brikana added.

"Yes," the Stäld replied, though the knights appeared to Domaren as if they were confused as to who they were answering. "Yes, into the mountain. Our home. We're welcoming you into our home."

Domaren continued for the entrances but stopped when he realized there were no footsteps coming from behind. He turned to his friends. Before he could address them, the Stäld spoke up.

"Will you be joining us?" They asked.

Domaren extended his arms and waved them over. One by one, they finally put the feet forward and joined him.

"We were just fighting these things, Domaren," Brikana said as she approached. "And now we're going to follow them down into a hole?"

"They could kill us if they wanted to," Domaren whispered back. "Or at least kept fighting us until we were out of energy. I'm inclined to trust them at this point."

"At this point?" She asked.

"Well, at least until we can't anymore."

Domaren looked up to his old friend and smiled as she waved the other knights along with her massive head. And after Domaren watched the Stäld enter the mountain, he watched his friends enter until he was the last left upon the mountain terrace. Before crossing one of the thresholds, he watched as the lit etchings snuffed themselves out, releasing small pinches of smoke as they did, above every circle, line, symbol, and symbol. The mammoth bonfire continued to punch at the sky and whip about until it too calmed down, slowed, and grew still before relinquishing its heat and life, succumbing once more to the stone that crept up from its logs and embers, to the boy and tips of its flames. A gentle thunder rumbled across the drum of the sky as Domaren stepped in.

When Domaren entered, he was immediately struck by a sight he wasn't expecting.

Rather than the primitive and constricting tunnels intended for an individual that Domaren was expecting, a few steps down from the door connected to an open walkway in the hollowed-out and cavernous center of the mountain. At the center of the huge chamber was a massive, constructed column connecting the peak high above with the floor of the room far below. Appearing to be carved from a black stone, the impressive monolith depicted countless shapes, scenes, and depictions that Domaren couldn't quite make out yet. All he could make out at that point were hundreds of torches burning intently, and mounted at evenly spaced distances around the entirety of the monolith. Knowing that his path would eventually come closer to the column and that he could review it more easily then, he scanned the rest of the humbling cavity for other wonders other features.

He could not only see his path, its shape, size, and direction, but he could also see each of the other paths and his friends traveling them nearby. Looking down, he saw the Stäld walking ahead and leading the way.

Each path never intersected with another and at first glance, meandered aimlessly with seemingly little thought given to how the paths descended into the mountain, other than the obvious need to avoid the monolith. But with each step Domaren took, he realized there was a definite intention with how the paths progressed. Rather than random twists and turns and spirals down, the paths eventually revealed their secret of what appeared to be a symmetrical root system. Though made from stone, the paths conveyed as much wonder and beauty as their natural counterparts.

Domaren, and, from what he could see, his fellow godknights and the Stäld farther ahead, continued their trek down into the mountain. With each step, Domaren grew closer to the center monolith and eagerly anticipated reaching it. He had watched as the other knights stopped to examine its artful representations and wondered what he would find.

Finally, he made it. He finally got close enough to see that the column was adorned with hundreds upon hundreds of square frames with rounded corners carved into the stone. Within each thin frame were characters and scenes depicting interactions and events. And in addition to the frames themselves, each symbol, figure, structure or natural element was inset with gold. The columns frequent torches reflected off the gold, making it appear almost molten, yet glassy. Living, but not.

At first, Domaren continued walking along, letting

his eyes wash broadly over the countless scenes, taken by the overall beauty of the interior of the mountain and the column, but shortly after, he slowed his steps and evaluated the depictions for their messages and meaning.

It soon struck him and stopped him mid-stride.

Each frame was similar in their intent as almost every scene in every proxy temples in the capital city of every race. But where the proxy temples devoted only short sections of their depictions to the creation of the world and birth of the virtues, this art seemed to have the opposite intent.

The Ständ's mountain column was, so far in Domaren's walk, committed completely to telling the story of the Ständ. He recognized the earlier frames. He was present for what the engravings conveyed. And in addition to the earlier frames, he recognized what was being shown in the golden images towards the center. Frame after frame, step after step, Domaren recalled specifics from his time as a Ständ in a time when *all* were Ständ, and when time was an undefined expanse where the nothingness of perpetual silence and lack of definition to every horizon could only be described as beautiful and peaceful. There was nothing else for comparison.

Domaren walked by rows and tiers of engravings that showed the Ständ population growing and spreading across the world. And after he passed a large number of scenes dedicated to the restlessness of a featureless people in a featureless world, Domaren saw the story evolve to depict visitations from and conversations with the Kihdai about suggestions on how their existence may be improved. What they could do to make their lives their own and lend somehow to the betterment of the world if there were only something to differentiate between one another. With each passing frame, they seemed to share a tale of the ideas for the virtues were communicated constructively, positively, with the wisdom and grace of an intellectual species, rather than mewling and whining from those who essentially amounted to the world's prepubescents.

Farther down Domaren descended, walking past more frames and advancing through the time represented on them. Much like the displays in the capital cities, the one created by the Ställd was lavish and ornate. And while Domaren found some humor and irony in the fact that all the life in the world had its own variation on the theme of creation, the birth of the virtues, and the transformation of the godknights, he found something to reflect on. Each of the world's races proudly displayed their origin, culture, and contributions in grand temples for the world to see. The Ställd's in comparison, was segregated away—buried under a mountain for only six beings to see.

Whether intentional or not, Domaren turned away from the column and focused on his steps. As he placed one front in front of the other, again and again, Domaren considered what he thought may be the absurdity of the moment. He wondered if the Kihdai knew he was trying to get help, much less from the Ställd. *Do they know where we are?* He thought. *Do they care?* But potential answers to his own questions would have to wait on extrapolation for the moment.

Domaren paid attention mostly just to the path ahead of him for the last one hundred steps. Before he realized it, he had reached the bottom of the path. There, the stone ended on top of a condensed and muddy ground, firm, but sparkling slightly with moisture. He looked up and found the assembled Ställd waiting stoically for the godknights to reach the bottom. Each of the godknights, Domaren saw, were looking back up through the intricate and winding paths. The central column's flames bounced gold reflections to the mountain's interior wall, also giving it the appearance of shifting slowly with life.

"Welcome," a Stäld said.

## Eighteen

"This is our most revered and cherished home," another Stäld continued. "As you can see, we made use of some of the natural features of this massive underground cavity to permanently document our early existence and relocation. We live here in peace and solitude amongst each other. We grow in our mutual bond but also grow in our knowledge. Throughout the ages we have reflected on that energy we have always had, practice it, document it, and share it between ourselves so that we may benefit. We are hopeful that we can share something with you that will be of benefit to your cause."

Domaren and each of the other knights offered sincere bows in appreciation.

"As you look around," the Stäld continued, "you will see passages carved into the walls at equidistant locations. These passages lead to our individual private chambers which none of you will enter unless invited or otherwise permitted. This open ring at the base of the steps and around the supporting column is our common area where we spend most of our time, gather together, engage in conversation and debate, or frequently sit and read texts we have either collected or created, retrieved from our library here, behind us."

As the Ställd explained the area around them before gesturing at the gaping opening to the library to the rear, the knights took in the sight of the shared area.

In an arrangement of perfectly appointed locations, dozens of identical, dark-stained tables stood around the cavern floor. Each circular table was topped by ancient slabs of dense cherry and were wide enough to accommodate seating for approximately twenty humans and their elbow space. In the center of almost every table, sat crafted oil lamps. The glass of each one twisted and curved up and out in odd configurations. No two were alike. Resembling something like neglected or shunned trees, the tips of each lamp's branches were covered by shades of glass leaves. As the walls of the cave displayed the curved and contorted light from the lamps, they seemed to take on the appearance of being riddled and diseased with colonies of persistent tree roots.

In addition to the occasional canvass painting of long-crumbled structures or long-transformed landscapes, the walls of the cavern were also decorated with carvings and paintings directly on the stone. Etchings and carvings stretched up and highlighted figures from the world's mythologies, literature excerpts, or in some cases, abstract experiments.The candle sconces on either side of every carving brought the depth of carvings and hues of life above ground to life below ground.

Also cut into the walls were deep holes, used to house items, or to be used as shelves. Here, the more decorative items or most frequently referenced books resided. And most prominently, at the base of the walls, four gigantic fireplaces provided the bulk of the area's light. Where smoke didn't find its way through the nooks and cracks at the back or tops of the fireplaces, it crept out and past the front edge and meandered lazily back up towards the entrance far above.

Every table was smothered mostly in books, but also documents in various states of stability. Some documents were made of stone. Some were scratches and fading ink on decaying sections of animal hide. Some of the more recent documents were made of processed reeds and bamboo, and more recent still, were pieces of more delicate parchment. Many artifacts also took up table space, and were undoubtedly strewn about to be used for various forms of study, documentation, or potentially, to simply *be used.*

"This is an amazing home," Nanutsi said sincerely. "There are temples, towers, and royal complexes that can't compare with this. It's beautiful, but humble. Modest and practical, but magnificent."

"That's a very interesting way to describe a prison," a Stäld said. Their tone was light and amiable, but cynical.

The knights all turned and met the sharp comment with expressions of confused contempt.

"Can it really be all that difficult to understand?" The Stäld asked. As they continued, some sat, while others tended to the fires.

"We tried to adapt. We tried to live among the rest of the world, and for a time, it was, in all honesty, an incredible experience. At first, we reveled in all of the wonder and variety. The different cultures, stories, music, or, the mountains and rivers, plains and glaciers. It was tremendous. We traveled through the world in our natural form. People and creatures ran up to us to thank us for our sacrifice. They honored us. Respected us. But after a while, the farther we got away from the birth of the virtues, and the generations became more apathetic about what they had and how it was realized, well, the more we became the outcasts. The different ones. The pariahs that were shunned and avoided. It got to the point where the world that we wanted, and the world we helped create was no longer anything we desired or desired to be apart of. So, we withdrew, and found peace amongst ourselves."

The knights let go of their silent animosity as their expressions relaxed. Domaren took a seat and gathered his thoughts in the dancing shadow of the table's mangled oil lamp. He stammered for a moment, searching for the right words for his question.

"Then... why? Why after generations upon generations and the world itself have wronged you, do you have any desire to help? Why wouldn't you be glad to be rid of it and see a new beginning?"

The Stäld stared at Domaren and answered immediately.

"Because that's what the Kihdai want."

The Stäld's justification stunned Domaren silent, not because it was a surprise, but because of the simplicity. As Domaren looked around to see what the others thought, some shrugged while Brikana lifted her eyebrows and nodded.

"But also, we do not wish for our sacrifice to be wasted," the Stäld continued. "We won't allow the many centuries and ages of being outcasts to be taken for granted and tossed aside casually just to please the Kihdai. No. They created this world and then allowed it to evolve. It, and those who live in it, will be allowed to end naturally."

Curious, Nanutsi walked over and pulled herself up

onto a chair at the table with the Stäld.

"How exactly are we to fight back?" She asked. "Is there a magic or power you will teach us, or a weapon of some—"

The Stäld interrupted with a playful, old, and ragged laugh.

"No, no, my dear knights," replied the Stäld. "We are not any more powerful than you, the Kihdai, and probably not even the proxies. There is no weapon in our home capable of more than Verikta there," they said as they gestured at Domaren, "or any magic more potent than Crizichial's decay magic. We have no greater command of the seas than you, Nanutsi, or skill with ax and soil, and we surely can not soar through the clouds and cook our enemies with flaming breath."

The Stäld stood up and after starting off with a slow shuffle, made their way towards the opening to their sprawling library. They stopped and turned around.

"What we have, is knowledge," said the Stäld. "If not all of it, close to that. Come," they continued, turning back to the library. "Follow me."

* * *

After sliding their chairs under the tables, the knights followed the Stäld as instructed. By way of a seamless floor, they passed through the library's impressive threshold which stretched up in an arch, to roughly half the height from the cavern floor to the entrance far above. The walls of the library were pristine rock at first, but after a few dozen paces in, the knights came upon dozens upon dozens of small staircases cut into the stone. An innumerable amount of books rested on additional chiseled shelves set just inside the stone enough to accommodate a single person's walking path.

Some of the inset nooks were deeper than others. Some could accommodate someone standing inside as they perused a book while someone walked by on the ledge outside. Some of the tiny rooms were flush with the stone wall and had to have books picked from them while standing off to the side. Numerous candelabras and sconces dotted the paths, the nooks, and sometimes, the sides of the stone stairs.

The initial height of the cave, closest to the table area, was the tallest, and allowed for some six, sometimes seven of the carved out bookshelf compartments. But as the knights and Stäld continued walking, the cave ceiling gradually lowered. The walls slowly encroached inward. But the decreasing scale of the overall area was so moderate, the knights knew it would take some time to reach a point where the library's dimensions became too close for comfort.

While the Stäld led the knights on, the group passed by writing and reading tables. Documents sat next to quills and inkwells while other tables had piles of books or a single one splayed open. Candles, long-since run out of wick or recently snuffed—the knights couldn't tell—littered each table as well. Some tables were accompanied by stools, others by benches. Some, had both.

The tables in the main hall, as well as the library, appeared ancient but well preserved. By only having to sustain the weight and burden of books, papers, and artifacts, the tables lasted longer than the various seating surfaces. The chairs and benches on the other hand, weathered day after day, after week, after decade, of the Stäld sitting up and down. Plopping down and launching up. Some had been replaced more recently than others and the finishes and condition of each reflected as much.

For a time, as they progressed through the library, Domaren found himself distracted and awestruck by the accumulated artifacts, annals, and towering walls of books. Like the other knights, he involuntarily marveled at the ages of wisdom gathered and stored about.

"Luckily," the Stäld continued as Domaren's attention returned, "we spent our initial centuries in and amongst the first proxies, knights, kingdoms and realms, and even the Kihdai occasionally. We documented many of the first histories of the world's inhabitants ourselves, or made copies of those made by others."

While she looked back and forth and soaked in the sights on either side of her, Nanutsi spoke up.

"How... exhaustive are these collections?" She asked.

The Stäld looked over her shoulder slightly with a reply.

"Exhaustive?"

"Oh, I'm mainly curious about how you have been able to stay apprised of everything that has happened since you became less... social," she clarified.

"Oh, yes, I see," the Stäld replied. "We have means of staying up to date. Whether we travel in disguise and in secret, or solicit input and materials from a few very confidential friends throughout the ages, I have a very high degree of confidence that our archives are by far the most complete in the history of this world."

The knights offered no reply, and for Domaren's part, couldn't think of one, much less cause to argue or dispute the Stäld's claim. After minutes of silent marching into the slowly narrowing cavern, Domaren was overcome with an epiphany that was at once comforting and simultaneously bittersweet.

"I have only just now remembered," Domaren said to any who would hear it," that I helped lend to some of this." He then shifted his eyes from aimless awe to the Stäld in the lead. "Is that right?" He asked. "Am I remembering that accurately?"

"That is accurate, yes," the Stäld replied. "I had doubted if you would recollect that at all. The collections you contributed to are towards the back of the library. You see, we have categorized our archives first by chronological creation. We sort everything first by when the physical item was created, followed then by a second classification by various topics.

"That seems as good a classification method as any," Crizichial said. "I wonder, what specific documents are we in search of?"

The Stäld sighed as if recalling their idea silently before sharing it.

"First, I would suggest we consult our very first chronicle,"theysaid."Specifically,informationsurrounding the construction of Prumo Hald, its features, and its powers. This is the oldest documented information of our making, begun shortly after the birth of the virtues. My hope is that we may recall information about the abandoned fortress that will provide clues on any potential way of restoring your strength."

As the Stäld outlined their idea, Crizichial listened intently and offered insight into a memory.

"I do remember shortly after the Redeemed were granted a knight, that for a time, the knights still received their restoration stones from Prumo Hald."

"That's right," Domaren confirmed. "Until Wrathlore, there was no grove and no disparate realm."

"But wasn't everything destroyed or at least removed

to the Grove when they left?" Kegli wondered.

"This is what I hope to reference and compare," the Ställd said. "Once we retrieve our first chronicle, we will then consult with our materials associated with Wrathlore. That was during a time when we still roamed above regularly, so much of it is firsthand of our creation, contemporary with events."

"I can probably contribute some firsthand, contemporary insight as well," Domaren said. His voice was flat and slightly agitated.

The Ställd abruptly stopped, sending the knights behind them sliding to a stop as well. The Ställd turned and looked back at Domaren and offered an acknowledgment in addition to a slow bow of the head.

"Yes. Of course," the Ställd said respectfully.

Domaren nodded at the Ställd's sincere recognition. He held no grudges or ill will towards the jaded Ställd and beyond understanding their justified resentment towards the Kihdai and how the world they requested treated them, he also appreciated the small note of acknowledgment that like the Ställd, Domaren had also been there from the beginning.

As the bond between the two ancient groups, or at least Domaren and the Ställd, strengthened, the knights and Ställd continued their march towards the back of the cave. It continued to narrow, and the ceiling grew closer. And while small side passages splintered off and meandered into the main library walls occasionally, the group maintained it's path through the primary section of the library. Finally, after a substantial amount of walking, and well-hidden impatience, the knights came to a stop when the Ställd did.

The Ställd turned around with a hand outstretched and addressed the knights.

"The first chronicle is just ahead at the end of the cave," they said.

The knights turned and stirred awkwardly while trading questioning expressions to see if anyone knew what was being implied. Brikana sought to clear the confusion.

"I'm not sure we understa—"

"It's very simple," the Ständ said. "From here, one must kneel, or shuffle, or crawl, depending on the creature, human, or animal, to the reach the back of the library."

The next batch of odd expressions were those no longer contorted in confusion, but ones waiting for a volunteer.

"Is there a problem?" The Ständ asked.

"No, but, um... How far back does it go?" Nanutsi asked.

"Not too much more," replied the Ständ. "If you kneel down and look, you can just make out the end."

Brikana smirked in humorous doubt.

"Is it safe way back there?" Brikana asked with a laugh.

"What?" The Ständ replied, genuinely stunned by the question. "How much safer can one be then being surrounded by knowledge?"

Brikana squinted her eyes and tilted her head as she considered the statement.

Silence followed again without a volunteer.

Kegli let go of a chuckle which in turn made Brikana grin.

Crizichial knelt down and leaned over, and upon seeing what lay ahead, couldn't help but skip the humor. He spun around on his knee to inform his friends of his appraisal.

"I am far too large to reach the back of this," he said.

The Ständ looked at Crizichial as if he had spoken a foreign language.The other knights erupted in spitting and rowdy laughter. Crizichial came to his feet, confused as to what triggered the outburst, and as the others caught their breath and settled down, Domaren ended the impasse.

"I'll go," he said to the Stäld. I'll go."

Domaren sunk down to his knees like Crizichial had moments before.

"Which book is it? Will I know it when I see it?"

The Stäld stepped closer.

"Yes, it should be extremely obvious. It is the book at the farthest end of this part of the cave. It is the only book in the entire library by itself and is in a small hole sequestered by itself. There is no writing, no inscription, no symbols or markings of any kind. Though it has been rebound and copied countless times to avoid disintegration over the ages, it is still extremely old. Please show it great care as you retrieve it."

"Absolutely," Domaren replied.

After looking back with a nod to the other knights, Domaren set out for the deepest corner of the cave. While hunched over, he walked regularly, but only made it approximately twenty paces in before having to go down to his knees. As he started crawling, he watched as the small shelves, practically at an arm's reach on either side, became smaller and smaller. By the time he started crawling, the book-holding spaces accommodated no more than three shelves and a few dozen books in total.

There were still, luckily enough, candelabras spaced frequently as Domaren crawled. Now on his knees and forearms, he had to stop frequently to light the candles with a set of flint, steel, and cloth the Stäld had provided. And between the lit candles and reflections of light from the moist rocks and rocky floor, Domaren could easily make out the desired chronicle.

"Everything okay, lad?" Kegli shouted. His voice reverberated and swelled raucously down to the confined space Domaren was in.

"Yes, fine, fine," Domaren said in response, not needing to yell. "It's gotten real tight and I'm lighting these candles, but I see the book. I'll have it shortly."

After slinging his piece of cloth ahead of him, Domaren crawled another ten feet. With another spark from the flint, Domaren lit the cloth, and then the next candle, and repeated the process.

The book shelf cutouts in the rock decreased from two to one, each increment spaced out with more crawling, and more flint flickers and lighting of candles. Soon after, Domaren found himself on his stomach and questioning the situation he had found himself in.

"There has got to be a slightly more accessible means of storing these books," Domaren grunted at himself.

Due to the acoustics of Domaren's confined space, the Stäld easily heard his complaint and offered a reply.

"It's intended to be challenging, Domaren. To keep the oldest materials the safest!"

Domaren rolled his eyes and only the darkened sliver of cave he was in could see.

"Couldn't hear that, hmm?"

"Hear what?" Nanutsi yelled from far behind.

"Nothing!" Domaren said after sighing. "Almost got it. Be out in a minute."

After crawling on his stomach for no more than another length of his body, Domaren had reached the book. Rather than lighting a candle, especially because there wasn't room for one, Domaren had just enough room to strike the flint onto the fabric he had been pushing ahead of him and held out in front of him. There, resting in it's own little square hole, was a simple book made of common materials. As the Stäld had described, there was no other discerning feature about it. Domaren dropped the linen and tapped it out with one hand and collected the flint and steel as well. With the other hand, Domaren reached out and wrapped his hand around its side, confirmed he had a good grip and started to wiggle backwards out of the tight quarters.

*I'm sure not going to say anything out loud, but I'm sure this looks as ridiculous as it feels,* he thought, as he squirmed to more open space. Once he felt the air flow change and saw one shelf to his sides increase to two, Domaren spun around to face the exit. When two shelves became three, Domaren crept back up to his knees and forearms, eventually to the kneeling walk, and finally, returned to standing completely up having returned to his friends.

"That was," Domaren began, with a slight heavy breath, "one of the most interesting and at the same time, irritating things I've ever done."

After a slap on the back from Kegli, Domaren handed the first chronicle to the Stäld.

"Well done, well done," they said. After taking it from Domaren, they rubbed the cover with gentle reverence before looking back to the godknight.

"This may be the hundredth copy, or more," they said. "But much, if not all of the information in here goes all the way back to the beginning, Domaren. The *very* beginning."

Domaren looked at the hefty book and dug deep into the farthest reaches of his memory.

"It's odd," the Stäld said. "It's almost no longer a set of memories that I can recall and remember myself in. The appearance of the land before the virtues, what the world smelled like in its earliest days. Conversations surrounding the newness and wonder of it all. It's almost all lost to me. Sometimes, it feels more like a story I've read ages ago, more than a life I experienced."

Domaren stepped back and reflected on the primordial beings words while keeping his eyes on the book.

"I can understand that," he said, with a soft chuckle. "I absolutely know how that feels. Perhaps that is a curse of immortality, hmm? Forgetting those moments that are special to you, only by way of the slow decay of time? At least mortals can die with their most cherished memories still relatively vivid."

The Stäld seemed to sigh, but made no noise. Only their shoulders seemed to raise and fall. They patted the book before moving on.

"All right," they said. "Let's find that Wrathlore book and see what we can learn."

The group lingered for a moment and took turns inspecting the exterior of the old chronicle before turning back the way they came. As they worked their way back out of the cave towards more recent collections, and specifically, the Stälds' Wrathlore collection, the knights took the opportunity to learn more about the materials that surrounded them. Occasionally, a knight or two would walk close to a side of the library and peek at titles, where there were some, or pause and marvel at a find before having to jog and catch back up.

"Can I ask you about something you said earlier?" Kegli asked at one point. The Stäld grunted in what sounded like the affirmative. Kegli continued.

"Did you say the works you collect here are entirely those of your own making?"

"For the most part," replied the Stäld. "Yes, but there

is a bit of an elaboration available on that point. While the majority of our library consists of chronicles, logs, and histories, we do often-times refer to or cite works created by the mortal members of various races. To that end, we try to keep a copy of what we refer to or cite as well. It's much easier to have a reference. That is also why you see so many artifacts, and some pieces of art. Those are also very often referenced in our documents."

"Ah, that makes sense," Kegli replied.

"But also," the Stäld continued. "We have also been gifted various items throughout time, either as simple gestures, or a request to house something and keep it safe."

"Hmm, interesting," Nanutsi said. "I don't intend this to be impertinent at all, but do you intend for this knowledge and tangible history to remain secluded and hidden for eternity?"

"Ha!" The Stäld laughed. "I don't find your question impertinent at all, but I find it curious."

"Curious? Why?"

"Well, you're a knight. While you aren't the first seaver knight, you've been around for a great deal amount of time. No? Think about how little it would make sense to show a mortal of today a peace treaty signed by two extinct empires that are no longer taught or sung about."

Nanutsi quietly processed the idea while the Stäld continued.

"It would be as insignificant and arbitrary to them as what the weather was like on a particular day forty-two thousand years ago."

Crizichial returned to the original question.

"So, you're saying you would not share this information with anyone outside your home?"

The Stäld replied immediately with a heightened

tone of agitation.

"We're sharing it with you right now, aren't we?"

Crizichial turned to reply, but had no words to say. The Stäld elaborated.

"What I'm saying is that it isn't a question of not wanting to share it. Only that we haven't considered it before."

Before anyone else could perpetuate the discussion, the Stäld gestured at the wall to their right.

"Right up here," they said, pointing up to a section of books. "It's in that fairly deep set of shelves, three levels up. Two columns before it goes from four to five levels."

"I'll get it," Nanutsi said as she bounce-jumped towards the first set of narrow steps. "Navigating damp rocks is my specialty!"

After a quick jog over to the wall, Nanutsi took a quick survey of the first set of steps and the narrow ledges between levels. Without any hesitation, she darted up the first set before tapping her flippers down the first ledge towards the closet set of steps leading up to the third level. Her feet splashed and slapped at the wet stone as she ran.

Once she ran up the second set of steps and reached the third ledge, she looked down at the group to confirm her destination.

"Which space?" She shouted. "How many columns before it goes to five?"

"Two," Brikana shouted, saving the Stäld the trouble. But the Stäld provided additional detail.

"It'll be just below your waist level," they yelled. "It's bound in gold leaf with black lettering that spells 'Wrathlore' on the spine."

Domaren recoiled with a slight snarl.

"Gold leaf?" He asked leaning towards the Stäld.

"Yes, I know," they replied. "We often re-use materials. The gold leaf cover was borrowed from a different book at some point when we made this latest copy."

"Very," Domaren said while tilting his head back and forth, "resourceful."

"Yes, thank you. We make every effort to minimize waste, especially when accumulating new materials is hard, given the arrangement we have made for ourselves."

"I can imagine, yes," Domaren agreed. As they wrapped up their discussion, Nanutsi scurried along the ledges and back down the steps, book in hand.

"Thank you very much, Nanutsi," the Stäld said. With the two books stacked in both hands, the Stäld addressed the knights as they made their way to the nearest reading table. "This should get us well on our way to getting you some information that will help."

The Stäld placed the books on a reading table, one beside the other, and reached for an oil lamp. They turned a brass dial to increase the wick and after it started smoking, backed it off a bit. Not satisfied with the amount of light to cover two books, they walked to another table and brought two additional candles back.

"Okay, Domaren," they said. "If you would, open up the Wrathlore book and begin looking through it. I would imagine you will be very familiar with the material. If you all want to look on, feel free. I'll begin reviewing our first chronicle."

"Sure, of course."

Nanutsi stepped closer to the table and leaned up to look over the Stäld's arm.

"What are you looking for?" She asked.

The Stäld pulled back from the table a bit and positioned the first chronicle so that Nanutsi could see it more easily.

"As for this book, anything that may mention what the original mechanisms were that restored the knights."

"And with this collection of Wrathlore information," Domaren said, "anything that might tell us what they did with those restoration tools."

Brikana's hands flailed in confusion.

"But don't you already know all of that?" She asked.

With wide eyes, Domaren rolled his head around on his shoulders and chuckled.

"Well, I'm sure we both did at some point, Kana," he said. "But it's been hundreds of thousands of years. I don't know about the Ställd here, but when it comes to a lot of those ancient events, my memory has gone blurry with many of the specifics."

Brikana only smirked and looked back to the Wrathlore book in response.

"Speaking of which," Domaren said. "Let's jog my memory."

But rather than opening it immediately, Domaren stared at the crisp, golden cover, entranced by its gilded facade that hid beneath it, the dark events from so long ago. Domaren was used to such meticulous and valuable treatments being reserved for holy texts found across the generations and cultures of the world, but he knew this book contained no such revered content. Instead, after opening the book's cover and skimming the initial summary of creation that he was all too familiar with, he found himself staring at the documented accounts of the Kihdai themselves at the onset of Wrathlore. After racing through that initial creation preface, Domaren slowed down to ensure he missed no details. As he started reading bits out loud, the hazy memory very rapidly came back to life.

"The following is a record of a portion of journals kept by the Kihdai and loaned to the Stäld for purposes of documentation for historical record. These specific excerpts from the Kihdai journals relate to the events leading up to, during, and subsequent results of what has become known colloquially as Wrathlore. The date of this initial documentation of collected and consolidated accounts is in the time of the 79th Ring."

Domaren paused. Unknowingly, he had let his mouth fall open, not in disbelief or shock, but from the magic of a mind rapidly recalling things it had long forgotten, or chosen to stow away. He looked over at the Stäld.

"I remember you coming to Prumo Hald," he said. "Well, I remember one of the Stäld or someone affiliated with you seeking an audience with the Kihdai to document this."

The Stäld paused their own reading and turned slowly to meet Domaren's eyes. In complete silence, the Stäld simply bowed his head.

Domaren's eyes darted about wildly before slowing. He then allowed himself to blink and returned to the Wrathlore book.

*All right,* Domaren thought as he continued reading, *these first pages... The first signs of a disturbance, of issues, came from a decrease in communications from the wider world. Less audiences requested. Less correspondence from monarchs, leaders, and politicians.*

As Domaren continued to read, he flipped pages and frequently blurted out significant notes or events. He also alternated between reviewing details silently and sharing spontaneous tidbits he thought the others would find interesting.

"Here, the Kihdai begin referencing the knights and their..." He said. He stopped and looked around at the others as he proceeded with an awkward but unnecessary correction. "...*our* behaviors. The knights who rebelled did so one by one and dispatched false correspondence to keep the Kihdai confused as to their motives. I remember that. There was so much confusion. So many questions. I was angry. The Kihdai were angry. No one knew what was happening."

Domaren looked back to the book.

*Right, here is where they begin mentioning the knights going silent. One by one they stopped responding. Reports were coming in from all over the continent referencing some of the knights being spotted at uprisings and invasions.*

Domaren read more and turned additional pages. A few of the knights walked back and forth to try and glean information from both the Wrathlore book, while others stayed with Domaren, or stayed next to the Ställd. After continuing to read the Wrathlore book silently for a time, Domaren lashed out angrily.

"Ah yes," he began. "Here is where they discuss how it came down to two knights. Domaren, and Isnyra."

With a face full of tense animosity, Domaren looked at Brikana, though they knew his ire wasn't for her.

"They describe here how it eventually came out that Isnyra was always intended to be the last one to reveal themselves as a traitor," Domaren said. "To help steer and misdirect me."

Domaren let Brikana loose from the uneasy stare and turned back to the book to shout at it instead.

"We went to Prumo Hald to report what we had found out up until that point and to get direction. She knew then she was a traitor and still went along with it. She turned on me just days later."

Domaren slammed the book shut, the force of the violent jolt sent the book scooting along the table a few inches.

"Please be caref—" The Ställd started to say. They were irritated and stern from the start of the request, but Domaren shouted over them.

"After that, I was the only one left. It was up to me to recruit and negotiate. Make alliances and make promises. Suggest others to be made new knights and help defeat the traitors. It was all up to me to do their bidding, and I did it! I made it happen and helped run a defense that allowed the Kihdai not only to escape a direct challenge, but also let them plan a betrayal of their own all these years later!"

Rather than hitting the book this time, Domaren slammed the bottom of his closed fist onto the table.

"Yes, but," the Ställd said, their voice now fortified with impatience. "Anything about restorations, changes to the grove stones?"

Domaren continued glaring at a bare spot on the table but finally shook himself out of his awakened, furious memories. He focused back on the Wrathlore text.

"I'm sorry," he said. He huffed the comment out in a gust of frustration. "I just can't believe they're doing this. But okay, yes, back to the book. Let's see, there are notes here where they discuss revenge, how to punish the knights, that kind of thing."

Domaren went silent as he continued running his finger down the list of notes and flipping pages.

"Here's where they reference the orcs and elves and how they were the two races that contributed the most from their general population towards the rebellion. Yes, and here is where they note the decision to deny them a godknight or proxy going forward."

Domaren resumed reading.

"Okay, everyone," the Ständ said. Their outburst was quick and loud as if excited to make an announcement. "I've found the original description of Prumo Hald's method of restoring the knights!"

Domaren peeled his widened eyes from the Wrathlore text.

"The main throne room," the Ständ said. "That's where it seems they controlled the Limb of Life and its extensions down to the world to restore you."

The Ständ looked up and clarified.

"Well, restore the knights, that is."

Domaren rolled his eyes and shook his head at himself, immediately remembering.

"Yes, that's right! Each throne rested atop a root which was connected directly to the tree at the center of the throne room. The limbs and tree only appeared when a particular Kihdai activated their connection with us. I watched the Kihdai do that a few times with other knights."

Domaren's eyes drifted away.

It's been so long..."

"Do you think that's all still there?" Brikana asked. "Do you think we can use it?"

Kegli leaned closer to the Wrathlore text.

"Does this say anything about what they did with it?"

After the possibility of a clue stung Domaren's nerves with excitement, he pounced back to the book. While seeking out a final confirmation, he mumbled the first few words of each sentence as he skimmed.

"Discussions on what to do with the traitors... the knights as well as the regular citizens... Here's a list of monarchs... kingdoms, that the Kihdai dissolved... Oh, and here are some additional changes to borders and geography... here's where the Vulgar Gap is created, as well as the Forgiving Sea..."

By this point in Domaren's ramblings, the other knights had repositioned and encroached on him and the Wrathlore tome with hopeful anticipation.

"Come on, where is it?" Domaren said. The silence between his mumbling grew. His finger flew down the pages faster. "No, no... more politics. Nothing here... Trials... Executions..."

And then without warning to those around them, or to their ears, Domaren picked his finger up and slammed into the book.

"Vals Hald!" He shouted. Ständ and a few knights alike jumped back. "Here it is! Their move to Vals Hald. Here, let me read it."

*And at last, the Kihdai felt as though they had tended to every traitor and those who aided them. Not only did they feel as though the traitors had been dealt with, but also felt they had taken measures to avoid such rebellions in the future, either by thought or by action. Whether by altering the continent, forcing renegotiations of political treaties and agreements, executing justice, punishing cultures, removing knights, or anointing others, the wave of Kihdai justice was swift, but thorough.*

*When the Kihdai achieved full confidence that absolute justice had been done and that all rebellion had been tended to, the creators of the world announce to all that as part of the continent's punishment, the Kihdai would leave their shared lands and exist apart. They would abandon their original fortress of Prumo Hald. They would leave from there, never to return, and take with them all of their belongings, furnishings, decorations, and any other sign of life that sustained them, those others who lived in or around Prumo Hald, as well as anything that friends and visitors depended on when visiting.*

*So too, they would remove their thrones from Prumo Hald, never to reign from there again. So too, they would remove their connections to the Limb of Life, as well as the Limb of Life itself. No more would Prumo Hald serve as the mechanism by which the Kihdai interacted with their godknights, empowered them, restored them, or otherwise communed with them. Indeed, all that had ever been attributed to the Kihdai would be removed and relocated to a newly created realm by way of a gate accessible only to those present at the beginning. This new realm, existing apart from the rest of the world, will be a great expanse of snowy hills and smatterings of forest groves. Set within this pristine breadth of snow, hills, and wealth of forest groves, will be the new Kihdai fortress of Vals Hald.*

Domaren stared for a moment, but stepped back. His mouth twitched as if he was waiting to hear himself say more. Explain more. But he said nothing else and stared down at the book with a squint of pain and confusion.

"That's it?" The Ställd asked. "Just those few sentences about the throne room?"

"Wait," Nanutsi said. "What was that bit about a gate?"

Domaren looked at Nanutsi and after a few seconds seemed to finally register the question. He shook his head and stepped back towards the book. He rubbed his eyes.

"Uh, relocated to a newly created realm by way of a gate accessible only to those present at the beginning," he repeated.

"What does that mean?" Brikana asked. "A gate? Have any of you ever heard of a gate?"

Brikana scanned the faces of her fellow knights. As they each shrugged or shook their heads, she quickly landed on the Ställd.

"I don't know anything about what the Kihdai did around that time other than what's in that book," they said, pointing at the book.

"Well, it definitely sounds like the old mechanism, or whatever it was, was removed," Kegli said. "What about this gate? Think it's still there?"

Domaren took a breath and flipped the book closed. He turned to his dwarf friend.

"There's only one way to find out."

# Nineteen

"We must leave," Domaren said to the Stäld. "We need to investigate the status of the old throne room, and whatever this gate might be."

"Yes, of course, I understand."

"If there is any opportunity to restore our power, we must act now," Domaren added, looking to the others. "I'm not sure how much longer we can proceed before being completely vulnerable."

"We should attempt to plan for any contingencies," Crizichial said.

Brikana chuckled.

"How?"

"Well, first, let us define the possible, and more than likely, probable, issues we will encounter," he said. "One, we should discuss what to do if we encounter the proxies again. Two, we need a plan if there is nothing in the throne room. And then of course three, what if nothing comes of whatever this gate might be?"

Kegli dipped and looped his chin around.

"One, we fight them. Two, we check for a gate. Three, we run," he said.

Nanutsi grabbed her forehead.

"That is definitely a... succinct response, Kegli," she said. "But what if any one of those veers off wildly in a different direction than we intend?"

"My point with that, Nanutsi," Kegli said, as he raised his voice, "was that there isn't a lot of variation we can plan for right now."

Crizichial, showing a rare sign of frustration spoke over his two friends.

"It is extremely poor strategy to not legitimately discuss alternative plans," he said, scolding them.

"Hey, wait!" Domaren said. The knights' arguing grew louder and the volume clashed into an increasingly painful glob of jagged reverberation. "Stop a minute. Hey, everyone, stop!"

With a few wild waves of his arms and an irritated yell, Domaren persuaded his friends to calm down.

"Look, there are no contingencies," he said, biting back at the arguments. "If there's nothing for us at Prumo Hald, that's it. There are no other allies. No one can restore us. There isn't anywhere we can go to be restored. Okay? All we can do is set out for Prumo Hald. Get there. Go in. Try and get restored. And you know what? Even then, even if we can get restored, all the Kihdai need to do is just wait us out again. Sure, we can be more careful and reserve our strength better, now that we know, but we'll still get weak again. But we'll handle that when the time comes. Okay? One step at a time. For now, we just need to get to Prumo Hald. If we find a fight, all we can do is fight until we can't anymore."

Domaren looked at Crizichial to see if he had anything

else he wanted to plan for, but he said nothing. After checking Kegli's demeanor, Domaren felt the dwarf had a bit more appreciation for the seriousness of the situation. Brikana's face was firm and serious. Domaren watched her clench and release her jawbones repeatedly, while Nanutsi appeared pensive and looked down with crossed arms.

"Very well," Domaren said. "Let's make our way back up."

* * *

The godknights thanked their hosts a final time and jogged out of the library before making quick work of the stairs back up to the surface. With very little conversation, they all mounted up and scrambled back down the mountain to the Vale. Once there, they worked their way back to Fimham Way. After meeting back up with the stretch of road close to where they encountered the Rifren, Domaren activated the road's lights once again before the group resumed their path east towards Prumo Hald.

"Crizichial, I may have spoken too hastily about not having a need to discuss other plans," Domaren said. His statement bounced along amiably as he sought to lessen some of the tension from their discussions in the cave.

"As we can see, the road condition is horrible," Domaren added. "Let's all just stick as close to the road as we can, and if we need need to veer off, so be it. The brush gets thick at times. If we get separated, just try to get back to the road or keep it in sight. It should stay lit for a full day from when I just activated it."

"While we are finally discussing contingencies," Crizichial said, his words dripping with a bit of lingering resentment, "what might our course of action be should we run into the proxies again before reaching Prumo Hald?"

The galloping hooves of the knights' mounts took over as Domaren considered his question. Their powerful slams into the ground pounded an erratic heartbeat into the land.

"Just keep riding. Ride hard and make it to Prumo Hald," Domaren said. "Don't stop unless they make us stop."

Domaren expected objections, but heard none, and had nothing to counter them with anyway.

The group raced farther through the forest. Now two and a half days after their encounter with the Rifren, the sky grew dark once again. Smoky clouds of charcoal prepared to unleash their rain as dusk approached. The paranoid riders took turns looking back over their shoulders or to the skies, looking, or more accurately, waiting for their next altercation with the proxies. But the altercation wouldn't come, and their ride proceeded without event, until at last, the group of knights reached the outskirts of the Firounda Plains. There, in the distance, stretched the ambitious spires of the once miraculous Prumo Hald. After a yell of attempted excitement to rally his friends, Domaren took the lead and sprinted towards the hills that lay between them and the old Kihdai fortress. But after cresting the hills, the group slid their horses to a halt.

Domaren's initial glimpse of the field ahead folded his brow in confusion before a sharp wave of dread poked at his stomach. He questioned himself mentally as to whether or not he was surprised at what was before him and dismissed the notion almost immediately.

Stretching out before the godknights was a sea of defenders waiting to repulse their attempts to breach the long-abandoned fortress. The mass of seething malice shifted slightly. Heaving and throbbing like a living organism, the field was blanketed by thousands of Tirngora orcs towards the front of the gathered army. The front rows of Tirngora were all Domaren could see, at least those at ground level.

Brikana sighed and let her head fall. Domaren turned and could only stare as the sound of the gathered armies' horns announced a sighting of the knights' arrival. Brikana looked up at her friend and slid out of her saddle. The dragon knight slapped her horse on the rear and turned to face the force standing between them and Prumo Hald.

"I guess this explains why we didn't run into the proxies," she said. Her voice dragged along with a dark reality. After a flash of her firestone, Brikana shifted into her dragon form. Domaren in turn pulled his vision back to the army ahead.

"What can you see, Kana?" Domaren asked. But his question was unheard, or ignored. The dragon's godknight had already unfurled her wings and begun hissing at the force opposite them. Her tail whipped about furiously and gave away small hints as to the taunting blasts of fire she let loose.

Domaren looked at Crizichial hoping to ask him the same question, but Crizichial anticipated it and shrugged.

"I don't have to be tall to see that there is a lot of, well, *everything* over there," Kegli said flatly.

Domaren huffed out a breath and scanned the landscape. After catching sight of a jagged outcropping of granite at the other end of his group, he ran over and shot up to its highest point. The others who weren't already nearby, followed.

As Domaren climbed, the mob of resistance ahead seemed to grow and stretch out forever, growing larger with each moment as dotted trails of additional foes joined the main force. Domaren drew Verikta and hollered back to his friends.

"Countless Tirngora," he yelled. "I see some humans... elves, dwarves... not sure how many. Mostly Tirngora. There's some Tirngoza orcs. Some Redeemed, and..."

Domaren trailed off as he first connected eyes with Nanutsi, and as he finished speaking, connected with Brikana, who returned the ominous stare.

"Dragons," he said. His voice fell weak as he spoke the word, turning back to look out blankly at the army, as if he spoke the word with the last pinch of air in his lungs.

"They gathered a little bit of everyone, it seems," Kegli said to his friends.

"I can't see any other seavers from here," Nanutsi began, "but I don't doubt you, Domaren. What a bitter feeling to have, to see this company, and those within it."

"Well, I swear this to each of you," Kegli added. "Kin or not, I'll do all I can to help clear us a path through."

Domaren turned back towards his friends and walked down closer to them.

"Friends," he started. "I don't know what power or time we may have left, but if you would stand with me once again on another of our countless fields of battle, it will be my single highest honor in all my many ages."

Instead of a spoken or gestured response, Nanutsi slowly pulled her tail up to her side. After reaching for her stowed flail, wrapped and attached to her pony, she looped the ends of its dangling chains through anchor points on her tail armor and secured it. She then stared ahead over the tops of the enemy army and focused her concentration on how best to harness the power of the nearby Firounda River. Kegli responded by pounding his ax handle on the base of the surrounding boulders in quick repetition. Crizichial calmly brought his hands up and slid them together before letting his lanky fingers fall in between themselves in what looked like the beginnings of a mischievous prayer. With his hands clutched, he grinned widely and slowly bowed his head in acknowledgment of his human godknight ally. As he bowed, his gaunt and pale flesh gave way to patches of disease and pits of decay, exposing teeth and bone.

Brikana, noticeably furious and insulted by the presence of any dragons on the side of the Kihdai and proxies, stood on her back legs and flexed her wings out as wide as possible once more. She stretched her neck high into the sky and let out a shrieking scream calling everyone to attention, and putting everyone on notice, that there was no superior being on the field.

She then slid her long neck back down to the ground and prepared to pounce while Domaren climbed a few steps back towards the top of the boulder.

"I will fight as long as I am able, friends. Do what you can to help us push through to Prumo Hald," Domaren said. "Making it inside is our primary goal. If for some reason you cannot or we get too separated, fall back. Regroup. There won't be any reasons to expend any additional energy at that point."

"Do we all need to make it in, or just at least one of us?" Nanutsi asked.

With his hands still clasped together, Crizichial shook his head.

"I believe our goal of making it in stands the most chance of success if we do everything we can to stay together," he said.

"I agree," Domaren said, looking over the heads of the Tirngora. "We should stay together as long as possible. But we will of course need to adapt as we push forward, and communicate if we can."

His friends didn't speak, but only squinted and peered at

the enemies across from them.

"This could potentially be the end for some of us, or all of us," he said to his friends. "Just like so many of the cultures we've seen crop up and disappear just as quickly over the centuries, it may finally be our time to fade into memory. The sun may finally set for some of us, after millennia of light. But that's a fate I can accept. I will accept it at your side, and give whatever I have left to give."

Domaren's friends stepped closer to him and kept their eyes trained forward.

"I'll see to that green one there," Brikana said with hissing contempt. "If I can dispatch it quickly, I'll at least draw its attention away from you all."

"Crizichial," Domaren started. "I'll strike an initial distraction, but try to keep up with some possessions and hauntings. Anything to keep them confused or panicked."

The Redeemed godknight rubbed his hands together and expanded his grin.

"Nanutsi. Kegli," Domaren continued. "Let's try to keep the main focus of the fight on us. All we need to do is maintain a steady pace forward. Our biggest foe right now is time, so we can't afford to get stuck or bogged down. We must keep moving."

The seaver and dwarf remained quiet and focused on the foes ahead, and nodded.

"Criz, can you help ward us against those other Redeemed out there?"

"Of course," Crizichial complied. He then held his open hands out to his side where his palms burst into flames that leapt up many feet in height. While the flames danced and rustled in Crizichial's hands, he closed his eyes and lowered his head. His lips began to move quickly. As he whispered an ancient Demith incantation, the flames in his hands shifted colors.

The flames that originally roared in expected bellows of orange and yellow shifted to a bright red, then a rich crimson, before somehow solidifying, molding over with a thin green texture. It continued decaying into a shade of brown and then black, before collapsing in on itself, dripping through Crizichial's fingers and spilling off into the ground. The dead flame that became a decrepit sludge splattered onto the ground and immediately sprang back up.

From the ground, the grotesque masses reached back up and grew into translucent shapes roughly the size of each godknight. Once Crizichial's specters finished growing, they shot over to their assigned godknight, and rather than entirely possessing them, lurked within them, on guard, on the defense, but without causing the godknight to lose control of themselves or of their free will.

"I'll clap a blinding strike off Verikta, and then we can begin. Agreed?"

Domaren checked for replies or disagreements on his left, and then his right before flourishing his blade and rolling his neck.

"Okay, then," he said softly.

Domaren took a final step to the highest point of the boulder. The Tirngora shot their sword and spear-wielding fists into the air, jeering at and taunting the knights. The nearest dragon in the Kihdai's army, a vibrant emerald dragon, hunkered down and prepared to strike. Though it wasn't as large as Brikana, Domaren didn't relish the thought of having to grapple with a dragon, or multiple dragons, in the knights' collective, weakened state.

He didn't look forward to facing their demons, either.

Or the Tirngora.

Or the Tirngozas.

Or any enemy seavers, men, and dwarves.

"Right," Domaren said. "I'll see you on the field, friends."

Brikana folded her wings back as she lowered herself in preparation of lashing out. Kegli walked up to the front of his friends and looked up to Domaren and waited on the blinding strike. Nanutsi and Crizichial stood ready.

Domaren looked up at the aggressive, bruised clouds, and held them in his sight as he sought their inspiration. With a deliberate move to grasp his old friend, he pulled Verikta from her scabbard and as he swung the blade up and felt the ancient blade's weight shift as he had so many times before, he gently pressed the black handlestone. With the blade's electricity activated by the onyx gem, he held Verikta out and prepared to strike the sky with a flurry of fire and light.

"Ready? Any final thoughts?" Domaren asked.

Kegli recoiled and looked up at Domaren with a cocked eyebrow.

"Poor choice of words," he said quickly. His scowl immediately turned to a playful smile. "But no," he added as he faced forward again. "We're ready."

The human godknight smiled and looked back his blade, poised to do battle with him once again.

"All right," Domaren whispered.

After the quickly muttered phrase, Domaren strained and gritted his teeth. He focused his entire being on the energy being beckoned and stored by his sword. After a final and instilled compulsion to flourish the blade with a quick twirl in his hand, as natural as a blink or a swallow, Domaren whipped the blade up out of the flourish and slammed the flat of the blade.

Just as it had countless times before, the energy of the sword exploded out and summoned to it, a web of accompanying light from the sky. Like magnets or primordial soul mates, the vibrant streams of fire ripped down out of the clouds and combined with the crackling beams from Verikta into individual ruptures of blinding light.

Punishing cracks of sound accompanied the wild sequence of flashes, sending the huge army to the ground in cowering balls of temporary blindness and deafness. Closing their eyes wasn't enough and neither was covering their ears. The brightness seeped through eyelids and crept through fingers. Shielding eyes with hands, paws, or wings didn't keep the punishment from finding its way through all cracks and crevasses.

Once the knights' foes had been stunned, Domaren jumped off the boulder and swung Verikta up to the sky and launched off at a sprint towards the Kihdai forces. The other godknights, who were mostly impervious to their friend's extreme and exaggerated light, joined Domaren in tearing off towards their enemies.

For a moment, the plains were eerily still and quiet, other than the group of sprinting godknights. The massive army had been forced into involuntary submission and cowered, quiet and still, appearing as though something had physically beaten them into the ground. Domaren's tactic to stun and seize an initial opportunity to pick the method and position of their attack was successful. But just a moment before any weapons clashed, the initial shock of blindness and deafness war off. One by one, each Tirngora or Tirngoza unfurled their arms and hands. They shot up in stubborn recovery and flung themselves back to their feet, agitated from being caught off guard and seething in hateful anticipation.

Dragons, no longer immobilized, pushed themselves back up to their feet and unfurled their wings, screaming at the sky in anger. Humans and dwarves beat their shields and clapped their blades and spears together. The clinking and rattling scratched at the cacophony of sound as the seavers rattled their flails. Demons hissed and poured black plumes of malevolent magic onto the field, preparing to unleash demonic nightmares onto the field.

But their preparations were delayed just enough by Domaren's distraction to matter.

The knights tore into the battle with the impact of thousands, rather than five. Domaren slashed at the front line of orcs with an enchanted strength, sending a dozen of the unsuspecting creatures dozens of yards back into the army. Between each subsequent attack, Domaren exhibited a dexterity that only he could have after ages upon ages using the same weapon.

The first attack that sent orcs flying was that of pure force. Having engaged the army and made a space to fight, Domaren changed to Verikta's amber handlestone and swung and deflected many defenses into place. With a number of obstacles in the way to control the speed at which the Kihdai and proxy army could attack, Domaren alternated between the brown stone purple stones to deal with large influxes of attackers at once, or deal incapacitating or deathblows in one blow, respectively.

Only after the introductory portion of the fight was tended to, and he felt as though he was in a fairly steady and predictable rhythm, did Domaren sneak quick glances to check on the status of his friend. Before he located any of his fellow nights however, Domaren felt a mist of water tickle at his skin. He smiled.

A massive torrent of water, undoubtedly from the Firounda River Domaren assumed, sailed over his head like a wave harnessed by the wind. As Domaren spun and dodged, attacked and parried, he watched the living river fly over head, dipping and cresting with anger. When he found a second to spare, he spun and watched as Nanutsi waved her hands like an expert but respectful marionettist, controlling the water. It flew just above the battle like a skilled eagle, dipping and crashing into segments of the Kihdai and proxy supports, before washing them out towards distant fields and forests.

A series of rapid whips of air flipping about nearby caught Domaren's attention next. Without having to or being able to look, Domaren recognized the rapid flights of Kegli's throwing axes flying by. A moment would come where the slicing flights stopped and it was then Domaren knew Kegli was retrieving his axes. Shortly after, the attacks would resume.

Brikana was of course the easiest to keep track of. Domaren frequently glanced up for quick checks on his friend. Still on the ground for the moment, Brikana spun about thrashing at the army with her tail, swiping at swaths of fighters with her wings, and of course, doing battle with streams of her most devastating weapon, the power of the Black Dragon's fire.

Whether against trapped clumps of orcs, humans, elves, or other dragons, Brikana showed no mercy. She shot out stream after stream of fire and sustained them until she absolutely couldn't. Like speaking until you ran out of breath, Brikana held her fire until the moment she felt a similar sensation as running out of air. Only when she absolutely had to, she breathed in and stimulated the fires and gases within her once again, before unleashing a new shower of fire further fueled by punitive hate.

And finally, in his continued effort to ensure the group was moving forward while staying fairly close, Domaren saw

Crizichial. The Redeemed knight appeared to Domaren as being the least busy by far, but most effective of the group. Crizichial's dead face still wore a grin, but was far more disturbing now that it was accentuated by the voluntary decay that fueled his destructive magic.

With the army being almost entirely made of mortals, whether humans or dragons or anything in between, the knights had little difficulty controlling the fight. In addition to the other knights easily holding their own, Crizichial conjured and called upon the entombed energies and remnants in the ground below to once again scratch their way to the surface. After popping up through the surface, they immediately went to work scratching and clawing at the knights's foes. As they claimed their victims, or sometimes only parts of their victims, the living were dragged down to suffocate in the soil, or slowly be broken apart by stones or roots.

The knights fought constantly, but fought well. Other than Brikana taking off to steer or draw certain parts of the battle in a particular direction with slow or rapid flyovers of flame, the group stayed close. They felt no need to communicate often, but occasionally shouted quick updates or changes to strategy. Much of what was spoken was from a code system or extinct language that meant nothing to those they fought now.

After a time, the fighting knights grew to within a distance such that Domaren could see the bridge over the Firounda River and that led to the entrance of Prumo Hald—the same bridge he crossed so many ages before to warn the Kihdai of what would become known as Wrathlore. In what he registered immediately as a lapse in sense from recalling the past, an elven foe smacked Verikta out of his hand and landed a well-placed piercing of a spear to Domaren's unarmored side.

With surprise registering first, and a substantial pain registering immediately after, Domaren crunched to his side and started to collapse to a knee. But rather than collapsing and staying on a knee, Domaren tucked to his side and rolled in the direction of Verikta. Though his side felt like someone had stuck their pair of hands in and started to pull at the wound, he completed the roll and came out of it with Verikta pointed in a defensive position.

The elf had jumped forward and pulled back to go for another devastating blow, but Domaren swatted the massive spear away and countered with a slice to the chest before stabbing the elf into the chest.

Domaren's side stung, and though the pain was more than manageable, he let a throbbing stab of concern seep into his mind.

Domaren turned to shout and ask his friends to push towards the bridge, but before he could spot any of them, his eyes landed on the proxies instead.

"Ah, there you are," Domaren said. "Was wondering where you were."

Maphikim leaned over, feigning a look of concern.

"Is that blood, Domaren? That can't be a good sign."

"Oh, no, this is Midovin's blood."

Vinlaza lowered her head and snarled while Tobati pulled his axes into an attack posture, and Bitano began spinning her tail flail.

Domaren tapped and slid his fingers along the handle. As soon as he chose one, the surviving proxies took off towards him.

The proxies raced ahead. Domaren scanned the field in a panicked search for the others, but it was too late, the proxies were upon him. But just as he raised Verikta to block Tobati's ax, a beam of fire shot in from the side and sent the proxies scrambling to dive or dodge. A huge wave immediately followed and sent the proxies tumbling.

Vinlaza rolled to a stop and staggered to her feet. In her fury, she thrashed her tail about, slamming dozens of their own combatants into each other.

"What do you think you can do to stop us?" She said, disgusted. "Don't you remember that it isn't just us you're fighting?"

As the other proxies clambered up to their feet, the sky cracked open in four distinct spots. Almost immediately, four streams of rocky debris shot down and struck each of the proxies, and not only hit them initially, but remained.

In what appeared to be a constant connection with the Kihdai or the Grove, or both, the proxies proceeded to unleash a relentless volley of axes, water, fire, and decay.

Axes met axes, and water met fire. Domaren's sword slashed and swiped at the living fire beasts conjured from the most obscene corners of Gru Glech and Maphikim's Nebulum. With each attempt at gaining an advantage, the proxies swatted it down with their temporary streams of unlimited power. And when Domaren found a second to reach for a different stone to change strategy, a massive wall of fire shout out from Vinlaza enveloping the knights instead.

Domaren took off in a sprint and jumped just in time to avoid it. After rolling on his side only to spend his accumulated momentum, he looked up in a desperate attempt to locate his friends.

The only sights for a time were those of jumbled foes caught in Vinlaza's blast, as well as some knights who hadn't been able to escape it. Crizichial and Nanutsi lay on the ground, at least partly charred and still. Kegli shuffled to his feat and almost at the same time as Domaren, looked up and saw Brikana hovering just above the fight. She had launched and avoided Vinlaza's attack.

Domaren locked eyes with Brikana. The dragon knight looked in the direction of Prumo Hald which prompted Domaren to do the same. The proxies had inadvertently pushed their way too far away from the bridge and left a clearing directly to it.

Domaren and Brikana looked to each other again. The Black Dragon the turned her attention to the proxies.

"What are you doing?" Domaren asked. But his question was only for his benefit. Before he could realize he hadn't asked his question loud enough for her to hear, Brikana whipped her wings back in a massive stretch and show of power and flew forward into a nosedive towards the proxies.

"What are you doing?" Domaren said again, this time, shouting loud enough for her to hear him, but Brikana made no effort to acknowledge him. Instead of responding, her huge throat glowed bright white, and a harsh wall of fire shot out towards the proxies.

"Domaren!" Kegli shouted.

He looked up and searched for Kegli. Upon finding him, Kegli waved him over with his axes.

"Domaren! Let's go! The bridge!"

Took stepped off slowly into a jog, only long enough to confirm the direct path to the bridge was still clear.

*But we were going to do this together!* Domaren screamed mentally at Brikana. But as he raced by his unconscious friends, Crizichial and Nanutsi, he came to understand Brikana's action. There wouldn't be a better time for any of them to attempt to enter Prumo Hald. After having his epiphany, Domaren dug in that much harder and sprinted all out as hard as he could for the bridge.

The bridge was just ahead and Domaren blocked out all goals or threats other than the few deflections or spins he needed to execute to continue his race for the bridge. But when a particular dragon's identifiable scream tore out into the battlefield, a fear more terrifying and extreme than he had ever felt, ripped into his heart.

"Brikana!" Domaren screamed.

He stopped just in time to see Tobati land a devastating slice to one of her wings while Vinlaza bit into the other one. Her wing's webbing tore, with fragments hanging loosely from bloodied bones and flapping in the wind. Her firestone glowed, but only partially, and pitifully, before fading and going dark. She hacked and wheezed as she attempted to strike up her unrivaled fire, but that mechanism also failed her. Domaren had already launched off at a sprint to save his friends, but Kegli grabbed Domaren by the shoulder.

"It's too late, Domaren! It's too late!" He screamed. "She did this to buy us time! Go! Go!"

Domaren turned and shoved Kegli away while keeping his eyes on Brikana. The mighty godknight of the dragons labored to flail and thrashed to her feet after being pulled onto her back. She tried to continue fighting with her tail and teeth, and managed to tear a critical chunk out of Maphikim's lower torso, but her extinguished power and strength were too great a loss. Between the axes, swords, flames, flails, and decay magic, from not only the proxies but the pockets of forces nearby, Domaren watched his friend fall.

"I'll kill you! I'll kill you all!" Domaren screamed.

Kegli tugged at Domaren's armor. "Domaren! We have to go! Now!"

"You will never know peace! I'll come back and kill you! I'll kill everything!"

"Domaren!"

Domaren didn't say anything to Kegli or even look at him. Instead, he finally turned and took off towards the bridge. Kegli was on his heels and the two standing godknights flew towards Prumo Hald's doors.

# Twenty

Domaren and Kegli leaned down and gave all they could for maximum speed towards the doors.

"Just run straight at 'em. Slam into them!" Domaren said.

"Right, here we go," Kegli agreed.

The two knights closed the distance and at the last moment, leapt into the air and flung themselves at the doors. Just before impact, Domaren noticed that the doors weren't fully closed.

They crashed into the doors and tumbled to the floor as they rolled through them, opening them enough to make it fully inside.

"Quick, get up and help me put these beams up," Domaren ordered. Still on the ground, they both rolled over and popped up to their knees before standing up. "Hopefully they're still here. Yes, here's one."

The two knights got on either side of the only beam they could find quickly and heaved into the holding brackets.

"That probably won't hold anyone long, but..." Domaren said. His thoughts trailed off and his head swung around to peer deeper into the fortress.

"The throne room is back there," Domaren said, pointing Verikta at it.

The two knights shot across the room towards the next chamber, but only after Domaren slapped his blade and made it surge with light. After crossing the threshold into the old throne room, they found nothing but an empty room.

"No. This is where it all was. This is where the thrones were and the flames. The Limb of Life. Everything."

But as Kegli looked around silently, Domaren thought what he assumed Kegli was as well.

*What now?*

Domaren continued his search of the room, but with so little light, the dimensions of the abandoned space were hard to determine. Only the area in Verikta's immediate vicinity could be seen.

"What's that?" Kegli asked.

"What? Whe—" Domaren started to say. But the sound of a significant smash back at the front entrance distracted them.

"Come on," Domaren said.

They crossed the room and stepped over the long-extinguished fire circle. Domaren looked up at the matching extinguished chandelier, remembering the bright flames that lit the room ages before. Piles of fine dust and particulate rested patiently where the old candle wax had long-since broken down.

With each twist or movement of Verikta, Domaren noticed a matching flicker come from the object they approached. After walking close to the back of the room,

Domaren and Kegli found themselves in front of a huge curtain of what appeared to be something similar to ice. Though it appeared like a wet wall of ice, there was no sign that any of it was melting, or had ever melted.

"What is this?" Kegli asked. He reached out his hand to touch it.

"Wait, Kegli!" Domaren shouted through a whisper.

But it was too late. Kegli pressed a few fingertips to the wall, and then quickly whole fingers, his palm, and his whole hand.

"It's ice cold," Kegli said. He then gently tapped the wall. "Solid."

Another, more crunching bang landed at the entrance door.

"That won't hold for much longer," Domaren said.

"Do you think this is the gate mentioned in the book?" Kegli asked.

Domaren's eyes widened.

"What? The Wrathlore text?"

Kegli grunted.

"Something about access to Vals Hald being accessible through a gate. Accessible only to those—"

"...at the beginning," Domaren said, completing the recollection.

As Domaren took off a glove, the most violent crash into the door yet sent a ripping echo throughout the hall. Domaren reached for the ice curtain to touch it. But rather than his hand landing on a firm, impenetrable surface, Domaren's hand went through it without resistance. Domaren felt no different in temperature, but only the slight feel of pressing through an incredibly thin film.

"That's it Domaren! Go restore our powers, or kill those bastard Kihdai, or both! I'll go back for anyone I can.

Go!"

The doors crunched again, and this time, noticeably crashed open against the walls.

"But they're here!" Domaren said. "Get out of—"

Before Domaren could finish, Kegli shouted a final, "Go!" and pushed Domaren through the ice gate.

Though he stumbled from Kegli's surprise push, Domaren found his footing and took stock of his surroundings. He saw, in all directions, far reaching hills covered in snow. Trees grew in frequent patches throughout this land and to the left, was a massive fortress that Domaren instantly assumed was Vals Hald, and to the right, was a grove of trees much taller than the others. Despite the fluffy crunching of pristine snow, Domaren set out as fast as he could for the distinct grove nearby.

Domaren waved his arms and hopped over a fallen log which helped him slow from his desperate sprint. When he reached the base of the hill he bent over, close to the ground, with Verikta poised and pointed forward. He looked up towards the Grove and set his sights on a noticeable clearing, still discernible despite the ravaged state of the surrounding brush and trees. Burned timber littered the ground. Other trees, hewn and split, mocked the knight with their whispered recollections of the recent betrayal. Yet, Domaren began the slippery trek up to meet those stories, avenge the Grove and the groveknights, and reclaim for himself and this friends the power they were robbed of and that belonged to no others.

The slope up to the Grove was covered in slushy snow and littered with muddy soil. Each of Domaren's stomps up the path was weighted with hate and defiance. Hate for the Kihdai. Disgust for the state of the Grove, and defiance of the ground beneath him. He punished the ground as he climbed. He stabbed it, claiming his traction, and ascended without doubt or fear. The world around him bounced slightly with each step but his sight remained fixed on the large gap in the trees ahead.

One foot forward followed another. With each step, Domaren's hate swelled and his defiance grew, and added to the burden he carried up to the Grove. This burden, further compounded by the sorrow of his lost dragon friend and those who fell in the Grove, as well as the despair of the forest, was only a sliver of that which weighed Domaren down. He had walked the world these most recent days with the creeping guilt of failing his people, his friends, and apparently those who gave everything to everyone, though his existing burdens only bolstered his hate and his defiance.

He continued trudging up the hill with a gait of a subconscious rhythm. But to an onlooker, it might have been easily recognized. To some, it could have appeared as though Domaren was treading the last steps of a solemn journey. Or, an exhausted march after expending himself in the last battle of the last lonely war. Occasional glances down caught sight of his wound spilling his blood onto the snow. He didn't care. Perhaps the godknight was fulfilling an ancient promise to be a pallbearer for the memory of a long-absent ancestor. Though maybe to some, and potentially to most, it could appear as though Domaren was playing his part in a grand or pitiful dirge. A funeral march. If not for himself, for the world, just before the rites are given and a eulogy for the dawn is spoken.

Regardless of what the imagined occasion may be, Domaren climbed the slope seething with intention and an aggravated urge to be a participant in the mechanism of justice. He gave no thought to whether he lived or died. He had no concern for victory or defeat. Instead, he walked up, forward, and toward a challenge to the unanswered and nihilistic will of the Kihdai. He went to confront their notion that such everlasting and final destruction would go unchallenged.

Domaren continued his ascent until finally his steady stare crossed the plane of the floor of the Grove. He slowed and tossed Verikta into his other hand and squeezed his fist to crack his knuckles. He tossed Verikta back.

He stepped higher and peered deeper into the jumbled and damaged grove. As he approached the Grove's opening Domaren saw that the outer rings of pine appeared to bear the brunt of the Kihdai attack with damage decreasing towards the interior. With Brikana's death, the remaining thread of doubt that the Kihdai were actively waging war against their own creation, was destroyed. Seeing the mangled trees strewn about was for Domaren, a fresh palm's worth of salt being poured upon the diseased scars and festering cuts the Kihdai had levied upon the world and the life within it. He pushed the distracting fury from his mind temporarily, if only to pay attention to the movement he thought he spotted within the trees.

He stopped and looked down and slowly moved his head from side to side. The feathery powder of snow on the ground hushed everything at first. His armor and leather fell silent. His feet were still. He listened and waited until a metallic clink pulled his attention forward once again. Without conscious effort, Domaren raised Verikta so that his sword was just at the edge of his peripheral vision. When the blade appeared, he looked to the blade and raised it a bit more. Though he knew Verikta's every detail, and was more familiar with the sword than anything ever created or imagined, he studied it and appreciated it like one might a discovered artifact, previously thought lost to the ages. He said nothing to the blade. Domaren thought nothing about it. He simply looked upon it and felt a longing, though for what, Domaren couldn't succinctly define. He felt ready for his and the sword's next fight, but hesitated to begin. There was confidence, but sadness.

After beginning at the pommel, Domaren deliberately took in the calling stones, the handle, and then the handlestones. After pausing only to consider how many individuals, creatures, cultures, and cities had met one of the sword's many possible fates, Domaren continued looking up to the cross-guard, and then finally, the blade.

The fuller and etchings looked up at him from where they had rested since the weapon was dawn-forged. They knew his face just as well as he knew how they reflected the various hews of the light of the world. And as his vision jumped up to the sword's point and started working his way back down, Domaren watched as a frozen puff landed on the blade. He watched it melt and looked up where he was pleasantly met with a rapidly proliferating whiteness of an incoming snowstorm. Domaren smiled as a calm came over him and blended his excitement and dread for the unknown.

The godknight resumed his march, looking up only after taking his next step. He didn't care where the step led him. He would proceed, regardless. He didn't care what his foot found when it landed. He would slam his whole weight down purposefully. He sought no assurance of a victory, had no concern over a loss, and had no desire to have the path or destination laid out before him. He slammed his boot down with a confidence. He took step after step forward and went to claim whatever awaited.

As he grew closer to the Grove, the tangled piles of gnarled trees grew taller, wider, and occurred more frequently. Scorched soil mixed with old and melting ice and bled the ground brown and black with the tears of the forest. If not for the meandering and lively streams of watery mud, the scene appeared stuck and frozen from a past war of an indeterminate age. The perpetual winter made it seem as though the destruction could have taken place a day, a year, or an eon prior.

The shock of the initial bombardment had been preserved. The vicious malice had been imprinted upon everything in the surrounding area. The futility of a potential escape or survival seemed to be dripping from each pine needle with mocking contempt.

Extinguished embers littered the ground with their top, ashy layers almost hiding them within the snowbanks. Split branches and wooden shards littered the path as though someone had split cord after cord of wood nearby. But these remnants were not made in the name of warming a home or a family. This hateful mess was made in the name of an ironic effort to deprive a world of itself.

Domaren continued towards the Grove, ready and resolute. He kept his eyes moving as he hunted the woods for more movement, more signs of who was there, and where. He wasn't expecting to be alone, and he wasn't expecting to make it to the center of the Grove without intervention. He expected a challenge. Challenges. Whether quick and easy, or involved and catastrophic, he anticipated *something*. And after reaching the outer edge of the Grove's outermost circle of trees, Domaren looked up the narrow but towering pine trunks and silently paid them his respects.

Domaren crossed through the outer layers of the Grove and the signs of the attack diminished. Fewer charred trees. Fewer split trees. So too did the signs of fire decrease, their signs of crisping the forest diminishing with each of

Domaren's steps.

With the center of the Grove approaching, Domaren found himself distracted, though only partially. His eyes continued scanning, and his ears remain flexed, but his thoughts turned to his friends. While he had no fear over the fate that awaited him there, at the Grove, he did however find himself mentally fighting exchanged volleys of doubt and reassurance over the decision to leave his friends behind, especially considering with Brikana being absent. But he quickly dismissed any worry. For them to have any chance, he thought, he knew he must be there at that moment.

"Kana..." Domaren whispered, proceeding the comment with a sigh. He spoke not with a gentle affection directed at the memory of his friend, but with a growling hate directed at those who robbed him of her.

Domaren walked deeper into the woods and at an increasingly faster speed. He stopped scanning as widely as he had been for movement but instead looked forward and focused. Quicker and quicker he walked until finally, while being surrounded by what appeared to be a mostly pristine interior part of the Grove, Domaren spotted a broad and flat clearing.

He immediately stopped. Then, with his thumb, he mashed the most lethal stone on Verikta's hilt. Whether flesh and bone, Kihdai, or pitiful creature, Domaren took no chance in risking his best chance to counter whatever he might find ahead. He leaned with his left shoulder just slightly, and resumed his trek forward, Verikta held out behind him.

Curtains of feathery snow cascaded down from a charcoal sky, seemingly suspended just inches above the thick pine canopy. Domaren took a long blink and drew in a massive breath to smell the trees, the wetness of the soil, and the decaying leaves. The clearing ahead grew closer and larger and its white blanket welcomed him.

The purity comforted him. The cold sterility focused his mind. He felt himself leaning in farther and increasing his pace as he excitedly anticipated what awaited him in the Grove.

He continued walking through the thick trees as his boots crunched the snow beneath him until finally, the forest sprawled open as he entered the open grove. The expanse of sound Domaren was aware of swelled rapidly due to the Grove being absent of trees. A slight metallic sound caught his attention, but he didn't immediately turn towards it. Instead, Domaren risked a few seconds to scan the interior of the Grove and noticed what appeared to be full, individual trees, each with the symbol of their corresponding knight. After quickly working to identify each tree, Domaren completed following the circle of trees around until his gaze came upon the source of the metallic sound.

Towards the opposite end of the Grove, was a surprise, and an expectation. It was a sight that at once frightened Domaren, and also relieved him. And in the face of competing and conflicting inclinations and feelings, however, Domaren found himself standing steady. He turned towards, and with arms outstretched, felt peace from the presence of Verikta's weight in his hand.

Domaren knew the figure. But he only knew the figure from what felt like a memory, or a dream. From something, the details of which couldn't be confirmed with certainty or clarity. Like a village elder struggling to remember the specifics of a childhood lesson, or parable passed down from the elder's elders, Domaren strained to place meaningful memories of the figure. But even without recollections of specifics of interactions from before the birth of the virtues, Domaren knew exactly who and what the figure was.

The human Kihdai stood across from Domaren and stared down at him from his additional height. He remained in place without producing a weapon and had it not been for the Kihdai's occasional and calm exhalations puffing out into the cold air, he could have been mistaken for one of the many inanimate trees behind him.

But his stillness was the only similarity to the trees.

Sitting on top of the Kihdai's head was the immense skull of Doja, the first ram killed by the gods during their first, and last, hunt. As Domaren recalled, the Kihdai swore to the beast as he dressed the animal, that he would honor the animal's sacrifice by wearing its skull as the top half of his helmet through all of eternity. Domaren couldn't help but focus on the skull's darkened eye sockets with an itchy anxiety of somehow being judged by the long-dead creature's absent eyes.

Jutting out from the Kihdai's lower jaw and chin was the skull of Frejnin, the raven that first called to the Kihdai and brought their attention to Doja's location. In a similar fashion, the god swore to Frejnin that once the raven had lived its natural life, it too would forever be immortalized as part of his helmet. Between the top and bottom skulls, Domaren could see only slight hints of the tissue and material that belonged to the actual god, which, it appeared, was skin.

The Kihdai's helmet was a macabre sight of sharp beaks, horns, and ghostly memories of haunted flesh and eyes. But, rather than instilling fear or dread like it might in any other witness, Domaren simply admired the god's continuing, honored promises to those first creatures of the world. But in light of the betrayal he sought to stop,

Domaren ended his admiration there.

The god's other armor was pristine, uniform in texture, color, and matte finish. The entirety of his black breastplate, dawn-forged at the birth of the virtues, was almost completely embossed with the first iteration of the Kihdai's first fortress. Stretching and winding down from the breastplate was an embossed forest root system that jumped down onto the legs and wound their way all the way down. Each embossed feature of the fortress and roots was as pure white as the skulls on the Kihdai's head and the feathery snow falling upon him.

The snow was big, feathery, and unrelenting. But even from the distance and the snow, Domaren could easily see what was strapped upon the Kihdai's back.

Like a prominent and beastly horn of its own, the hilt of the creator's sword stuck up in the air behind him, it's ebony handle and unpolished cross-guard easily distinguishable above the skulls. This sword was a sister to Verikta, also dawn-forged, but where Domaren's sword had various options available to its wielder, the creator's sword only had one. Lethality.

And though the entire vision ahead of Domaren was familiar from ancient recollections, he had more than enough time to review every detail of the Kihdai, his weapon, armor, and posture, and even then, gave the human Kihdai a few following moments to speak before taking the initiative to begin the encounter.

"Yes, they are all still here," the Kihdai said. As he spoke, he held his hand out in the direction of all the knight trees. "Even Crizichial's. It is almost hard to tell that it was planted after the others. See how its branches—"

Domaren's adrenaline spiked. He launched off towards the closest knight tree, Kegli's. A dozen steps felt like one, but before he could even extend his hand out in hopes of pressing his palm to Kegli's symbol, the Kihdai's imposing mass shot into view. His blade had been drawn, and the god brought it down in the first swing of what seemed to be a destined battle between a god, and his knight.

Domaren drew Verikta and brought it up in time for the two sister blades to clash. Together with his momentum and the force of the clashing swords, Domaren rolled forward. Snow found the small divisions in his armor and raced in as he tumbled. Once he spun and jumped to his feet, he felt the snow tickle and scratch at his neck.

"—are starting to curl upwards?" The Kihdai finished asking.

"I'm going to press each one of these," Domaren responded, matching the god's irreverence.

"It seems pressing Brikana's will not be necessary," said the creator.

The Kihdai turned slightly to face Domaren straight on again after their first encounter. Domaren rolled his shoulders and shivered not from the snow, but from an involuntary and primal surge of hate. The Kihdai's head tilted down slightly, the ram skull appearing to preemptively mock whatever Domaren might reply with.

But before that, Domaren took a moment to focus once more on the snow. The peace of its steady and icy fall felt as though existence was deliberately picking and placing each of the frozen blessings. Domaren always considered it to be sentient. He liked to wonder if it could ponder where it would go, where it would fall, and what elements of filth it could aggressively tear away from Domaren's existence. He found it much more efficient and deliberate than the haphazard placement of rain, and Domaren found no greater peace in the snow of that or any moment, even then, in the presence of the Kihdai and his condescension.

"I find it interesting," Domaren started as he casually examined Verikta, "that you all started this effort like a dense child might. The Kihdai," he continued, smiling towards the snow-covered tree canopy, "feeling compelled to sneak and hide from their own creation. Almost as though, from the start, that you couldn't escape the stench of shame and obviousness of how backwards some of your decisions were."

"We do not expect you to understand," the human creator replied quickly. "You have never expressed gratitude for your lives. Never expressed gratitude for what your lives contain, nor made any significant efforts to preserve them, or improve yourselves. You do nothing but lay in apathy and pitiful beds of mediocrity. You try us. You bore us."

"Stop saying *you* as though I haven't been here roaming this world longer than you all have been absent from it, doing every bidding and enforcing every will asked of me." Domaren said.

"And would you equate your and the other knights' efforts with success?" Asked the creator. "To find our world in the state it is currently in?"

"I would equate the state of the world, whatever it may be, with the point where it has naturally arrived," Domaren answered.

"And we are not satisfied with where it has naturally arrived," the Kihdai said, his voice snapping back in defiance.

Domaren lifted Verikta and quickly pressed one of the handlestones. The blade swelled, if only marginally, and began to ring with a sound similar to that of a low tuning fork.

"Dissatisfaction does not justify total destruction," Domaren said.

"That is not for you to say."

"You created me, all of us, with the ability to defy you. I am here. And I *am* saying it."

"Yes. You can defy us," the Kihdai acknowledged. "You can persist. At least, for a time. It appears however, that the time available to you is near exhausted."

"But not yet," Domaren said.

Domaren raised his sword as another blossom of snow landed on the flat of the blade. He looked up and into the empty recesses of the skull but then let his head tilt slightly to connect with the Kihdai's actual eyes, barely visible behind the skulls.

Domaren stepped away and marched toward the god. He nodded and held his sword out to the front in a two-handed posture. As he approached, Domaren looked around once more to confirm which knight tree was where.

*Mine is straight behind the Kihdai. Crizichial's is to my tree's left. Kana's is on the other side, with Nanutsi's next, followed by Kegli's tree. He can pivot to respond to any direction I choose. I need to engage him, maneuver around him, and then strike out for one of the trees.*

The godknight lunged into a sprint towards the Kihdai and brought Verikta over his head before heaving his and the blade's exponentially increased power down at the creator. And though he blocked in plenty of time, the combined energy of Domaren's and Verikta's jarring force slammed into the Kihdai's blade, sending the defender's arm flying back. The deflection sent Verikta bouncing off slightly, but Domaren immediately recovered and arced the sword down for an attempted slice to the Kihdai's side.

Having quickly learned what to flex and reinforce to better absorb Verikta's accentuated power, the Kihdai flipped his wrists and turned the blade upside down, defending

Domaren's attack once more. After slicing upwards and sending Verikta sliding away, the god let his deflection's momentum continue slicing around before bringing his own blade down towards Domaren's neck.

It too was blocked. After a flurry of subsequent attacks and expertly executed parries, the two combatants quickly settled into an intentional and calculated rhythm. The Kihdai and godknight exchanged slice after swipe, and thrust after vicious counter.

The Kihdai met Domaren's attacks with perfectly executed defenses and Domaren in turn anticipated the creator's attacks. Each slice or parry resulted in an impasse. A stalemate.

But it shouldn't have been so. As the snow was increasingly painted with Domaren's blood, they were both aware of his increasing weakness. The Kihdai enjoyed a far more balanced experience in his fight with Domaren and it should never have been so. The knights were created to be stronger and more powerful than the Kihdai in most circumstances, but that was of course not the case now. The Kihdai simply entertained Domaren's attempt for his own pride and entertainment.

Domaren continued cycling through stones and sought out any opportunity to execute something the Kihdai could not predict. And after an especially quick switch between handlestones, Domaren skirted past the Kihdai and made contact with Crizichial's grove tree. Domaren slapped his hand on Crizichial's carved symbol and woke the tree, sending a grove stone down to hopefully restore and heal his Redeemed friend. The symbol glowed brightly with the colors of fire as it did so.

As the Kihdai let a growling huff shoot out in a heated cloud from under the bone helmet, Domaren's fleeting flame of hope found new oxygen with which to grow brighter. His wound hurt and though he had continued bleeding, the pain was manageable and was no longer increasing.

"It isn't so much that you succeeded in reaching the Redeemed tree that infuriates me, Domaren," the Kihdai said. "It's that you defy our will as if you can. That, and we have to wait until the knights' power is spent again. But no worries, we have time."

Before Domaren could reply, the Kihdai shot off across the Grove and met Domaren with a flurry of rapid attacks that Domaren could only barely respond to in time. The momentum of the attack swung Domaren around and sent him stumbling back. And in an unintended consequence, Domaren found himself tumbling back, straight towards the dwarf tree. With a mouth hanging open, gasping desperately for gasps for air, Domaren clawed his way up the tree and back to his feet before pressing the symbol. It in turn lit up and extended a grove stone for his dwarf friend.

"Your will means nothing to me. Your will lost its value when you decided to destroy a world because you failed it," Domaren said. He spoke softly between his labored breaths but maintained all the animosity and contempt that he could. "Perhaps you should think twice about creating a new world. Maybe the fault is with the creators rather than the created. What kind of creators bring so much to life only to kill it?"

"The kind who don't wish to reward those who live only to destroy that which they have been given."

Just as the Kihdai finished replying, Domaren shot up from his crumpled posture and raced at the creator. Having pressed many of Verikta's handlestones, Domaren attempted to sprint the most direct path straight to Nanutsi's tree. In a blur of combined speed, mirrored offense, and multiplied power, Domaren flew past the Kihdai, simultaneously attacking, deflecting, and distracting. After Domaren's chaotic flurry came to an end, he found himself sliding down the trunk of Nanutsi's tree. He had pressed her symbol and activated a grove stone for her. As the relief of having activated the living knights' trees registered, so too did a new pain. It was new, and much more severe. As Domaren darted towards the Kihdai and ran past, the creator had found a sliver of time and vulnerability to thrust his sword through Domaren's chest. Domaren slumped down to the base of the tree and turned to face the Kihdai, gurgling.

Domaren squinted at the ground before relaxing his eyes. After a long and rattling sigh, he loosened the muscles around his eyes even more before allowing his sight to slide completely out of focus. Domaren stared through the Kihdai, past the visual smear of blurry nothingness, and into the reality that his reality would soon be ending.

The godknight was shocked physically, though he found a peace in knowing he had restored those knights that he could. As he fell into a hateful pit of sorrow over the loss of Brikana and the failure he felt in being unable to save her, his emotions sent a flood of tears and phlegm pouring out of his face to mix with the blood of his wounds. He sighed harshly again before gasping quickly and settling into shallow, rickety panting. He curled Verikta into view, slowly lowering his stare as if preparing to bow his head in deference to the truth of futility. His focus sharpened and landed on his sword.

The Kihdai let a breath go.

"You did everything right," he said to Domaren. He continued speaking slowly. The weight and volume of his voice made his words ring ironically sincere to Domaren.

"By us," he continued. "By them. By Verikta there. No one and no weapon has done more for this world."

Domaren's head wobbled up. He squinted again. This time, at the creator.

The Kihdai stepped closer and knelt down. Before speaking again, the other Kihdai raced up through the Grove's clearing and slid to a slushy stop. Their eyes scanned the Grove with random jerks back and forth to the trees and blood-stained snow.

"What is this?" The orc Kihdai asked. "He activated the trees? You let him?"

Domaren listened and watched through fading sight as the human Kihdai whipped a hateful glance over his shoulder.

"I didn't *let* him do anything," he said. "The dragon is dead and Domaren is dying. But, he did get the other three activated."

"Well, our side of the gate needs destroyed before anyone else comes through," another Kihdai said. "Let's go. He's gone."

Before the human Kihdai could reply, the others ran off to see to the gate. Domaren's foe stood up and looked down at the dying Domaren.

"It's slightly impressive you found the gate. It had been so long even we almost forgot about it. But unfortunately, I don't have time to discuss how you learned it was there."

The Kihdai stepped back before turning towards Vals Hald. As he approached the path leading out of the Grove, he turned to address Domaren a final time.

"We'll close that gate so that can't happen again..." the Kihdai said, before glancing at Domaren's tree. "And since we have to wait out the others you restored, we can wait you out again, too."

With a hint of a dark grin and a slap of his hand onto Domaren's tree, a grove stone quickly rumbled out from the ground. Domaren's eyes found energy to pop wide open as he dragged himself over to the grovestone's indentations. As he reached up to the rising stone and slid his hands into the perfectly sized recesses, he felt his strength return, and his wounds close. His stomach felt full and a cold wave of refreshment spilled down through his body.

As a wall of watery sediment quickly obscured the Kihdai and the Grove from view, Domaren was thrust out of the Grove and returned to Prumo Hald where he once again found himself staring into the gate made of ice. Just as he reached up to test it once more, to return to fight the Kihdai with his full strength, the ice gate cracked and sent webs of weakness rapidly racing throughout the gate. Just as Domaren's hand would have landed on the gate, the slick panel of ice shattered and crumbled into a pile of frozen rubble. While attempting to sort through and settle a million thoughts, he could only stare at the remnants of the gate to the Grove. But within seconds, the ongoing battle outside Prumo Hald stole his attention.

He turned and spun in circles, examining the ancient and dark room as he gathered his thoughts. After his third or fourth circle, he stopped and set his vision on the field outside, the ongoing battle just visible through the open doors and across the bridge.

When the compulsion to find Nanutsi, Kegli, and Crizichial entered his mind, the thought of seeing Brikana's body again immediately followed. Domaren then sprinted back outside. Full of power, and full of wrath.

# Epilogue

Once the surviving, restored knights sent the proxies and allies of the Kihdai fleeing, and the Battle at Prumo Hald ended, the field resembled a paralyzed ocean of red flesh to the distant eye. But those intimately trapped in its riptide of death, wounded but still alive, watched as others slipping away from life slid helplessly down the crimson-stained hills. Surprise waves of survivors brought attention to the healthy, as they crawled up and over the dead. The humps and lumps of dragons and the larger demons created artificial hills of their own, stretching back to the horizon of casualties.

The sounds coming from the battle's floor were initially dominated not by the peaceful rush of Firounda River, but by the gurgling rattles of those choking on their own blood, or a combination of choking and damaged vocal cords. Usually attributed with mortal wounds to chests and necks, those most chilling sounds thankfully dissipated the quickest as those lives dissipated the quickest.

General groaning and pleas for help soon took over as

the predominant sounds and lasted until they expired, or, in most cases, were removed from the field for treatment. While some cried out in agony from compound fractures, slices, or dismemberment, others called for their friends by name, or their respective godknight. Many simply cried out "Help!" over and over again, and sometimes provided direction on where on the field they were.

There were also those unfriendly to the godknights. Indeed, the adversaries had their own wounded who screamed and begged for help, or mercy. Others cursed, or attempted to curse, those who supported the godknights and their position. Many died using their last breath to antagonize and insult the godknights, or to champion the Kihdai and the proxies.

But the sounds of the deviant and their efforts to cause additional horrors were dealt with quickly. As is customary after a battle, especially those who presented extraordinary risk and opportunity for a future, additional conflict, the surviving knights and their allies spent hours scouring the field to dispatch any surviving combatants.

It was only then, when the ocean of war had fallen truly still and peacefully quiet, that Domaren and the others made their way to Brikana's lifeless body.

The march to her was a slow one. It was made without organization or coordination. No one spoke a suggestion to gather near her, but that is what they did. Many, including Domaren, stomped slowly and deliberately. They told themselves that they wanted to step carefully to more easily tread through the waves of dead, but they all knew the truth. No one wanted to reach her. They didn't want to look up at their friend, their godknight, or their symbol of power and potential, until the absolute last possible moment.

But they all eventually closed in on the dragon. And

they all eventually looked up.

Even in death, the Black Dragon was mighty. Even in death, she instilled fear. Even in death, she made her allies entertain that thought in the back of their mind, that should they anger her in just the right way, she might incinerate them where they stood.

But also in death, survivors recalled her as a proud and worthy champion of the dragon race. They remembered her not only as a bastion of primordial power that represented the interests of all dragons at all times, but also as a friend and ally to anyone that gave a legitimately fair amount of deserved respect to her and her kind. They saw in front of them, not just a dragon's corpse, but the corpse of Brikana, Godknight of the Dragons, defender of her race, and willing ally to all who would strive for and help others strive for, the greatest potential for all life.

Across the battlefield, hearty warriors sobbed. Like bursting spores of sorrow, the sounds of grief peppered the area in every direction. Elder beasts succumbed to their emotion and collapsed into a pile of disbelief. Proud men and women, still shimmering in sweat and blood, comforted each other with hugs, or by clinging desperately onto the shoulders of their friends.

There were some who, whether by an overwhelming need or a stubborn sense of devotion, found within themselves the ability to step closer to Brikana's body. They slowly crept through and over the piles of bodies, all the while looking up through tear-flooded eyes, to approach the corpse of their stalwart champion and beloved friend. One of those to approach, was Domaren, who through a combined need and devotion, mustered the will to stare down his sorrow. He stepped closer still, and extended his hand out to touch her.

The Black Dragon was still, and her scales were cold. Domaren's touch yielded an unexpected surprise of frigid bite that sent a fresh wave of emotional pain scratching through his skin and new tears to his eyes. She had always been a symbol of life to Domaren, as well any who knew her. She used to symbolize life, warmth, heat, and energy. But, no longer.

* * *

Even as the wounded were dispatched or tended to, and the mourners gathered around Brikana's body, there were already efforts underway to pursue the fleeing Kihdai loyalists. Not wanting to reignite a battle with the proxies until planning could take place to take advantage of the restored, surviving knights, it was quickly decided that a small force of quick infantry and fighters would follow, with the intent of tracking and gathering information. They were to obscure their numbers and spread out so as not to give away how small their force was. Though, after a few hours, the retreating force dispersed with little to no organization and broke off towards regions in all directions. The trackers ended their pursuit and returned.

The restored godknights, those that survived, walked the impromptu camps and spoke with those who fought alongside them. They shared their appreciation and provided reassurance that the final outcome of the conflict was still to be decided. And after stabilizing and preparing their wounded for travel, the knights and their allies abandoned the outskirts of Prumo Hald.

In the subsequent days once everyone returned from the battle, the majority of waking hours were spent by godknights, kings, elders, and other leaders discussing their next steps. Some wanted to regroup and reequip their combined forces and strike back out immediately, to hunt down proxies and their conspirators, if not prioritize a way to somehow reengage the Kihdai.

Citing what they perceived as overwhelming odds and the futility of resisting the will of the Kihdai, others wanted to abandon their cities. They wanted to flee from all they had ever known and seek safety in hiding, though many pointed out that given the Kihdais' goal of a complete rebirth of the world and all who inhabit it, that there was little guarantee of living in safety.

Others proposed the notion of offering an understanding of some type. They suggested that the Kihdai might accept an offering of peace, or an agreement to meet whatever demands they may have in exchange for their lives. These ideas were largely dismissed as well, with the counter argument that the Kihdai couldn't be trusted in such an agreement. Or, that should they decide to resume their efforts to obliteration, that they need only wait out the godknights again. Those that were still alive, that is, and Domaren referenced his direct conversation with the human Kihdai to support that.

Before any significant decisions were reached however, there was an unrelated agreement between all parties. A funeral would be held for Brikana. Not a common funeral. Not an uncommon funeral. Nor would it be a funeral for kings or heads of state. It would instead be a ceremony worthy of the Black Dragon. A dragon's send off for the grandest of dragons. A funeral for Brikana, Godknight of Dragons.

The general process of a dragon funeral ceremony was long established, but many hours were spent discussing how to alter the customs so that they would be worthy of so grand a being as Brikana. Dragons conferred with each other in spite of the obvious absence of their proxy, and in a rare display of humility, brood leaders, elders, and members of the tribunal, sought out the opinions and suggestions of the surviving godknights. After three days of discussion, Brikana's body was retrieved from the Fields of Frigid Fire, where it had been kept for preservation, and kept safe in the heart of Kimozoa until preparations were complete.

Scribes and volunteers dispatched verbal as well as written invitations across Stä Bläsjä. Most invitations were obvious or sincere. Some were attempts to win the support of those thought to be yet uncommitted to any particular side of the conflict. They were also considered by some to be exploitive of the occasion, and thinly veiled anti-Kihdai propaganda, but few voiced any meaningful concerns. Regardless, the primary sentiment was intended to convey that all were invited to memorialize Brikana.

After the significant efforts in logistics, communications, planning, and staging had been completed, the first godknight in thousands of years would be put to rest.

When the sun had set on the fifth day, and any remaining light in the sky had exiled any hints of reds, oranges, or yellows, the citizens of Kimozoa lit large torches lining each side of the main thoroughfare. These torches, each a fully grown tree only roughly shaved of its limbs and bark, were wrapped in yards and yards of dense linen and soaked in oil. When lit, they roared to life and resembled the wafting wave of fire erupting from a dragon. The lighting of the fires signaled to the city, its residents, and the guests, that the funeral was about to begin.

Humans and bears, dragons and orcs, Redeemed, seavers, elves, and dwarves trickled quickly onto the sides of the expansive street. Their bobbing heads and collective movements looked like drunken fireflies under the flames of the tree torches. While the crowd was not boisterous or joyful, it was also not quiet and somber. All forms of life were still angry at losing one of the world's godknights, and proud to be involved with her funeral. Once dragon patrols high above signaled to their superiors that the majority of the crowd had entered the center of the city, the formal memorial event commenced.

The beginning phase began with bringing even more fire to life. In addition to the torches, tall strips and meandering patterns of specially confined material were ignited, bringing the most impressive and interesting architectural features of the city to life in roaring flame. Beginning at the Kimozoa's theatre, each structure, gargantuan in all manners of height, width, and overall scale, burst into flames. Slowly at first, and then faster, the entire complex of structures along the road were set aflame. The city roared to life in simulated destruction, far down to the distant end of the road. Symbolically, the deceased dragon godknight had engulfed the world in a final eruption of heated fury.

Once the guests and mourners had craned their necks, stood on their toes, and peered over the heads of those nearby to see the extent of the fiery display, a blanket of of music crashed upon the city.

Beginning with an ensemble of one hundred musicians and one hundred vocalists, the theatre blasted out an initial drone of low finality with a simple harmony. Like two companions making the journey towards death together, the two blasting pitches sounded the way towards death for the departed. But then, to remove all doubt as to the location of where the dead dwell, the majority of the remaining ensemble provided aural roadsigns of sorts, trumpeted into existence by rattling brass and punching percussion. With a musical path put forth, and accompanying musical roadsigns established, the vocalists then started to sing out the directions.

In an impressive display of logistics and scale, the ensemble played a morbid game of call and answer with smaller ensembles scattered throughout the city. The larger group asked questions as to what road to take, or mountain to climb, or river to cross. The singers would sing their questions, and the smaller groups would answer:

*What is your destination?*
  *I seek a place of rest.*
*Do you know the way?*
  *I have only taken the first step.*
*First, follow the fires.*
  *Yes, I see them.*
*Climb the mountain of rest.*
  *But where do I go then?*
*Cross the river of peace.*
  *But where do I go then?*
*You only need keep walking.*
  *Should I continue towards flame and its light?*
*Walk. There will be only one direction.*

The entire musical conversation repeated five times. With each repetition, the number of instruments playing increased. The harmonies became more complex, but the low drone—that pair of pitches outlining that path to death—remained. In addition to added players and vocalists, each individual player or singer increased their volume with each repetition. The richness and power of the music escalated to a point that some of the onlookers and listeners began to worry. A sense of dread overcame them that crept up their back and made their necks uneasy. Many considered for a moment that they were not there only to show their respects, but that they might even join Brikana in her final journey. But those feelings were few and fleeting.

The city's shadows and fires mangled themselves into an orgy of death while the accompanying musical instructions serenaded them. The five choruses of questions and answers blasted out from the theatre before being bounced about with answers from all over the city. The music continued to build and pound at the city's ears. The fires grew brighter, and hotter, and blinded the city with a threat of death. Over and over the musical conversation was had, until finally, the final word of the final chorus was performed.

As the musicians unleashed their ending final combustion of sound, the massive doors at the top of the theatre shot open.

Six dragons ruptured out from the massive doors before launching into the sky and disappearing into the night's darkness. As soon as they slipped out of view, another dragon appeared at the theatre doors. It was Brikana.

Though lifeless, she appeared to launch out from the doors as well. Tethered to the six preceding dragons, Brikana's body shot out and took to the air and defied gravity. Working together with expert precision, the six dragons not only kept her body aloft, but synchronized each of their tethers to move her head and neck, and beat her mended wings through their full body of motion.

Brikana would rule the skies one final time.

In a smooth coordination, the unseen accompanying dragons let Brikana's body dip down to within feet of the towering tree torches. The departed godknight then flew down the length of the street slowly and proudly, as the onlooking crowds cried out with mournful tears or cheered out in affectionate shouts. She continued flying down the street for miles until onlookers lost sight of her behind buildings, behind those in front of them, or simply due to distance. As Brikana's body slipped out of sight and into the night, the sprawling cacophony of music cadenced into a lush and furious chord. The performers sustained the finale for such a time that would have required the performers to stagger their breaths two or three times, until at last, the music concluded.

The music echoed and reverberated beautifully like the persistent aftertaste of a fine wine. It stayed with the city for many seconds, until eventually, silence cleansed the palette. Within moments of the music ending, attendants for the funeral standing at the base of the tree torches pulled on long lengths of thick rope attached to large bronze cones attached above. As they pulled, the cones swung out and up before landing on the tops of the torches and snuffed them out. Other attendants splashed large barrels of water against ignited ornaments, and unfurled massive blankets to extinguish other fiery displays. The city fell into a dark and somber hush. No one spoke. No one cheered. There was no crying, and no one moved.

Then, as if a ribbon of clouds had dissipated and revealed an obscured star, a bright point of energy appeared high in the sky. Appearing towards the far end of the city, it wasn't quickly noticed by anyone gathered at the street. But the distant shape of light grew. It grew in size quickly and appeared to pulse and whip with energy. The object continued to grow and flicker more wildly, yet the crowd showed no signs of disruption or dispersing.

The light grew larger still. First it was a point, then an oddly shaped mass, and then finally, it took on a noticeable form.

As the bright shape rapidly grew brighter, it became obvious that it was racing speedily back towards the heart of the city. The crowds at the end of the city roared in cheerful approval. With each passing moment, the passionate shouting cascaded farther and farther back up the main road as the shining shape approached.

The shape raced back towards the heart of the city with impressive speed. It flew through the heart of Kimozoa at a rate usually reserved for dragons. And so was the case now.

Brikana departed the city for her journey towards the afterlife moments before, and after finding death, she was symbolically escorted back through the city to an eternity of soaring through the skies. The escorting dragons that helped carry her body out of the city now raced her back at their best combined speed. And the light seen at the end of the city that only grew brighter as they flew back through was due to the rumbling flames fully engulfing Brikana's body. Not only was Brikana *a* fire dragon, but now in death, the Black Dragon was now *the* fire dragon.

In the crowd standing next to Crizichial, Nanutsi, and Kegli, Domaren cleared his throat in an effort to remove the mass of sorrow that had accumulated into an uncomfortable annoyance. Without a glance or a cut of the eye, he addressed them all.

"Even if it means condemning existence to a future without creators, we *will* kill each of the Kihdai."

"We will need to find a way to fight them much sooner, rather than later," Crizichial said.

Kegli continued with Crizichial's line of thinking.

"If not, they'll just keep contriving ways to make us waste our power," he said.

"I doubt there are many new options available to us," Nanutsi said.

Domaren turned towards her.

"I don't know that we necessarily need new options," he said, before looking back to the display in the sky. "There are plenty of old options, and I think the Stäld can help us with remembering or finding them."

The entirety of the city, now at full volume, sang, cried, cheered, and shouted at the sight of the magnificent Brikana disappearing into the heights of the skies, forever alight in the pure majesty of her cherished flame.

## Acknowledgments

While the Wrathlore series isn't explicitly based on Norse mythology or Scandinavian themes, I am extremely passionate about the people, cultures, and histories of the region. Throughout this book, you may have read things that reminded you of a Scandinavian or Norse element, and in many of those types of situations, those little pinches of familiar flavor are intended to be subtle tributes. With that said, I want to express my gratitude for the Scandinavian region for being an inspiration to me, especially in the areas of warmth, wonder, and strength.

In addition to the people, cultures, and history of Scandinavia being an inspiration, so too is the brilliant music and art created by Forndom, Wardruna, Myrkur, Heilung, and Danheim. I lean on their music frequently to imagine what may have happened in the world so long ago, as well as imagine what may be possible in the future.

Lastly, I want to extend a massive amount of appreciation to the team at Vulgarlang.com. Their robust constructed language application provides hours upon hours of imagination-stimulating and world building inspiration. It is is not only one of the most exciting tools I've ever used, but it provides deep and complex content that helps immerse not only a reader, but the writer as well, into fantasy worlds.

Thank you for buying Wrathlore #1,
*Eulogy for the Dawn.*

*I hope you enjoyed it!*

Please be sure to leave a review!

Visit JeramyGoble.com and sign up for my newsletter for occasional book news!

Feel free to visit me at jeramygoble.com or on most social media: @JeramyGoble

www.ingramcontent.com/pod-product-compliance
Lightning Source LLC
Chambersburg PA
CBHW020352310726
48979CB00015B/2561/J
* 9 7 8 0 9 9 9 0 4 3 5 6 1 *